做
好
了

THE
PEAK

Sam Guthrie writes international political thrillers based on his experience working at the nexus of business, politics, and international diplomacy.

His character-driven fiction explores the human desires and frailties that shape world-altering events, drawing on an insider's knowledge of the machinations of power, political intrigue, and the geostrategic challenges confronting the global order.

Prior to publishing his first novel, *The Peak*, Sam had a twenty-five-year career in international relations serving as a trade envoy to China, an Asia Pacific corporate affairs adviser and political lobbyist and a senior government official.

He has worked extensively across Europe, the US and Asia, and has spent close to a decade living and working in Shanghai, Hong Kong and Prague. He has a master's degree in international relations.

sam_guthrie_author
www.samguthrieauthor.com

做好了

THE PEAK

SAM GUTHRIE

HarperCollins*Publishers*

HarperCollins*Publishers* Ltd
1 London Bridge Street,
London SE1 9GF

www.harpercollins.co.uk

HarperCollins*Publishers*
Macken House, 39/40 Mayor Street Upper
Dublin 1, D01 C9W8, Ireland

First published by HarperCollins*Publishers* Ltd 2025
1

A catalogue record for this book is available from the British Library.

ISBN: 978-0-00-874735-0 (HB)
ISBN: 978-0-00-874736-7 (TPB)

This novel is entirely a work of fiction.
The names, characters and incidents portrayed in it are
the work of the author's imagination. Any resemblance to
actual persons, living or dead, events or localities is
entirely coincidental.

Set in Bembo by HarperCollins*Publishers* India

Printed and bound in the UK using 100% Renewable
Electricity at CPI Group (UK) Ltd

MIX
Paper | Supporting
responsible forestry
FSC™ C007454

This book contains FSC™ certified paper and other controlled
sources to ensure responsible forest management.

For more information visit: www.harpercollins.co.uk/green

To lifelong school friends.

PART ONE

Charlie

CHAPTER ONE

So now I'll tell you what happened, as best I can. No spin. No agenda. If I get something wrong, it's not because I'm being evasive or trying to protect Sebastian. It's simply because I don't understand what happened today either. I don't understand why there's police tape around his office, why his wife has been sedated or why the lights no longer work. I'm sitting here by torchlight, with a yellow lawyer's pad, trying to craft a statement about the unthinkable, but I'm still not sure myself what has occurred. This all just happened today. In fact, it's happening now, it's happening to us and I'm writing what I know to explain, as best I can, what Sebastian has done, and why tomorrow when you wake up it will be the end of the world.

Just another sitting week, the third of the year. Since the last Parliamentary session, we'd attended the Pacific Islands Forum, had discussions in Geneva about our WTO case against China's economic coercion, participated in a roundtable on supply chain resilience in Toronto, led a business delegation to the Sea-Air-Space Exposition in Maryland, then headed home, with the usual stop over in Hong Kong for investor calls. All the sort of trade diplomacy policy wonk stuff that floats Sebastian's boat.

Floated his boat.

Nothing seemed out of the norm. Seven am in the office, first floor of the Senate Wing, Parliament House. I swung by Aussies and bought him a coffee. (Long black. No sugar. No milk.) I had a cappuccino and a bacon-and-egg roll, and I dripped egg yolk over a pile of ministerial submissions.

'Jesus, Charlie. It's not the school dining hall.'

Sebastian threw me a handful of tissues from the box on the windowsill beside the framed photos of him with Kurt Campbell and Graham Allison. Judy had been busy: new pictures from the last US trip had appeared already. Sebastian with the Secretary of State, the Secretary of Defence, the Secretary of Trade. A new one of him with his arms over the shoulders of his buddies Kai Birch from the Innovation Expansion Unit at the Department of Defence, and Henry Mallet of Deep Pacific Capital, whose bloated face I couldn't look at without a shiver of resentment. Still no photo with the President. Sebastian had been angling for one, but of course that was the PM's special relationship. Not for an assistant minister of Foreign Affairs and Trade, not even a thruster like Sebastian.

I grinned my apologies, bobbing my head and mopping up egg yolk and crumbs with the tissue. It's been this way since school. I'm the fat, dishevelled creator of mess, to his Robert Redford charisma. Maybe that's why I'm the one who does the tactics, the spin, the knife work in the dark. He is the charmer with twinkling eyes and a wide smile that wins every room he walks into.

Until today.

It was the first meeting of the day. Judy, the diary secretary, had scheduled it early, 7.30 am, as the day was full. I was there to hurry it along. The advisors never bring the curtain down soon enough. They're too deferential to Sebastian, who loses track of all time when his insatiable curiosity is triggered. I've known him since we were thirteen, and have no qualms cutting his meetings short. This one risked running long. It was about Hong Kong, or inevitably Sebastian would turn it into a discussion about Hong Kong. He couldn't resist talking about what had become of the city he loved. I intended to give him fifteen minutes to deliver the official talking points, then shut it down.

❖

Mr SK Tang, of Tung Shing International, came to the office alone. He was in his late sixties, an affable grandfatherly figure in a three-piece suit. He had dyed-black hair that reflected the ceiling light. His round, pockmarked cheeks bounced as he smiled with teeth that were yellow and peppered with fillings. We'd seen him only a few weeks ago in Hong Kong. He'd hosted us for a breakfast of dim sum and corned beef sandwiches (white bread, no crust) at the China Club, insisting we return again for dinner to watch the jazz band and the noodle show.

Tang had been lobbying for the approval of Tung Shing's acquisition of a gas pipeline out of the Beetaloo Basin, south-east of Darwin in the Northern Territory. It was all very awkward as we knew the Foreign Investment Review Board would reject his bid. Foreign ownership of critical infrastructure is particularly sensitive. Electricity assets or gas pipelines are primary targets for sabotage or cyberattack. If an enemy state or non-state actors wanted to coerce the government, they'd do it by plunging our citizens into darkness, turning the power off until we capitulate.

Of course, we acknowledge little of this publicly. As an assistant minister for Foreign Affairs and Trade, Sebastian's job is to promote foreign direct investment. We do the sales pitch, then when the transaction is rejected on the advice of the security agencies, we shake our heads and say it's not our fault, it's the Treasurer's decision, it's out of our hands.

Tung Shing was certainly out of the Foreign Minister's hands; knowing Tang's reputation for aggrieved gasbagging, she had become unavailable and hand-balled the meeting to Sebastian, her star assistant minister.

Tang lectured us, without pausing for breath, for thirty minutes, detailing Tung Shing's vast contribution to the Australian economy. He wore a confused smile, head shaking, his hands open like a supplicant, entreating friends who had betrayed him.

'Minister, this decision has hurt my company. Our shareholders want to know whether the Australian Government trusts us, or thinks we are no different to some mainland Chinese state-owned enterprise.'

Sebastian smiled and recited the meagre talking points prepared for him by the department.

'Tung Shing has been approved to invest twenty billion dollars into some of our most critical infrastructure, SK. That should show we have no problem with your company.'

'Yes, but that was before, wasn't it, Minister? Before these problems. Before Australia started talking about going to war with China ...'

'That was the previous government, not ours. We have sought to identify areas where we can work with China.' The other talking point. But Tang wasn't listening. He had his own key messages.

'I am a businessman, Minister. So, I leave the politics to you. If Australia wishes to follow the United States into a cold war, that is, of course, its prerogative ... My interest is business. Tung Shing is not a Chinese company or even a Hong Kong company. We are an international company, with shareholders. In fact, if you want us to be, we can be an Australian company. As you know, we employ Australians. Some four thousand in fact, and yet somehow your Treasurer cannot see past the colour of my skin.'

Sebastian was tense next to me. I heard him sigh with displeasure. Following his cue, I added my own disapproving theatrics, stiffening and folding my arms. For the first time in half an hour, Tang stopped speaking and looked between us, startled by the change in our manner. Sebastian leant across the table, a strand of sandy-blond hair falling over his forehead.

'As you know, SK, I lived in Hong Kong for many years. The greatest ... friendships ... of my life have been with people from Hong Kong. I don't make decisions based on skin colour.'

I glanced at him, trusting this was confected emotion to shut Tang down. Too many years have passed since Chloe for Sebastian's voice to tremble like that about 'friendships' in Hong Kong.

With relief, I saw the anger disappear from Sebastian's face as fast as it had arrived. He waved a hand, again his pragmatic self.

'But of course, I understand and agree with your concerns, SK. I'll relay them to the Treasurer. Our government needs to be consistent, and we can't forget our friends ...'

Tang nodded his head, relieved. 'Thank you, Minister.'

That was my cue, and I pointed to my watch.

'I'm sorry, Mr Tang. The Assistant Minister has a committee meeting. We appreciate you making the time.'

'Of course.' He grinned, getting to his feet, and we were the best of friends as we ushered him into the foyer.

'Thank you for seeing us today, SK.' Sebastian smiled and shook Tang's hand.

'It is my pleasure always, Minister. It is good to have a friend of Hong Kong in this government. Someone who knows and loves Hong Kong.' SK's eyebrows shot up as a thought occurred to him. 'Ah, and Minister, speaking of your connections. I almost forgot. I met some friends the other night for dinner. I think you know one – Mr Zheng, from China Overland Group.'

Sebastian flicked a glance at me. Then back at Tang, the smile on his face resolute.

'Did you, SK? I haven't seen Zheng in years. Where did you see him? In Australia?'

'No, in Beijing at the CPPCC. I mentioned I was seeing you ...'

Sebastian retained his smile, but I knew him well enough to translate panic from the way he blinked and refocused his eyes.

'Mr Zheng was Head of Logistics at Overland when I was posted in Shanghai. He was a good friend of the Consulate. I understand he is now CEO.'

I nodded, feigning ignorance. Zheng. Of course I knew who Zheng was. He was Chloe's father. Chloe Zheng. And now that breathlessness I feel when threatened and preparing for a battle clutched at my chest like the hands of the bullies that persecuted us at school. I kept smiling as Sebastian continued his unnecessary explanation.

'China Overland is the second largest state-owned enterprise in China. They've become even larger because of their involvement in Belt and Road projects across Southeast Asia, Africa and the Pacific.'

'It's now the number one in construction and logistics.' Tang nodded, ignoring my hand on his back pushing him towards the door. I turned and nodded at Judy, who marched around the reception desk to accompany Tang back to the marble foyer and get him the hell out of Parliament House. But with a strange choreography, Tang pirouetted from my grasp, reached out and took Sebastian's wrist, pressing a plain white business card into his hand. 'Zheng sends his regards. He asked me to give you this.'

There was a pause, in which Sebastian spun the card over and stared at it. He didn't speak, and his smile, at first indulgent, turned to confusion.

I looked at the card as it hung limply from Sebastian's fingers — blank on one side, with three characters penned in clean black-ink calligraphy on the back.

做好了

'What is this?' he asked.

Sebastian's Mandarin was perfect. It couldn't be he couldn't read it. His face had gone white. His eyes were wide and wild, panicked.

'Zuò hǎo le,' Tang read. 'Does that make sense to you, Minister? It doesn't to me. He said you'd understand.'

Clearly, Sebastian understood. He seized Tang by the shoulder. 'When was this? How long ago was this?'

'The night before last.' Tang winced.

'Saturday night? He knew you were coming, and he said to tell me that? Anything more? Any other message you've forgotten?'

'No ... I don't think so, Minister.'

'You must be sure!' Sebastian shouted, shaking Tang.

I was stunned. Sebastian never lost his cool like this. Not even with staff or other ministers. It was the diplomatic training. Something was wrong. Could it be happening? After all this time? Now, after years in opposition. Now, the ghost of yesterday. Of what had happened to Chloe.

I stepped forward to break his grip on Tang, but Sebastian shoved me with his elbow.

'Tell me, did he say anything else?'

'Nothing else. Nothing else, Minister. I'm sorry if I have upset you. That wasn't my intention,' Tang said, touching Sebastian's lapel as if trying to soothe him.

'He's not upset,' I interjected, prising Sebastian's hand from our guest and putting my body between them. 'We just have a lot on. Judy here will accompany you down.'

'Thank you, Minister. Goodbye.' Tang waved awkwardly, and I almost felt sorry for him. He looked like a schoolboy leaving the principal's office.

I turned and saw Sebastian rooted to the spot, pale and visibly trembling, staring wide-eyed towards something I could neither see nor guess.

Taking his arm, I marched him into his private office and slammed the door.

'What the hell is wrong with you? What was Zheng's message?'

He stared at me, and there were tears overflowing in his eyes, coursing down his cheeks. His whole body was shaking.

'Sebastian, what does "*zuò hǎo le*" mean?'

'It means … it's done.'

❖

Sebastian doubled over and groaned like some tremendous weight had been lifted from his shattered body. I locked the door, fearing the staff would come rushing to his aid.

'Is it about Chloe?'

His hand shot to his mouth and he lurched forward, staggering towards his bathroom, collapsing over the toilet and vomiting hard, his shoulders heaving. I was next to him, holding his tie, rubbing his back. I found a towel, wet it and wrapped it around his neck.

It was happening. We'd always known it would come to this. This was about Chloe. About what happened that night as they drove from the Peak in Hong Kong. It would be blackmail. The secret relationship. The undeclared vulnerability.

Sebastian ground his head against the toilet seat. Inexplicably, he was laughing now, a hysterical cackling. Then, with a terrible violence, he headbutted the porcelain cistern.

'Jesus! Stop it,' I cried, dragging him to my chest. 'It's going to be okay. We'll work it out.'

No more laughing. He was sobbing against me. Just like when Chloe was killed.

I felt his tears seeping through my shirt, his body trembling in my arms. He stuttered when he tried to speak, unable to frame words. The stink of his vomit filled the air. Christ, he couldn't be seen like this. I raised him to his feet and walked him to the couch.

'Lie down. I'll be back.'

'No.' He grabbed me by the lapel of my jacket. 'Get the guard. Get the guard.'

I reeled away from the stench of his breath, not comprehending the instruction.

'Who do you mean? What guard?'

Sebastian's face contorted with impatience.

'The fucking AFP. The Federal Police. The guard outside. Get him.'

Sweat broke out across my spine. I looked at him aghast. 'Why do you want the AFP, Sebastian? What are you going to do? Let's discuss it first. If it's about Chloe, we need to be careful. Okay?'

But he'd already gone far beyond a place where my entreaties could reach him. He threw his head back and shouted loudly enough for all the staff in the office outside to hear.

'For Christ's sake, Charlie, get me the fucking guard!'

As ever, I was cowed by his distress and the fear of making a scene. I couldn't have others seeing him this distraught. I tried to comfort him, apologising and pressing him back down on the lounge.

'Okay. Okay. I'm sorry, Sebastian. I'll go. I'll get someone.'

Satisfied, he slumped back down. I rested a cool towel over his eyes. Touched him on the shoulder. Told him again it was going to be okay. Then I rushed out the door, through the office and into the hallway to fetch Albert from the guard station.

Albert was a mate. We sometimes shared a covert smoke in the garden courtyard. He had a grey crew cut, a goatee beard and a tattoo of his mother's name, Enid, across his forearm. He was in his late fifties and already a bit frail for an AFP officer, but he'd seen everything. I passed three other AFP guards before I found him. I knew he'd be discreet. As I led him back to the office, I was already trying to frame the situation.

'I don't know what's wrong with him. If he says anything strange, just ignore it. He's having some sort of episode.'

Excuses on the fly. But I couldn't be sure what Sebastian would say or do. If this was about Chloe, the blackmail I'd long feared, then it was only the opening salvo. It was my job to protect him, even when he was like this. I'd done it before, when he was much worse. When it was my fault. That was the deal: I ran defence and managed risks, always ready with the spin and the outright lies. Anything to protect my boss, my best friend. And that included getting rid of the evidence.

I tore up the card with Zheng's message as we walked, depositing the shreds into the garbage outside Sebastian's private office. Then I pointed the way inside for Albert.

'Just go straight in. I'll come in a minute.'

I turned back to the staff, who were looking worried and waiting for an explanation.

'Tell Judy when she gets back, no appointments. He can't see anyone. He's not well. He feels unwell. We'll need a pair for the Senate —'

A cry echoed through the office, then sounds of a struggle, then something heavy collapsing on the floor. I broke the stillness first, turning on my heels and running for the door of Sebastian's office.

Albert lay unconscious on the floor, a heavy metal paperweight shaped like a Virginia Class nuclear submarine beside his head, which was gashed open and disgorging blood.

'What have you done?' I cried in horror at Sebastian's back as he crouched on his hands and knees over Albert's unconscious body. 'Sebastian!'

He ignored me, instead tearing at the clasp on Albert's holster. The holster that contained his sidearm. In a fluid, nightmare movement, Sebastian released the weapon and thrust it into his mouth. My body froze. I was unable to move, unable to save him from himself.

'Sebastian! Jesus! No!'

Our eyes connected, and he let out a breath. I didn't recognise his expression. It was calm, almost relieved.

He pulled the trigger. A whip-crack fractured my ears. The smell of smoke stung my nose. Christ! Christ, Jesus.

Sebastian's body crumpled onto the coffee table, draped half on the floor, half on the lounge, the gun still in his mouth. Blood from the back of his skull seeped out onto the pale leather.

You think you've seen blood? Your own, most likely. Or your child's. A bleeding nose. A cut finger. A grazed knee. You don't know blood. Not until you're slipping in it as you grasp for your friend's body, not until it wells between your fingers as you hold the shattered pieces of his skull in place, or you find yourself dragged away by armed Federal Police, throwing you in a corner, and you raise your hands to find your best friend's blood congealing between your fingers, on your shirt, on your face, in your mouth.

I was sobbing and rocking and tearing my hair. The staff were looking at me in horror. Alarms ringing. Judy standing in the doorway, screaming. Advisors shouting at the AFP, who had their weapons out and pointing between me, Albert and Sebastian. They were explaining it wasn't me. It wasn't me who killed my friend. Killed? But was that right? Could that be right? Sebastian was dead? He couldn't be dead. He couldn't have left me behind. We've been together for thirty years. Even when he abandons me, he always comes back. We are connected. I'm nothing without him. He is the one on the stage and I hold the spotlight. He is the minister, I am the advisor. He'd been my brother from the first day we'd met. That was my brother lying there. Why had he done it?

Why had he left me alone?

CHAPTER TWO

There are friendships you make in childhood that last a lifetime. They are fused to your soul.

Sebastian and I were friends for thirty years. We were at school together. You might have seen us on the bus or at the train station. The uniform would be familiar to you for its absurdity. The Akubra slouch hat, the black tie (a mourning tribute to Queen Victoria). The blue trousers with red stripe, which matched the red piping at the sleeve and lapels of our Boer War-era blazer, impractical for the Australian heat, yet worn on the threat of dire punishment should we be caught without it beyond the sandstone gates.

It was worse for us as 'day boys' (or 'day fags' to the boarders), meaning unlike the other students we didn't live in a boarding house and instead travelled from home each day, ridiculed and gawped at by commuters on public transport.

I was a state-school kid and had grown up seeing the occasional boarding-school student from the window of my mother's car, wondering at these strange soldier boys haunting train stations and bus stops. It was a shock when my mother told me I was to be enrolled. News got out among my primary-school peers, most of whom would attend the local state high school.

'Charlie's a snob.'

'Charlie thinks he's better than us.'

I was ostracised. A class traitor. I would be attending the oldest independent school in the country. A school of privilege, of sandstone chapels, Olympic swimming pools, endless sporting fields, land worth hundreds of millions (yet still a registered charity with prime ministers and premiers among its alumni).

I did as I was told and sat the scholarship exam, ignorant of what success would bring. My father was an electrician. My mother a secretary. They must have had to borrow and scrape to cover the gap left over in those formidable fees. I can't imagine what they sacrificed. But at no time – during our interview with the school bursar, the outfitting in the dusty school clothing pool, the orientation day when I spoke to no one – at no time did I believe I would actually end up at that school.

And so, the morning I first met Sebastian, I was sitting in my mother's car, refusing to get out, still staring with confusion at the boys in their uniforms as they walked into their houses for morning roll call, refusing to accept that I too must join them. They'd hate me. I was fat. I was common. I was afraid. I didn't want to go in there. I didn't want to leave my mother's car.

Then a boy whom I'd seen before, when we were both with our parents buying uniforms in that dusty hall, a boy who already looked confidently at home in the grounds, a boy named Sebastian, was knocking on my window, *Are you okay?* and my mother, already late for work, sighed with relief and ushered me out and into his care.

'Go with this boy. He'll look after you.'

CHAPTER THREE

I was left in a corner of Sebastian's office and forgotten. I don't know for how long. Maybe hours passed. Time stretched into a despairing purgatory. Two AFP guards whispered by the window, waiting for the coroner, unable to meet my eyes. Sebastian was as I'd left him when they pulled me away, between the lounge and the coffee table, slumped on the floor as we had in his rumpus room watching videos, age thirteen. All those lifetimes ago.

While I knew the back of his head yawned with gore, his face was unmarked save a rivulet of blood drying on his chin.

He wore a curious expression, his eyes wide, brows raised, lips pursed: a conspiratorial stare, as he had fixed on me in his Shanghai lane house, confessing his clandestine relationship with Chloe. 'I need you to keep a secret for me ...' And of course I had.

I sat gazing at him, the almost-telepathic connection that we'd shared for a lifetime now lost to the static, white noise divide between the living and the dead. *Why did you do it? Was this all for Chloe? What do you want me to do now?* A transmission came back from my mind, or from his?

I need you to keep a secret ...

❖

I must have sobbed or called out to him or something, as the guards were triggered into action. They gave me a blanket and led me from the room to sit in the outer office, my clothes and hands still covered in blood.

The other staff had been told they could leave. Only Judy remained, wearing the beige cardigan that usually hung on the back of her chair. Her salt-and-pepper hair tangled in the rainbow lanyard that held her Parliamentary pass as she dusted her computer keyboard. She arranged a cup filled with pens, straightened a box of papers, then stepped from her desk and sighed. There was nothing left for a diary secretary to schedule.

The stillness of the room was disturbed by murmuring in the corridor, where members of the Protective Services Unit stood watch. A nasal voice cut through the quiet as the door wrenched open. I braced myself, knowing who it was.

'The media have to be kept away from this area. Not a sniff, you understand? Tell them there's a bomb threat or something, but keep them away from this office.'

Two men entered. One was tall, in the blue short sleeves, epaulettes and matching tie of a high-ranking AFP officer. The other, short but pugilistic, in a slim-fitting black suit, stood half in, half out the doorway, berating with a finger whomever stood outside. 'You work it out. Just keep them away from here.'

He slammed the door and barged past the AFP officer he'd entered with. He was all angles: elbows, shoulder blades, gestapo knees, a body like a coat hanger sharpened into a prisoner's shiv. Ronnie Durban. I'd known him since university, when we'd sat on either side of a Political Science 101 lecture theatre. We'd also been on either side of every issue before the Student Representative Council, later the Party Conference, not to mention the recent felling of our party leader. (I'd done the felling.) We'd been enemies for the best part of twenty years. I thought he was a pig. He also happened to be the current Prime Minister's Chief of Staff and, by extension, in a roundabout way, my (other) boss.

Ronnie stared in unveiled horror at my bloodied shirt and hands as he strode across the room. No word of greeting. No consideration for my welfare. Icy rage took me by the throat, and I felt my lips twist into a snarl.

'Yeah, Ronnie. Thanks for asking,' I barked as he reached the door of Sebastian's office and wrenched it open.

The cop with him was more civilised. He nodded to me. 'Julian Woods. Security Controller.'

'Fuck me!' Ronnie's voice made us both turn. Beyond him, I could see Sebastian's legs twisted on the floor. Woods followed him into the office.

'What fucking happened?' Ronnie spun on his heels and stalked over to me. 'What did he do?'

'He shot himself.'

'I can fucking see that, Charlie. What the fuck with?'

'He took a gun off one of the AFP guards.'

'Took a gun ...' His face creased in perplexity.

'Knocked him unconscious first.' I shrugged, finding his distress somehow numbing. 'With the paperweight from his desk.'

'Christ,' he muttered, lowering his head and displaying a widow's peak that traversed the distance from his crown to his forehead, like the beak of a crow ready to peck out your eyes. His head shot up again, and he hissed in a low voice that the cops wouldn't hear. 'You realise it's a fucking sitting week, Charlie. Right? And that this place is crawling with fucking journos? They're all asking what's going on in the Senate wing. What with the alarms and the fucking AFP trampling up and down the stairs like elephants in heat ...'

I dragged myself to my feet, ready to shout and spit and punch him in the mouth. Not for the first time. But Woods had walked back into the room and now appeared beside us, making Ronnie jump.

'Sorry to interrupt. But I need to get some basic details here, sir.' He was broad, mid-forties, and had the slightest crease across his forehead as he consulted his notebook through gold-rimmed glasses at the end of his nose. 'Now, may I just confirm your name?'

'I'm Charlie Westcott.'

'How did you know the deceased?'

I shuddered at the word.

'We work together. I'm his Chief of Staff.'

He nodded. 'I understand you were first on the scene.'

'I was out here. I heard a shout. I ran inside.'

'Who shouted?'

'At first I thought it was Sebastian. But when I got into the room I realised it was Albert ... I'm sorry, I don't know his last name.'

'Rossi.' Woods made a note. 'What did you see when you entered the room?'

'What the fuck do you think he saw?' Ronnie said, agitated. 'He saw precisely what I just saw, precisely what you saw. He saw what Sebastian had done to himself.'

'Not precisely,' corrected Woods, as if Ronnie had hurt his feelings. He nodded at me. 'You saw him pull the trigger?'

I felt the blood leaving my face. I nodded.

'Did he say anything to you?'

'No.'

But I could still see Sebastian's expression. Like the runner's relief at the end of an endurance race.

'There's other witness statements saying you cried out.'

I felt a flare of anger. 'Of course I cried out. My friend had a gun in his mouth.'

'So, you were his friend. Not just his staff.'

I gritted my teeth and listened to the sound of his pen adding this to the notebook.

'Was Mr ... Abler upset about anything?'

'Adler,' I corrected.

'Was he depressed about anything? Experiencing any more stress than usual?'

'No,' Ronnie interjected, eyes wide and alert. 'Of course not.'

I shook my head too, smothering the memory of Sebastian sobbing and cracking his skull against the toilet cistern, his shoulders trembling in my arms as he wailed and repeated Zheng's message. *It's done ...*

'Did he have a history of depression? Any previous suicide attempts?'

'No. No. No. Of course he didn't.' Ronnie again.

'Any depression in the family?'

I pressed my lips together.

'Absolutely not.' Ronnie glared at me, his eyes darting back to Woods. Ronnie was lying, too. That was fine. I wasn't going to be the first to bring up Sebastian's father.

'Anyone threatening him? Any aggressive altercations?'

I shook my head.

'How about any recent unusual contacts?'

My eyes flicked to Judy. She opened her mouth to speak, but seeing my expression closed it again. Ronnie watched the exchange and frowned. 'Nothing out of the usual, right, Charlie?'

'Nothing.'

'I see. Now let's talk about the weapon that was used to strike Officer Rossi.'

'It wasn't a weapon. It was a paperweight,' Ronnie snapped. 'Tell him, Charlie.'

'It's a replica Virginia Class submarine. He kept it on his desk.'

'Why?'

'He got it at the Sea–Air–Space Expo. We were there last month, in Maryland.' Woods' creased brow suggested he needed more explanation. 'The assistant minister is involved in the AUKUS program, the trilateral security partnership between Australia, the United Kingdom and the United States —'

'Involved?' Ronnie snorted, unable to help himself. 'Barged his way, in as usual —'

'The senator was asked by the minister to help connect Australian industry to AUKUS related opportunities,' I continued, ignoring Ronnie. 'AUKUS has two pillars. Nuclear-powered submarines and partnership on advanced military technology capabilities.'

'And he was focused on submarines?' Woods asked, jerking his thumb back, presumably towards the paperweight.

'No. That's his wife, who works in defence,' said Ronnie.

'Senator Adler's focus is the second pillar, on advanced technology capability. He met with representatives of the US

Innovation Expansion Unit at the expo, they're part of the Department of Defence. They gave him the paperweight as a momento. Kai Birch, the director of IEU, is an old friend of the Senator.'

It was this relationship with Kai that had allowed Sebastian to justify his AUKUS involvement to the minister, despite Ronnie's suspicions (no doubt shared by the PM) that this was more overreach by an ambitious upstart with longterm leadership ambitions.

In truth, I could have done without our involvement. I couldn't stand Kai Birch. Meeting him in Washington, or at IEU in Mountain View, California, was a staple on every US trip. As was Sebastian spending an evening with Kai, more often than not joined by Henry Mallet, who had relocated from Singapore to Silicon Valley with his firm, Deep Pacific Capital. Inevitably, the three of them would end up at Kai's Los Altos Hills villa, where the old Shanghai threesome would spend the night playing poker and watching cable sports. Hating sports, and hating Henry Mallet, who had been at school with us, even more, I refused to attend these evenings and retreated to the hotel. Sebastian didn't mind. He didn't want me there anyway.

'Still, it's a bit of a strange thing to keep on your desk, isn't it?'

'For fuck's sake! Are you moonlighting as an interior decorator?' Ronnie scoffed, seemingly distracted as he held up his phone searching for reception. Woods' eyes flickered. He ignored Ronnie, but at last changed topic.

'Do you know if there were any issues between Mr Adler and Officer Rossi?'

'What the fuck type of question is that?' Ronnie stuffed his phone into his jacket. Impatient now, about to get punchy.

Woods took a beat. When he spoke, his voice constricted. 'I'd like to interview Mr Westcott, without you interrupting. If you don't mind.'

But Ronnie tipped his chin at him.

'Actually, I do mind Mr Security Controller. In case you've forgotten, you're in Parliament House, under the authority of presiding officers. And the presiding officers, the Attorney General and the Minister for Justice, all work for me. If you don't like it, I suggest you go familiarise yourself with the Parliamentary Precincts Act.'

'I'm aware of the jurisdiction, Mr Durban.'

'Good. Then please fuck off and work out how we clear the Senator's body out of here without turning it into a parade for the television cameras. Meanwhile, I'll see to the welfare of my staff, who are in shock and unfit for your bullying.'

Ronnie marched from the room, pausing only at the door to shout back at Judy and me. 'You two. Follow me.'

Now the real bullying would begin.

CHAPTER FOUR

Sebastian and I had experience with bullies. The boarders were the worst. Sons of the sons of the landed gentry, sent to the city for their education. Nine years away from home living in a boarding house. Day boys had the benefit of leaving the school each afternoon. They had other influences in their lives. There was no such civilising force on the boarders. They were a product of their institution. They'd lost any capacity for gentleness, having to adapt to the pecking order of dormitory rooms and dining halls, corporal punishment that was still dealt out with canes, rulers and sandshoes, even in 1990.

Stripped of privacy, they experienced the gratuitous traumas of puberty amid leering peers, boarding houses filled with pimple cream, pornography, masturbation and homophobic intrigue.

They could not escape the institution. It was on their clothes, in their hair, the way they smelt, the way they spoke. Where our blue shirts were crisp and ironed, theirs were faded and stank of the industrial laundry on site. Their hair was long and tangled or cut by a razor belonging to a boy in an older year. Even their farts, which they'd share by holding us down and sitting on our heads, seemed to stink more due to only ever eating the slop in the dining hall.

They hated us day boys.

Of course, they hated me more, and they bullied me mercilessly. I was a natural target for them. I was fat. I was common.

They'd wait for me at the end of recess, in the narrow hallways outside the classroom. They'd sit facing each other with their legs out, their feet almost touching. When I tried to shuffle between their shoes, they'd swing their legs, sweeping me off my feet, or worse, kick me in the balls as I attempted to step around them. I'd end up in a heap on my back, weighed down by my backpack, legs scrabbling to climb back to my feet. Henry Mallet christened me 'the fat cockroach' and made a personal project of my torment.

Mallet was tall for his age, with broadening shoulders and muscle already filling out the excess flesh on his arms and neck and fists. I can recall his sneering face. He suffered from rosacea, which made him always appear to be flushing, not from shame but with anticipation. He was from a long generation of aristocratic wool growers near Cowra, but he spoke like a bushranger, a broad accent that distinguished him further from the city boys he despised.

It was Mallet who, getting creative with the violence one afternoon, brought things to a head.

I was walking across the quadrangle, outside the library, when I noticed a group following me. I fought the urge to run, knowing to show fear would only incite them. Mallet darted in front of me, bringing me to a halt by the vacant block cleared for the construction of the school theatre. He gestured for his acolytes to surround me.

Six boys grasped my arms so I couldn't struggle. Then Mallet's hands were inside my trousers, grasping the elastic of my underwear and dragging them towards my chin. I felt my testicles separating along the crotch of my boxer shorts and wailed for him to set me free.

But Mallet's meaty face only beamed with delight. He grunted orders to his gang. 'Pull it harder. Pull it further.' My feet left the ground.

It was then that Sebastian came around the corner from his piano lesson and called my name. I couldn't reply. They had me held aloft in the air, screaming in pain. Tears of humiliation blinded me. I heard the seam of my boxer shorts rip. Mallet roared in glee and pulled harder. The biting constriction up the crack of my arse was finally released with a cathartic heave. I dropped to the ground as Mallet waved my torn underwear like a flag of triumph above his head.

What happened next, I was too delirious to see. I heard Sebastian cursing, then Mallet crying out. I looked up and saw my friend between me and the boarders, his hand clenched into a fist.

He rushed forward and punched Mallet in the face. His blow was weak, but it shocked Mallet, who let out an effeminate squeal that made his acolytes glance away.

Mallet recovered, regrouping to his full height and snarling at Sebastian. 'I'm gunna fucken kill you.'

Sebastian put up a brave fight, but Mallet was stronger and brought him to the ground with a series of vicious punches to the head. Boys pounded him, jumping on top of him, rucking him over, kneeing him in the face.

Mallet turned his sneering face back to me. There was time for a last humiliation. They dragged me, kicking and struggling, to a metal garbage bin that stank of food and dog shit. They stood in a circle spitting in globules of phlegm before grasping me by my arms and legs and thrusting me headfirst into the bin.

It stank and turned my stomach. But I stayed there in the dark until I felt Sebastian's hands on my back drawing me to my feet. I blinked in the afternoon sun and saw Mallet and his crew in the distance, walking towards the boarding houses, shoving and laughing.

'We've got to go. Dad is picking me up.' Sebastian's face was swollen and bloodied. 'Are you okay?'

I couldn't speak. Seized with shame, the tears fell. I let out a sob.

'Stop that, okay?' He was trying to be comforting but struggling to control his own voice. His hand was on my back, urging me towards the carpark. 'We've got to go.'

As we turned the corner and the cars came into sight, we saw Sebastian's father standing beside his silver BMW. He wore a dark suit, fresh from the office, but with his aviator sunglasses and his slicked black hair I thought he looked like Tom Cruise in *Top Gun*.

'Don't tell my dad,' Sebastian muttered to me as we approached the car.

'What?' I asked in outrage.

'Say nothing,' Sebastian repeated, urging me forward.

'Why?' I stopped, grabbing his arm. 'Why not tell him and get him to do something about it? He's going to ask anyway when he sees your face.'

Sebastian shook his head. 'Say it happened in sport.'

I was shocked.

'Sebastian,' shouted his father. 'Hurry up, I've got to get on a conference call.'

'Tell your own parents,' Sebastian hissed, and he pulled away, walking towards the car.

I stumbled after him, still arguing. 'I have. They said there's nothing they can do. I should "appreciate the privilege of coming here." I'm a charity case, I can't do anything. Your dad could if you told him.'

'I don't want to tell him.'

'But why?' I grabbed his arm again. 'Why keep it a secret?'

He spun around, his bruised face now taking on a frenzied twitching that distorted the usual calm. He spoke through gritted teeth. 'Because he'll think I'm a weakling and that it's my fault.'

'Your fault?' I shouted. 'How is this your fault or my fault?'

But Sebastian was shaking his head. 'He's an old boy. He knows what it's like. It was the same then. Worse. He says to never show weakness. Hide it. If you show you're scared, that's when they attack. You can't let on. You just have to do more, work harder, say nothing and keep it all to yourself.'

My mouth was wide, staring at him.

'But it's not our fault. We did nothing.'

'Doesn't matter.' Sebastian shrugged, grabbing my bag and drawing me towards his father's car. 'It's our mantra from now on. Don't show it. Don't show it. Don't show it. Don't show it.'

'Alright, what the fuck happened?'

Ronnie had dragged us into a small meeting room down the hall. He'd given me a moment to wash my hands and face of blood in the bathroom adjoining the meeting room, but when I came out he was waiting impatiently, standing with his hands on his hips at the end of the table. I collapsed in a chair, my arms and legs folded. Judy hovered by the door. I kept my eyes on her as she wrapped her lanyard around her hand and stared at her toes. We were both still in shock, but I was counting on our shared loyalty to Sebastian to keep it together in front of Ronnie.

Don't show it.

Ronnie dispensed with any pretence of caring about our welfare.

'I mean, Jesus Christ, why would he do this?'

'I don't know, Ronnie.'

He was panting, marching back and forth in front of the table. I followed his passage with my eyes. As a professional political operative, I was long past being surprised by the capacity of people in our field to dispense with common human empathy in the face of political risk or opportunity. But Ronnie was something else.

He tossed his head towards me. 'Charlie, you must have known something was wrong with him.'

'He was his normal self.' I shrugged. 'He was enjoying the job. He'd enjoyed the recent travel.'

'Any issues on the trip?'

'Not at all. The Sea–Air–Space delegation was a success. California was really positive. Kai Birch had a whole bunch of Australian AI and Quantum companies pitching into a project the IEU is running. That was a win for us. Sebastian was delighted.'

'That's it?' Ronnie barked.

A brief flash of memory. Sebastian's sweating face in the Four Seasons lobby in Hong Kong Central.

'Food poisoning.'

'What?'

'He had food poisoning, on our last night in Hong Kong. Had to take a few days off after we got back …'

'Jesus, I don't give a shit about that. You.' Ronnie clicked at Judy and she flinched. 'You didn't think anything was going on with him?'

'Nothing.' She shook her head. 'He was his normal self.'

Judy's eyes darted to me. I gave her a reassuring nod.

'So, what the fuck happened? Why does he do that today?' Ronnie kept on. 'In a sitting week, for fuck's sake. In Parliament House, with so much legislation going through. That's not suicide, that's a spectacle. Why did he want to make a spectacle? Was everything alright at home? Cassie? The kids?'

'As far as I know, everything was fine at home.'

'As far as you know ...' He shook his head in disgust. Ronnie hadn't wanted me for this job, but Sebastian had insisted. 'As far as you know. Well, you know who is going to want to know, don't you? Not just the gallery journos sniffing around downstairs, not just the lumbering AFP. McCubbin ...' He opened his eyes wide and growled, the name curling back his lips. 'McCubbin is going to want to know.'

The name was like an incantation. Black splotches crept across my vision. The breath left my chest. Keeping Sebastian's secret from Ronnie was one thing. Hiding it from Sebastian's father-in-law would be another matter.

Alec McCubbin was Director General of Security. The Prime Minister's intelligence tsar. Head of the Australian Security Intelligence Organisation, ASIO. Ronnie was right. He would want to know what had happened to his son-in-law, and why his daughter and grandkids had been left without a husband and father. He'd want to know what information I was hiding.

'I know nothing, Ronnie. There's nothing to tell McCubbin. It's just a tragic —'

'Nothing to tell him?' Ronnie looked at me as if I was mad. 'His fucking son-in-law has just killed himself. You don't think we need to tell him anything?'

'I didn't say that.'

Ronnie stepped forward, his chin thrust out like he used to in younger days, when we'd scream at each other across a university branch meeting. 'Now you listen to me, right Charlie? The only fucking reason your beloved Sebastian Adler was in the position he was in was because we wanted to keep things nice with McCubbin. Can I put it any clearer than that?'

I looked away, grinding my jaw.

'As you know, McCubbin is not our greatest ally. He was appointed by the last government. He has files on all of us, including the PM, and he thinks we're all Manchurian candidates in Beijing's pocket. He hates us. The only reason he hasn't either quit or found some spurious secret intelligence reason to undermine our agenda is because his little girl's husband is among our ranks. Now that's changed. What do you think he's going to do?'

'He'll be looking for a scandal,' Judy volunteered, staring at me with raised eyebrows.

'That's right. McCubbin will be all over this, asking the same questions I am, only worse. Was he depressed? Was he in trouble? Was he on drugs? Jesus, did he have debts? Were there other women?'

'Sebastian's dead, Ronnie,' I snarled back. 'How about you have some respect and give us a moment?'

'I don't have time for fucking respect!' Ronnie bellowed. 'This shit is going to break, and it's going to be a national fucking news story. I need to know if there is a scandal coming that can damage the Prime Minister or the government …'

'Or his family,' Judy whispered, turning accusing eyes on me.

Dread balled in my gut. I didn't like the way Judy was looking at me. I'd presumed she would be loyal. She'd been with Sebastian and me since opposition. But if I thought about it, she'd been assigned to us by Ronnie. She'd be loyal to Ronnie, particularly now she needed a new job. And she'd seen it all. The altercation with Tang. Sebastian's manic reaction.

As she opened her mouth, I leapt in.

'I'm still wondering why you lied about his father,' I said to Ronnie.

'What was that?'

'His father's suicide.' I shook my head. 'It's public knowledge. It was a stupid move to lie to the police about it.'

A plan had formed in my head. It was a Machiavellian plan, but this is how my brain works, and my priority was to draw

Ronnie off the meeting with Tang, the spectre of Zheng. Protect Sebastian. Keep his secrets. Even if it meant being a prick to his memory.

'I was stupid, was I?' Ronnie was up on his toes again, rising to my bait. 'Do you have any sense of the scale of this fucking mess, Charlie? There's going to be wall-to-wall coverage. I'm not giving those pricks any additional angles to kick the story along for another few weeks.'

'I'm saying' – I raised a placating hand and spoke to him as if he were a moron. He was my superior in rank, but we both knew I was the superior political mind – 'isn't that the better explanation? His father killed himself. Now Sebastian kills himself ...' I swallowed the lump in my throat.

'What about it? So what?'

I persevered. 'So, it suggests mental health issues. Something running in the family. It explains things. It doesn't point to anything else we don't know about. Any ... scandal.'

Silently apologising to Sebastian, I braced myself. This could now go one of two ways. Ronnie would either seize on the idea of a scandal and demand to know what I was hiding, or he'd take the gift-wrapped explanation I'd just offered. It was a betrayal, of course, but it would keep Sebastian's secret out of the vulture's grip.

Ronnie had become still. When he spoke, his voice had calmed. 'Now that's a useful contribution ...' He nodded and flared his nostrils. 'How old was he when his old man killed himself?'

I breathed out. 'Fifteen.'

'How'd he do it?'

I swallowed again, my throat dry. 'The same way. Gun in the mouth.'

Ronnie licked his lips. 'Jesus. You sure?'

'I was there.'

He paused, staring at me. I thought for a moment he was realising how insensitive his language was, how much like brothers Sebastian and I were. But, of course, he was just calculating. He eased himself into the seat next to me, almost salivating. I knew him so well.

'That's pretty compelling.' He tapped his teeth. 'There's a story in it, don't you think?'

My eyes flicked to Judy, who had folded her arms and was grinding her heel into the carpet. Looking back to Ronnie, I nodded.

'It ties it up neatly,' he said. 'Some mental health issue running in the family. Like father like son.'

It had become his plan. My voice was gentle, like comforting a child. 'That's right. Not our fault. Not the PM's. Not a scandal for the government. Not something that needs to be probed or investigated.'

On cue, his mobile buzzed.

'Shit, this is the PM. I'll tell him the plan.' He grabbed a yellow legal pad off a shelf and tossed it onto the table in front of me. 'Write it down.'

'Write what?'

'You said you were there when his dad killed himself. You knew Sebastian as a kid. Write about how it affected his life from that night. Like you said. We've got to give the journos and the feds reasons. Give McCubbin reasons for what he's done. That way, we control the story. Just get it all down.'

'Can I speak to you a minute?' Judy muttered to Ronnie as he steered her towards the door.

I sprang out of my seat. 'Judy, I could use your help ...'

Ronnie turned back, phone already at his ear. 'Just get on with it, Charlie. Give me reasons. And don't leave this room until you're done. You owe us.'

The door closed.

I turned back to the yellow legal pad, trying not to obsess over what Judy might be saying to Ronnie as they walked down the hall.

CHAPTER FIVE

Even before he killed himself, Paul Adler's ghost haunted us at school.

Sebastian showed me his photo in a glass cabinet in the trophy room. He'd been in the rugby firsts and was a rower in the first eight that won Head of the River for three consecutive years. The school commemorated the name of each crew member on a special plaque outside the Main Hall.

Sebastian sought out these vestiges of his father's success to shape himself in his image and win his approval. In the school museum, the curator recognised Sebastian's surname and produced his father's colour blazer and a box of photos of his third regatta triumph. We also found his sixth form yearbook, which contained a photo of the sharp-jawed young rowing champion and a brief interview about his post-school ambitions: 'I'm going to row at the Olympics, then make a million bucks before I'm thirty. Then give back. Politics. Diplomacy. Military service – officer class.'

But by 1990, Paul Adler was a disappointed man. In his first year at Sydney University, during a drunken night at St Paul's College, he'd fallen from a window and suffered a severe spinal ligament injury requiring him to wear a brace throughout months of rehab. His doctors told him to prepare for a lifetime of reduced endurance, and they medicated him for chronic pain. He never played sport at a competitive level again, and never went to the Olympics.

After this humiliation, the success of Adler's early career gave him some relief. He had leveraged the old boy network to land a role at Macquarie Bank, earning considerable commissions and bonuses, but by the time Sebastian and I were entering first form the nineties recession was worsening and Adler's job was under pressure.

At thirteen, I had never heard of narcissistic personality disorder, but I was familiar with the shadow Adler cast over his son. It seemed that, with his career on the rocks and his own dreams dashed, Adler clutched jealously at his memories of high school triumph.

He'd strut up and down the sideline on the football fields as if he owned them. He shouted the loudest of the parents, vocalising his disappointment with the referee, the other team or, most of the time, his own son. At the end of the game, when other parents were putting a congratulatory arm around their boys, Adler would be poking his son in the chest, pointing out the multiple faults in Sebastian's game and contrasting his performance to when Adler last played in the firsts.

The teachers only encouraged this sort of behaviour. It wasn't just those older generations that fawned over him, but the newer masters too. On learning of the Adler pedigree, they found every opportunity to venerate Sebastian's father, with invitations to old boys' soirees and motivational speeches in the sandstone chapel, and with VIP seating at the head of the river or to the cadet corp passing-out parade on the manicured oval.

At parent-teacher night, Adler would spend half of each interview regaling Sebastian's tutors with stories of his own exploits at the school. His mood would darken when teachers more interested in his son's development (a minority) would force the conversation back to Sebastian.

Outside of school, if Sebastian wanted Adler's attention he had to insert himself into his interests. He spent weekends chasing after his father: orienteering, obstacle racing, skeet shooting, mountain biking. This often meant on Monday morning he'd show up with bruises, cuts or, in one instance, a broken arm. He'd recount stories of his adventures with his dad and the other boys would be in awe of what a cool father he had. But as time went by I saw the bruises and imagined Sebastian's gritted jaw grinding through the weekend, determined to keep up, fearing of being called weak by his father, who always reminded Sebastian that he was the one suffering through chronic pain.

Sebastian worked harder to secure his dad's attention. By the end of second form, Sebastian was in the best rugby team and the A-grade cricket team. He was a champion swimmer, an accomplished pianist, the star of the junior musical, the top of all his classes.

Then Adler played his cruellest card. Without warning, he absented himself from the school, as if his son's success was too much for him to stomach.

It devastated Sebastian. All he cared about was making his dad proud, and I saw the look on his face as he scanned the crowd from the stage, singing in the choir, accepting an award, losing concentration as he ran the ball up the sideline, only to be tackled into the dirt knowing that his father had failed to show up for his final football game of the year.

While at the time all this felt like a cruel and deliberate neglect, we would find out later that Adler was distracted with darker, more impulsive enthusiasms.

❖

One Saturday, after another game from which Adler had been absent, Sebastian emerged from the change rooms with a bleeding lip and a black eye. I hadn't noticed him receive a blow on the field, so I asked what had happened.

'Mallet,' he answered with a shrug. 'Let's go home.'

We walked out of the sandstone gate and over the main road to his house in the nearby suburb. It had become our Saturday ritual. I'd go over after sport, we'd play *Castle Wolfenstein* on his computer, we'd watch movies on video: *Young Guns, Terminator, Flying High*. Then I'd sleep there for the night.

As usual, we raided his kitchen for chips, ice cream and Milo, and we were settling down to watch TV in his rumpus room when Adler staggered into the doorway, sniffing and touching his nose. I didn't know then that he'd been absent from the house for almost a week.

'What happened to you?' he asked, pointing at Sebastian's lip.

'Nothing.' Sebastian stood to attention in front of his father. 'You missed my game. We won.'

Adler didn't reply. He looked wired. His black, oiled hair was a mess. He had bags under his eyes and swayed where he stood.

'You've been fighting?'

Sebastian shook his head.

'Don't bullshit me, son. Did you win the fight?'

Sebastian was silent.

'For fuck's sake.' Adler groaned. 'Can't even protect yourself. When I was your age, we fought back.'

'I fight back.'

'Yeah? Show me how. Come on.'

His father raised his fists and assumed a sparring stance.

'Come on. What did I show you? Jab, cross, slip, roll.'

As if triggered by a stage hypnotist, Sebastian began performing a boxing drill. He jabbed his left fist towards his father's head, stopping short of connecting. Threw his right across his body. Then moved his torso to the left. Then around in a circle, as if dodging a punch. Adler only sneered.

'Too fucking slow. Do it faster.'

Sebastian increased his pace, breathing through his nose, giving off the sound of a panting animal.

'You're not going fast enough. No wonder you're losing.'

Sebastian increased his pace. This time when he rolled, his father's hand shot out and slapped him across the face. Sebastian staggered backwards.

'Hold your stance,' his father shouted. 'Don't break. Do it again.'

Sebastian, his face glowing red, fronted up again to his father. He moved through the drill, faster and faster. I could see the sweat on the back of his blue shirt. But again, his father's hand shot out and found its mark.

'Stop it,' I cried, dropping the chip packet and clambering to my feet. But they ignored me and focused on their strange, violent dance. With every jab and roll from Sebastian, Adler would move in time, dodging and mirroring his son's movements. It occurred to me they must have sparred like this before. Another activity Sebastian had thrown himself into to spend time with his father. Another slap. The sound of a fist connecting with skin.

This time it was Adler who backed away, holding his cheek.

'Fuck!' he roared, staring with hatred back towards his son. 'You little shit.'

'Sorry.' Sebastian stepped closer, concerned for his dad.

'Get your fucking hands up.' Adler was back in position. 'Faster,' he snarled, now throwing punches at his son that were intended to connect. They were ferocious, and Sebastian dodged and rolled and blocked to avoid being hit. Adler wheezed, clearly beginning to tire. Whatever he'd been up to over the last few days was catching up with him. But the fixed look in his eye only hardened as he flailed his punches and movements, losing any sense of control or style. Sebastian kept dodging. I could see he was holding back. He didn't dare hit his father again. Another minute passed and Adler's breath was ragged. But rather than giving up, he cheated. Snapping out of the choreography of jab–cross–slip–roll, he sucker punched his son in the belly.

Sebastian bent over, gasping for air. Adler stood, hands on his hips, panting. Sweat dripped into his eyes and onto his upper lip, which he licked away.

I'm not sure how long Sebastian's mum had been standing at the door, but she was there now. I'd never seen a look of such hatred. When Adler saw her, he called her name, but she was gone. I heard them chasing each other through the house. Sebastian sat down on the couch, shivering. I moved closer to him, but he shook his head and turned the volume of the television up, trying to drown out the noise of his parents fighting with the sound of an afternoon game show. He didn't take his eyes off the screen. Not even when we could hear his mother's furious voice and words like 'traitor' and 'betrayal' pierce through the floor. My eyes rolled from the board games we'd played in here a hundred times before, to the computer and the television, which he turned up again with the remote control. Then I looked at my friend and saw tears dripping down his face.

Hours later, when I climbed out of the sleeping bag on Sebastian's bedroom floor and crept out to use the toilet, I saw a light on in Adler's study. I was passing the open doorway and glanced in to see him with a target-shooting pistol in his mouth. His eyes locked on mine. To this day, I swear he only went through with it because he was worried about looking weak. Ashamed that I'd seen him like that. Maybe he'd acted it out on other nights in a similar desolate mood. A sort of Russian roulette with himself. He was slumped on his desk, leaning on his elbows. The pistol in his mouth. Only when he saw me did he straighten. His eyes opened wide. And he pulled the trigger.

We didn't go back to school for a month. Sebastian's mother paid for us to see the same counsellor. We went together.

Sebastian was less affected by his father's death than by the betrayal that was revealed in the funeral's aftermath and the reading of the will. Debts wracked up and bank accounts drained paying for gambling losses, a cocaine addiction, prostitutes called to casino hotel rooms. Not only was there a lover, but there were newborn twins with a woman from his office, a secretary. June. Sebastian had a brother and sister.

There was a fight over Adler's estate. Sebastian and his mother lost half of everything, including a trust account set up for Sebastian's university and the deed to the house.

Sebastian never recovered.

He swore he'd never do that. To anyone. He'd be loyal. Most of all to his wife. To his kids. He'd never betray them like his father had.

We returned to school, and the boarders didn't dare touch us. A mysterious aura of grief and death surrounded us.

Of course, it was Mallet who broke the taboo. He made some comment about a dead dad.

Sebastian beat him to a pulp.

❖

I put my pen down and breathed out. Somehow, writing about it was comforting. Maybe it was just being together with Sebastian, even in memory.

But the relief was short-lived. The meeting room door was flung open.

Ronnie entered the room, his face shrivelled in fury. Judy stood behind him, her hands clasped in front of her, head down, only glancing up to catch my eye.

'You didn't tell me everything,' Ronnie snarled.

CHAPTER SIX

In the time it had taken to write out the tragedy of Sebastian's father, Judy had resolved to throw me under the bus.

I lurched to my feet.

'She's in shock Ronnie. Whatever she's said, it's nothing.'

'He needed to know,' Judy said, unrepentant.

'Tell him what you've told me,' Ronnie barked over his shoulder.

Judy blushed and stepped back through the door. 'I told Ronnie that something happened today …'

'Today? It's not even lunch time. What could have happened today?' Ronnie asked sarcastically. 'In fact, I recall Charlie telling me nothing fucking happened today, so I'm all ears.'

'The Assistant Minister had a meeting —'

'Judy, it was nothing.' I implored. Ronnie stepped between us so she couldn't see me.

'Who did he have a meeting with Judy?'

'SK Tang of Tung Shing International.'

'The Chinese company.'

'Hong Kong,' I corrected.

'And? Come on.' He rotated his fingers, prompting. 'What about him? Tell us what happened.'

'He handed something to the Assistant Minister. There was an altercation. Sebastian grabbed Tang by his jacket.'

'That's an exaggeration,' I protested.

'I saw what I saw, Charlie,' Judy said stubbornly.

'Why did Adler grab him?'

'They were talking about Tang having met someone who had a message for the Assistant Minister.'

Now Ronnie turned to confront me. 'So? What the fuck is she talking about?'

I shook my head, but Judy was still going.

'His name was Jing or Jong or something.'

'Zheng,' I corrected.

'Jing, Jong, Zheng ... What the fuck happened, Westcott?'

I looked up at him, feeling anger course through me. I hate being called by my surname. It plunges me back into memories of school. Mallet spitting in a garbage bin and throwing me in.

I sucked in a breath, making calculations, assessing the threats. It was out now. I had to switch from hiding the truth to containing it.

'Well, Charlie? What the fuck have you got to say for yourself?'

I nodded at Judy. 'Go home Judy.'

Ronnie didn't stop her, but as she left he said, 'Not a word to anyone ... you understand?'

'But if they ask —'

'You shut your fucking mouth.'

She nodded and left, closing the door behind her.

Silence in the meeting room.

He leant against the door, staring at me. His face had turned white.

'What the fuck is going on? Why was he so distressed about this Tang bloke's message?'

'Judy's exaggerating. Tang is a friend. We know him from Hong Kong. We've met him hundreds of times.'

'She just said Sebastian lost his shit and grabbed him.'

I pressed the heel of my hand against my forehead, calculating whether I could risk trying to use him.

'Tang said he'd seen an old acquaintance of Sebastian's in Beijing.'

'Zheng.'

I nodded. 'Sebastian knew his daughter. When he was on posting in Shanghai.'

'Knew his daughter?' He cocked his head to one side. 'What does that mean? Was she a colleague, a stakeholder? Did he fuck her?'

I folded my arms and looked away.

'Jesus,' he muttered. 'Okay then, Charlie, what was Zheng's message?'

I scrunched up my face, thinking hard whether to tell him. I wanted to protect my friend. But I knew I couldn't do it alone. The truth was emerging, and I needed to slow it down. To contain the damage. Ronnie would help. Not because he cared about me or Sebastian. But to defend the Party against a scandal that seemed to be threatening to emerge from a history I thought we'd long outpaced.

'He said ... "it's done".'

'It's done? What's done?'

I shrugged.

'He'd done something for Adler?'

I shook my head. 'I don't know.'

'You do know, Charlie. Stop being so fucking obtuse,' he shouted, leaning over the table at me, then glancing towards the door and lowering his voice. 'What did the message mean? What was the bloke telling him? Why would he kill himself directly after?'

'I don't know.'

'Jesus. Do you want to explain it to me? Or do you want to tell McCubbin?'

I shuddered. Not McCubbin. That was exactly who I didn't want to tell.

'I think it was blackmail, Ronnie.'

'Blackmail? By a mysterious fucking bloke in Beijing?' He slumped into the chair and put his head in his hands. 'What could this bloke be blackmailing Sebastian about?'

I sighed and gripped the table, sending a silent prayer to Sebastian, hoping, if he was watching, he'd know I was doing it for him. To protect his reputation. To protect Cassie and the girls. And to protect the memory of Chloe.

'What did Zheng have on him, Charlie?'

I cleared my throat.

'Sebastian killed his daughter.'

❖

Ronnie sat, looking at me with a dumbfounded expression as I told him what Sebastian had done. Of course I didn't tell him everything about Chloe. About the length of their relationship. About all of the time in Hong Kong and Shanghai. I didn't tell him they'd been together during Sebastian's posting in China. I made it sound more like a one-night stand. Something grubby and fleeting, which for years I had wished it was.

Images of Chloe played in my head. The sleek bob of black hair she curled behind her ear. The thick black rectangular glasses that reflected the fireworks during the handover celebrations. The white of her teeth as she smiled, sharing an earbud and listening as Eddie Vedder sang 'Indifference' on my mix tape.

Ronnie's voice was sharp. 'What did Sebastian do?'

I swallowed. I knew every excruciating detail.

'It was when he was at the Australian Consulate in Shanghai. He was on leave in Hong Kong, where his mother had lived during the handover to China. He went to a party in one of those colonial villas built by the British on the Peak. He was with a girl.'

'Zheng's daughter?'

'Chloe.' I nodded. 'They'd both been drinking, possibly more …'

'More?'

'A few lines of coke. I don't know what else.'

'Jesus. Go on.'

'They left together. Sebastian was in better shape than she was, so he drove her car. A black Porsche. The roads up there are narrow, and the descent, late at night, curling round the mountain, surrounded by darkness and jungle … It's dangerous at the best of times. The thick fogs can be fatal. The edge of the road vanishes, and cars go over the edge.'

I swallowed, unable to keep the tremor out of my voice.

'They took the turn too fast on Magazine Gap Road, went through the railing, into the jungle. Sebastian was thrown from the vehicle before impact and miraculously walked away with only cuts and bruises to his body and face.'

'And the girl?' Ronnie stared at me, arms folded, his face creased with horror.

'Incinerated in the car.'

I had gone to the scene. After Sebastian had returned to his job in Shanghai, three days later. Three days ...

I had stood looking at the buckled barrier where the dark skid marks across the asphalt ended. I'd found a metal maintenance ladder and descended into the jungle, pushing into the dense vegetation through vines and aerial roots of banyan trees. I'd followed the smell of petrol across the uneven ground, in the sweltering humidity, clutching at vines to keep my balance. There had been an area of burnt ferns and crushed bamboo exhibiting the drag marks where they'd hoisted the vehicle out with a crane. They'd cleared the site, but I'd found evidence of the crash, of the paramedics. Packaging for IV fluids, suction catheters, defibrillator pads. She hadn't died on impact. They'd fought to keep her breathing. To keep her heart beating. I'd fallen to my knees in the jungle and wept.

'Was Sebastian arrested?' Ronnie asked, pacing the room.

'No. Zheng managed it.'

'What does that mean?'

'He didn't want a scandal. He was Deputy CEO in a Chinese SOE. He didn't want the shame of his daughter out with a westerner, on drugs ... a one-night stand.'

'You're saying he covered it up?'

'He did what he needed to. He paid off the right people. Sebastian spent a night at the Central Police Station and was released without charge.'

'And then what? He just went back to work at the Consulate? He didn't tell anyone? No one at Foreign Affairs knew it had happened?'

I shook my head. Ronnie's mouth fell open further.

'And this girl was a Chinese national?'

I nodded

'Jesus Christ! So, Sebastian was totally compromised. This Zheng had him by the balls.'

'They had no contact after that night. Not a word. Sebastian tried. He was desperate to apologise. Zheng refused to meet with him.'

'None of this was in Adler's record when you brought him into the party ... when you stacked branches to get him pre-selected over my candidate' – he spun around, pointing his finger at me – 'whose reputation you trashed with gossip about infidelities to sway the preselection ... all that time, your candidate was infinitely more compromised.'

'Yes.'

'You hypocritical grub,' Ronnie spat. 'You've betrayed the party. You sold us a ticking bomb, Westcott.'

I stared at the table and said nothing. Ronnie sucked in a breath, trying to get himself under control.

'So, this morning ... Zheng gets in touch after years —'

'Decades.'

'— decades of silence and says "it's done". That can only mean blackmail, right?'

'It would seem so.'

Ronnie clutched his head. 'We form government after ten years in the wilderness, and in the first six months, because you have given us a fucking bomb, we get compromised like this ...'

'We're not compromised, Ronnie.' I was getting angry now. 'Sebastian just killed himself to protect us!'

'You think splattering his brains all over a parliamentary office was some honourable act to protect us?'

'To remove whatever leverage Zheng had. To put an end to whatever was coming.'

Ronnie took a step back and snorted with contempt. 'You think this goes away because he's dead?'

'Why can't it?' I shrugged. 'There'll be a media storm about his death, but we can keep a lid on everything else.'

'And what about when they find out about Zheng and all your secrets?'

'They won't.'

'You think journos won't dig into this? The likes of Judy there will stay schtum?'

'She will if you tell her to. She won't tell the police or the media anything. None of the staff will.'

'I'm not worried about the fucking police. I'm worried about McCubbin, for Christ's sake!'

He'd hit it. McCubbin was the danger. He always had been. This was why I needed Ronnie's help.

'If McCubbin gets wind of any of this shit …' Ronnie circled his finger disdainfully at me. 'Jesus. He'll fuck us … Sebastian's fucked his family, his daughter, his grandkids. He'll fuck us because he'll be furious. Worse, he'll be embarrassed.' Ronnie was clutching his head now. 'Jesus, he'll fuck us because it'll look like McCubbin's dropped the ball. That Sebastian's fucked him.'

'He'll fuck us because he's wanted to all along,' I said coldly, pushing back my chair and flicking lint from my trousers. 'He'll leak it all. He won't even leak it. He'll call a press conference to confirm everything he said about us in opposition was true … that we're soft on national security and we've been infiltrated by Beijing.'

'This could bring the government down,' gasped Ronnie.

'You're right.' I nodded, continuing to hustle him. 'And so, we lock it down. This stays tight between you and me. We don't breathe a word of it to anyone. Not the PM. Not the police. Not the media. Not McCubbin. If ASIO come asking questions, you shut them down. Same with the staff. We keep Sebastian's secret between you and me. That's how we protect the Party.'

Ronnie's head now twitched on his neck, and he recoiled as if I'd struck him. His face flushed as he raised a trembling finger. 'You conniving cunt …'

'What?' I asked, watching realisation dawn over his stupid face.

'You've set me up. You've told me this, knowing I would need to help you cover it up. You've made me as compromised as you are.'

It would have been pointless to deny it. The contingency plan had formed in my head as soon as Judy had spilled about Tang.

'It's going to be alright, Ronnie. We will contain it. As long as we leave out the stuff about Zheng and what happened in Hong Kong.'

He shook his head. 'You think you're a political mastermind, don't you, Charlie?' He curled his lip. 'Even if I give you cover, even if we batten down the hatches and let this blow out as a tragedy and call your mate a hero, do you really reckon we've heard the last from Zheng? If this was an attempt to blackmail Sebastian and fuck with this government, they're still going to want to cash in on their intel after waiting all these years.'

'It's possible,' I agreed. 'But I don't know what else we can do.'

I'd lanced the wound. I'd dealt with the immediate threat after Judy's disloyalty. I'd proved my loyalty to Sebastian by making Ronnie our accomplice. *I need you to keep a secret for me.* That was as far ahead as I could think. I just wanted to go home, to some dark room, and grieve the friend I'd lost.

But Ronnie wasn't having a bar of it.

'I'm not sitting here waiting for the other fucking shoe to drop, Charlie. I'll keep your filthy secret because, unlike you, I'm loyal to this government. But nothing else has changed. There's a scandal coming. We have to get out in front of it and find out what's going on. And by we, I mean you.'

I grabbed the yellow legal pad and threw it at the table in front of him. 'I've given you your alternative narrative. What else do you want me to do?' I was desperate for a cigarette and my patience was wearing thin. 'There's enough childhood trauma there to explain it all.'

Ronnie lifted the yellow notepad and flipped through its pages.

'Read what I've written, for Christ's sake. I've done it all for you. It's a diversion. A decent narrative for the journos to get their teeth into. I don't know what else you expect me to do.'

Ronnie dropped the pad back on the table, having not read a word. 'Well, for a start, you can go find the bloke who brought the message.'

'Tang?'

'Yeah. Find him. Find out what he knows.'

'You want me to start randomly questioning members of the public to find out why Sebastian did it?'

'No, Charlie. I want you to ask the cunt that triggered all this to explain himself. I reckon, given the circumstances, that's fair fucking enough.'

We stared at each other in silence. His punchiness had returned. I had no choice but to do what he instructed. Tang wouldn't know a thing. He was nothing but a messenger. In fact, he was a friend. But fine. Fuck it. I'd do it.

'Fine,' I said, standing up and moving towards the door. Ronnie followed me, his eyes filled with hate. When my hand was on the door knob he stopped me, his voice quiet.

'And Westcott ...'

I turned back.

'Change your fucking shirt. It's disgusting.'

I left the room, realising with horror that I was still covered in my best friend's blood.

CHAPTER SEVEN

The AFP officer waiting outside the meeting room accompanied me back to the office, where I was able to grab my jacket and change into the clean shirt I kept in my bottom drawer. Then I walked quickly towards the Senate entrance, head down, eyes scanning the corridors, wary of journalists, members of the opposition or colleagues who would ambush me with questions about the growing disturbance outside Sebastian's office.

I was in a daze, trying to comprehend what I'd just done.

I'd spent much of Sebastian's preselection battle, then during the election campaign, dreading the day I read of his Hong Kong secret on the front page of *The Australian* newspaper.

Now I had volunteered the information. To Ronnie Durban, of all people. What would Sebastian have thought of my decision?

Maybe he would have understood. I'd explained all the risks years earlier, when first he'd raised the prospect of running for office. He hadn't wanted to hear.

We'd sat on the private balcony of the Australian Consul-General's residence in Hong Kong.

The sound of the Ocean Park roller-coaster carried across the gentle currents of Deep Water Bay, across the junks and private yachts that cruised out towards the South China Sea as lights from the luxurious villas scattered up the hillside twinkled in the dusk.

Consul-General in Hong Kong was a diplomatic posting not of the significance as to Beijing, Tokyo or Washington, but high profile given the hundred thousand Australian passport holders in the Hong Kong community.

This was my second trip to marvel at his life of cocktail receptions, speeches at the Jockey Club and endless ministerial visits. It was a long way from when I'd been with him in Hong Kong, years before, in the excruciating week after Chloe's death. When we'd gone to ground in a small rental on Lamma Island so he wouldn't be seen walking by the sea, tearing at his clothes as he struggled with the horror that he had killed the girl he loved.

May, the housekeeper, brought our drinks out on a silver tray. Gin and tonic for me. Sebastian had lemon, lime and bitters. For the most part, he hadn't touched booze since that night. Or at least that's what he always pretended.

'Christ, what is this appalling music?' I pointed at the portable bluetooth Bose speaker that was connected to his mobile.

'It's the playlist we use for functions. I put it together myself.'

I grimaced at his predictable choice of classical, elevator music.

'What do you want, Charlie? The Smashing Pumpkins, Pearl Jam, Blinding Love?'

He'd always mocked my musical taste. Not like Chloe. She and I had bonded over alternative music. I could still see her, sharing the earbud of my Discman. Swaying beside me. Swapping smiles and nods of recognition. *You're like me. We're the same.*

Not wanting to have the same old fight, I gestured out to the bay before us.

'How could you walk away from this?'

May returned and placed an ashtray with a gold Australian coat of arms on the coffee table in front of me. Sebastian waited for her to leave before responding.

'Time's almost up.' He sighed. 'And I don't want to stick around in Hong Kong, after what I've seen ...'

I presumed he was speaking about the summer of protests that had abruptly concluded only a few months earlier with the introduction of Hong Kong's draconian national security law. I'd watched footage on television of the street battles between riot police and protestors, and I'd wondered how it had affected him. But he didn't want to talk about that.

'I've done too many diplomatic postings in a row.' He shrugged. 'When I'm done here they'll send me back to Australia and stick me in the RG Casey building to rot.'

Of course, it was about his career. He'd always been a thruster, and I could imagine how the Department of Foreign Affairs and Trade expectation for onshore time between extended postings would be anathema to him.

'But why do you want to get into politics all of a sudden?'

'My life for ten years has been pressing the flesh, making speeches and networking. What's the difference?'

'That doesn't answer my question.'

'Well, Charlie, I'm presuming my application wouldn't be unappreciated.'

That hit a nerve. Back home, the Party had just been routed at the election and our best and brightest were already deserting us, unable to spend another three years in miserable opposition. We'd lost the unlosable election, or in fact, I'd lost it. Despite the PM being incompetent, despite the government being mired in sleaze and scandal, it turned out the public hated my party more.

I'd fled to Hong Kong to drown myself in gin and tonics. A self-imposed exile as detractors back in Australia wrote a post-mortem on my failings as Campaign Director, compounding my earlier sins as one of the faceless men who had torn down a sitting PM.

I confess, when Sebastian confided he wanted my help to win preselection, my first thought was that this could resurrect my career in the party.

'You should be careful what you wish for.' I licked my lips.

'You think they'd go for it?'

'I know they would. It would be a coup for us.'

'Because I'm a public figure.'

'Because of your father-in-law.'

He sighed, and I could tell I'd bruised his ego.

'Recruiting you would stick it up the other side.'

'McCubbin isn't political.' Sebastian grimaced as I laughed. 'I mean, he isn't a politician.'

'Your father-in-law was Secretary of the Department of Prime Minister and Cabinet for three conservative PMs, the last of whom refused to let him retire and appointed him ASIO boss. He's called us soft on terrorism and soft on China ever since. He is totally partisan.'

Sebastian shrugged. 'So if I joined your party, that would be a win for you, right?'

'And a betrayal for your father-in-law. That's some enemy.' I chuckled, still not quite willing to believe he wanted to do it.

Sebastian sucked in a breath. 'I will do … what I need to do.'

I sipped my gin and tonic, feeling my legs jitter as they always did when an idea took me. It was strong. A well-needed win, and a humiliation for the PM. I could picture Sebastian in parliament. He had the intellect, the charisma, the social networks to go a long way. Maybe all the way. We could do it together.

It was only then that my dogged caution kicked in. I stopped speaking, ashamed, realising I was only thinking about myself. I looked at the glass of gin, wondering if it was my second or third. I forced my knees to be still.

'It would bring scrutiny …' I turned to find him looking at the lights across the bay. I wasn't sure if he had heard me. 'How many times have you renewed your security clearance since …'

He shrugged.

'You've never disclosed it? What happened …'

He looked away. 'It's nothing to do with them.'

'They would say …' I picked my words. 'That you failed to disclose a vulnerability. They would say you are a security risk and vulnerable to blackmail by foreign intelligence services because you have never declared what happened —'

He turned to me, his eyes flashing. 'It wasn't their business. It wasn't anyone's business.' He thudded his forefinger into his chest. 'I had to go on living.'

I had to go on living. It was not the first time he'd said that phrase over the years, justifying not only his aggressive social life and the stellar diplomatic career that took off in Shanghai after her death, but also the fact that I was pretty sure he'd repressed all emotions about what had happened, that he'd never confronted the guilt for what he'd done. He had gone on living.

I nodded, raising my hand to calm him. 'I know. And I supported you.'

He took a breath. 'It's been over ten years. It's in the past.'

I sipped my G&T, still trying to balance my moral compass.

'I'm just saying, if it came out, if something happened and it came out, being in politics is going to make things ten times worse. It would be a scandal, exploited by the other side. The media would pile on. McCubbin would swing his axe.'

Sebastian breathed through his nose.

'I can live with that risk.'

On cue, Cassie walked out of the girls' bedroom, and we watched through the window in silence as she poured a glass of water and sat down in front of the television, as usual giving Sebastian a wide berth when I was around.

'What about your family?' I chided him.

'They know nothing. And you would protect them. Just like you've always protected me.' He turned, and I saw a familiar tightness of his lips, unblinking eyes and pupils like needle points. 'And you owe me that, Charlie.'

In the awkward silence, I felt the usual pang of guilt. I had my own ghosts and buried shames.

I looked to the hillside, watching car headlights follow the curving road towards the Peak.

'Do you ever think of her?' I asked, watching him stare off into the dark horizon.

'Who?'

'Chloe.'

'No,' he responded, and I remembered how sometimes, despite my love for him, I hated Sebastian.

CHAPTER EIGHT

It was a relief to get in my old Mazda Astina, 1990, filled with McDonalds wrappers and empty bags of Twisties. I fumbled in the glove box for the emergency cigarettes and lit a Marlboro Gold with shaking hands. The nicotine hit was further relief. I inhaled it in three breaths, then, before lighting the next, checked to see if there were any leftovers in the Twisties packet. There weren't, but as consolation, I found some Fruit Tingles and popped two into my mouth, then some sour Jubes. I lit another cigarette and snapped on the stereo. The Smashing Pumpkins: 'Soma'. A deep but beautiful cut from the 1993 album *Siamese Dream*.

I rested my head back on the car seat with my eyes closed, then pulled out my phone and searched for Tang's number.

He answered after a single ring.

'Did I forget something, Charlie? Does the Minister have another question?'

'No, SK, I have something personal I'd like to discuss with you. Can we meet?'

'Of course. I am available at the Hyatt in an hour ... What's wrong, Charlie?'

I opened my mouth, then closed it again, feeling foolish and annoyed with Ronnie for sending me on a goose chase. SK sounded so normal. He wasn't part of any conspiracy. He'd just passed a message on.

'I'll see you there, SK.'

I hung up and breathed out through my nose, feeling my

heartbeat slowing for the first time since I saw Sebastian with that gun in his mouth.

A fist beat at the passenger window, and I jolted forward, thinking of Sebastian.

Go with this boy. He'll look after you.

Andrew Swann, political journalist for the *Herald*, gestured for me to roll down the window.

'Have you been sacked?'

'What?'

'I'm trying to work out why else you'd be sitting in your car, smoking in the middle of the day.'

I checked my watch. Sebastian had been dead for just over three hours.

'I heard The Smashing Pumpkins and knew it'd be you.' Swanny grinned. 'What are you doing out here?'

Swanny was a friend. One of the old pool journalists I got on well with. He liked to share a cigarette or a late-night Chinese meal. He had a narrow head with fire-engine-red hair, and an unkempt beard on his chin. He never wore a tie and looked perpetually dishevelled. We used to joke we shared the same stylist.

Swanny stood back as I opened the door and got out of the car. Before I could say a word, he leaned in, muttering in a conspiratorial tone.

'Mate. What's going on at the senate offices?'

'What do you mean?' I played dumb, shaking my head as I lit another cigarette.

Swanny looked sceptical. 'Something's going on. Paramedics have been in, and the AFP has shut down the corridors, so I can't see what office it is.'

I smoked and looked him in the eye, offering nothing. It was my well-practised journalist stonewall. Unfortunately, he'd seen this look before and wasn't deterred.

'You sure you don't want to share anything?'

'No.'

'Off the record?'

'No.' I said, throwing the cigarette butt on the ground and grinding it with my foot. 'I don't know what you're talking about.'

Swanny touched my shoulder, his unshaven face close to mine. 'No one else in the Press Gallery has twigged yet, Charlie. But they will. You sure you don't want to set the record straight before people start making shit up?'

My heart beat faster. He already knew. Someone was leaking. Who? Judy? The DLO? Maybe the AFP. Woods, whom Ronnie had so brazenly insulted?

It was only a matter of time then until the story broke and Sebastian's suicide would lead every bulletin.

I concentrated on keeping the panic from my face. But Swanny was a veteran: he smiled, knowing he'd caught me. I gave up any pretence to normality and got back in the car. I needed to get away.

'No comment then, Charlie?'

'No comment, Swanny,' I growled, slamming the door and reversing out of the parking space as The Smashing Pumpkins' distorted guitars ravaged the cabin and Billy Corgan began to wail.

❖

SK Tang pushed back from the table, his mouth open in shock.

'But Charlie … this is awful.' He mopped his head with a napkin. 'I don't know what to say …'

I remained silent and watched him, wary of any sign he may be feigning surprise about Sebastian.

We were in the tea lounge at the Hyatt. An art deco dining room with ornate plasterwork, high ceilings and marble floors. The clinking of fine china and silverware surrounded us. An American family of four stared into iPhones and iPads at a table by the door. A Japanese couple talked, their heads close together as they flicked through a Lonely Planet guide.

Tang and I were in a corner as far from listening ears as I could find.

He reached across the table and tugged at my sleeve.

'But why would he do this?'

'I was hoping you could tell me, SK.'

'Why would I know?'

'The message from Zheng. It seemed to trigger him.'

He blinked his eyes a little. Then stuffed his forefinger and thumb into his sockets and massaged, shaking his head as he spoke. 'I don't understand what you mean by "triggered".'

'*It's done.*' I repeated, anger unexpectedly making my voice tremble. 'Clearly, that meant something to him. It disturbed him.'

'But to make him do something like this? Why would he do that?' He widened his eyes, pausing for a response. Was he sincere? Or was he provoking me? How could I accuse him without revealing the substance of the presumed blackmail? I pulled back. Worried I was being too rash, giving too much away.

'I was hoping you could tell me what that message meant, SK.'

'I don't know anything about that, Charlie. I just passed on the message. I thought they were friends. Maybe I lacked tact. My chairman always tells me I am not subtle … but it was an innocent thing.'

'They weren't friends, SK.'

'Maybe there was more to it than I thought.'

I rolled my eyes, rising to the bait. 'Sebastian hadn't heard from Zheng for over twenty years, SK … and Zheng sends a message like that. It's intended to get a reaction.'

He stared at me, then shook his head. 'But they were friends, Charlie.'

'They weren't friends. And they hadn't spoken in twenty years.'

I could see Sebastian, in the villa on Lamma Island, his head in his hands, recounting his last sighting of Zheng. It was in the police station garage, where they'd been brought after Chloe's death. Sebastian said he'd never been looked at with such hatred. He could feel the heat across the space between them. He'd tried to speak to Zheng, but the door closed in his face and they'd thrust Sebastian out into the street.

Tang's low voice brought me back to the table.

'But that's not right, Charlie.'

'What's not right?'

'You said they hadn't seen each other in twenty years. The Minister saw Zheng last month when he was in Hong Kong.'

'No, he didn't.' I squinted at Tang, wondering if his age had caught up with him, whether all the doddering mannerisms were less a funny eccentricity and more the signs of early onset dementia. 'I was with Sebastian in Hong Kong. He never met Zheng. We met you, SK. Don't you remember?'

'Of course I remember, Charlie.' He wrinkled his nose, annoyed.

'We had breakfast and dinner together, you remember?' I urged.

'I know that, Charlie. I'm saying after. After we said goodnight. Some hours later ...'

'What are you talking about? We returned to the hotel. His room was down the hall from mine. We said goodnight.'

'Then he went out again. I saw him.'

'Where?'

'Back to the China Club.'

'But we all left together, SK. Are you telling me you went back later? That Sebastian went back too?'

'Yes, but for different reasons.' Tang blushed. 'I have a young lady friend. We meet there. In the Long March Bar.'

'Sebastian came into the bar?'

'No, he went into a private room ... with Zheng. As you can imagine, I was embarrassed. My friend, she is ... younger than me.'

'So, you didn't approach him.'

'No.'

I shook my head. It sounded absurd. Impossible. Why would Sebastian go back to the China Club? Why would he have a secret meeting with Zheng after some twenty years?

Then, with a tremor in my gut, I remembered the morning after that night in Hong Kong. Sebastian had arrived in the Four Seasons lobby looking pale, unusually unshaven. Bags under his eyes. Complaining it was something he ate. Unsteady on his feet.

I felt my face twitch.

Food poisoning. Nothing more.

I pushed back, refusing to let myself be distracted by Tang's absurd claims.

'Sorry, SK. I don't believe you. He wouldn't have gone through such a charade. He would have told me about Zheng if he'd shown up after two decades and invited him for a nightcap. Anyway, that night he was unwell. He told me about that the next morning.'

I stopped speaking, realising that again Tang was staring at me with grandfatherly confusion. There was more to come.

'But Charlie, it wasn't the first time I'd seen him with Zheng. I'd seen them before. Other times you visited. They went to the China Club late at night.'

I frowned.

'Zheng acknowledged it. He sought me out at the CPPCC. He asked if I would be seeing the Australian Assistant Minister. Our friend in common. I remember I was shocked. Like you now. I didn't know how he knew I was travelling to Australia or that I was scheduled to see Mr Adler. But he seemed relaxed and natural and told me if I was seeing Mr Adler to hand him that message. "*Zuò ha'o le.*"'

'That's rubbish, SK.' My legs were bouncing under the table now. 'Even this morning, Sebastian said he hadn't seen Zheng in years.'

'I wondered at that too, Charlie.' He shrugged. 'I didn't want to contradict him.'

That was all I could take. I dragged myself to my feet, shaking my head. I needed to get away from this. Tang's words were poison. Sebastian wouldn't have lied to me.

'I don't know what you're talking about.' I said, feeling my body tremble. 'I just need you to tell me. Is there anything else coming? Are there any other messages? Is there anything to come out?'

'To come out?'

'A scandal.'

'I don't —'

'Are you fucking blackmailing us, Tang?' I burst out, at last unable to contain myself. 'Is Zheng? Is this some sort of political thing?'

SK's body seemed to deflate.

'Charlie, I thought we had a trusting friendship. I am sorry you have such a low estimation of me.'

'Answer the question. Is anything else coming?' I struggled to contain my rising panic.

'I have no idea, Charlie.' He straightened his back and looked at me with clear eyes. 'What else was your friend hiding from you?'

❖

I stormed out of the tearoom and into the foyer of the hotel.

Secret meetings with Chloe's father? It was impossible. Sebastian had been unwell the last night in Hong Kong. I'd seen how terrible he'd looked the next morning. He hadn't been sneaking back to the China Club for secret meetings with Zheng. He'd been curled up over the toilet bowl. He wouldn't have kept a secret like that from me. He never would. If Zheng had made contact, if it was blackmail, if he was threatening Sebastian, Sebastian would have come to me first. He would have demanded my help, insisted I protect him. *You owe me!*

But then … if they were friends? If it were some kind of secret relationship? A secret friendship?

I stopped dead on the steps outside the Hyatt.

It would not be the first time Sebastian had hidden a secret friendship.

As if responding to my growing sense of dread, my phone vibrated with incoming messages. My heart sank as I read the list of names. Journos. Journos asking for comment. On what? Ronnie had texted, too.

<*The story has broken. Fucking Swann has it.*>

I followed the link. Just as he'd hinted. Swanny had the story. The headline: ASSISTANT MINISTER SUICIDES IN PARLIAMENT HOUSE OFFICE.

My phone was ringing. I declined the call. It rang again. I glanced around the steps of the Hyatt, fearing I'd see people I knew; journalists with cameras and microphones running towards me.

Head down, I stumbled across the road to my car, my hands searching through the pockets of my jacket and overcoat, trying to find my damn cigarettes. Juggling the lighter, the cigarette. My phone was still ringing, and I placed it on the roof of the car, dismissing the call, as I unlocked the door.

Jesus, Ronnie now. Decline. Another journo text message. A number I didn't recognise. Turn it off. Off. Off.

Fuck!

I'd answered a call.

I could hear her voice. Tiny, out of the speaker, yet still filled with bitterness.

'Charlie? Charlie, are you there?'

Cassie Adler. I couldn't hang up.

'Sorry, Cassie, I can't talk right now ...'

'Shut up, Charlie. Don't be an idiot.'

I sighed. I didn't want to talk to her. I never wanted to talk to her. I swallowed down the usual bile and reminded myself her husband had just killed himself. *Husband.* The word stuck in my throat.

'You didn't think to call me, Charlie? You don't think that's the normal thing the Chief of Staff would do, or a best friend would do? They wouldn't call to check on their friend's family?'

I opened and closed my mouth, not knowing what to say. 'I didn't think —'

'About us? Of course not. When have you?'

'— that you'd want to hear from me. I was giving you space.'

'I don't want space, Charlie. I want to know what happened to my husband. I want you to come over.'

I began to protest.

'Now, Charlie. I swear to God you better get here.'

'Okay, I'll come. But I don't have any answers, Cassie.'

'You knew him best. You'll know more than me.'

But after the conversation with Tang, I wasn't so sure.

CHAPTER NINE

When we were sixteen, Sebastian became a boarder at the school.

His mother had never really recovered from his father's betrayal. When she began a new relationship, she clung to her partner like a drowning person to a life buoy. Six months later he was offered a posting to his firm's Hong Kong office, and she decided she was moving with him, not pausing to consider the effect it would have on her son. It all happened so fast.

Sebastian confided the news to me in a corner of the library one Monday morning.

'She's leaving and wants you to board?'

He nodded. 'I'm already enrolled in Monash.'

'That's Mallet's boarding house …'

A chill passed between us.

Sebastian had beaten Mallet bloody after his father's suicide, and we had walked about the school unaccosted ever since. But going into his boarding house? Living with Mallet? Sleeping in the same dorm room as him? Anything could happen.

On the last night in his family home, we sat in the rumpus room, as we had hundreds of times before. Removal boxes were everywhere. They had already packed most of the other rooms. We tried to pretend nothing had changed. We watched *Star Trek: The Next Generation* and played *Dungeons & Dragons*. I had made him a mix tape of alternative bands, and we listened as we turned on *Castle Wolfenstein* for the last time.

The tracks on my mix started heavy, distorted, fast. I'd

discovered listening to grunge triggered the testosterone in my adolescent body. It made me feel somehow wilder, stronger, more confident and ready for the world. I wanted to share that strength with Sebastian as he went off to the boarding house.

The opener was, of course, Nirvana's 'Smells Like Teen Spirit'. Kurt's jangling power chord opening was sent into orbit by the booming entry of Dave Grohl on the drums. From there I kept up the pace. Straight into 'Porch' by Pearl Jam, the bristling tempo, like the accelerator of a car, hitting the floor. Eddie Vedder seething about love and regret and freedom. Then the next track, slower but so much heavier, Soundgarden's 'Outshined' and Chris Cornell's multi-octave voice wailing above that muddy distortion swamp. I couldn't help but nod my head in time with the power chords.

Sebastian smiled, looking at the tape cover. I'd made a collage of magazine cuttings and coloured pen spirals. I'd called it the *Nothing Will Change You* mix tape and had written the name of each band and track on the other side.

By the time J Mascis was singing 'Get Me' in that shoegazing drawl that defined Dinosaur Jr.'s sound, Sebastian was laughing out loud.

'What the hell is this?'

'Just keep listening,' I urged him, trying not to feel hurt but pleased I'd at least distracted him. I wanted him to concentrate on the next track. I thought it was poignant: Buffalo Tom, 'Taillights Fade'. A miserable choice really, given the circumstance, but in the weary sadness of Bill Janovitz's voice, I'd heard something warm and reassuring. Sebastian glanced at me out of the corner of his eye, and I thought maybe he felt it too.

He stopped playing the computer when Billy Corgan's second guitar part swelled out of the intro to the anthemic 'Snail' from the Pumpkins' debut, *Gish*. 'This is cool.' He grinned, and I blushed with pleasure, delighting in sharing with him the discovery of this music that I felt was rewiring my brain.

Neither of us spoke after that. I'd followed up with 'Everybody Hurts' by R.E.M., then Pearl Jam's 'Release', which concludes their debut album, *Ten*. Vedder's agonising lyrics, longing to connect with his deceased father. Sebastian hung his head as Vedder's gravelly voice articulated the way I imagined he would feel, awake in the boarding house longing for a father who would recognise him and be proud.

His whole body shook, and tears streamed down his face.

'Do you want me to turn it off?' I asked.

'No. Leave it on.'

Sebastian was driven to the boarding house the next day. I stood on the driveway watching the car pull away.

On Monday, I waited for him outside the library. When he appeared, he didn't look me in the eye.

'How did it go last night? What happened?'

'Don't ask,' he replied without looking up. Now it felt like it was my turn to give back the same life-saving support and love that I felt Sebastian had shown me in those dark days when we were both new boys at the school. Perhaps it was only in my imagination that this need existed, but it made me feel strong to be there for my friend. My best and only friend.

From then on I stayed at school late after class, even when we didn't have sport. We'd hang around the library together until it closed, and then sit on the steps as dusk fell, giving him as much time as possible away from the boarding house.

I found I couldn't sleep. I lay awake listening to a copy of the mix tape I'd kept for myself, imagining that he might be hearing the same song, at the same time, lying in his bed, and that somehow the music connected us, that he felt less alone, like I had that day he helped me out of my mother's car.

Go with this boy, he'll look after you.

I kept getting to school earlier and earlier. Waiting for him before class. When I saw him, my heart lurched. He was a forlorn figure. Always by himself. His shoulders hunched. The once crisp blue shirt that his mother had ironed, now drab. Over time his smell changed to that of the institution, the industrial laundry, just like the other boarders. I felt powerless to help him. I stayed late and came to school early to be with him, and it went on like that, until one morning when I was waiting at the dining hall and I saw him walking back with a group of boys, including Mallet.

Sebastian caught my eye, then looked away, pretending he hadn't seen me. Some of the boys jeered at me, as they usually did. They kept walking.

He avoided me all day, then in the afternoon he was late to the library. He finally came, but muttered excuses about needing to get back to the house for prep.

'That's not for another hour.' I showed him the new *Dungeons & Dragons* campaign book we'd been waiting to arrive for weeks.

He shook his head and said he needed to go.

The same thing happened the next day. He told me before the bell that he couldn't meet that afternoon. I'd organised with my mum to pick me up late so I could be with him. Instead, I found myself alone and wandering around the school with my Walkman, listening to the mix tape.

The music was comforting, still a connection to my best friend, even as I struggled to understand why he was growing distant.

I drifted along the bush track that led up towards the large sports fields. In the evening light, students were playing football. It wasn't training. It was just play. Mallet. Boys from his group. From the boarding house. And there was Sebastian in among them. I turned, and he caught my eye. He stopped running for a moment. Then one of his new friends called and passed the ball. He swung round, caught it and ran up the field as the other boys clapped and chanted his name.

The next morning, I didn't wait for him, and he came looking for me. In class, he sat next to me, pretending that nothing had happened. Mallet called, encouraging Sebastian to sit with him. He refused. It was almost like he was ashamed of his behaviour. Like I was an obligation he needed to attend to.

But after school he muttered his excuses, unable to look me in the eye, and was gone.

Sebastian and Mallet remained friends up to the end of school, and into adulthood when Mallet, following the well-trodden path of old boys from our school, became an investment banker and moved to Shanghai during Sebastian's diplomatic posting.

Starting from those later years of high school, Mallet opened a whole new vista of social groups to Sebastian, which included weekends away to watch football games, or discos with girls from a nearby girls' school, and double dates on Saturday nights as we entered our last year of school.

It set a pattern for our relationship that lasted for the rest of his life.

There were always other friends in other compartments of his life, closed off to me. Friends with whom he could have fun and play sport, with whom he could let loose, when he wasn't acing his exams, winning academic awards and being offered scholarships to all the best universities. The need to be loved seemed to be as much a driver for him as the need to perform and achieve.

I always wanted Sebastian to myself: talking into the night, sharing music, spending time alone together. But he was an extravert by nature. He needed people around him. He needed people to approve and applaud him. He was the life of every party, to which I was not invited. There was a whole side of him I couldn't keep up with, nor did I want to.

I kept walking miserably around the school, now alone, the music blaring on my Walkman.

It was amid that loneliness I first realised how awful my jealousy could be. One afternoon I saw Mallet walk out of a bathroom near A-block. I had Nirvana in my ears. 'Territorial Pissings'. The driving guitar and distorted bass, the pounding, ferocious drums, seized me with a violent inspiration. I marched into the bathroom, picked up the heavy metallic garbage bin filled with paper towels and hurled it at the mirror, which fractured and burst into shards across the floor. I then left the bathroom and reported to the school sergeant that I'd heard the smash and had run in to see, following Mallet. The teachers checked the cameras to corroborate. Of us two young men, I was the least likely to be lying. I hoped Mallet would be expelled. He was only suspended, during which time I think, but can't be sure, Sebastian spent a weekend at his house in Cowra.

CHAPTER TEN

It was just after 1 pm by the time I arrived at Sebastian's home in Forrest. When Sebastian and Cassie first moved to Canberra, after Sebastian won his seat, I'd shown them some grand family homes in the leafy suburb, but Cassie opted for something different, and chose an impressive but starkly contemporary building. Its clean lines and open-plan functionality struck me as cold and anonymous. Sometimes, I suspected she chose it just to annoy me.

Cassie had never liked me. I had gone to extreme lengths to engineer Sebastian a Senate seat, including assassinating the character of the much-loved sitting senator. But in Cassie's mind, I had co-opted her husband into a job that separated him from his wife and kids.

Or maybe, to be fair, Cassie just knew that I didn't like her. In my mind, I had always compared her to Chloe. I know this is hypocritical considering my jealousy of Sebastian and what I did to try to fracture his relationship with Chloe, but there it is. If my best friend was to marry anyone, it should have been the woman I loved.

Cassie was, in her way, more successful than Sebastian. She was one of the most accomplished bureaucrats in the country. She was a deputy secretary at Defence, with responsibility for the AUKUS nuclear submarine program. Her career had taken off the moment she'd left the Defence Force Academy. She'd deployed to Timor-Leste, then been part of the F-35 Joint Strike Fighter Program. By the mid 2000s she was involved in Iraq War planning, contributing to the Defence White Paper and Afghanistan surge, then she was seconded to the Australia China Defence Strategic Dialogue.

It was in Beijing that her relationship with Sebastian got underway. He was at the embassy and she was coordinating the Australian delegation's participation in military-to-military discussions on defence cooperation.

Sebastian pursued her with the same drive with which he'd once chased Chloe. It was another relationship I knew nothing about. Only later did I learn he'd proposed to Cassie in the Qantas lounge at Hong Kong airport. A wedding invitation landed in my inbox, announcing they would tie the knot a month later at St Christopher's Cathedral in Canberra. The reception would be at the National Gallery, overlooking Lake Burley Griffin.

A week before the wedding, he introduced us at Aubergine. It was a rushed audience, as if he needed to go through the motions of seeking my blessing, despite having kept the relationship a secret. Cassie resented it as much as I did.

I found her appearance plain and her conversation dull. She looked so much like her father, whose politics were repulsive to me. I couldn't help hating her.

She left after dinner, and Sebastian and I went to Molly, a shadowy speakeasy hidden away in a Canberra CBD back alley. Sebastian, breaking his usual abstinence, drank himself stupid, and at some point in the night reached across the table and clutched my jacket.

'I love her so much.'

Not knowing what to respond, I shrugged and said, 'You'll be very happy together.'

He looked away. 'I don't mean Cassandra.'

I hated her more then. I felt she must have trapped him somehow. Played to the grief that wreathed his soul since Chloe's car left the road.

Cassie was an interloper. A thief.

❖

I endured the wedding. Sebastian's guest list, and those who made speeches (I was not among them), made me feel like a stranger. It was that familiar nauseating feeling I'd had glimpsing his compartmentalised life on the school football fields.

Mallet was there. Older, his head shaved. His suit probably worth a month of my salary. He made a speech with another former banker leaning ridiculously on his arm, Kai Birch. A Ken doll lookalike from Michigan, who revealed they'd spent a six-month secondment in Shanghai with Sebastian (he pronounced it *'Bastion'*) going to bars and playing rugby union against British expats. All information that Sebastian hadn't shared with me.

Other long-forgotten acolytes were there from the school, people who I'd just presumed Sebastian had severed contact with. DFAT grad mates, other business people. All loud and back slapping and overly familiar. They spoke about him with such confidence, but I didn't recognise him in their speeches. How could I? They knew nothing about the boy who had wept in the rumpus room of his house in the suburbs, nor the hysterical grieving man in my arms on Lamma Island. And when, in his own speech, Sebastian referred to me as his 'childhood friend', I struggled even to see myself. 'Charlie is someone I can always share deep and meaningful conversations with … just not his music taste.' As if our friendship were a joke. As if the music I'd shared with him was just for a laugh. As frivolous as what he shared with those impostors at the reception, with Mallet, with his business chamber buddies, with Cassandra fucking McCubbin.

'Some wedding.' Kai Birch was next to me, holding a glass of red wine by the base. He wore a double-breasted blazer that should have looked absurd on someone in his thirties, but on Kai it made him look even more the American hero. He had cropped, jet-black hair, and his skin wore a healthy Californian tan that money couldn't buy at a solarium. He gazed at me with blue eyes that were almost translucent. I could imagine him as a fighter pilot walking across the tarmac from his jet, a helmet under his arm, and later I learnt he had in fact achieved senior rank in the US Navy Reserve. He told me all about his accomplishments at

Yale, life as a Rhodes scholar to Oxford, his five years making millions at some investment bank I'd never heard of, investing in tech companies across Asia, then on to management consulting in New York and Washington (one of the youngest partners ever). He was about to move to a global tech giant ('look out for the announcement on Bloomberg').

'And how do you know the happy couple?' he asked me.

'I went to school with Sebastian.'

'Oh really? You must know my Henry.'

'Henry?'

'Henry Mallet. He was great pals with Sebastian at school too. We were quite the trio in Shanghai.' I wondered whether the bitterness was visible on my face as Kai effortlessly plucked a passing guest from a group beside us and drew him forward, a languid arm draped over his shoulder. I saw the bald head and meaty cheeks, and immediately felt the old rage rise in my belly.

'Henry. I've met an old school chum of yours,' Kai crooned, oblivious to the torture he was putting me through.

'Hello, Charlie.' Mallet's voice was soft, almost – absurdly – shy. It was the first time he'd ever used my Christian name.

I saw Sebastian striding across the reception hall. But when he caught sight of us talking, he came to a jerking halt, spun on his heels and walked off in the other direction.

I was saved by a techno track blasting from the speakers beside the dance floor. A cheer went up from the wedding guests. Then Cassie was amongst us, a dervish of white chiffon, her hands in the air displaying splotchy shaved armpits. She bustled Kai and Mallet onto the dance floor, ignoring me. Sebastian was already up there, beneath the lights, busting out moves like a man without a care in the world.

I left the wedding, furious with Sebastian, loathing his friends, hating Cassie. I didn't see him again until they gave him the Consul-General role and they moved to Hong Kong. His diplomatic career evolved. It couldn't have hurt being Cassandra McCubbin's husband and Alec McCubbin's son-in-law. The cynic in me wondered whether this was why he had chosen her. By that stage in our friendship, I didn't know why Sebastian chose anyone. Including me.

❖

The door opened before I could knock, and there was Cassie, still in the dark suit she would have worn to work that morning.

She was, as ever, impeccably made up, but the eyeliner was smudged and her concealer patchy around the eyes. She was holding a glass tumbler of what I presumed was gin. She stared at me a moment as she took a sip, then turned, gesturing with her head for me to follow her into the house.

'The girls are still at school. They wanted to send them home, but I said to keep them there. Why rush back? To what?'

I had only been to their house a few times. It looked like a showroom or something from a magazine spread. Perfect, but cold. Their labradoodle, Bradley, slept on his bed in a corner, the non-moulting hypoallergenic breed as characterless as the house.

I couldn't imagine Sebastian here.

I followed Cassie through to the kitchen, which opened onto a deck overlooking their pool and manicured garden.

'Do you want a drink?' Her voice was constricted, as if she had a chest infection. She pointed at a glass table on the deck, where I saw open bottles of Bombay Sapphire, Fever Tree tonic and a freezer tray of melting ice.

'Are you alone here?' I asked, watching her walk in a crooked line to fetch another tumbler from the cupboard.

'You're here,' she said, gesturing for me to sit down.

'Yeah, but you need to be with someone ...'

'You're someone, Charlie,' she snapped, cracking the glass down on the table. 'And I've got plenty of time for friends with sympathy. Right now, I want you to tell me why the fuck Sebastian would do this.'

Her sharp features, like the ice in the tray, melted. Her lip trembled, and she thrust a finger to her eye, staring up at the ceiling.

'I need you to make sense of it ...'

I rubbed my face with my hands, already tired to the depths of my soul with being asked to make sense of Sebastian's actions. I was still reeling from the conversation with Tang, trying to bury the notion he'd planted in my head of a secret friendship between Sebastian and Zheng.

'I'm sorry. I don't —'

'Don't fucking tell me you know nothing, Charlie.' She stamped her foot. 'You always know everything. Everything I don't. Everything he doesn't share with me. You *know*. So now you must know about this. Tell me. Explain it to me.'

She sat down, folding her arms. I knew she hated showing vulnerability in front of me. She had the same steel in her as her father.

I was wondering how much I could say. Whether I should trust her. Whether Sebastian would want me to. And yet a piece of me wanted to compare notes. *Do you feel betrayed by him too?*

'I think maybe it had something to do with his father.'

'Oh, Jesus.' She rolled her eyes and stood up.

'I don't know if they told you. The method of ... the suicide ... it was the same ...'

The twins' towels were hanging over the fence around the pool. She pulled them to her, folding and rolling them while shaking her head.

'Fuck off, Charlie. Don't give me some trite line about what his daddy did thirty years ago. I've read that rubbish the PMO is putting out. It's bullshit. We've been together for almost ten years and he's probably spoken about his dad maybe six times. He did not kill himself to be like his father.'

'I'm not saying it was to be like him,' I persisted. 'But if you think his dad's suicide didn't affect him, then you didn't know him at all.'

She spun around. 'Why the fuck did you come here?'

'You asked me to.'

'You've never liked me. You never thought I was good enough for your best mate, did you? Now I'm not even worthy of being told the truth.'

I folded my arms. The urge to smoke was overwhelming. Christ, she pissed me off. She could play the bereaved wife as much as she wanted. But I'd known him longer.

'What do you want me to say? I don't have an explanation for you, Cassie. I was hoping you could tell me something. I have my own questions —'

'I'm not answering any more questions.'

That slowed me down.

'Who else has been asking?'

'Take your pick, I've had an endless procession through. First the ACT police, then AFP, then Defence, and the others …'

I felt my chest constrict, but I tried to suppress any sign of panic on my face. She wasn't watching me as she strangled the towel.

'What did they ask you?'

She shrugged. 'What do you expect? Last sightings. Was anything going on with him? Was he troubled?'

'Was he?'

She dragged another towel down and shook it at me. 'He was swimming with his girls this morning. They were playing Marco Polo.' She slapped the towel and folded it again. 'He was happy with his kids. He's always happy with his kids.'

Something struck me in her tone.

'Just his kids?'

Her shoulders slumped. She dropped the towels into a basket and returned to the table, pouring herself a gin and tonic. Half gin. A splash of tonic. She took a large sip.

'Give me a cigarette,' she sighed. I handed over the packet and she lit one. Glancing up, she curled an eyebrow and spoke with the cigarette hanging from her mouth. 'Don't look so shocked, Charlie. You don't think we smoked in Iraq?'

I shrugged and watched her blow a cloud of smoke towards the sky, the fingertips of her free hand tracing the rim of the already half empty tumbler.

'I've never known what was going on with him,' she breathed.

'What does that mean?'

She looked up at me with a challenging expression on her face. 'How about that after twelve months into our marriage … he refused to touch me?'

I kept my eyes on the flame as I lit my own cigarette.

'Eighteen months of frantic pursuit, seduction, courtship, long distance relationship, dirty weekends in Hong Kong in little rented cottages on the islands. He would have told you …'

'He told me nothing.'

Her eyebrow twitched at this, but she continued speaking, staring into her glass. 'Then twelve months after we were married, he was like a stranger. At first, I thought he was being considerate after the birth of the twins. But it went on. It didn't stop. We were in separate bedrooms in the Hong Kong residence. The only time we slept in the same bed was when you came to visit.'

She finished her drink and poured another. Her hands were unsteady, and I reached out, still avoiding her eye, and mixed the drink for her. She tapped her finger on the glass, requiring a more generous helping of gin.

'So then when the AFP are asking me, "Did you see a change in him? Was anything different? Was he distant?" What could I say? He's been distant for years. He goes into his study and I go into mine. He sleeps in his room, I'm in mine. I was always worried about how we'd explain that to the girls when they were old enough to ask. I guess no need to worry now.'

I poured myself another gin, knowing I couldn't let myself get drunk but already feeling the sweet fingers of the booze dragging me forwards. I mixed it with similar proportions to hers.

'Had he met anyone different recently?' I blurted this out, not knowing how to question her about Zheng. What the hell could I say? Had he popped over for a barbecue? Had they both gone off to The Dock for a beer?

'How would I know, Charlie? You manage his diary. Even when I'm out with him at a function or something, it's because you've put me there as a prop.'

'He attends Defence events with you too, Cassie.'

'Sure.' She shrugged. 'Part of the bargain. We look after each other's careers. That's the bargain I didn't realise I'd signed up to.' Her eyes narrowed. 'Did you put him up to it?'

'To what?'

'To bagging me, so he'd have the protection of my father. To advance his career.'

I shook my head and breathed smoke out of my nose. 'I knew nothing about your relationship until the wedding invitation.'

She laughed through perfectly white teeth.

'Well, that's something. Having you in our lives, Charlie, has been like being in a polygamous relationship. He was married to you, too. Maybe there were others. How does a man go years without an urge to be with a woman?'

'You think he was having an affair?'

'Probably. He was always up late. On the computer. On his phone. All that travel. I presumed you knew. I imagined you were procuring him whores in Hong Kong. He came home from the last trip so haggard and strung out, I presumed you'd both spent the weekend fucking hookers in Lan Kwai Fong. That would explain why you were both there so frequently.'

She jutted out her chin, wanting to be provocative, wanting to appear strong. But I could see she was half crazed with grief. I knew I should find words to calm her, but she'd reinforced my memory of how out of sorts Sebastian had been that last morning in Hong Kong, and now presumably the days that followed. I couldn't get Tang's words out of my head.

'You think he was seeing other people? Other people he kept secret?'

She shrugged. 'If he was, it'll all come out now. It'll all be another trauma. For me. For the kids. That's the selfishness of suicide. Not only has he abandoned us, but he would have known that now all his secrets will be dredged up for us to hear. I'm just waiting for the next shoe to drop.'

Ronnie had used the same expression earlier in the day. There was a pressure building in my chest. I pushed the tumbler away and cleared my throat.

'What do you think will come out?'

'I have no idea. But ASIO turned his study over pretty thoroughly ...' She swallowed more of her drink. 'No stone left unturned. They carried at least three boxes out of there, including his laptop, papers, albums. So, I'm sure further humiliation will follow.'

My mouth fell open. I felt my heart thudding. I'd underestimated how quickly ASIO would ask the questions that Ronnie and I had feared. How quickly our smokescreen about Paul Adler would be dismissed by professionals much better acquainted with misdirection than the ignorant constituents Ronnie and I were used to manipulating.

'But surely, your father won't let you be humiliated ...'

She looked at me over the rim of her glass. 'Are you asking about me? Or on behalf of the government, Charlie?'

'Both,' I said, finishing my drink.

Cassie narrowed her eyes. 'Well, you can ask him yourself. He'll be around soon enough.'

I leapt to my feet, feeling the urgent need to flee. There would be nothing worse than interrogation by McCubbin in Sebastian's house. I knew I'd wilt in front of him. I'd tell him everything. I had to get out. But my eyes moved to the study doorway again, and I imagined stony-faced men and women in suits carrying boxes. What had they found?

'Mind if I look?' I asked, nodding towards the door.

Cassie shrugged in response. 'Why not? Our life is an open book now, anyway.'

CHAPTER ELEVEN

Sebastian's study was spacious. The curtains were drawn over the two large windows, keeping out the natural light. Two standing lamps in opposing corners of the room illuminated bookshelves stuffed with Chinese language texts, an ancient tape recorder, and photographs, including one of Sebastian and I singing in the school choir. Next to it was a photo of Sebastian in the first fifteen rugby team, standing side by side with Mallet. Another a photo of the three amigos: Sebastian, Kai Birch and Mallet standing on a bar street in Shanghai.

The walls of the study were a deep scarlet, matching the rugs that covered the floorboards. It was as if he'd tried to recreate the character of a Beijing hutong amid the contemporary banality of suburban Canberra.

I turned on the shaded lamp. His large oak desk was vacant of clutter. The wood was lighter and free of dust in an area the size of his laptop, now seized by ASIO. His in-tray was a neat pile of Ministerial Submissions in red folders and other papers that I flicked through, checking for any that were classified SECRET in red on their header. Unless ASIO had already taken them, he was fine. He had nothing at home that he shouldn't have.

I looked back across the room and a framed painting caught my eyes. A leather armchair was angled to face it. I turned on the desk lamp so it illuminated the image on the wall. It was familiar, like the Ming Dynasty cabinet beneath it. I remembered both from Sebastian's CG residence in Hong Kong, but like everything else in the room it now seemed to carry more significance. The leather armchair seemed to be angled to fixate on it. The lamp, if tilted, illuminated the image as if for inspection on the stage at Christie's.

It was Chinese ink and colour on rice paper. A view of Hong Kong Island from Kowloon, or perhaps closer. Floating on the waters of Victoria Harbour. I could imagine the rising swell of the current, and the Star Ferry peaking the little waves, pushing towards the shore.

The cityscape (what was it? Causeway Bay? Sheung Wan? Wan Chai?) was outlined in confident black strokes and blotches. Minor details like windows in the skyscrapers had been implied with jabs of the brush. The ripples across the surface of the water were similarly presented in curling lines. Neither land nor sea were shaded, and as the city ascended towards the mountains beyond, the outlines ceased, leaving an inexplicable white expanse, as if the city were evaporating into clouds of steam.

Above the city loomed Victoria Peak. The only part of the landscape that was coloured. The shading brought a weight to the shadowed mountain, a brooding darkness, like a violent storm was about to roll down the cliff face towards the metropolis, a typhoon of rock and wave, moments from breaking across Hong Kong.

I returned the lamp to its original position, letting the shadow again gather around the frame. I sighed. Was it just me? Was it always just me that saw the profundity in such things? Photos of me, then Mallet and Birch on the bookshelves, speaking volumes of Sebastian's disloyalty. This ink painting, representing what? His conscience? The brooding guilt related to Chloe, of what happened that night on the Peak?

I could feel the gin spinning in my head. It made my assessments harsher.

Rubbish. It was rubbish.

Sebastian was brilliant, but he never felt things like I did. He never felt meaning like I could. That's why he never understood my music.

The photos were there to take up space. They were decoration and meant nothing more. The image of the Peak, a beautiful artwork. Not even that beautiful. It would have been as meaningless hanging on the walls of a motel, or a rented shack on Lamma Island, or indeed the walls of the Australian Consul-General residence in Hong Kong, as it did here in a stuffy study in a suburb in Canberra.

I was kidding myself to attach so much goddamn meaning to everything.

Charlie is someone I can always share deep and meaningful conversations with ... just not his music taste.

Well fuck you, Sebastian.

No. No, I can do better. How about this?

Do you ever think of her?

Who?

Chloe.

No.

Beside the armchair, I noted a small table with a tumbler. I smelt it. Scotch whisky. Now I was furious. So, he drank? Despite claiming to have abstained 'with only minor lapses' since the crash. It seemed to confirm all my suspicions.

I poured myself a drink from the decanter and sat down in the armchair. Fuck McCubbin. Fuck Sebastian. Let the papers write what they goddamn pleased. Let McCubbin discover it all. I'd even tell him what Tang claimed about Zheng. Let ASIO sort the truth from the lies. I'd tell poor Cassie anything she wanted to know too. Why should I care? Why should I care after what Sebastian had done to us all with his hideous, selfish act?

But then, something about the Ming-style cabinet caught my eye. I remember it had stood just inside the door of his private apartment in his Hong Kong Consul-General's residence. The housekeeper, May, had used it to display vases filled with orchids, lilies and gerbera daisies, all intertwined with sprigs of greenery.

The cabinet was low, dark red, with an orchid pattern sprayed across its two doors. One door was ajar, as if someone had rifled through it.

I got down onto my knees and looked inside. It was almost empty. Maybe ASIO had been here first. All that was left was a document box file containing miscellaneous crap. Serviettes, business cards, scraps of paper. I withdrew to the armchair and adjusted the light so I could see the contents more clearly.

A sharp intake of breath.

So maybe Sebastian had a sense of nostalgia after all.

Beneath the gentle orange lamp, I realised the file held not junk but artefacts. Just the sight of them plunged me back into those steamy nights of excitement and discovery in 1997. We were twenty. Hong Kong was being handed back to China. And we'd just met Chloe.

There was a matchbox from Joe Bananas in Wan Chai, a sleek design with the club's name printed in bold letters; another from JJ's nightclub in the Grand Hyatt Hotel. I could still see Chloe dancing through the crowd with her hands in the air. A flyer from The Globe in Central. A ticket stub to the Fringe Club. A serviette from Lan Kwai Fong Beer Bar with illustrations of beer mugs and the bar's name. A flyer from The Underground, where Sebastian disappeared with some Canadian girl amid the writhing bodies. A ticket stub from the Peak tram. I had a matching one in my wallet. Chloe and I had gone by ourselves. Listening to music. Sharing secrets.

My heart lurched. A handwritten note with directions to Ah Mei's Claypot Rice at the Temple Street Night market. A rendezvous of which I was unaware.

My pulse quickened as I sifted my way to the bottom of the file, recognising beneath all the debris a familiar shape that made me bite my bottom lip and feel again a twenty-year-old's outrage. How the hell did he have this? Where had he found it and why had he not said a word to me?

It was the mix tape I made for Chloe. I'd called it *Just Waiting to Be Free*. It was for her. Not for him. I'd spent a day making it when Sebastian was out with his Canadian girlfriend. Down on my hands and knees in his mum's apartment in Hong Kong, my travel case spilling CDs across the spare bedroom floor. I glanced at the portable stereo on the bookshelf. It may even have been the same one, with an inbuilt CD and dual tape player that could record. How could Sebastian have kept this from me for all these years?

I smiled at my handwritten track listings. I'd put so much love and meaning into the songs. 'Disarm' by The Smashing Pumpkins, 'Indifference' by Pearl Jam, 'Street Spirit' by Radiohead. 'Landslide' by The Smashing Pumpkins again. Multiple tracks with coded messages. I'd hoped to God she listened to the lyrics. Side A ended with 'I Alone' by Live. That big, angsty chorus telling her explicitly what I couldn't say to her face. And the tape named after the lyrics which we'd both sung aloud to each other at Victoria Peak. Blinding Love's 'Restless'.

While they're sleeping
we'll be wild in the streets.
They've got names for kids like us.
It's called restless.
And I'm just waiting to be free.
With someone else like me.
I'm just waiting to be free.

And in my youthful ignorance, I completely missed the meaning of what this girl from mainland China saw in the lyrics, supposing only she felt the same deep yearning I had when I walked alone around an empty private boys' school in Sydney with the music in my head – a yearning for freedom from loneliness, for companionship, for friendship.

I'd made the cover and slipped it into the plastic tray. A picture of two hands clasping each other. I'd cut it from a detergent advertisement in *South China Morning Post*. I shuddered, reliving the nervous thrill of such an obvious statement.

I'd poured so much anxiety and courage into creating this. I'd carried the mix tape in my pocket as I moved through the crowd, searching for her among thousands of people. She'd said she would meet me near Central Pier 4. Chloe. Chloe and I amidst the celebrations. I'd searched all night, only to find them together. To realise Sebastian had compartmentalised me again.

'You won't find it.'

I looked up, my eyes still clouded with memories, the mix tape still in my hands.

'Find what?'

'The photo album. I told you, they took it.'

'What was in it?'

'Don't play dumb.'

'What was in the album, Cassie?'

'Pictures of her.'

'Who?'

'His fucking Chinese girlfriend,' she spat.

'You knew?'

My phone was buzzing violently.

'Of course I knew. She was the one he was having an affair with. When I came in here.'

I sat looking at her, stunned.

'I wish I'd caught him watching porn. Or having a real affair. Rather, he was exactly as you are there. In his chair. Sifting through memories. Having an affair with a ghost.'

My phone beeped with a message from Ronnie.

<Get back here immediately.>

I ignored him and looked back. 'You knew about Chloe? All this time? Did you tell anyone else? Did you tell ASIO? Your father?'

Cassie was staring at me and said nothing as my phone vibrated again and I looked down. Another message from Ronnie.

<ASIO is here.>

CHAPTER TWELVE

I was back in the meeting room down the hall from Sebastian's office in Parliament House. I hadn't made it as far as the office before Ronnie appeared, grabbed me by the arm and dragged me inside.

'What do they know?' I whispered. He turned his icy stare away and pointed to a woman standing against the wall.

'This is Katrina M from ASIO.'

Katrina M. No surname. They don't have surnames.

She wore a black suit over a dark grey blouse. Her long brown hair was tied in a sensible ponytail. Her glasses were wide, with a translucent frame that magnified her mascaraed eyes, blinking and cartoonish.

I took it as a positive sign that Ronnie was still doing all the talking.

'Katrina has been to Sebastian's house.'

'I've just come from there,' I volunteered.

'Her colleagues are down the hall in Sebastian's office right now.'

'I see,' I said, looking at Katrina. 'I presume that's standard procedure.'

'It's far from standard, Charlie,' Ronnie muttered, turning to pick something up from the end of the table.

My eyes flicked to Katrina. Her silent gaze felt like an accusation. I looked back to Ronnie, trying to question him, to communicate as I had with Sebastian. *What's happening?*

'Cassandra Adler handed this over. It's a photograph album.'

Ronnie placed it on the table in front of me. I braced myself. Cassie had obviously thought I was looking for it when she found me with Sebastian's box of mementoes. How bad could it be? She'd given it up to ASIO with some relish. I'd told Sebastian to get rid of the evidence – maybe Cassie thought she was punishing him.

Ronnie turned a page, and I felt my chest constricting …

Chloe's smiling face. She was eighteen, wearing a Dinosaur Jr. T-shirt and smoking a cigarette, leaning up against a wall. Sebastian and I were standing on either side of her. We were twenty. A lifetime ago. Still the look of schoolboys to us. My hair was long, free of the school's dress code and modelling the Seattle grunge look that by 1997 was already out of style. Sebastian looked just the same as ever with his short back and sides, although he wore a Union Jack vest. He was in his first year at London School of Economics, on a semester's exchange to Peking University in Beijing. I hadn't seen that youthful grin on him in years.

I shrugged my shoulders. 'This was in 1997. We were in Hong Kong, visiting his mum.'

Ronnie pointed at the girl. 'And who is that?'

I looked at him, trying again to read in his eyes whether we were putting on a show for the spooks.

'Just a girl we met when we were there.'

'Just a girl?' he asked.

I gave the slightest rise of my eyebrows. What the hell was he doing?

'Yes, just a girl.'

'Not Chloe Zheng?'

My heartbeat increased. Surely not. Surely he hadn't told them. 'I told you, I don't know who that is.'

Ronnie placed both hands on the table in front of me and recited, his voice a loud drone, his eyes unblinking.

'Chloe Zheng. Died in a car accident. Sebastian was driving. Her father just sent a fucking blackmail message to Sebastian, and then he topped himself. "It's done." Remember now, Charlie? Remember? You fucking liar.'

Black dots coursed across my vision. I couldn't understand what he was saying, only that it was a calamity. That his voice was getting louder, and every word exposed us further to Katrina M of ASIO, who leant, motionless, against the wall with her arms folded.

Ronnie kept shouting.

'You made out that she had some kind of one-night stand with Sebastian. Turns out she was the love of his fucking life. You're a fucking liar, Charlie,' he repeated.

I wanted to punch his treacherous red face. He had buckled under the first bit of pressure they'd applied. All that bullshit about protecting the Party. As soon as it got tight, he'd protected himself and told them everything. What had they threatened him with?

'You are a piece of shit, aren't you, Ronnie?'

Now Katrina spoke, calmly plucking a tissue from the box on the table to clean her glasses.

'Mr Durban was just responding to my questions, Mr Westcott. I hope you will be as cooperative. Please look at the album. Tell me what's familiar.'

Her eyes glowed with a restrained excitement, but even that scared me. I felt like a specimen under examination. Parliament House was a bell jar.

I turned back to the album and flicked through pages. There were more photos of Chloe. Not just Hong Kong. Lamma Island. Shanghai. And I was no longer with them. It was an album of their life together. Those years after the handover. Sebastian had been a fool to keep it. But I was pleased and so envious he had. I wanted time with it. I wanted to study every page.

I forced myself to close the cover and sat back, folding my arms.

'I'm not clear about what you're asking.'

Katrina stared back, waiting, as if she had already asked a question.

I tried to hold the pause, but broke first. I was speaking too loud, too fast, gesturing too much.

'I have no idea about this. Or whether it was the same girl who was … We met this … this Chloe' – I touched the album – 'when we were visiting his mum during the handover of Hong Kong. I have no clue what happened to her after that. If Sebastian and she had some kind of relationship, if that's what you're surmising, I have no idea. If you're asking if it's the same girl who was in the crash, I don't know ...'

'So, there was a car crash,' she deadpanned, and I stiffened, then pointed at Ronnie.

'Ronnie said they were in a car crash.'

'And you had no contact with her, beyond that meeting in 1997? I won't find your photo anywhere in this album?'

'How could there be photos if I never saw her again?'

'You had no contact with her?'

'For God's sake, how many times do I have to say no?'

'Oh, stop fucking talking, Charlie ...' Ronnie sniffed and turned away. My breathing was the only sound in the room. Humiliated, I realised I was sweating, and cursed my body for giving me away.

Katrina of the silences, her head on one side, placed a pile of A4 printed pages on the table in front of me. Her voice softened.

'You knew who she was. And you knew the ongoing nature of Chloe Zheng's relationship with Sebastian Adler.'

'I did not ...'

She pointed at the pages. 'You wrote her almost a hundred emails, Mr Westcott.'

I gripped the table as I looked down at the pile in front of me. Sure enough, they were my emails. Emails I'd kept all these years, private correspondence, that I couldn't throw away. Safe keeping. Mementoes. Artefacts. Evidence. Locked in a folder on my hotmail account. I had also not followed the advice I'd given to Sebastian.

'You hacked my account.'

'We did.'

Outside, it was getting dark. It was already late afternoon. I was shivering now.

'These emails show you knew the nature of the Assistant Minister's relationship with Chloe Zheng. But not only that,

Mr Westcott ...' She walked around the table and took the chair next to me, bending forward as if sharing a confidence. 'You were involved with her too.'

I tried to scoff and threw a wary look at Durban, who was pacing, one arm across his chest, the other running over the short hair of his widow's peak.

Katrina kept going, her voice gentle and consoling. 'You loved her.'

I winced and refolded my arms. I glanced at her from the corner of my eye. She'd come closer. Her hand was on my shoulder now.

'You loved her and he betrayed you. Didn't he?'

I shook my head. Not looking at her. Not letting her get inside my mind. Was this how they did it? Could she read my thoughts?

Her varnished short-cut fingernails touched the printed emails.

'I haven't read every line yet. We have people doing that now. But it's clear to me, Mr Westcott, your best friend betrayed you.'

A surge of anger and jealousy – like I'd felt that day by the edge of the football ovals, or as I hurled the garbage bin against the bathroom mirror, or watched the speeches at Sebastian's wedding. She was right. She was right.

'And Charlie ...' Using my first name now. Her hand on my wrist. 'We've read your draft emails, too. The ones you didn't send.' She squeezed my wrist. 'The ones you wanted to send. What you wanted to say to her. But dared not. The way you felt for her. And how you felt about what your friend did. You say it yourself. Your friend betrayed her. He betrayed both of you. There's no reason you should protect him. What he did covering up this relationship was wrong, and he knew it. Sebastian Adler's lies, betrayals and negligence killed Chloe Zheng. Who knows what else he has done? So now, we need to know. We need you to tell us everything and not hold back. Not protect your friend, because ultimately, he wasn't your friend. He betrayed you and the girl you loved.'

I lurched to my feet, purging her from my head. I wanted to run out of there, but Katrina was on my left and now Ronnie was edging between me and the door. I looked between them, and then sat back down, reached inside my jacket and pulled out a cigarette. 'You're wrong,' I said, lighting it and speaking while exhaling through my nose. 'Sebastian didn't betray me. I betrayed him. I'm the reason she's dead. It was because of me. I killed Chloe Zheng.'

PART TWO

Chloe

CHAPTER THIRTEEN

Katrina and Ronnie leant across the boardroom table, their eyes hungry. Between us, the photo album was again open at the picture of Chloe. They wanted to know what happened in Hong Kong and insisted I tell it from the beginning.

'When was this photo taken?'

'I told you. It was the night we met, in June 1997.'

'Who took the photo?'

'I don't remember her name. Carol. Caroline. She was Canadian. She was with Sebastian.'

'With?'

'They were sleeping together.'

'He wasn't with Chloe?'

I snorted. 'Chloe thought he was a sleaze.'

'Why were you there, Charlie?' Katrina asked. 'Why were you in Hong Kong?'

She peered across the table, her eyes magnified through saucer glasses, urging me to betray my friend. But a sense of calm had descended over me, like when the bullies had thrown me in that garbage bin with the dog shit and phlegm.

I would confess. I'd tell them everything that happened. And when I was done, they'd see that my treachery far surpassed any betrayal Sebastian had inflicted on me.

I owed him.

❖

I'd gone to Hong Kong in 1997 because I wanted to see my friend. The final years of high school had continued a similar ebb and flow as the pendulum of Sebastian's attention swung between Mallet and me. Many times I thought my best friend had abandoned me permanently and I would be left to the company of a few fellow rejects as Sebastian pursued his social, sporting and academic glory through myriad scholars' study trips, holiday debating camps, cadets expeditions, sporting tours, school dances and end of year house parties.

But he always came back to me. Right through to the end of school. It was as if his drive for popularity and excellence included me too. I think he could feel me drifting away, and that triggered him. He couldn't not excel at being my best friend. He'd be back, wanting to reconnect, as familiar and engaged as ever, as if he hadn't ignored me for weeks on end. And I know this makes me pathetic, but I would always forgive him. Tentative at first. Only to be pulled into that false sense of security born of long, earnest conversations, the sharing of more music and the return of that feeling that he and I were brothers, alone in the world. And I would forgive him the world, and I still would. I'd forgive him like he would one day need to forgive me. But then, of course, inevitably, it would happen again. Mallet would lumber into sight. Maybe Sebastian felt him slipping away too, and so the pendulum would swing the other way again and off he'd go. He couldn't let any one of us down, and so he let us all down.

He had received a scholarship to the London School of Economics to study international political economy, and he left Australia to travel in Europe before commencing his course in September 1996.

Our last weeks together were a gentle tug of war. I wanted to be nostalgic. His mind was on the future. I made him a mix tape. He responded with a back-slapping hug and a grin, then was gone.

As if driven by an opposing force, I took Political Science and Sociology at Sydney University. I joined the Party and set about addressing the character flaw that was my school pedigree, devouring the works of Marx, Engels, Gramsci and Foucault.

Over the following year and a half, the occasional emails I received from Sebastian made me resent him and miss him in equal parts. He still compartmentalised his friendships. He'd talk about going out to raves, or nights on the town, a few gloating inferences to his blossoming sex life. But never any details, or names of his new friends, as if he was worried I might reach out and introduce myself, and tell them about his past.

For the most part, his emails were an attempt to convert me to his new neoliberal philosophy. He'd send me book lists. *The Road to Serfdom, Capitalism and Freedom, The End of History and the Last Man* ... The correspondence depressed me. I imagined his emails to be a weary obligation to an old friend.

Then, true to form, he surprised me by throwing open the doors and windows and inviting me back into his life.

He wrote about a semester transfer to Peking University. He would be living in Beijing. Would I like to meet him in Hong Kong and stay in his mother's apartment the fortnight leading up to the handover on 1 July 1997?

Landing at Kai Tak airport, the plane turned forty-five degrees over Victoria Harbour before descending through a forest of high-rise towers, eye to eye with people staring from apartment windows.

The taxi from Kowloon brought me out of the Cross Harbour Tunnel on Hong Kong Island at Central: an orderly chaos of glass office towers, luxury boutiques, and neoclassical colonial buildings.

Pedestrians in suits and designer brands navigated the footpath beside peasant cleaners pushing wagons of rubbish and building-site debris. Buses, taxis and sports cars blasted horns, and trams rattled over tracks laid only a few years after the death of Queen Victoria.

The streets were adorned with red and gold banners and lanterns with intricate designs. Everywhere the Union Jack, alongside China's national flag, evoked the peaceful transition of power, and reassured the people of Hong Kong that they would preserve their unique way of life under Beijing's rule.

It didn't take me long to realise I had made a mistake leaving the taxi. I struggled on foot up the hill towards Mid-Levels, following the instructions Sebastian had emailed. The weather was humid, and I was still dressed in clothes for the Australian winter. I could smell my body odour beneath my long-sleeved Pearl Jam T-shirt. My hair was wet with sweat that dripped into my eyes.

It was a relief to know Sebastian's mother and stepfather had left town to avoid the handover. There'd be, at least, no lectures about my personal hygiene or surprised exclamations that I'd lost weight on my university diet of potato chips and beer.

After a nine-hour flight crammed into economy, and now the blazing heat and sensory overload of Hong Kong, all I wanted was air-conditioning, a cold drink, and a catch-up with my oldest friend.

The door to Sebastian's apartment opened, and a young woman my age greeted me in a bikini and sarong. She had long blonde hair, wet and slicked back as if she'd just combed it with her nails, drawing attention to her high cheekbones and amber eyes. A white-toothed smile broke from between her pink, bow-shaped lips as she looked me up and down.

I blushed, humiliated by my rancid appearance. She smelt like lavender and sunscreen oil. I forced myself not to look at her breasts, but neither could I hold her eye.

'I'm sorry. I think I have the wrong apartment.'

'You're Charlie?' she gushed.

I nodded.

'Come in. Sebastian's in the shower. We've just come back from the pool. I'm Caroline.'

Disappointment, like a rash, fired across my skin. He'd said he wanted to spend time together. I should have known.

Sebastian appeared, still wet from the shower. His chest was absent of any hair. Was he waxing? He clutched a towel low around his waist and hugged me.

'You've met Caroline?'

I nodded.

'She's a marine biologist. Backpacking to Thailand next, but I'm trying to convince her to detour via Beijing.' He reached out with hungry arms around her waist and pulled her to him, her breasts pressed against his naked chest. It was like a Calvin Klein advertisement, and I looked away, covering my discomfort with a scowl.

'You have a shower, babe. I'll get Charlie a drink. It's gin o'clock.'

She grinned and left. And Sebastian whispered in my ear. 'Don't worry. She'll go when she's had a shower. She has to get her stuff from the backpackers at Causeway Bay. Then we can spend some time catching up.'

'Get her stuff?'

'Yeah, she's going to crash with us. But don't worry, she's with me. You've got the spare room.'

I sighed. So, nothing had changed. I still had to share him with strangers.

❖

Nothing had changed, which meant that, despite my disappointment, within minutes he had me in stitches, and after half an hour, I loved him again.

He mixed gin and tonics with huge wedges of lime and gave me a quick debrief about his life in London and Beijing. LSE was brilliant, and he'd become a globalisation zealot. He was learning Mandarin. He was captivated by the reform of China's economy and was already talking about looking into the Department of Foreign Affairs and Trade graduate program and becoming a diplomat, as his father had once aspired to be.

He'd also realised that he was attractive to the opposite sex, and he catalogued the various girlfriends, trysts and affairs he'd had over the last twelve months.

More gin and tonic. Then some more, and it felt like we'd parted only a day before.

❖

'The girl. Chloe.'

Katrina tapped the photo, and the smile drained from my face. 'When did you meet her?'

That night. It was a bar in Lan Kwai Fong.

Sebastian proclaimed it was time to get out on the town. He was wearing a ridiculous Union Jack vest. Caroline was in a traditional Chinese silk dress, cut so short I wondered if she'd collected it from the tailor too soon.

Dance music spilled from bars lining either side of the street. Men in polo shirts crowded the footpath, holding pint glasses. Women in high-heels teetered on the cobblestone road.

Sebastian gestured towards a British-themed pub, screening rugby union for patrons, mostly British or Australian.

'It's the rugby tens.' He grinned. 'We can go watch tomorrow.' Caroline rolled her eyes just as a roar went up across the pub. The British Army team had scored against the Hong Kong Police.

As Sebastian stood with punters in front of the television, I took my Guinness outside to watch the street.

I felt impatient to explore the city. The air was thick with alcohol and perfume, the aroma of kebab shops, overflowing garbage bins, and that indescribable scent of incense, spice and ocean spray. The Fragrant Harbour.

The street was a sea of people, snatched conversations were in English, Cantonese, Mandarin, Russian, Japanese, German, French. The bodies of beauties and beggars pressed against each other as they moved by hole-in-the-wall bars and clubs amid that chaotic clash of colonial architecture, modern glass towers and traditional Chinese shanties with tiling and balconies that seemed liable to collapse in a strong wind.

And then I noticed her. She was leaning against a wall, further along the street near the entrance to a club, smoking and staring at passersby.

She wasn't much over five feet, with a bob of black hair and a fringe that ended just before her thick-framed glasses. She wore a denim skirt and black Converse. I did a double take at the image on her T-shirt. It was the cover of the Dinosaur Jr. album *Where*

You Been.

I was smiling when our eyes met.

I'd never in my life spoken to a woman in a bar, let alone sidled up to a stranger in the street. But there was something freeing in that warm Hong Kong night. I could be anyone here. No longer the scared, bullied boy at school. Nor the earnest student politician at Sydney Uni. Here I was an adult in a kaleidoscopic city, a world city of infinite disguises and possibilities. I could be whoever I wanted to be.

She stiffened as I approached, and glanced towards the African bouncer.

I pointed at her shirt and gave a thumbs up. She scowled, glancing down at her chest. With horror I realised she thought I was commenting on her body and, desperate not to be misunderstood, I stepped forward.

'I meant Dinosaur Jr., *Where You Been*. I love that album.'

She gave a half smile. 'Good choice.'

'Have you heard?' I persisted. 'They split up.'

She looked surprised, then shrugged and said, 'J Mascis played all the instruments on the last album, anyway.'

'Like Billy Corgan on *Siamese Dream*,' I offered, and now she smiled.

'You like them?'

'The Smashing Pumpkins were everything to me in high school. I was alone a lot, and they sort of kept me company. They made me feel free.'

It's cringeworthy recounting it now, but it struck a chord with her. She blinked, and pushed her hair back as if emerging from a wave.

'Same,' she said, her eyes glazing a moment. Her voice was constrained. 'They make me feel free, even when I'm not.'

Her face briefly darkened, and I saw grief and loneliness close to the surface. Then, as suddenly as it appeared, the darkness was gone. She was nodding, her smile now one of recognition and fellowship. The ice broken. A connection formed. All awkwardness stripped away.

She wanted to know what other music I liked. Had I heard the new Foo Fighters album? What about Mad Season? What did I think about Radiohead's *OK Computer*? Did I think The Smashing Pumpkins would break up after they kicked Jimmy Chamberlin out of the band? It would be an end to an era, with Soundgarden breaking up too. Not to mention Blinding Love after the death of Shannon Hearn.

'Shannon Hearn dying was so sad.'

I nodded my head and tried to explain how I'd listened to their first album walking alone around my high school. Before I could feel like an idiot, she smiled and sang, 'And I'm just waiting to be free ...'

'With someone else like me ...' I chimed in, mangling the key but too elated to care. She laughed, then lifted the hem of her shirt and pulled a pack of cigarettes from the pocket of her skirt. I glimpsed a momentary flash of her olive skin and looked away.

'Do you smoke?'

'I'll try one.'

She lit the cigarette and handed it to me. Her lips were full and free of lipstick. She had a small mole just beneath her nose, which, along with her pronounced cheekbones, rose and fell when she smiled.

She poked the Pearl Jam stick figure insignia on my T-shirt and mentioned she'd seen Soundgarden and Pearl Jam in Seattle and for an encore Eddie Vedder and Chris Cornell had sung 'Hunger Strike' from the *Temple of the Dog* album.

I choked as I inhaled on the cigarette, and she laughed.

'One benefit of studying in the US.'

'You're American?'

'I'm Chinese. From Hong Kong. Well, Beijing. My father sent me to study in the US. I'm at MIT.'

Now she had said it, I noticed the velvety tone to her accent, the rolled 'r' sound.

'You speak perfect English. I'd never have thought you were from the mainland.'

'I'm not anymore. We moved to Hong Kong in 1990, when I

was twelve. I'm a Hong Konger now. I went to DGS, the Diocesan Girls' School.'

I shrugged, not knowing it. 'Why did you move?'

She looked away, the red light of a street advertisement tinting her glasses so I couldn't see her eyes. 'My father came for work.'

'And you've come home from university to celebrate the handover?'

She snorted and was about to reply when Sebastian and Caroline stumbled out of the bar. Sebastian's fists were raised in the air. 'Victory!' he chanted, then did a double take noticing me across the street. 'Charlie? You've made a friend?'

'This is Sebastian,' I said.

'Nice vest,' Chloe said with a sneer, the cigarette hanging out of her mouth.

Sebastian glanced down at his chest, a brief look of puzzlement crossing his face.

'Your name's Charlie?' she asked me, ignoring Sebastian. 'I'm Chloe.'

'Picture. Picture,' cried Caroline, stumbling across with a camera.

'Pass,' Chloe said, but Sebastian fell on her, his arm around her shoulder.

'Oh, come on. Do it for Charlie.'

He stood beside Chloe. I was on her other side. In the photo you can see I'm blushing. Chloe looks like she thinks we are all fuckwits, and we probably were.

After the photo, she extracted herself and began walking away. 'It was nice to meet you, Charlie.'

'Let's go somewhere else?' I called after her, in the most daring gesture of my life.

'I'm not into football.'

'Neither am I. Where do you want to go?'

A small smile played on her lips.

'You want to see some live music?'

I glanced at Sebastian, and he grinned back at me as if reading my mind.

'Sure.' He winked. 'Charlie is all about the music.'

CHAPTER FOURTEEN

There was an abrupt knock at the meeting room door. A man in his forties with short blond hair appeared.

'Excuse me a moment,' Katrina said, stepping outside.

Ronnie sat motionless, glaring at me across the table. I took the opportunity to chide him.

'I thought we had a deal, Ronnie. We were going to protect the Party.'

'Oh, fuck off. Protect the Party,' he spat, turning his head. 'Don't blame me for this. They had it all, anyway. I wasn't going down with your fucking ship.'

'You've always been so loyal, Ronnie.'

Now he lunged across the table, his chin jutting out.

'Don't talk to me about fucking loyalty. If someone's going under the bus here it's not me, and it's sure as hell not the PM.' He stabbed his finger at me, as if aiming for my eyes. 'That's your fucking job now, Charlie. You've worked for this party for twenty years. You reckon you're a true believer? Well, now's the time to show you're not just a private school fuckwit expecting everyone else to pay the bill. Get under the bus. Own what you and your mate covered up and whatever else they've got on you.'

He fell silent for a moment, staring wild-eyed across the table at me. Then, with an exaggerated sigh, he changed gears, waving a dismissive hand. He forced his voice into a conciliatory tone. 'Look Charlie, I mean it was years ago, right? We all do stupid things in our youth. You met a girl. He met a girl. She died. Shit happens.' The door opened. 'Own it. Quarantine it,' he hissed.

'Mr Durban, can you come out here a moment?'

Alone in the meeting room, I took stock of my situation.

Despite a lifetime of being on opposing sides of the Party, Ronnie and I were the same. We were both consiglieres, him for the PM, me for Sebastian. Our instincts and sense of responsibility were the same. If our principal was under threat, we did everything to get him clear, up to and including throwing ourselves under the bus. That's what I was trying to do with the mid-flight manoeuvre when Katrina had caught me out with the photographs and emails. Fine. They knew about Chloe. So, contain it. Reframe the story. It was about me. It was about what I did that led to her death. The more appalling they found my story (and it *was* appalling), the less they'd focus on Sebastian's cover-up.

But there was more to it than loyalty, wasn't there? By stepping into the spotlight, what was I hoping to leave in shadow? I wasn't sure yet. But I knew it had something to do with Tang's claim that Sebastian had been meeting Zheng. It made no sense that Sebastian would have continued to meet with him, let alone become his friend, in the aftermath of Chloe's death. Politics 101 suggested that where logic failed, something else was at play. That's where the threat would be.

Ronnie had said to own what Sebastian and I had covered up and *whatever else they've got on you.* But what was that? What else did ASIO have? How much did they know? And did they know something that I didn't?

The door opened and Katrina returned with Ronnie, whose head was bowed, followed by the same blond-haired man, who took up a position by the door.

Katrina sat down and turned pages in her notebook without looking up. Ronnie leant against the wall, grimacing, and turned away when he caught my eye.

Katrina spoke, and I felt heavy with dread.

'Charlie, before we continue would you mind handing over your phone?'

My gaze shot to her. 'What?'

'Your phone. We're following up all leads. It's procedure.'

'Procedure? What are you talking about?' I growled and leant back in my chair, my palm covering the breast pocket of my jacket.

Katrina looked across at me, a cooler tone creeping into her voice. 'Nobody wants to be heavy-handed here, Charlie. Your phone may contain information as to other possible threats we are confronting. We are also freezing yours and the Assistant Minister's email accounts. This is all standard procedure.'

'Procedure for what?' I snapped, gripping the arms of the chair so my hands wouldn't visibly tremble. 'What other threats are we confronting?'

'Hand over your phone, Charlie,' Ronnie said, taking a threatening step forward.

Stunned, I looked at the sweat dripping off his top lip. He was losing the plot. Surely, Ronnie more than anybody should understand the risks of handing over my government phone. We fought tooth and nail against even the most bland Freedom of Information request for an email or a text exchange. There was no way I was handing over my entire mobile.

'What did he say to you?' I pointed savagely at the man standing by the door. 'Whatever he said, I've got a right to know. You can't just come back in here demanding my phone. What is the nature of the threat you're talking about?'

'Hand over your mobile, please, Charlie.' Katrina's eyes were unblinking through the windscreens of her glasses. She turned her palm to me. I looked at the thin-strapped gold watch around her narrow wrist and wondered if it was a gift from someone.

'Am I under arrest?'

'You can be, if you don't wish to cooperate,' she said calmly.

'I am cooperating. I have been …'

'Then hand over your phone, please.'

I was fighting to keep my independence. I couldn't obey. I couldn't let myself assume the role of a prisoner. I turned furious eyes on Ronnie. This was what happened when ASIO were involved. This was why I'd had him promise he'd keep them under control, keep McCubbin and his goons off the scent, because as soon as it started there was no going back.

'ASIO has no jurisdiction or powers of arrest. You can't detain me in Parliament House. You can't seize my property. Ronnie, tell them. ASIO can't arrest me.'

Katrina sighed and clenched her fingers into a fist, which she then clasped in front of her.

'Charlie, I can have the AFP in here in less than a minute. I suggest you don't test me on that, otherwise what is currently an unofficial conversation is going to turn very official very quickly and we will conduct you to more suitable accommodation for someone arrested under the ASIO Act.'

I swallowed hard. The ASIO Act? Espionage charges? The room darkened. Those black splotches, again in front of my eyes. I stared frantically into the darkness. What was it? What was it they knew? What had they discussed outside that door? *Whatever else they've got on you.*

'Give her your fucking phone!' Ronnie bellowed, shocking me back to consciousness. Shaking, I passed it over, my stupid fat hand getting caught in my inner pocket. Katrina took the device and handed it to the wispy-haired bloke, who left.

'Thank you, Charlie,' she said, nodding to Ronnie, who, trembling with fury, lowered himself into his chair and cradled his forehead in a hand. Katrina turned back to me, wiping her hands on her trousers.

'Charlie. My job is to assess and understand threats to our national security. What Adler did constitutes a threat. I'm trying to understand how it relates to other threats that are emerging right now ...'

'What other threats?'

'You don't need to know that, Charlie. It is my job to know. And right now, I don't know. So my people will take a look at your phone, and meanwhile I want you to continue your story, please. I want the details. I want to know what occurred in Hong Kong with this girl. I want to know what happened between you and her, and her and Sebastian. And most of all, I want to understand why her father was sending messages to an assistant minister twenty-five years later, after you all met in Hong Kong.'

I sighed and shook my head heavily. There was no point in arguing further. I could feel the shadow in the room. They suspected something. I didn't know what. But I had no time to dwell on those mysteries. I had to persevere, to try and win back control of the narrative. Just as Ronnie said, I needed to throw myself under the bus.

❖

The Wanch was a street-level bar off Jaffe Road in Wan Chai. We could hear the music before we got inside, no longer techno, but guitar rock.

It had a grungy vibe, with walls covered in posters from past performances, a chalk board listing Jam Nights and an enormous Hong Kong Tramways sign along the far wall. There were a few small chairs and tables near the bar, but it was mainly standing room only, with the audience clustered close to the band.

Chloe shot me a look, and I grinned. This was my kind of place. It reminded me of the Annandale Hotel or the Hopetoun in Sydney.

During the set, it was too loud to talk. Sebastian adapted, by making eyes at a girl in a black halter top at the table beside us.

When the band broke into a cover of 'Restless', I roared with delight and grabbed Chloe's arm.

'Blinding Love!'

She leant her shoulder against mine and shouted in my ear. 'I saw them live twice.' I threw up my arms in mock outrage as she laughed and nodded and danced in her chair.

Between sets, Caroline stormed off to the bathroom and Sebastian tried to kick off a conversation with Chloe.

'So your family is from Beijing? Did Charlie tell you I'm living there? I'm at Peking U for a year, on exchange from LSE.'

She wrinkled her nose. 'Why would you leave London for Beijing?'

I grinned, enjoying how impervious she was to his charm. Sebastian felt it too, and redoubled his efforts. 'I'm fascinated by China's economic reform. Deng Xiaoping's legacy. The Southern Inspection Tour. It's going to be a brilliant decade as the country liberalises.'

Chloe snorted. 'You think China is liberalising?'

'"Poverty is not socialism,"' cried Sebastian. '"To be rich is glorious." That's Deng Xiaoping.'

Chloe's face twisted. 'Dead students in Tiananmen Square. That's fucking Deng Xiaoping.'

Sebastian glanced at me. I looked at Chloe, ripping her empty cigarette packet.

'Anyway,' she said, not looking up, 'how can you learn anything about China if you don't speak the language?'

'I'm studying Mandarin.'

She snorted. 'You can't learn Mandarin in a year.'

Sebastian leant forward, lifting her chin and looking into her eyes. '"Wǒ xūyào xuéxí ránhòu néng gàosù nǐ, nǐ hěn měilì."'

I couldn't understand. But Chloe did. I saw her contain her surprise, then she shrugged.

'Your accent is shit.'

Sebastian cackled. 'Oh, come on, Chloe! I've only started learning.'

Chloe hit me on the arm. 'Come get more cigarettes, Charlie.'

'Since when do you smoke?' called Sebastian after us. He winked at me and turned back to the girl in the black halter top.

'Your friend's a sleaze and he doesn't know shit about China,' she said as we walked down the road to the 7-Eleven. 'But he's got good Mandarin.'

'What did he say to you?'

'Some shit.' She waved her hand.

'What did he say?' I persisted.

'He told me I was beautiful.'

I halted and looked at her, feeling my face burn with anger.

'What's wrong?' she asked, blinking at me. Then she realised, and she laughed and touched my hand. 'Charlie, you just met me.

You can't be jealous already.' She paused. Tilting her head to one side, then checking her watch. 'Okay. Don't be jealous. Do you want to come home with me?'

My heart pounded. My eyes must have been wide as she started laughing again.

'I don't mean for sex, Charlie.' She reached up and tweaked my nose. 'Something much better.'

'Oh come on, Charlie. I knew you then.' Ronnie blurted. 'You might have been skinnier. But you were as butt ugly as you are now. You want us to believe some young girl you'd met for thirty seconds invited you home?'

'I was astonished as you are,' I responded wrly, turning again to the photograph of the three of us and looking at Chloe's eyes through her black-rimmed glasses. The sadness, that hollow feeling she talked about so often, it was there in her gaze. I don't know if it was always there. Maybe it was the loneliness of an international student living between two worlds, an isolation that she'd brought back with her from MIT. Maybe the isolation ran deeper, to a sort of depression, the product of her traumatic past, the strained family life she shared with her father, her increasing anxiety, which swelled as the days ticked by towards the handover of Hong Kong to Beijing. Maybe for any of these reasons, she was looking to embrace a new friend, to cling to someone who didn't know her. Maybe it wasn't me at all, but the music we shared, which somehow expressed and responded to her longing to be free, to share a moment of release in this soundtracked middle ground. Whatever it was, it appeared to be exactly the relief she was looking for, and I wasn't about to reject her invitation.

❖

Our hands rested on the back seat of the taxi, amid the shadows, fingers touching as the driver hurtled around the treacherous hairpin turns towards the Peak.

We arrived at Chloe's house, surrounded by jungle. The

twinkling lights of the city were distant beyond the tangle of banyan and rubber trees, the occasional elm. The frenetic energy of Central and Wan Chai was reduced to a hum, melding with sounds of mountain streams and anonymous creatures scurrying in the foliage beyond the road. She led me down a driveway to a colonial mansion, art deco style, surrounded by a large verandah.

'This is your home?'

'It's where my father lives. It's owned by the company. They bought it off a British trading house.'

At the glass front door, she pressed her hand against my chest and whispered, 'When we're inside, walk straight up the stairs. My room is first on the right. Go in and close the door.'

I raised my eyebrows.

'Tina, the maid, has a big mouth. She'd love to tell my father I had a western boy in my bedroom.'

'What would he do?'

'He'd have you shot.'

I presumed she was joking, but didn't have time to ponder. She opened the door, calling to distract the maid. I walked up the stairs, into her bedroom.

My heart was pounding. The double bed was all I could focus on. She'd said no sex, but what else could this be? Better than sex? My mind swam.

To distract myself, I surveyed a small desk on which she had a pile of textbooks bearing the stamp of MIT. *Geotechnical Engineering: Principles and Practices*; *Construction Planning: Equipment and Methods*; *Reinforced Concrete: Mechanics and Design*.

I laughed to myself, struggling to align such dense subject matter with the cool alternative girl I'd left downstairs.

The book on concrete was filled with incomprehensible graphs showing 'stress-strain curves', 'moment-curvature' and 'load tables'. In its cover she had slid a Moleskine notebook. At first I thought it must be her notes, but as I flicked through the pages, I realised it was a diary. She wrote in English. I only glanced at a line.

||*Life lived, locked-inside my head. Freedom isn't betrayal.*||

I wondered if they were her words, or a lyric she liked. It sounded like the angsty music we shared in common.

I was replacing the Moleskine when a small colour photo slipped from between its pages. A woman in her late thirties, wearing a white coat, stood in a tiled hallway near a noticeboard. She was holding hands with a little girl, who I recognised as Chloe.

'The coast is clear.' Chloe entered behind me and locked the door. I returned the Moleskine to where I found it. She glanced at the textbook in my hand. 'Want to quiz me on concrete?'

'What do you study?'

'Civil and Environmental Engineering,' she said, taking the book from me and squeezing my hand. 'Sit down.' She beckoned to the bed and waited for me to sit, then began to lift her T-shirt. I felt my throat constrict. But her hand went to her skirt pocket again, and this time withdrew a plastic bag filled with marijuana, shaking it at me and smiling. 'Welcome to my bedroom, Charlie.'

She rolled a joint and handed it over, from her lips to mine, as she busied herself levering open the windows.

'This is the only reason I visit fucking Lan Kwai Fong these days.'

'Do you smoke a lot?'

'I don't drink. I have to chill out somehow.'

She took the joint and inhaled, her eyes closing.

'But is it better than sex?' I questioned, not wanting the subject to drop.

'Not that. This.'

She handed me a CD cover. It was an unauthorised recording of The Smashing Pumpkins. She came and sat close to me on the bed, pressing a bud into my ear and hitting play on her Discman. It was the distinct opening riff of 'Rocket', not the usual electric guitar distortion, but an acoustic version.

'*This* is better than sex.' She grinned. 'It's from the *Siamese Dream* album release at Tower Records in 1993. No one has a copy of this.'

I'd never heard those versions of their songs. It sounded intimate. Billy Corgan's voice was rich and the guitar parts were all extended, wide open for improvisation. We smoked and listened and got stoned. Sharing the headphones meant Chloe rested her head on my shoulder, then on my chest. My fingers played with her hair.

'Why don't you drink?' I asked in a haze.

'Wha?' Her eyes were closed.

'You said you don't drink.'

'Because if I start to drink, I will drink and drink and drink ...'

'Are you sad?'

'Desolate.' She wet her lips with her tongue. 'I lost someone, Charlie.'

'The woman in the photo? In your concrete book?'

She glanced towards the desk, as if only then realising I had snooped. Then she nodded. 'My mother. I lost her in Beijing. When I was twelve. This month is the anniversary. I come to Hong Kong to remember.'

'Why Hong Kong? Why not Beijing?'

'Because remembering is not allowed in Beijing.' She rolled onto her back, holding the earbud in place.

'My mother was a nurse at Peking Union Medical College Hospital. Have you heard of it, Charlie? It's where they took the students.'

'The students?'

She was about to tell me more, but then the acoustic guitar strummed and Billy Corgan interrupted her confession.

'This is a cover of a Thin Lizzy song.'

'"Dancing in the Moonlight",' Chloe cried, dragging me up. 'Dance with me, Charlie.'

Her body was close against mine. Her hair smelt like shampoo and her chest and hips pressed against me. I locked my arms around her waist and her fingers splayed on my back.

I've thought of that moment all my life. Playing and replaying the scene. Wondering what else I could have done to prolong it. To kiss her. To make her mine. And if I had – if I'd had the courage, none of the rest of it would have happened.

But then there was the sound of a car engine. Doors closing. Male voices. Chloe pulled away and went to the window, dragging the earbud from my ear and winding the cord around the Discman.

'It's my father.'

'At least finish the song.' I was stoned and filled with desire. Immune to her concerns.

She shook her head, then hid the Discman beneath her mattress 'You must go.'

'Why are you hiding it?'

'My father doesn't like me listening to western music.'

She then pulled off her T-shirt and threw it into a corner. I may have groaned out loud seeing her small breasts cupped in a white bra. But she was in no mood to be ogled. She pulled a shirt from the wardrobe and began buttoning it up. 'You have to go, Charlie.'

I tried to embrace her again, but she grabbed my wrist and dragged me towards the door.

I wasn't afraid. I thought, in fact, I should stay and meet her father. Tell him I was in love with his daughter. That would impress Chloe. I was ready to declare my love, having only met her a few hours before.

It was too late. We heard the front door close, her father's tread on the stairs. He was ascending, as if he knew I was in his daughter's room and was coming to catch us.

He'd have you shot.

Chloe pushed me into the wardrobe as a voice called on the stairs.

'Měi? Měi? Měi'er?'

Her face was close to mine, beseeching me not to make a sound. She swung the wardrobe door closed from the outside and spun around, not noticing the door was still ajar.

I could see her standing in the middle of the room, preparing herself for her father. She brushed at her shirt. Finger combed the back of her hair into place. Then, remembering the locked door, she opened it and allowed a beam of light from the hall to shine into the room, illuminating her as if she were about to perform.

He called again. This time, she answered.

'Shì de, bàba?'

'Měi'er?'

Heavy footsteps on the wooden floor. '*Měi?*'

'*Wǒ zài zhèlě, bàba!*'

And the beam of light from the corridor disappeared. He was in the room. I couldn't see him, but that voice was enough to fill the space. It was a deep, resonant authority, ravaged by cigarettes and a life hard lived.

They began a conversation I could not understand. It was less a conversation, more instruction. He spoke. She nodded and said '*Shì de*', which I presumed meant yes, she was agreeing with him.

At first, I thought he was angry. That he knew she'd been out to Lan Kwai Fong. That maybe the maid had ratted on her. But then I realised this must be a normal exchange. Instruction and affirmation were the way they interacted.

It ended with him saying '*hǎo de*'. He turned to leave, and I let out a breath of relief. Chloe did too. I saw her lean forward, exhaling.

But then he stopped. I could see his body now. In a suit. He paused at her desk. His long thin fingers reached for the textbook on concrete.

My stomach sank. I knew what it was. I hadn't put the photo back inside the Moleskine notebook. It was jutting from between the textbook pages.

The excruciating sound of him teasing it halfway. Then snatching it with a shout.

Chloe lunged forward, trying to seize it from him. But he was too fast and held it away from her like a bully in the playground, fending her off with his free arm.

All the while, he shouted at her. That ravaged voice, now trembling with fury. It was a reprimand to which she responded with her own unbridled anger, an anger that shocked me. She shouted and wept and tried to strike him with her fists.

He silenced her with the back of his hand, whipping her across the face.

She didn't collapse. She took it standing. Swayed a little. Then hung her head in silence.

Her father's voice became a hurried murmur, like a priest reciting a catechism. His hand on her shoulder counselling her, educating her. Now urging her to speak with a gentle push and a word like 'eh?'

'*Duìbuqǐ. Duìbuqǐ, bàba,*' she mumbled, and he began his coaching again. '*Duìbuqǐ,*' she repeated.

At last, he stopped lecturing. Sighed. Then embraced her. I watched as Chloe's arms hesitated, then clasped him in return.

When he left the room, he took the photo.

❖

When Chloe opened the wardrobe, her eyes were red and her cheek was swollen.

'Are you alright?' I whispered, but she put her finger to my lips.

'He's in his study. You have to go.'

We slunk like prowlers downstairs and through the house. She pushed me out the back door.

'Go around the side. There are steps that lead to a walking path through the forest to May Road. You can get a taxi there. Don't go to the front of the house.'

I clutched at her. 'I'm sorry he hit you. It was about the photo, wasn't it? It's my fault.'

She grabbed my cheeks in her hands. 'Listen to me, Charlie, focus. Do not go up to the front of the house. Liu Hui will still be out there.'

'Who is Liu Hui?'

'His security.'

'Your father needs security?' The marijuana was making a confusing situation worse. 'Why was he so angry about the photo, Chloe?'

'Just go.' She pushed my chest. 'I'll tell you tomorrow.'

I leant forward, tilting my face down to hers. She turned her head and my kiss glanced off her cheek. She kept pushing.

'Go. Go. I'll see you tomorrow.'

'Where?' I was not usually this forward. She grimaced and rolled her eyes in exasperation.

'Lin Heung Tea House. For breakfast. Okay?'

She pressed the door closed in my face, and I was alone in the night.

I crept along the side of the house, but couldn't resist peeking over the stone wall towards the front. Two men sat in a black BMW talking through the driver's side window to a third man. I presumed this was Liu Hui.

They finished their conversation, and the BMW drove off. Liu strolled back towards the Mercedes parked in the driveway. He was of indistinguishable age, but with the cropped hair and muscular posture of a soldier. He wore a dark-coloured suit, and pulled cigarettes and a lighter from his jacket. The flame illuminated his face, and I saw his cheek was discoloured by a birthmark.

There was something about the way he smoked, the confidence of his gestures, the focus of his eyes as he stared into the darkness, that suggested strength, even violence. He frightened me. I slunk away.

I made my way back down the side of the house, through the fence and towards the stairs that formed part of the walking trail down to May Road.

As I was about to descend, something caught my eye. I glanced back at Chloe's house. I was on a level with the lighted window of Zheng's study. I could see him now. He was tall, but slender, with ever so slightly hunched shoulders, as if he tried to disguise his height. He reminded me of a priest. Maybe because I'd heard him whispering like that to Chloe, or maybe it was the traditional Chinese jacket, clasped at the neck. But there was an elegance, almost a vanity to him too. He held the photo of his wife between two fingers, like a curator setting an exhibition. His skin, in the lamp light, was a rich olive colour. He was bald and his scalp seemed perfectly smooth, as if oiled. He touched it with his free hand as he gazed out at me. He had sharp features. Chloe's cheek bones. An intelligent face. As much as I tried to move away, to pretend I was just a passerby on the track, I lingered too long. I couldn't break his stare.

CHAPTER FIFTEEN

'Wait a fucking minute.' Ronnie was on his feet. 'So you met this Zheng?'

'I never met him.'

'But you fucking saw him, Charlie, right? That's more than you said before. He's not just some mystery man Sebastian told you about.'

'I guess not.'

Katrina nodded and drew an A4 image from a manilla folder. 'Is that him?'

It was Zheng. Older than when I saw him that night. Perhaps thinner. A few more lines around his mouth and forehead. His head was no longer bald but now covered in a few tufts of grey, as if with age he'd grown disinterested in the vanity of close shaving his scalp. But it was definitely Zheng.

Zheng. In the Great Hall of the People in Beijing.

Zheng. Standing in front of the Chinese President.

Zheng. Who SK Tang claimed had clandestine meetings with my best friend in Hong Kong.

'Is that Zheng?' Katrina asked again, pointing at the image.

I nodded.

'Wait, ASIO has a file on Zheng?' Ronnie turned to Katrina. The same question was in my mind, and that same dread was forming in my guts. If they had a file on Zheng it wasn't just because of Sebastian. They couldn't have assembled it just as a result of Tang's message. They had another reason to be interested.

But what? It was that truth in the darkness again, and as much as I wanted to reach it, I felt compelled to stay away, to stay clear. It was a dark contagion from which I felt I needed to distance myself and Sebastian, even if I didn't know why.

'This picture was taken at the Chinese People's Political Consultative Conference earlier this year,' Katrina said, ignoring Ronnie.

Fighting to regain my composure and keep the concern from my face, I shrugged dismissively.

'That doesn't surprise you, Charlie?'

'Why would it?'

'The CPPCC is a central arm of the United Front Work Department.'

'And Zheng is the CEO of one of the largest Chinese state-owned enterprises,' I argued, feeling an urgent need now to head off any conspiratorial assumptions that Katrina was working towards. 'The CPPCC is a consultative body made up of Chinese elites talking about policy. It's not a secret society.' I knew my voice was too loud. I took a beat and dialled it back. Then continued, more restrained. Slower now. 'The CPPCC draws in the views of academics, diplomats, party elders, and' – I folded my arms – 'senior business leaders, like Zheng. There's nothing surprising about him attending in his capacity as CEO of China Overland.'

'Are you sure that was the capacity in which he was attending?'

I opened my mouth to respond, but nothing came out. I wasn't sure. I had no reason to be sure about anything. I had seen Zheng but once in my life. All I knew of him other than that came from Chloe and then Sebastian. And it seemed Sebastian had been lying to me, which meant Zheng could be anyone. But not just anyone shakes the hand of the Chinese President.

'Let's put that to one side for now. I'd like to talk about the capacity in which he was in Hong Kong when you met him.'

'I didn't fucking meet him,' I repeated, unable to control the tension in my chest. 'I hid from him in a cupboard.'

She curled an eyebrow and drew a sheet of paper from the folder beside her. I noticed again her long, slender fingers and sensibly short, varnished nails.

'I'll tell you what we know, shall I?'

The smile in her tone made me squirm in my seat.

'Zheng Liang, graduated from Beijing University in 1974, having studied engineering and logistics. He was recruited as a junior engineer by China Overland Group and by 1977 he was working on major infrastructure projects in Guangdong province, including a new highway connecting several cities in the region.'

'What is that you're reading from?' Ronnie asked.

'It's from his biography. Taken off the Overland website.'

'Jesus, is that the extent of ASIO's intelligence collection?'

Ignoring him, Katrina continued.

'In 1982, he was promoted to manage a large-scale dam and hydroelectric power generation project in the Yangtze River. He seems to have had a reputation for delivering on time and within budget, and was regarded as a capable leader. Three years later he got a promotion to senior management, overseeing multiple infrastructure projects in Western China.'

Katrina scowled at the paper in front of her.

'This is where it gets strange. In 1990, he transfers to Hong Kong and takes a lower-level position. Why would he do that? He's been climbing up the tree, and then he seems to be demoted. Did something happen that made him leave Beijing? Was he just desperate to get to Hong Kong? I mean, it was no small demotion. If it was a decision to take some time out after his wife passed away, it took him until 1997 to rebuild his career back to managing South China infrastructure projects.' She narrowed her eyes. 'Just in time for you two to come into contact with him in Hong Kong, I might add.'

I watched Katrina fold the page and push it into the notebook. I wanted to argue, to dismiss whatever dots she was connecting. But once more I had the distinct impression she knew more than me. Not only about Zheng's history, but about his present. About who he was now. They knew something and it was bad. Possibly very, very bad. And Sebastian was at the heart of it. The truth in the shadows, just out of sight.

Katrina leant over the table with her arms folded, watching me.

'Why had Zheng brought his daughter to Hong Kong, Charlie? Did Chloe tell you? Did you meet her the following day? We need to know everything.'

❖

I did meet her. The next morning she was waiting, as promised, at the Lin Heung Tea House on Wellington Street. She was alone at a table amid the bustling breakfast rush, wearing a white polo shirt and white shorts with a blue stripe, as if she were coming from a tennis club. Her head was bowed, and I feared she would be in a dark mood after the events of the night before. To my relief, when I reached her she was just writing in her Moleskine notebook. When she noticed my arrival, she beamed at me, beckoned to the seat in front of her, then poured milk tea with one hand, flagging down the dim sum trolley with the other.

If anything, she was hyper effusive, providing a detailed history of the hundred-year-old Hong Kong breakfast institution, pointing at the traditional Chinese calligraphy and landscape paintings on the walls, the locals eating breakfast around us.

'It's famous for its dim sum and Chinese pastries. You have to try the steamed sponge cake and the egg tarts and the pineapple buns,' she said, scooping plates off the trolley. 'Otherwise you can never say you've been to Hong Kong.'

I ate and nodded my approval.

'Much more authentic than bullshit nightclubs in LKF.'

She ragged me about wasting time in typical expat haunts, but then in her rapid-fire way talked about bars she'd frequented around Wan Chai, LKF and Tsim Sha Tsui, in what seemed to be a pretty rebellious youth. Before she could get further into the drugs and party scene that had disrupted her final years at the Diocesan Girls' School, I interrupted her, wanting to focus on what had happened last night.

'Chloe, about last night …'

'Yeah. By the way, which one did your friend take home? The one in the half a dress or the one in the halter top?'

I laughed and, successfully distracted, told her the truth, that the sound of Sebastian and Caroline having sex had kept me up most of the night.

'Thin walls?' She smirked, slurping noodles into her mouth. 'Or good sex?'

My heart skipped, pleased we were back on the subject of last night and fired to be lingering on something intimate.

'One of those.' I blushed. 'But then when I left this morning, there was a woman in our kitchen getting a glass of water. Guess who …'

Chloe's eyes widened behind her glasses. 'Halter Top!' She laughed. 'Fuck. Your friend is a sleaze, Charlie.'

'Yep. Turns out Caroline slept the night at the hostel with her friends. I've been sworn to secrecy, of course.' I laughed and felt pleased to be shading Sebastian's reputation after his flirtatious Mandarin display.

'What about your father?' I pushed. 'Was everything okay last night?'

'Fine,' she said, pouring more tea.

I reached an arm across the table and lightly touched her hand. 'It got pretty intense last night. I don't understand why he was so angry about the picture of your mother.'

'He overreacts. He doesn't like to be reminded of her.'

'He hit you. Just because you had it.'

I saw the briefest look of pain cross her face. Then she shrugged. 'Relax Charlie. It looked more intense than it was. It's just family stuff.'

'Chloe, I saw him —'

She waved her hand at me, wanting me to stop.

'It's always intense with my dad, this time of year. I'm all he's got for family now, and he's protective. I can handle it. Trust me, I've done the therapy.'

I halted, not knowing what to say in response to this, then tried to lighten the mood by ribbing her.

'Is that why you have to study concrete?'

Her face clouded.

'No. I want to be an engineer, Charlie. I want to build infrastructure that ends poverty and makes people's lives better. It's how I want to spend my life.'

I nodded. Surprised but respectful of this serious side to her.

We ate on in silence. I tried again.

'I saw that Liu Hui last night.'

'Did he see you?'

There was a look of such fear in her eyes I didn't dare tell her I thought her father had noticed me walking down the stairs. I shook my head. 'He looked like a thug.'

She scrunched her face. 'He's not a thug. He's just always there. He was assigned as security to my father.'

'Is your father in danger?'

She shrugged. 'Assigned security guards have various functions.'

I found this very confusing, but blundered on regardless. 'Well, your father must be important if he needs security. What does he do?'

'My father is a minion. A logistics minion. For Beijing. He makes the trains run on time, more like Mussolini.' She crumbled the rest of the tart with her finger.

'Is that why he's in Hong Kong? Working on the trains?'

She looked at me, confused for a moment, then laughed, reached over and pulled my nose. 'No stupid. It's just a turn of phrase. He works for an SOE. The company does a lot of development in Shenzhen. Highways, bridges, land reclamation, ports.' She listed on her fingers. 'My father manages the logistics. People. Material. Contractors. Shipping. Utilities. He organises everything. I guess he is good at it. His bosses in Beijing seem to have realised he's some kind of genius. He keeps getting summoned for his advice.'

'Is that why you moved to Hong Kong from Beijing? Because he was working on infrastructure projects?'

'You have a lot of questions this morning, Charlie.'

'I've been thinking about them all night.'

Chloe pursed her lips, looking at me.

'We moved here after my mother died. It's hard to explain. The way my mum died. It fucked us both up.'

I wanted her to trust me, to let her know she could rely on me to listen and support her. I wanted to feel her head on my chest again.

'I know what that's like. I've seen it before,' I said. 'Sebastian's father died when he was fifteen. I was there. I helped him through it.'

'How did he die?' she asked, pouring soy sauce over a dim sum. I could tell she was listening intently.

'He took his own life,' I said, feeling guilty for using my best friend's tragedy to connect with a girl. But it had the right impact. Chloe stared at me, her chopsticks hovering in front of her mouth.

'He killed himself?'

I nodded. 'His dad was intense. Controlling but damaged. A bit like your father, maybe.'

She bit her lip a moment and didn't respond, then leapt at a passing dim sum trolley and put another flaky pastry with a soft centre on the table in front of me. 'There. Give that to him.'

'What is it?'

'*Lǎopó bǐng.*' She winked. 'Sweetheart cake.'

CHAPTER SIXTEEN

At first, we were a little group. Chloe and me, Sebastian and Caroline. We went to exhibitions at the Hong Kong History Museum, watched live bands playing in Central. We even acquiesced to Sebastian's demands to watch the Hong Kong Rugby Tens game, where his frenzied cheering for the New Zealand team (there was no Australian side represented) drew a smile from Chloe, who called him a maniac and asked him to explain the rules.

But Chloe's moods swung. When she was happy, she was full of joy and enthusiasm, eager to show us her Hong Kong. She walked us around the Tsim Sha Tsui Promenade, pointing at the Hong Kong Island skyline; took us to the Mong Kok Night Market, where she made Caroline buy clothes and accessories; and delighted in showing us street food after insisting we go sing at Neway Karaoke Box.

Then there were days when it was hard to get her to come out with us. Her mood was bleak, and she hardly spoke a word, instead just scribbling away in her notebook.

It didn't help there was a frenetic atmosphere in the city. For Sebastian, Caroline and I, it was a sense of being at the centre of a historic event. For Chloe, something darker loomed, and she became more anxious as the days went on.

She didn't like the crowds on Hong Kong Island. I often saw her scanning faces as we walked, perhaps looking for Liu Hui or another member of her father's 'security' who would inform him she was out with westerners.

'They don't know if they're mourning or celebrating,' she said as we pushed through a group watching traditional Chinese opera and folk dancing, only to find a small Hong Kong Alliance protest with posters and T-shirts depicting the famous 'tank man' image from the Tiananmen Square protests. I felt her stiffen at my side.

To relieve the tension, I asked her to show us the real Hong Kong. Where were the food districts we needed to see? She agreed and toured us through markets in Sham Shui Po for bamboo pressed noodles and wantons, into Yau Ma Tei District for claypot rice with sausage and chicken, and egg waffles. Then there was the seafood tour of Lantau Island. First to Tai O fishing village with its stilt houses, then a drive to the Mui Wo market and a lunch at the Wah Kee restaurant: razor clams, typhoon shelter crab, and silky smooth tofu fa pudding.

On the way back, she made us stop to admire the new Tsing Ma bridge that had opened earlier in the year, connecting Lantau to the rest of Hong Kong. She explained the stability challenge of the longest suspension bridge in the world, exposed to high typhoon winds, and how the foundations had been constructed in the Ma Wan Channel's soft marine clay. Her voice carried a tone of wonder I'd heard her use to describe Billy Corgan's guitar work on *Siamese Dream*.

'Charlie said you were a cement nerd,' Sebastian teased.

'It's not about the fucking cement.' She snorted. 'It's about the lives of the people the bridge connects, and how it makes them better.'

If I had been jealous of Sebastian flirting with Chloe in Mandarin that first night, it allayed my concerns that the two of them couldn't go ten minutes without bickering. Sebastian, used to being the smartest person in the room, insisted on singing the praises of Deng Xiaoping's economic reforms and lectured us on the coming Chinese century that would lead to the strengthening of a Chinese middle class, demands for political reform and, ultimately, democracy in China. Chloe called him naive. When I made the mistake of trying to wade into these debates with a Marxist defence of why the Party would better protect the Chinese people from the forces of rapacious capitalism, she groaned and covered her ears.

'Can the two white boys please stop lecturing the Chinese girl about China?'

If it wasn't about politics, or music, she'd be squabbling with Sebastian about what bar we'd visit that night, or what we should do the next day. It was as if they took pleasure in arguing with each other. Chloe always took Caroline's side or mine in any disagreements, and never missed an opportunity to tease Sebastian about being a 'player'. When he remarked he found Chinese girls attractive, she snorted.

'A Chinese girl would eat you for breakfast.'

'Hopefully lunch and dinner too.' He'd laugh, and she'd grimace with theatrical disgust.

'He's so gross,' she'd say to me, and I was relieved by her scorn.

I loved Sebastian, but I wanted Chloe to know I was different to him. I wasn't a flirt. I didn't 'pick up' women. I could be trusted. I was the one who understood music and could have deep and meaningful conversations.

I was sure she felt it too. We were connecting on a deeper level.

And yet, every now and then I'd catch her watching Sebastian. I couldn't read her expression, I didn't know what she was thinking. But it made me slightly sick in the guts. Despite how dismissive of him she seemed, her eyes always tracked where he was in the room.

After a while, the weird tension between Sebastian and Chloe impacted on Sebastian and me too. One morning when I was fixing coffee in the apartment's kitchen, Sebastian emerged from his bedroom.

'Chloe doesn't like me, does she?'

'How can you tell?'

'She gets pissed off and argues whenever I speak.'

'You don't need everyone to love you, Sebastian,' I chided.

He picked up the coffee I'd made for him. 'Well, she's hanging off your every word.'

I felt a flush of anger.

'Is it so much of a problem that she enjoys being with me?'

He ran his finger around the rim of the coffee. Apparently it was a problem.

❖

A Unity Rave was to be held at the International Trade & Exhibition Centre in Kowloon Bay. It would be an all-night party going through until the morning of the 29th. I wasn't interested, and hoped if Sebastian and Caroline went off it might give me time alone with Chloe, maybe in Sebastian's apartment. But she surprised me and seemed excited by the idea of the rave.

'I need to blow off some steam. All this tension is killing me.'

'But will you be able to get away?'

'I'm an adult, Charlie. I don't need permission.' Her eyes lowered. 'And my father's in Beijing.'

We arranged to meet around nine. Doors opened at ten, but it was common knowledge the actual event wouldn't kick off until at least midnight. Sebastian, Caroline and I went out for drinks. I was eager for Chloe to join us, but she didn't show.

At midnight, I kept checking my watch. I was wearing my Blinding Love T-shirt. It had a picture of a little girl dancing in the rain on the front, and the lyrics to 'Restless' on the back. Chloe had said she was jealous and wanted one of her own. She'd joked about stealing mine. I guess I was hoping that come the morning she might be wearing it. But I tried not to think about that, as I kept glancing towards the door. Where could she be?

The line to get in pushed forward into the enormous hall, intended for trade shows. It was packed with dancers, arms in the air, heads thrown back, wearing top hats with Chinese and British flags, glow sticks wrapped around necks and shoulders and wrists and thighs. Strobe and colour lights fell across grinding bodies, like fingers caressing the surface of the water. The drum and bass music was so loud I felt it as a pain in my chest.

'Chloe's not coming. Let's just dance!' Sebastian cried, grabbing Caroline's hand. She gave a rodeo whoop, and they plunged into the writhing throng.

I ordered a Guinness at the bar and leant against the wall, watching the door. I was worried about Chloe. Had something happened? Had her father not let her come?

A little before 1 am, she appeared.

'Fucking Liu Hui. He wouldn't let me leave. He sat downstairs by the door until midnight. He's such an arsehole. It's got nothing to do with him if I want to get fucked up.' She grabbed me by the shoulder. 'And I do want to get fucked up, Charlie.'

She had shunned her usual grungy clothes and was wearing a midriff top, tight black pants and shiny shoes with a massive heel. She wore bright red lipstick; her eyelids were shaded lilac blue, with black eyeliner that made them look catlike.

'Nice T-shirt.' She winked. 'I still want one.'

'You look amazing.'

'It's the end of the world, right? Might as well try. Come dance with me.'

I raised my hands and backed away.

'Oh no. I don't dance.'

'Just this once? For me.'

I never danced. The closest I came was listening to live bands, where I would headbang along in a mosh pit, or occasionally crowd surf.

'Oh, come on, Charlie! Why don't you want to dance?'

A lumbering fool, I refused, and with a shrug she plunged into the sea of bodies. I was left on the shore, holding her bag.

She was possessed. Dancing beneath the light, throwing her head back as if releasing wild spirits. They cleared a circle around her. She didn't dance with anyone, but was just lost in the music's freedom. Free of her father, free of her mother and whatever burden they'd heaped on her shoulders. Free of the handover and all its uncertainty.

After half an hour, she bounced from the dancers back to my side and kissed my cheek.

'Oh my God, it feels so good. I feel so good. Touch my arm. You can literally feel everyone in the room.'

I saw how much she was sweating. Her dilated pupils filling up the entire eye.

'Are you on something?'

'I took a little ecstasy before …'

She took her bag from me and rummaged for water, drinking half the bottle.

'Get me another one, Charlie?' She kissed my mouth. Biting my top lip. Closing her eyes. Moaning a little. 'God, that feels amazing.'

Then she was off. Back onto the dance floor.

I stood there holding her bag. Feeling the tingling sensation of her mouth on mine as I waited in the queue for water. But when I returned to the hall, I saw with horror that Chloe was dancing with Sebastian. She had her back to him, and he closed the gap behind her. His hands on her hips. Grinding himself into her. Her head tilted back into his chest. His mouth opening, eyes closing. I wanted to stride into the crowd and punch him. He was betraying me. There was no other way to describe it. Right there in front of me.

But then she opened her eyes and saw me and smiled. As spontaneously as she had left me, she was back. And Sebastian was calling her name from the dance floor.

She ignored him and took my arm.

'Let's get the fuck out of here.'

CHAPTER SEVENTEEN

We took the Star Ferry back across Victoria Harbour, then a taxi to the Peak, stopping near Lugard Road. Chloe wanted to get away from people. No more sights and sounds of the handover.

I was still holding her handbag as we wandered around the Morning Trail, the paved walking path that winds through the lush greenery at the highest point on Hong Kong Island. First staring at the lights of the city, then further out, as we followed the looping path into the darkness of the South China Sea.

Up here, the British colonialists had once strolled to escape the heat and the colonised masses in the city below. Now aerial roots of banyan trees curled over stone walls, choking wrought-iron railings and street lamps. Park benches, once situated towards the view, stood a blind vigil overwhelmed by scrub and clinging vines, as if the reclamation of the island by its own nature was already underway.

I checked the time. It was 2.40 am. The sky was an inky blue; the wind was still. Jungle sounds in the darkness, our shoes scraping the pavement. We held hands and walked in silence. My mind was elated and alarmed in equal measure. She kept coming back to me, wanting to be alone with me, so surely that meant something. And yet when I closed my eyes, I saw her with Sebastian. Her head leaning back against his chest, moments from a kiss.

'Can I tell you something and you promise not to freak out?'

I nodded, my heartbeat increasing as I expected she might be about to confirm how I thought we were feeling about each other.

'My father saw you leaving the other night.'

I stopped and looked at her. 'How do you know that?'

'He told me.' She smiled with just one side of her mouth. 'He said he'd seen a young foreigner staring at the house. He asked if I knew anyone of your description.' She turned and kept walking, speaking nonchalantly. 'He was watching my reaction. I denied it. But he's suspicious. That's why Liu was being such a dick tonight. My father told him to watch me.'

I hadn't started moving again, but this last part made me launch forward.

'Liu kept you home because of me?'

'My father warned me to stay away from foreign boys. He threatened to pull me out of school.'

'That's ridiculous.'

We were at the furthest point of the headland, which stretched out towards the water. The track now looped back towards the city. She paused with her hands on the iron railing, staring at the dark waves.

'I've been in trouble before. It's one reason he sent me away from Hong Kong.'

'What sort of trouble?'

'Drugs. Alcohol …' She looked down. 'Boys …'

'Sounds pretty normal,' I said, stifling my jealousy of these faceless boys.

'I was a bit like Sebastian, I guess … with all his flings. Maybe losing a parent makes you wild and need more … connections with people.'

I scowled in the darkness, lamenting telling her about Sebastian's father.

'My father thinks I'm rebelling against him. Nothing scares him more than that. He says he won't let me shame him. He says he can't afford to lose face again after what my mother did.'

I could see freighters in the distance. Their lights blinking through the haze. There were people on those ships. But I couldn't imagine them as anything but a backdrop to this moment with Chloe.

'My father blames her. It hurt him. Not only his career. He loved her very much and, in his mind, what she did, what they all did, was a betrayal. A product of foreign influence. He suspects foreign ideas. He calls it "black hands". He wants to lock me away from all of that. Protect me against that.'

'By sending you to the United States for university?'

'You don't know how isolated you can still be as an international student. I live with students whose parents work with my father. I need to sneak out at night to see a band, or escape their spying eyes. It's no different from being here.'

'What happened to your mother, Chloe?'

'It was after Tiananmen. The students came to her hospital. She spent days treating wounded young people. Caring for those that would recover. Mourning for those she couldn't help.'

She sighed and turned, as if she couldn't explain while looking out into the dark sea. We began walking back towards the Peak Tower.

'My mother became depressed. She and my father fought. She was angry about what the government had done. He was angry that the students had driven them to it. He left for a business trip. She stopped eating. Or going to work. Or caring for me. Then she locked herself in her room.'

I clutched Chloe's bag to my chest as we walked, watching the way she picked at her knuckles. She was no longer looking around us. Her eyes were those of a little girl in a Beijing apartment, worrying about her mother.

'I begged her to open the door. Pounding until my knuckles bled. And when she did, she slapped my face and told me if the neighbours complained we'd be arrested. She said the army was executing the student troublemakers who had survived. Dragging them from their homes and their hospital beds into prison to be tortured and shot. She said we would be executed too if I made a fuss.'

Chloe shook her head, grinding her knuckles into her eyes.

'She wasn't political. It wasn't intended as a statement or any kind of protest. She loved China. She respected the Party. But she knew some of these young people. She knew their families. She knew them as her patients. She'd treated their wounds. And they were young. Our age. Younger. Just students. Suddenly troublemakers, counter-revolutionaries, black hands. I don't know what she saw in the hospital when they brought them in on stretchers or when the authorities dragged them away in handcuffs. But she said she heard their screams in her sleep. I'm sure it was this that made her do what she did.'

'What did she do, Chloe?' I urged.

'I don't know. They never told me. She took something, I guess. She didn't wake up. Not even when the flames were biting her skin. The entire apartment was ablaze. I was screaming, trying to move her. There was fire everywhere. I would have been burnt alive. I was only a girl.'

'How did you get out?'

'Someone rescued me. He carried me out. I wish he hadn't.'

'Don't say that.' I reached out and tried to draw her to me. But she shook her head and increased her pace. It was as if she wanted to get back to the lights of the Peak Tower. To outpace her story and leave it in the darkness.

'My father refused to mourn,' she continued. 'I don't know what pressure he was under. What my mother had done was not an explicit criticism of the Party. But it was close. It could be inferred. He needed to be distanced from it to save face. His career suffered. He almost lost his job. The work in Shenzhen became his priority. He brought us to Hong Kong. Which, for me, was a relief. I don't think I could have lived on the mainland where it was illegal to talk about what happened. You need to talk, right? That's what my shrinks have said. To process tragedy? So, in Hong Kong, at least they acknowledged June 4. People here have freedom of speech. They are allowed to remember.'

She kicked a rock from the road.

'Not my father. We brought the silence with us. I was not to speak of her. I was not to speak of June 4. I was not to swallow the western lies that wanted to hurt the feelings of the Chinese people. But Charlie ...' She stopped and grabbed me by the wrist.

'That's what drove my mother mad. She did what she did because she couldn't talk about what she'd seen. It was gone. It had not happened. And yet it was inside her like a cancer. It's inside me like a fucking cancer.'

I began to speak, but she placed her finger over my lips.

'You can't say anything, Charlie. You're not Chinese. You know nothing. You understand nothing.' She pointed at her bag. 'Give me a cigarette?'

I rummaged in her bag like it was our shared possession, locating the carton of cigarettes and pulling one out for her. She leant forward, and I held the lighter with trembling hands. She touched my wrist, looked into my eyes and mouthed the words *thank you*.

We smoked. I remained silent as she'd instructed, which was fine. I didn't know what to say, anyway. She exhaled the last of her cigarette and crushed the butt on the ground. Then snatched her bag from me.

'We need music now. Music helps.'

She waved for me to come close to her, then pushed an earbud into my ear. She clicked through tracks on her Discman, then looked up at me and tried to smile through tears welling up in her eyes as the organ swelled and Jeff Ament's upright bass began 'Indifference' by Pearl Jam.

As the song soared, she let her bag fall to the ground and covered her face with her hands, supressing a sob.

'Hey,' I said, 'Chloe, please don't ...' I clumsily tried to put my arm around her to comfort her. She twisted and pressed herself against me.

'It's just ... unbearable sometimes,' she muttered into my chest.

I held her body against mine. Her tears on my shirt as Eddie Vedder sang about holding a candle and burning his arm, how little difference any of it made.

We swayed beneath the lampposts on the deserted Lugard Road.

I told myself: *Now. Now. Kiss her now.* But I couldn't. It wasn't right. She was still high. She was emotional. The story she'd told was overwhelming. I couldn't just take advantage of her. I nuzzled into her hair. I held her cheek against my chest.

Then I felt her sigh heavily.

'When will you leave, Charlie?'

'The first of July.'

She shook her head and may have sobbed again. 'Everyone's deserting us.'

'Don't say that.' I felt her tears through my T-shirt. 'We'll go to the fireworks tomorrow.' There was still tomorrow. To kiss her. To tell her how I felt.

She was turning her head up to mine to answer when there came the squeal of brakes. We were exposed in piercing headlights. A black Mercedes mounted the pavement, screeching to a halt in front of us.

Chloe screamed. We both backed away.

A figure leapt out of the car. Tall, strong. In a leather jacket. Balling his fingers into fists. Liu Hui. He grabbed Chloe by the wrist and dragged her to the car. She screamed and fought against him, punching him on the chin. He took her blows as if they were from a child. Even when she drew blood across his forehead, he didn't stop moving.

'Charlie. Charlie!' Chloe screamed.

But I was frozen. A coward. Staring. Unable to move.

He dragged open the back door of the car and thrust her inside as if she were a bag of groceries. She pounded on the window, still calling my name, muffled through the thick glass.

Liu Hui turned to confront me, and I prepared to be beaten, maybe killed. The retribution demanded by Chloe's jealous father. I looked behind me and considered running back the way we'd come. But I knew he'd be able to outrun me and the idea of being stuck with him in the darkness was no relief. I wanted to cry out. Call for help. But who would come? He stalked towards me, his face illuminated in the streetlight. I could see the discolouration on his cheek and as he drew closer I realised now it wasn't a birthmark. It was scarring from a burn. The whole side of his face appeared like melted wax. I knew then who had carried Chloe out of the flames.

He bent down beside me and retrieved Chloe's bag. I wanted to speak. To tell him to let her go. That he couldn't do this. She was an adult. She was free to be with whoever she pleased.

'She's free to choose what she wants,' I stuttered.

It was meek. It was shameful.

And Liu Hui silenced me with a cautionary finger. I froze in terror. He held my gaze as I closed my mouth. I lowered my head. I let him take her away.

CHAPTER EIGHTEEN

'Well, at least we know why her father brought her to Hong Kong.' Ronnie yawned. 'His wife sympathised with the protestors. Even dead, she would have imperilled Zheng's career. So, was that it? Was that the last you saw of her?'

Katrina answered for me with a shake of her head. 'It wasn't, was it, Charlie? One more betrayal to come. Finish it for us.'

❖

It was the last day of British rule over Hong Kong. Sebastian watched me from the doorway. My CDs spilled out across the floor. His old stereo beside me. I'd bought a blank cassette tape from a street market in Wan Chai. I'd cut an image of hands clutching one another out of the South China Morning Post.

'Mix tape?'

I nodded and continued writing the track listing.

'For Chloe? Doesn't she already know all your songs? You guys are like musical twins.'

I looked up at Sebastian. He didn't know the half of it. I hadn't told him what had happened.

'Where did you go last night?' he asked.

'To the Peak for a walk.'

'Why didn't you bring her back here?'

'What do you mean?'

He grinned. 'Well, if you guys got together … . why didn't she spend the night?'

'We're not a …' I knew I was blushing. 'We're not that.'

I had no time to bother with Sebastian. It was always so basic to him. Did you get it on with her? Did you get her into bed? It was so puerile, so fucking schoolboy. I'd outgrown all that in the last week.

Now all I cared about was helping Chloe. Helping her the only way I could. With music. A mix tape. Just as I'd made one for Sebastian when he went into board at school.

Saying it now seems pretty feeble. But it felt important then. It was all I could give.

'Well, are you two just music twins, then?' There was malice in his voice. 'That's why you didn't make a move?'

'What does "make a move" even fucking mean?'

He shrugged. 'You didn't make a move. That's all I'm saying.'

'I didn't make a move, Sebastian. We're friends.' To say anything more would have been a betrayal of what I felt for her. What I felt we had together. I had to believe that, just like I had to believe that last night we didn't kiss because I didn't want to take advantage of her. I had to believe in my moral superiority over Sebastian, otherwise I was simply a coward. A coward for not kissing her. A coward for letting Liu Hui drag her away.

'We're just friends.'

'Best friends, it sounds like.'

I wondered for a moment if he was jealous of me being with Chloe or Chloe being with me. Ridiculously, I felt the need to reassure him.

'We just walked and listened to music, okay? It was nothing else. We're not like that.'

He nodded and his voice became low.

'Okay. I just wanted to be clear. You didn't make a move. You're not like that.'

❖

And then it was the night of 30 June 1997.

The sovereignty of Hong Kong was to be transferred from British rule to Chinese control. Ceremonies were being held across the city. Dignitaries gathered at the Hong Kong Convention and Exhibition Centre in Wan Chai. The media broadcast the event live to the world. The end of the British colonial empire, live on television screens across the planet.

At midnight, they lowered the Union Jack as the Chinese national flag was raised. The Hong Kong police band played the Chinese national anthem and a hundred-and-one-gun salute rang out across the night sky. Prince Charles and Chris Patten boarded the royal yacht *Britannia* and sailed out of the harbour. The handover was complete.

And I didn't care.

I was looking for Chloe.

I was winding my way down to the harbour, and along the waterfront. Once more wearing my 'Restless' T-shirt. I was searching for her. We'd said we would meet around Pier 4. I searched for her, navigating my way through endless people gathering for the fireworks.

They filled the harbour with boats. Junks. Yachts. Ferries.

Music and voices filled the air, then cheers and cries as the largest fireworks show in Hong Kong's history exploded in the sky above us.

I felt an urgency pounding in my chest as I peered through the crowd, Chloe's mix tape in my pocket. The brave track listing. Telling her how I felt. Trying to give her relief.

I didn't even know if she would be there. But Christ I hoped she would be. I needed to see her again. I needed to apologise for letting Liu take her away. To tell her I didn't make moves. I wasn't like Sebastian. But we shared the music. The music would tell her. She'd know when she listened to the tape.

And I'm just waiting to be free.

With someone else like me.

Fireworks pounded in the sky. Colours bursting like a mad artist's box of paints hurled towards the stars. The air filled with smoke, people cheering and clapping, some crying, children screaming. I pushed through them all. Looking from face to face. Imagining I saw her, chasing a stranger, clutching at shoulders, only to find I'd been chasing a phantom. It wasn't Chloe. Where was Chloe? My heart pounded. Where was she? Had her father returned? Was she being punished? Was she locked in the house? Pulled out of school? Sent back to Beijing? It was all too horrendous to consider. And I increased my efforts, thrusting through groups of cheering friends and families. Dragging people out of my way, shouting, 'Move. Move. Please move.' My breathing wild. Panting. Panicking.

And then everything became still.

The fireworks were silent.

The surrounding cries were hushed.

Darkness filled my head and my heart burst inside my chest.

I saw them, sitting on a wall, back from Pier 4. His arm was around her. Hers around him. For a moment, from a distance, I grasped onto the illusion that it was a friendly embrace. Like the handover, a friendly new embrace. Just friendly. I didn't believe it. I couldn't believe it could be anything more.

I walked closer, forcing myself forward. Needing to know. Beyond denial. Needing to see. But what else could it be? Like secret friendships revealed on the edge of the school football field. I stood by Victoria Harbour, the sky exploding above me. I saw them clearly: Sebastian and Chloe, in a passionate embrace, their lips together, his hand upon her cheek, her eyes closed.

Sebastian had made his move.

CHAPTER NINETEEN

Silence in the meeting room. Ronnie shook his head and muttered, 'What a prick.'

I folded my arms across my chest, stifling the emotions that my recollections had restored. I hadn't meant to tell it in such detail. To let the old feelings out to run.

'My God,' Katrina said. I turned, expecting her wide-eyed sympathy, but to my disappointment I found her scowling at her phone. 'Do you have reception?' she asked Ronnie.

'What?' He blinked at her, surprised by the abrupt change of subject.

'Do you have mobile phone reception?' she said, a hard note creeping into her voice. Ronnie checked.

'No bars.' He shook his head. 'That's weird.'

'Who is your mobile provider?'

'Optus,' he replied, beginning the process of turning his phone on and off again.

'It won't help,' she said standing up. 'Their network is down across New South Wales and Victoria. And now here.'

'It's been on and off all day. I was getting low bars before. Now it's SOS Only,' Ronnie said with a frown.

Senate bells broke the silence. The little red light blinked on the wall clock. I instinctively got to my feet, forgetting I no longer needed to get Sebastian into the Senate chambers for the vote. I must have startled Katrina with the movement of my chair, as she looked at me with alarm.

'Sit down please, Charlie. We're not finished.' Her body was tense, her stare no longer detached but fierce. I didn't understand this change in her demeanour.

'I need a break.' I tried to assert myself. 'We've been going for two hours.'

'I said sit down, Charlie.'

'I need to stretch my legs,' I insisted, feeling increasingly desperate for a cigarette.

'Sit down.' Katrina's voice was raised now. The door opened, and a well-built young man in a cheap suit with a sea admiral's beard appeared.

'Is everything alright in here?'

'Everything is under control, Jacob. Charlie is about to resume his seat,' Katrina said not taking her eyes off me. 'What do you need?'

'Director-General needs you on a call ...'

'About the network outage?' she asked.

Jacob glanced briefly towards me, then back towards Katrina. 'Yes, and other matters ...'

'The situations are linked?'

Both of them were looking towards me now, glares accusing, as if I was somehow responsible or I was one of the 'linked situations'.

'Looks like it,' Jacob said.

I turned to Ronnie for an explanation but he was staring at his phone.

'Reboot didn't help.'

Katrina nodded and turned to walk with Jacob out the door. Irritated by their mysterious behaviour, I walked around the table and followed Katrina, speaking to her back. 'I'm going for a smoke then.'

She spun on her toes so abruptly I had to pull up short to avoid colliding with her pointing finger.

'Charlie, I don't have time to indulge you.' Her tone was sharp. 'I have already told you we are in the midst of assessing a serious threat. You're not leaving this room until we work out what is going on. Do you understand?'

I was shocked. First they'd taken my phone, now the supposedly 'unofficial' conversation had shifted to one in which I appeared to be detained.

I swallowed and looked back towards my seat at the long table. I could see the coffee mug where, hours ago, I'd ashed my cigarette after a single rebellious puff to show them they did not intimidate me. I'd thought I was to be questioned on a decades-old security breach. A breach that would embarrass the memory of my friend, lose me my job, potentially humiliate the government, and even damage the party to which I'd dedicated my life. But nothing more consequential than that. Yet now Katrina was speaking as if I were linked to some imminent threat. She'd earlier taken my phone and referenced the ASIO Act, and now the young sea captain stepped back into the room as if limbering up to make an arrest.

'I just want a cigarette,' I said, certain that I couldn't submit to whatever this was, that to comply would be an admission of guilt for a crime of which I was still to be accused.

'For fuck's sake, I'll take him.' Ronnie sighed, getting to his feet. 'Come on, Charlie.'

'No.' Katrina gestured at the sea captain. 'Jacob will take him. Be quick. We reconvene as soon as I am off this call.'

I walked down the corridor, Jacob looming over me like a prison screw. A few staffers glanced in my direction, but no one approached. Everyone seemed distracted. There was a tension about the place. The usual sitting week urgency, the news of Sebastian's death, but something more. I saw a few MPs at a distance, running down corridors clutching briefing books. Public servants hovered outside ministers' offices, their phones raised as though, like Ronnie, they were unable to get any network connection. The AFP presence had been reinforced and the guards now openly cradled firearms at each checkpoint we passed.

We went out the doors towards the Senate carpark, pacing the requisite five metres away from the building entrance. An aeroplane flew low over the city, its engines loud in the quiet capital. It was a grey and cold afternoon. Snow on the mountains. I'd left my jacket upstairs. At least the cigarette was comforting.

Smoking was a habit I'd brought back from Hong Kong with me. A quiet nod to Chloe. Every time I opened a pack, in my mind I offered her one, like we had in those weeks together, when we referred to them as 'our cigarettes'. *Let's go get more cigarettes.* Our excuse to go off together and leave Caroline and Sebastian behind. I hadn't thought of that for a long time, but everything was again so fresh in my mind. I smoked, and the memories were like an addiction.

Another aeroplane flew overhead, and I glanced up at the noise from its engines.

'You got a light, mate?'

I turned. Swanny was waving an unlit cigarette towards me, his other hand hiding his press pass. I offered my lighter, indulging in the artifice that we were strangers.

'Thanks, mate.' Swanny nodded, catching my eye as he bent over the flame. Jacob hadn't recognised him and, thinking we were just two old blokes sharing cancer sticks, stepped away to avoid the stink.

As soon as he was out of earshot, Swanny was whispering at me.

'Your phone dead too? I've been trying to call. The Optus network is totally down. But Telstra's still up.'

I shrugged. 'No idea. They took my phone off me.'

'Who's "they"?' He frowned, then looked towards Jacob. 'AFP?'

I didn't respond.

'What's going on?'

'Can't talk about it, mate. I saw your article.'

'Any comment?'

I shook my head. Swanny was a mate. I could see the concern in his eyes, but there was also that hunger. These gallery veterans are born with it. Bloodhounds on the scent. They'd sell out their brother for a story on the front page, their mother too if it was above the fold.

'Doesn't matter anyway. I've got a few more leads now, and I reckon I'm on to a whole new yarn,' Swanny said slyly, watching for my reaction.

'What yarn?'

'About a Chinese lover and a cover-up.'

My heart leapt. I stared at him and tried to keep the emotion from my face. I desperately wanted to deny it, to mock him, to demand his source, but I was afraid my voice would shake. How could he already know about Chloe?

'I've got a source,' Swanny continued, not waiting for my response, 'suggesting Adler may have been involved in a cover-up regarding the death of a Chinese girlfriend in his youth. My source suggests Adler was being blackmailed and this explains the suicide. Care to comment on that angle, Charlie?'

'Jesus, Swanny, you can't write that.' I tried to grab his arm, then remembered Jacob watching us at a distance. Blackmail? That was an allusion to the message from Zheng. How could any of this have got out so fast? Judy knew nothing about Chloe. Ronnie wouldn't have leaked it. Cassie didn't want it out. 'If you publish that, Swanny, you're going to do irreparable damage to the government.'

Swanny nodded his head sadly. 'I know, Charlie. It's not a good look. A bit hard to claim your government is tough on national security when your Assistant Minister for Foreign Affairs and Trade is being blackmailed over a secret Chinese girlfriend. Someone's sending a message.'

I gritted my teeth. Another aeroplane flew overhead. Was this the threat Katrina had referenced? Had the blond-haired bloke interrupted the interview to tell Katrina and Ronnie that Swanny was about to break the story?

'Mate, I'd be very careful if I were you, throwing around unsourced bullshit like that. You never know who you're going to piss off.'

'I've got a credible source, Charlie.'

I couldn't help myself and started pointing at his chest, throwing my weight around like I was known for when it came to getting these fucking journos under control.

'All you've got is a source with some bullshit story motivated to hurt the government. Where's your professional integrity, Swanny? This is clearly a political hit job. Someone is feeding you a line to damage the PM. I'm sure your editor won't be too pleased if you let your column become a vehicle for a grubby political attack by leveraging a good man's tragic death —'

I stopped speaking abruptly as I could hear the tremble in my voice. There were tears in my eyes, and I knew he could see them. I had to persevere. Reclaim the narrative.

'This is fucked, Swanny. My best mate is dead. We're in shock. I'm in shock. His wife is a mess. Are you really going to let some opposition source turn this political?'

Swanny sighed. I could see the lines of concern wrinkling across his forehead. He was deliberating. I knew he voted for us. I knew he wouldn't throw us under the bus.

'My source isn't political, Charlie.' His voice was quiet, and he didn't look at me.

'Bullshit mate. What do you call this, if it isn't fucking political?'

'A cautionary tale.'

I inhaled hard on my cigarette so I didn't have to look at him. He'd just given me his source. We both knew it. But it was shocking. A cautionary tale? Who had access to information about Chloe and an interest in exposing undeclared relationships and vulnerabilities as a cautionary tale?

'Your source is ASIO?' I asked, incredulous. 'Fucking ASIO leaked to you?'

Swanny shrugged, non-committal, but I knew I'd guessed right. It could only be ASIO. The agency in recent years had become proactive in explaining the risk of foreign interference. Where once they would have squashed any coverage of arrests made under suspicion of espionage, McCubbin's ASIO now went out of its way to promote details of people arrested under the Espionage and Foreign Interference Act, referring to these drops to the media as 'cautionary tales'. The most recent had been a young marketing executive charged with reckless foreign interference after being co-opted by handlers 'Ken' and 'Evelyn' in Shanghai to 'write reports' on AUKUS and lithium mining in Australia. Rather than covering up these cases, ASIO promoted them as both a demonstration of its investigative success, and a threat to any trusted insiders thinking they could get away with betraying the country to foreign intelligence services.

I stared at Swanny, unable to frame my words. I knew the question I wanted to ask, but how to broach it? If his source was ASIO, who from within the agency would have given the order to leak the information? It could only have been Alec McCubbin. Given the hurt to his daughter, the humiliation to him personally, only with his sanction could the story get out. But would he really do that? Was his desire to see the government fall so profound he'd be willing to throw his family – and his own reputation – under the bus? Again that feeling of dread. Stumbling in shadows. There was more going on here that I couldn't make out, as if ASIO knew more about the story they were forcing me to tell than I knew myself.

Someone's sending a message.

The sound of screaming aeroplane jets filled the sky.

A dreadful realisation pierced me.

McCubbin would only have given up the truth about Sebastian, at such a cost to himself and to his family, if he was covering up something worse … if there was another truth.

'You haven't denied it.' Swanny's voice snapped me out of my thoughts.

'What?' I blinked. 'I deny it.'

'Okay, well you're lucky with all this shit going down in Sydney we've got time. Editors don't want to hear about anything but traffic chaos. So if you want to give me your side we've got a few hours —'

'What's going on in Sydney?' I interrupted, unable to think straight, still dazed as I studied the crystallising realisation in my head. *There is another truth.*

Swanny cocked an eyebrow. 'Jesus. How long have you been in there with them?'

'A few hours. This is about the phone networks or something?' I asked vaguely.

He shook his head. 'It's more than phones, Charlie. Transport is fucked. Rumour is that it's a cyberattack. They haven't made any comment, but I'm hearing there has been a massive coordinated DDOS assault on the transport system.'

Now I was focused. 'A cyberattack targeting what?'

'Targeting everything that moves. Air traffic control systems, traffic management and rail control systems, ferry and port operations.'

'Fucking hell.'

'That's what that is,' he said, pointing towards the sky. 'Planes are being redirected to Newcastle and Canberra, as well as interstate.'

Realisation dawned on me as I stared at the usually quiet sky over Australia's bush capital. It was filled with aeroplanes circling the city, awaiting an opportunity to land, like a flock of lost birds searching for dry terrain.

❖

Jacob, continuing his disconcerting impression of a jail warden, deposited me back in the meeting room. Katrina was frowning into an iPad and Ronnie, finishing a call on his personal phone that seemingly was able to connect to a network, gazed out through the Venetian blinds.

'Did you hear what's going on in Sydney?' I asked as he ended the call.

'Of course I have,' he snapped. 'I should brief the PM for NSC, but he wants me here managing your fucking mess.'

I had considered warning him that ASIO had given Swanny the story about Chloe, but his sneering remark, along with the fact he had betrayed me only a few hours earlier, sapped me of any loyalty I felt to him or the PM. My objective now was to keep my head down, not let on what I knew (which wasn't much), and get out of there as soon as possible.

'Please sit down, Charlie,' Katrina said, looking up from the iPad she'd been scrolling through. 'Where are you going, Mr Durban?'

Ronnie looked agitated and lingered near the door. 'I just need to call someone.'

'Can it wait? We're in the middle of something here.' She gestured at me.

I was the something.

'This thing in Sydney is getting worse,' Ronnie growled, looking at his phone. 'Transport for NSW and the Civil Aviation Safety Authority have been hit with a new ransomware attack. I've just got to check in.'

Katrina folded her arms.

'I'm aware of that, Mr Durban. But if you leave we will conduct the meeting without you. We do not have time for delays.'

Ronnie hesitated: clearly he'd been ordered to stay. The PM didn't trust (rightly, it seemed) ASIO to talk with me alone. Ronnie turned back to us. His voice had lost its usual belligerent edge. 'Look. It's my dad. He visits Mum mornings and evenings. He never misses. He's insisting he needs to go. I just need to call …'

For the first time in years, Ronnie was a human being rather than the PM's enforcer. That alone told me whatever was happening in Sydney was serious.

I'd met his father at branch meetings many moons ago. I knew his mum was in a care home with dementia. Maybe sensing how extraordinary this rare show of vulnerability was, Katerina's tone changed. 'Tell him to stay home,' she said, almost gently.

'I just said that's what I'm …'

'I mean, prepare to stay home for the next little while. Order in groceries, non-perishables. If he can't use the internet to buy provisions, tell him to fill buckets and other containers with as much water from the tap as he can.'

We both turned to stare at her.

'What do you know?' Ronnie asked.

She sucked on her lips a moment, as if deciding whether to say more.

'AEMO report a virus has been unleashed into the National Energy Market systems and perhaps other utilities. There could be blackouts. The water could stop running. Our people are over there now.'

'Is it going to get bad?' Ronnie's face was paling.

'People fought over toilet paper during COVID. If the power goes off, it will be bad.' She pointed at us both, suddenly stern. 'That information is not to leave this room.'

Ronnie nodded and closed the door.

❖

The certainties of daily life seemed to be collapsing around me. First Sebastian. Now the transport system. The electricity network. The second largest telecommunications provider in the country.

Katrina's advice to Ronnie's father sounded unbelievable. It was the sort of extreme paranoia you'd expect from survivalists or conspiracy theorists. Not a senior ASIO operative.

And yet, what I'd learnt from Swanny about ASIO leaking to the media was also unbelievable.

I sat in silence, watching Katrina check her phone. She must have known about the leaks, and whatever the hell it was McCubbin was hoping to gain from them. Maybe she leaked the information herself. Maybe tomorrow I'd wake up and the transcript of our entire discussion would be on the front page of the paper under Swanny's byline. What game were they playing? And why were they doing it in the middle of an emerging crisis?

'Is McCubbin directing the response?' I asked, hearing the venom in my words.

'The Director is splitting his time between comforting his daughter and grandchildren and, yes, managing what is emerging as a significant national security emergency.' She gave me a meaningful stare. 'Otherwise, he would be here asking these questions of you now.'

'Has he had any time to speak to the media?'

'ASIO resources are strained as they are. It's not his role to talk to the media.'

'I agree,' I growled, scouring her face for a sign she knew to what I was alluding. There was nothing. I breathed out, frustrated. 'Look, I'm happy if you want to wrap this up and go contribute to the effort.'

'I am contributing to the effort, Charlie. And so are you by continuing your story.'

She consulted her notes, and we were off again.

'Let's return to how you left it. Sebastian has betrayed you in Hong Kong with a girl you had genuine feelings for. You didn't see him for two years …?'

'Five,' I said, feeling the old bitterness. 'He'd stayed on in China, then finished his degree back in the UK.'

'And then it seems he suddenly made contact. Correct?'

She looked at me with eyes magnified through those fishbowl glasses. I knew she knew more than me, so didn't bother arguing.

'Yes, he made contact,' I replied, folding my arms.

'And convinced you to lie on his security screening.'

'What? No. What are you talking about?' My scalp was itching. It happened when I was nervous. I didn't like where this was going.

'You deny it?' she snapped.

'Yes, I bloody do.'

Katrina sighed like a disappointed school counsellor, then pushed the iPad across the table.

'Do you know what this is?'

'It's a scan of an Australian Government Security Vetting Agency form …' I scrolled down, and my stomach lurched as I read the scrawl in the box marked 'Candidate's Details'.

'It's Sebastian's security clearance.'

'It's the report from the Assessment Officer,' Katrina said. 'Scroll to appendix D. What does it say?'

I saw my name filled in with the same handwriting.

'It's the transcript of my referee's interview.'

'You gave him a character reference? Why would you do that after what he did to you?'

'I have no idea,' I deflected.

'Question four. Can you read it aloud?'

With a trembling hand, I scrolled further through the document.

'Read it out loud please, Charlie.'

'Has the applicant to your knowledge had any relationships with representatives of a foreign government, or their families, that may represent a potential risk of undue influence or compromise?'

'And you answered?' Katrina raised an eyebrow.

'Not to my knowledge.' I sighed, not needing to read what I had said to the harried officer in a telephone interview twenty years ago.

'You provided misleading information.' She shrugged.

'Oh come on,' I said, covering my nervousness with bravado. 'Zheng wasn't a representative of a foreign government. He was a businessman.'

'He was a senior representative of a major state-owned enterprise working on government projects. It is equivalent to a representative of the Chinese state.'

I leant towards her, determined to call her bluff.

'Well, how the hell was I to know that as a twenty-something-year-old? There is no way you can suggest I lied on that form.'

'No way?' She raised a threatening eyebrow. 'I presume you're aware that under Section 137.1 of the Criminal Code Act 1995, the offence of knowingly providing false or misleading information to a Commonwealth entity carries a maximum penalty of ten years in prison.'

I could feel my heart beating in my ears. My throat was so constricted I couldn't respond. She was threatening me with jail time. Ten years in prison. Is this what my loyalty to Sebastian would cost me? Was this the price of redemption for my betrayal?

'Why were you protecting him, Charlie? After what he'd done to you.'

'I wasn't protecting *him*,' I snapped, folding my arms and looking away.

Katerina leant back in her chair, steepling her fingers like a shrink sensing a breakthrough.

CHAPTER TWENTY

Five years had passed since Hong Kong. Sebastian, for all I knew, had finished his time in Beijing and returned to London to graduate LSE. We hadn't spoken. And then, out of the blue, he left a message on my answering machine saying he had followed through with his ambition to enrol in the Department of Foreign Affairs and Trade graduate program. That he was back in Australia and wanted to catch up.

My first thought was to delete his message. Then I realised I wanted to see him. I wanted an apology. I wanted him to acknowledge what he'd done.

We met at Badde Manors cafe on Glebe Point Road. A walk from the Sydney University campus where I was teaching political science. Everything about the cafe added to my agitation: the sound of the coffee machine spraying steam, the grinder chewing through beans, the portafilter belting against the knock box, the baristas shouting and living up to the name of the establishment.

Sebastian had outgrown such grungy Inner West cafes. He was older, more sophisticated, a man of the world. His hair was thick and styled, a manicured strawberry blond stubble across his cheeks and chin. His sky-blue eyes locked onto mine from across the cafe as he zeroed in for a hug – best friends, reunited.

'How are you, Charlie? It's been too long.'

I didn't return his embrace, and when we sat down, I folded my arms against my chest.

If he noticed my coldness, he didn't acknowledge it. He was all easy charm. No mention of what happened in Hong Kong. No reference to why we hadn't seen each other in years. He brushed past it all, talking about his new life as a diplomat in training.

I couldn't bear it.

'Was there something you wanted to say to me, Sebastian ... after all these years?'

He paused, only for the slightest moment, perhaps processing the surliness of my tone. Then he leant forwards, cutting to the chase.

'Well, you see, Charlie, I'm aiming at an early diplomatic posting on the back of my grades and language. But I'll need an NV2 security clearance. I'm being screened by the AGSVA. And I have to provide referees, who aren't family, who have known me for ten years or longer.'

I rolled my eyes. 'So you're asking permission to put my name down?'

'Well ...' He grinned.

'You've already put me down.'

'They'll call you this week. Look, it's no big deal. They'll just want to check if I am who I say I am. They'll ask you if I have any vulnerabilities that could compromise me. If I'm an alcoholic or a problem gambler or closeted homosexual ...' He laughed, then grew serious. 'They'll probably ask about Dad. There'll be questions about whether all that fucked me up. If it had any lasting impacts on my character.'

'Did it?' I couldn't hide the spite in my words. 'Fuck you up?'

He shrugged. 'Well, I'm not an investment banker and I haven't fathered any secret love children.'

'That you know of ...'

'Fuck off.' He grinned, thinking I was joking. 'So will you do it, Charlie? Will you do it for me?'

His capacity to compartmentalise was dazzling. I ground my knuckle into the leg of the table, hesitating only a moment before letting him have it with both barrels.

'Are you actually fucking serious? You turn up five years after what you did in Hong Kong and ask me a favour? I thought you were here to apologise.'

He jerked backwards, as if he'd sat down at the wrong table with an aggressive stranger. 'Charlie, what you are talking about?'

'Oh, come on. Don't pretend you can't remember? Hong Kong? 1997? Chloe Zheng?'

His face hardened. 'What about Chloe?'

'You knew how I felt about her!' I exploded, unleashing years of repressed anguish. 'I saw you that night … the night of the handover … on the pier with Chloe. You couldn't help yourself. You muscled in. You were kissing her. You fucking betrayed me.'

Sebastian slapped his palm against his forehead. 'That's why you left without saying goodbye?'

'You knew how I felt about her.'

'Charlie …' He was shaking his head as if I was crazy. 'Don't you remember? I asked you if there was anything going on between you and Chloe, and you said, "We're just friends." You and Chloe were just musical twins.'

I remembered the conversation. I'd dwelt on it endlessly, just like all those moments with Chloe. The night in her bedroom, the walk around the Peak, the confrontation with Liu Hui. I'd lain awake at night, replaying scenes. Replaying what I *should* have said.

I *should* have told Sebastian that I was in love with her and to back off. Just as I *should* have told Chloe how I felt, and I *should* have done more to keep her from Liu Hui.

But all I had done was make a fucking mix tape.

It was pathetic. And my impotence made me furious.

'So that gave you a fucking green light, did it? You didn't give a second thought to whether or not my feelings went deeper? You just took what you wanted. Another conquest.'

People at the surrounding tables were turning to look at me. I didn't care.

'You knew we were meeting at the pier and so you rushed in and got there first …'

'Charlie.' He said my name softly. I hated him for the sympathy in his eyes. 'I didn't go looking for Chloe. I'd lost Caroline in the crowd and I came across Chloe by chance. She was crying. She'd had a fight with her father. He'd returned early from a business trip …'

I blinked my eyes, processing Sebastian's words. She'd been crying? It could only have been because of what Liu Hui had done. He must have told her father about finding us at the Peak. And despite that, Chloe had still somehow got out of her house. She'd still come out looking for me. She'd wanted to see me.

'So you took advantage of her being upset and kissed her ...'

He was shaking his head, no longer smiling. 'No, listen, Charlie. *She* kissed *me*.'

The blood drained from my face. I heard it rushing in my ears.

'She was sobbing ... the fireworks were going off. She kept talking about her mother ... "Everyone leaves," she said.'

I swayed in my chair, punch drunk. No words.

'She was talking about her mother's suicide. Those last weeks of the handover ... with everything going on ... you know, it brought up a lot of this stuff for her. Everyone was leaving. The British were leaving. We were leaving.'

I grimaced, remembering her asking me when I would leave Hong Kong. I *should* have told her I would stay.

'I told her I didn't need to leave. I was trying to comfort her, Charlie ... I said I could stay in my mum's apartment as long as I needed. I wasn't going anywhere.' He leant back in his chair and shrugged. 'That's when she kissed me. It was just in the moment, you know? She was overwrought.'

It *should* have been me.

'So it was just a kiss ... when she was upset that night? Nothing else happened after that?'

Sebastian paused too long and my guts flooded with dread.

'I fell in love with her, Charlie.'

I could have reached over the table and punched him.

'I fell for her hard. All the time we were together in those weeks leading up to the handover, I'd thought she was beautiful, self assured and razor smart ...'

I hated the way his eyes lit up as he reminisced.

'But after that night ... after she told me what she'd been through with her mother ... Her life was like a mirror to mine.

Not just her mother's suicide, but the way she had to live with her father. We both know what it's like to fail a father.' He reached over and grabbed my wrist. 'You can't understand what it's like to find someone who's lived that same experience ... I've never had a connection with anyone like her, Charlie. Not even you. That's why I loved her.'

I felt desolate. As if somehow he'd raided the shrine I'd established for Chloe in my chest. He loved her. Sebastian, who had only ever spoken of conquests and pick ups and one-night stands. And now they shared this profound connection? She'd told me all the same things. About the loss of her mother. Her controlling father. I understood it. I'd shown her empathy.

But Sebastian had *lived* what she'd lived. How could I possibly compete with that?

'And, so now, you're ... what? With Chloe?' It was a struggle to make a sentence. 'Have you been with her all this time – are you still with her?

A shadow fell across his face.

'It got complicated,' he said.

A warm current of hope broke across the ice in my chest.

'You're not still with her?' I fought to keep the smile from my face. 'You and Chloe ... are no longer together?' I wanted to throw my head back and laugh with relief. 'What happened, Sebastian?'

'Her father happened, Charlie.'

I leant forwards, hungry for all the gory details about how their relationship fell apart.

'The trouble started almost straight away. I'm sure it was the maid. She'd heard a man in Chloe's room and ratted her out.'

I thought he was talking about me. I could hear Chloe's instructions as I raced up the stairs to her bedroom that night. 'Chloe said she had a big mouth,' I said.

'What?'

I took pleasure in the look of confusion on his face. 'The maid. She was probably talking about when Chloe took me to her room. We smoked pot and ...'

Sebatian's eyes were wide. 'You had sex in her room?'

My heart lurched. 'No. We just ... talked.'

'Ah,' he said, a small smile playing on his lips. 'Well, we did a little more than that and I guess, in the moment, we weren't as careful as we should have been, and the maid heard ...'

I could no longer hear him. Static filled my ears as I imagined them writhing on her bed.

'I reckon she told Liu Hui.'

'Liu Hui.' The name drew me from my reverie. His fierce stare in the darkness on Lugard Road, his finger threatening me as he drove off with Chloe pounding on the window in the back of the car.

'Yeah, late one night, as I was leaving her house, he was standing at the top of the stairs, leading down that jungle path to May Road. He was smoking under a streetlamp and gave me this accusing stare, like he was disappointed to have shown up too late to catch us together. He tried to be intimidating. He started sniffing, as if he could smell Chloe's perfume on my clothes. I just looked him in the eye and walked past.'

'Jesus.' I choked, contrasting Sebastian's mad courage with my cowardice. 'And that was it? He just let you walk away?'

'That was just the start. The next day outside my apartment, a black Mercedes slows beside me. The driver's window comes down, and it's Liu Hui again. He calls out and says, "Someone wants to talk to you." I look through the window and there's an old bald guy in the back seat. It's Chloe's father, and he tells me to stay away from her. He was pretty agitated. He reminded me of my dad. You know, the way he got when he just wouldn't stop lecturing, like he was drilling the point into your skull.'

He pressed so hard on his forehead I saw the knuckles of his fingers turn white.

'Zheng knew we'd been seeing each other and said it had to stop. That I was compromising his daughter. That Chloe had a substance-abuse problem, mental health and trauma issues. All this long list of shit. He said I wasn't the only guy she was seeing, that there'd been another western boy …'

'*That* would have been me,' I said, raising my eyebrows.

Sebastian licked his lips and continued as if I hadn't spoken. 'And then he started threatening me. He promised if I didn't leave her alone, he'd get my visa revoked. He knew all about me. He had my name. My address in Beijing. He said I wouldn't be able to finish studying at Peking University. I'd have to leave China, and if I still didn't listen, he said he could have me arrested.'

'That's crazy,' I said, shaking my head and leaning back in my chair.

Sebastian's face darkened. 'Chloe was already in a pretty dark place. The handover seemed to trigger something. And then Zheng followed through on his threat.'

'He didn't let her go back to school?'

He shook his head, spinning a teaspoon with his fingers. 'It was fucked.'

I felt heartbroken for Chloe. I knew how passionate she was about her studies. She'd dreamed of becoming an engineer and building infrastructure that would change people's lives. It was a brutal move by her father.

'I tried to support her. I didn't go back to Beijing. I delayed a semester. But she wasn't in a good place. She got into a lot of weed and pills and she'd come over to my apartment and just be desolate. I didn't know how to cheer her up.' I noticed the teaspoon bending in his fingers.

The roar of the coffee grinder muffled his voice. I leant forwards.

'What did you say?'

'I said, then they started trying to terrorise us.'

'What do you mean terrorise you?'

He threw the teaspoon onto the table. 'Every time I left the apartment, Liu Hui would be there, across the street smoking, or reading a newspaper. Really obvious. Not trying to hide. He'd follow me when I went out to get a coffee, or the shopping. Or a restaurant. If I confronted him about it, he'd just stare at me and sniff. If I was out late at night, he'd be following me along the pavement. I started planning routes based on the knowledge that he'd be following me, and I needed to give him the slip so I could meet Chloe somewhere. But that got harder.

'One night Chloe and I went for a walk on the harbour front, and she saw him and went over and started screaming at him. He and I would have got into a fist fight if the police hadn't separated us.'

'Fuck, Sebastian.'

'Yeah. It was crazy. I was determined not to leave Hong Kong, or her, because she was in such a state. But I got a call from Beijing and there were issues with my visa, with my enrolment at Peking U. I had to go back for urgent conversations with the university, then the visa office, then the police. It was a total stitch up.'

'You think that was Zheng?'

'I know it was. And while I was away, Chloe got packed off to some remote village in Yunnan Province. She started a role with the China Foundation for Poverty Alleviation. She was helping them build a bridge or something. Can you imagine, from MIT to fucking Yunnan?'

He was trembling with rage, but I could imagine Chloe appreciating such a shift. She'd wanted to help people. Maybe this was her way. Maybe it was her decision. But Sebastian hadn't accepted that. He went to find her. They met in Kunming and spent a weekend together in a guest house in Xishan District on the shores of the Dianchi Lake.

'She'd lost weight, if you can imagine it. I just wanted her to come back with me. To Beijing. To Hong Kong. To the UK or Australia. She just seemed so intense and sad. We argued, and she refused to come. She agreed to meet every few months. Either in Kunming, or on Lamma Island where we'd found a room. It was something for her to look forward to, you know?' He sighed and cracked his knuckles. 'I transferred full time to Peking University so I could stay on in Beijing. It wasn't perfect, but we saw each other regularly, and that was our relationship over the next few years.' He sighed and pushed the hair out of his eyes. 'Then fucking Liu Hui showed up in Beijing.'

'Jesus. Did he know you were still seeing her?'

'He must have. I was walking out to uni one morning and there he was, smoking outside my apartment, just like he had in Hong Kong.' Sebastian's voice quietened. 'But in Beijing it felt worse. Less safe. One night I was coming back from a meeting with my thesis supervisor, and I saw him with a group of friends, drinking Tsingtao beer from long neck bottles on the street. He was drunk and with other guys who looked as aggro as him. As I passed, they all stopped talking and glared at me. When I went in the door of the building, they started pissing themselves laughing. When I got into my apartment, I knew why. They'd trashed it. They'd torn up my books, slashed my clothes and sheets and mattress. Smeared shit on the wall. The door wasn't forced, so someone had obviously let them in. When I complained to the landlady who lived downstairs, she called the cops, and they all made out that I'd done it to my own apartment. When I wrote and told Chloe, she ended it. She said we couldn't fight them and that she didn't want to put me in danger. She refused to see me again.'

It sounded awful. I couldn't imagine the toll it had taken on Chloe.

But I was impressed by Sebastian. He had pulled out of LSE, altered the whole course of his studies and his life for five years, just to support Chloe. It was out of character for my friend, who I was so used to seeing pursue his own pleasures and ambitions at all costs. As I looked across the table at him, it struck me that Sebastian cared deeply for Chloe. For years I'd known him as someone who could easily discard friends and lovers, but now he seemed to present a stubborn, diamond-hard loyalty towards the woman he'd loved, and I couldn't help thinking back to those nights in his bedroom after we'd learnt of his father's second family, when Sebastian had sworn into the darkness: 'I will never do that. I will be loyal to the woman I love.'

Maybe I had underestimated his love for Chloe. Maybe he loved her just as much as I did. Maybe more, given all he had suffered for her. I wondered whether I would have dared put so much on the line for her. I hadn't that night on the Peak when Liu Hui came. Was that the reason she chose Sebastian? Did she want to be with someone who would fight alongside her, not freeze and let her be dragged away?

'You can't hide all that from DFAT and the vetting interview,' I said, not knowing what else to say. 'It's a vulnerability. A person who has significant pull in China has targeted you.'

Sebastian shook his head.

'You can't tell them, Charlie. That's why I needed to speak to you. You can't tell them anything about Chloe, or her father.'

'What if they ask?'

'They won't. I won't mention her, so she won't come up.'

I'd never gone through a security clearance process, but it was clear to me that saying nothing about Chloe or Zheng was a significant omission that his employers at Foreign Affairs would frown on. It was very likely DFAT would think he was compromised.

But before I could protest, Sebastian reached across the table, clutching my shoulder and beaming at me.

'But, Charlie, listen. I'm not finished. Chloe might come out to Australia, to finish her study here in Sydney. We talked about it in Yunnan. Her last project finishes midway through this year. I said to her she could get her degree here and we could all be together.'

His eyes were wide, and he was breathing hard. If I'd had my wits about me, or maybe just more life experience, I'd have realised I was looking at a salesman, a huckster, a confidence trickster. But all I saw were bolts of brilliant light bursting into my brain.

Chloe was coming? I was going to see Chloe again?

I couldn't believe it. It was the second chance I'd dreamt of.

We were going to be in the same city once more.

In a heartbeat, the fleeting respect and compassion I'd felt for Sebastian's struggle with Zheng dissipated. The competition for Chloe's affection burst back to life. This would be a chance to set things right. Finally, after so many nights imagining and replaying scenes of my failures in Hong Kong, now I'd have an opportunity to succeed. A real second chance to show Chloe that our connection was just as deep as whatever she'd experienced with Sebastian.

I knew I could win her, if I had another shot.

Sebastian grasped my wrist.

'But Charlie, if my relationship with Chloe and all this stuff about her dad and Liu Hui is on the record, because we put it there, just for my security clearance, well, who knows? It might compromise her. You can imagine it, right? They might not let her into the country. She might not get a visa and end up working on shitty projects in rural Chinese villages for the rest of her life. Or worse still, she'll be back with Zheng in Hong Kong. That's why you need to know about all this. We've got to protect her. You've got to keep it a secret. And not say anything when AGSVA calls this week. Not for me. But for Chloe. You've got to protect Chloe.'

❖

In the months after Sebastian had betrayed me in Hong Kong, I tried to pursue other relationships, usually drunken affairs with quiet girls in the Party, who could do no better. I compared them all to Chloe, and judged them harshly, always ending it before it really began. I was less chasing romance than wanting to replay time and again the sense of abandonment I'd felt that night as Hong Kong was handed to Beijing. Feeling loss repeatedly gave me an opportunity to revisit losing Chloe. I couldn't get her out of my head. Like smoking, it was a destructive habit which I knew would ultimately kill me. But I was addicted.

Things changed after Sebastian's revelation that Chloe might come to Australia. I grew obsessed. I stopped wasting effort on new friends. I just waited impatiently for Chloe to arrive. Every night I'd lie awake dreaming about her coming to Sydney. I wondered how she'd look after five years. Was her hair still cut in a bob? Did she still wear that Dinosaur Jr. T-shirt? Would we have the same connection? How would it feel to stand in front of her? How would her skin feel? Would her perfume be the same? Would we share a cigarette? Would she lean her head against my chest?

Every day I'd go to work, distracted by the prospect. I couldn't stop imagining what it would be like to be in the same city as Chloe again.

I hounded Sebastian for news. Did he have a date? How many weeks until she arrived?

I phoned. I emailed.

At first he indulged me, spinning reasons for her delay (new projects with the Foundation, some issue with her visa), then he told me to be patient, we'd just have to wait.

I asked for Chloe's email address and started writing drafts. He promised he would send it through. It never happened. Nothing ever happened.

All the resentment from his betrayal in Hong Kong, resentment I'd deferred given the prospect of seeing Chloe again, now came welling up.

Half the reason I took my first job in Canberra, advising that idiot Don Watkins, the then-member for Blaxland, was to hound Sebastian until he gave me the good news he'd promised. Of course, I was no fool. It took a month to realise that he'd been full of shit, and simply strung me a pack of lies to get my support on his security clearance. But rather than packing my bags and getting as far from Sebastian as I could, I stayed in Canberra to haunt him. It was his punishment. I seethed and wanted revenge. I gave him no choice but to continue the lie, calling him regularly and faux-naively asking for news. When was Chloe coming? Did he have a date yet? He must have thought me a gullible fool, but I knew my incessant chasing for updates made him uncomfortable, because each time he needed to repeat his original lie, then commit to it again and again. I became fascinated with just how many times he could lie to my face, to betray me time after time. It was an experiment that offered some relief from my brooding and seething. I wanted to expose him. To drag him into the light as the liar I knew him to be.

After a while he avoided me. He'd compartmentalised himself into the DFAT grad program. It was all he cared about. He'd grown obsessed, wanting to be not only the smartest, but the most popular in his year. Always the life of the party. Never any time to see me.

But of course, Canberra is a very small town.

It was inevitable we'd be invited to the same event at some stage.

Mutual friends were getting engaged and had booked out the Ambassador Hotel in Manuka for a party. I came from a late sitting at Parliament House and the party was already in full swing.

They had decorated the room with balloons, streamers and pictures of the happy couple. On each table was a disposable camera, and guests were encouraged to take pictures of the night. When I arrived, many had their cameras pointing towards Sebastian, standing on the head table, reciting the St Crispin's Day speech from *Henry V* to a crowd of adoring grads.

We few, we happy few, we
Band of brothers

Drunk and ecstatic and full of himself. I didn't approach. I watched from afar as everyone cheered and Sebastian bowed, then slipped, clambering off the table.

Just like his father.

But a group of his DFAT peers, roaring their approval, caught him.

He landed on a blonde woman in a beige blouse, slipping again in spilt beer and wine, and this time taking her with him. Crashing back onto the floor. Her skirt tangling in his trouser legs. Him on his back. Her straddling him. The crowd cackling. What a mess.

I didn't approach.

I'd helped him learn the lines for that speech back in high school. In second form. When he was trying to impress his dad by taking the lead in the junior play.

I snapped a photo of him on the floor with one of the abandoned disposable cameras, for posterity, then left without letting him know I'd been there, pushing out into the night.

I developed that film more out of a morbid curiosity than anything else. It hadn't been Sebastian's party, but whoever had the camera before me must have been smitten with him. He was in almost every image, moving between the tables, shaking hands, back slapping, hugs and kisses. As ever, the life of the party.

But the photo I had taken made me gasp.

Rather than a clumsy drunken moment of action, the photograph had created a phantom scene, where Sebastian lay on his back and clutched the waist of a woman straddling him. Her blonde head was thrown back, her laughing face now flushed and ecstatic, her white blouse tight across her chest as her back arched, and she appeared to be grinding against him. Sebastian's face was red. He wore an unfamiliar smile, like the jaws of a dog, wide and salivating into the wind. But unlike the woman who seemed oblivious to everything but the pleasure of the moment, Sebastian's eyes were open, turning from her, looking out at the room, his gaze blank and cold and calculating, caring only about how he was perceived, considering his next move, calibrating who he would seduce next with his charm and friendship. It was the very vision of treachery, infidelity, inconstancy.

I threw the other photographs out. This one I kept. I wanted to show him, I wanted him to see himself as I saw him. That cold, nihilistic stare, caring for nothing, for no one, amid his endless pursuit of vanity and the indulgence of his own pleasures and ambitions. I wanted to hold it in front of Sebastian like a mirror, and tell him once and for all: 'Look at yourself, you care for no one but yourself.'

Of course, I never did.

This furious pursuit around Canberra went on until he left. Posted to the Australian Consulate in Shanghai.

He went without saying goodbye. Thinking he'd got off free. That he'd avoided a confrontation with me.

He was wrong.

I followed him to Shanghai.

CHAPTER TWENTY-ONE

Neither Katrina nor I heard Ronnie come back into the meeting room until the door closed and we turned to find him leaning against it, his eyes wide, lips pale.

'The lights have gone off in Sydney.' His voice trembled.

'Christ.' I stood up. This was bad. Ronnie looked scared.

'I was talking to my father. He said everything was dark. He said he could hear people calling outside in the street. Then his phone went dead ...' He gestured. 'I called the neighbours, I don't know how I got through, they said they'd check on him.'

Katrina pushed past him and disappeared out of the room. I glimpsed people running in the corridors, but before I could look out, Jacob took up position in the doorway with folded arms, like a bouncer at a cheap hotel.

Ronnie was pacing, glaring out the window.

'And they're still circling up there.'

His fear stoked my own feelings of dread. My mind and body could not take any additional panic today. My best friend had killed himself. ASIO was threatening me with espionage charges. The world was already ending, regardless of whatever was going down in Sydney. I needed to keep my head.

'If it's a cyberattack on the National Energy Market and it's caused an outage in Sydney, Canberra will not be spared.' Ronnie addressed this to Jacob, who remained expressionless. 'It's an interconnected grid across eastern and southern Australia, including both Sydney and Canberra. Disruptions in one have a cascading effect on neighbouring regions.'

I recalled long ago Ronnie had advised the Shadow Energy Minister.

'I'm saying if there's a significant power outage in Sydney, it will impact the broader NEM network, including Canberra. We'll have power outages here too. There's no doubt.'

He didn't need to spell it out for me. I knew that if the NEM went down it wasn't just a matter of the lights being off. Other essential services would be impacted. Water and sewage, hospitals and health care, petrol stations, supermarkets, emergency services …

Jesus Christ. Law and order.

'Who do you think's behind it?' I asked, looking at both Jacob and Ronnie for an answer.

'The source of the attack hasn't been attributed,' Ronnie replied. 'If it's some sort of ransomware attack, like on the Colonial Pipeline, there'll be demands coming. Payment in cryptocurrency most likely.'

Before I could ask any more, Ronnie's phone chimed. A puzzled expression came over his face as he pulled it from his pocket.

'It's the Optus one. It still says SOS but there's … messages.'

I moved so I could see the screen. The dread in my stomach grew heavier as I distinguished 'breaking news' notifications. The familiar logos of the mastheads we read everyday, the *Sydney Morning Herald*, *The Age*, the *ABC*. But rather than headlines, the notifications were blank. Or, stranger still, filled with error messages.

503 Service unavailable: Server Overload Detected.

HEADLINE_NOT_FOUND: Could not retrieve latest story. Please try again.

ERROR: ☒☒☒☒☒ *Unrecognized data stream.*

'What the fuck does that all mean?' I asked, the anxiety sending chills over my arms and chest. More unknowns. More incomprehensible threats.

'I have no idea,' Ronnie said, showing the screen to Jacob.

'They've been targeted too,' Jacob muttered. 'The media's been hacked.'

Ronnie and I caught each other's eye then. Something passed between us.

He looked away as the door opened.

Katrina walked back in, looking determined. 'We're to keep going.'

'Have you confirmed the electricity is off? Is it widespread?'

'No, it's just parts of Sydney.' She swallowed. 'A large chunk of Sydney ...'

'Jesus.' Ronnie bit his lip a moment. Then, as if deciding something, strode towards the door. 'I have to go to the PM.' But Jacob, having let Katrina back in, remained in place. Ronnie glared at him, but the younger man was impassive and refused to move.

'Sit down, Ronnie. We're to keep going.'

'Seriously?' Ronnie's face was scrunched in doubt. 'They seriously still think this is relevant to what's happening in Sydney?'

A sharp buzz began to pulse in my ear. The room felt claustrophobic. What had Ronnie just said? Was that what they thought, that somehow my story about Sebastian was linked to a cyberattack and Sydney losing power?

'Why would this be relevant?' I shouted, unable to contain myself. 'What is actually going on here? What do you think Sebastian has done?'

I looked between Katrina and Ronnie; neither of them spoke. They stared back blankly.

'Is this why ASIO is leaking to Andrew Swann?' I spat. 'You want to use Sebastian as a fall guy for your own incompetence in keeping out a cyber threat? What else are we going to blame on him – interest rate rises? The housing crisis?'

'What are you talking about?' Ronnie barked.

'Sit down. Both of you.' Katrina's voice was sharp and brokered no opposition. Ronnie and I slunk into our seats. Katrina continued in a constrained tone, as if she too were trying to manage her own panic. 'We have been told to continue the interview. And that's what we will do.'

'Interview?' I said. 'I thought this was unofficial.'

'Parts of Sydney are indeed dark.' She spoke over the top of me. 'Whoever is behind the virus now has unfettered access to the NEM. If they want to turn the lights off in the rest of New South Wales, or anywhere else, they will. But we will not leave here until you finish your explanation about Chloe and Zheng. Those are my orders.'

'Orders from who?' spat Ronnie.

'From the Director-General of Security. From Alec McCubbin,' she said, turning back to me. 'Now Charlie. Tell us what you did in Shanghai.'

Getting myself to Shanghai was easy. Rivers of gold were flowing from China to Australia and delegations buzzed between each country on a monthly basis. I got Don Watkins on a Foreign Affairs and Trade parliamentary study tour.

I took a vengeful glee, emailing Sebastian that I'd be in Shanghai for a week before travelling to Shenzhen. I was ready to confront him for his lies about Chloe.

Not unexpectedly, I got a less than friendly response. He would 'see' if he was in town and able to catch up. He 'might' be travelling with the Consul-General. I knew this was bullshit, as my delegation was scheduled to get a briefing from his CG, so he had no place to hide. After a week of silence, he agreed to meet, but even then, I had to get his address from someone at the Consulate. To make things more mysterious, I realised Sebastian, unlike all the other Consular Officials, didn't live on the diplomatic compound. He was in Luwan district, the old French Concession. The bottom floor of a Shanghai deco lane house, somewhere off Hua Hai road.

I was suspicious as soon as I got there. It didn't look like a bachelor's apartment at all. I entered through a gate into a little walled courtyard, where a table and two chairs were set next to a water feature, surrounded by bamboo, then followed through

French doors into a sun-filled lounge and dining room, with antique Ming era furniture and a soft material lounge. There were black and white images of cityscapes, bridges and elevated highways across all the walls. Off to the right from where you entered, with no door, was his bedroom, which looked out into the courtyard.

After the requisite embrace and welcome, Sebastian looked abashed. 'So, you found me.'

'You didn't make it easy.'

I was about to chastise him further, but he held up a hand. 'Before you say anything, I have a favour to ask?'

I scowled. 'Another security clearance?'

'No.' He shook his head. 'I need you to keep a secret for me ...'

He nodded behind me. I turned, and a woman stepped out of the bedroom.

I let out a sharp cry of surprise. I felt heat rushing to my face. I wanted to punch him, I wanted to shout with outrage. But I did none of these things, because when I turned back to the figure that had emerged from the bedroom, none of that mattered. I wasn't dreaming. It was no longer a fantasy. It *was* Chloe. We were back together again.

❖

In the years we'd been apart, she'd matured. She'd lost weight in her face. Her hair was longer, and she wore it up. She'd ditched the grungy T-shirts, and now wore a Japanese designer dress with big pockets and buttons that made her look both artistic and stylish. She'd swapped the black-rimmed glasses for contacts.

For a moment she looked embarrassed, but then a grin lit up her face and she rushed over and embraced me with such strength it knocked the wind out of me. Her hair still smelt like the shampoo she'd used in Hong Kong and clutching her to my chest I was transported back to her bedroom in the Peak, swaying in time to 'Dancing in the Moonlight'.

They confessed the whole story. Or she did, as Sebastian made himself scarce in the kitchen getting drinks.

It was all remarkably similar to what Sebastian had told me in Badde Manors cafe. They'd 'connected' the night of the handover.

'I was so low, Charlie,' she said, frowning as if it was painful for her to recall. She placed her hand on my wrist. 'You saw how I was.'

The thrill of her touch made up for the heartbreaking memory.

'I'd had a big fight with my father. Liu Hui had reported to him that I'd been spending time in the company of "western boys".'

My face flushed red when she said this, but she pretended not to notice.

'As usual one of us brought up my mother. I said, "No wonder she did what she did – to escape you." It was cruel of me. But he replied saying she'd betrayed us, that she was a traitor and she'd abandoned us, I think ... that week of all weeks ... it just hit me hard.'

Chloe squeezed my wrist and smiled sadly, as if she hoped I could understand and forgive her for the things we obviously were not going to talk about.

'Remember, you told me what happened to Sebastian's father. You remember? That morning in the Lin Heung Teahouse.'

'I remember,' I said, the words choking in my throat.

'To be honest, I thought he was a jerk, a "player" until then.' She paused. 'But, I guess ... similar experiences in childhood, gave us a certain connection. We spent the rest of that handover night and the days after talking and sharing. It helped me, Charlie.'

She had come to rely on Sebastian. Having had a controlling father of his own meant Sebastian offered her not only empathy, he helped her stand up for herself. Not just against Zheng, but Liu Hui too. And when she couldn't stand up, he offered a place to hide at his mother's apartment, or in a guesthouse on Lamma Island.

'He kept his promise too,' she said, nodding at her lover, who glanced across from the kitchen. 'He said he wouldn't abandon me. And he didn't. He stayed in Hong Kong and cared for me. Then, after my father sent me to work for the Foundation, Sebastian followed me around China.'

Now Chloe blushed.

'He fought for me, Charlie …'

She said it so tenderly, it couldn't have been a reprimand. But I was reprimanding myself, and I couldn't hold her eye. I stared at my feet and bit my lip.

I wanted to tell her how sorry I was that I hadn't fought for her that night on the Peak. That if I had my time again I would have thrown myself on Liu Hui and taken any amount of beating to protect her. I wanted her to know I was as much of a man as Sebastian. I would sacrifice everything for her.

But it was clear by then that she loved him. That they were committed to each other. And even when Sebastian was forced out of China, that commitment continued.

They'd had a long-distance relationship. They'd kept it a secret, worried about Zheng and Liu Hui, and about Sebastian's diplomatic career. Chloe's job with the China Foundation for Poverty Alleviation had concluded, just as Sebastian was posted to Shanghai. They'd moved in with each other.

'You lied to me all along,' I growled to Sebastian, choking on jealousy, as he carried in gin and tonics. The joy of sitting next to Chloe softened my anger, but I was furious and wanted him to know it.

'I know. I'm sorry.' He handed over my drink, unable to look me in the eye. 'We just had to be so careful, Charlie. What I told you about Liu Hui was all true. It rattled us.'

'I told him he should tell you,' Chloe scolded. 'I wanted you to know, and find a way to stay in touch. I missed you, Charlie.'

'I asked him for your email address a thousand times,' I said, wanting her to know how selfish her 'boyfriend' had been.

'But we couldn't trust emails,' Sebastian said, putting his arm around Chloe. 'I didn't know what AGSVA would look at during my vetting, nor whether Chloe's dad could get into her emails.'

Chloe closed her eyes. 'He wouldn't have done that.'

'Liu Hui would have,' he said.

Chloe grimaced again. This time, she nodded. 'Anyway, when he told me you were coming to Shanghai, I insisted,' Chloe said.

'And so no one at the Consulate knew?' interrupted Katrina.

'He hadn't declared this relationship or the living arrangements to AGSVA, or the Consul General?'

I don't think he'd declared it to anyone. He wouldn't have told me. It was Chloe who forced it. She was pleased to see me. She wanted to know all about what I had done at university and where I was working. She was impressed I was advising an MP.

Sebastian too was enthusiastic, feigning interest in stuff about my career that I'd told him, and he'd forgotten. He couldn't keep it up, though. He played with his phone when Chloe and I inevitably got into music. She wanted to know my thoughts on Pearl Jam's latest album, *Riot Act*, and put Radiohead's *Hail to the Thief* on the stereo as we talked.

'Oh God. You two and your music.' Sebastian groaned and walked off to mix more drinks.

'And what about girlfriends?' Chloe asked, touching my knee. 'Are you dating any lucky girls?'

I felt my face burning and shook my head.

'Charlie, not even one?' Sebastian shouted from the kitchen.

'Not even one?' I scoffed at him. 'We can't all get around as much as you, Sebastian.'

The impact of my words was immediate. He stopped chopping limes and glanced back at me as if shocked. Chloe's face creased.

'He's not like that anymore,' she said in a quiet voice. I'd struck a raw nerve.

We'd mercilessly mocked Sebastian in Hong Kong for being such a dog. Chloe had told me so many times how disgusted she'd been by him cheating on Caroline. Maybe, despite everything she said, a small part of Chloe still had suspicions; such were the sensitivities of a long-distance relationship. It wasn't until later I discovered she had other reasons to feel vulnerable. But in the moment I just filed the information away.

'Why don't you tell me about your work with the Foundation?' I said, changing the subject. She beamed and went to fetch her portfolio from the bedroom.

'Don't encourage her with the Foundation stuff,' Sebastian hissed, sitting down and folding his arms.

'Why don't you shut the fuck up?' I whispered back at him.

Chloe returned with a large black folder, from which she drew A4 images, unrolled terrain maps and aerial photographs of the projects she had worked on with the Foundation. A highway in Sichuan. A school in Xinjiang. A community centre in a rural village in Guizhou Province.

As she talked me through each project, I could see the passion in her face. Gone were the shadows I'd seen in Hong Kong. She'd found her calling. Sebastian, meanwhile, sat with his arms folded across his chest, his foot tapping.

'And in Guangxi Zhuang,' she said, 'the project was a rehabilitation of water supply systems so rural people could access clean water. Oh and Yunnan was electrification projects. I designed the infrastructure to integrate solar renewable energy because the villages are so remote.'

'This is amazing.'

She nodded. 'It's my purpose, I think.'

'Will you do more? What happens now you've left the Foundation? How are you going to pursue it?'

This was too much for Sebastian. He leapt to his feet and announced he needed to leave.

'Where are you going?' Chloe asked, looking hurt.

'To the Consulate.' He gestured at his phone.

'But we only have a short time with Charlie. You're leaving tomorrow.'

'Yeah, sorry Charlie.' His eyes were cold and angry. 'I'm travelling with the CG to Jiangsu for the next few days. He's texted and wants to go over the briefing before we leave tomorrow. I'll leave you two to catch up.'

He left, slamming the door behind him.

Chloe let the images from her portfolio slip from her hands back onto the table.

'What's his problem?' I demanded, not disappointed to see him go, but still hurt he didn't want to stay. 'He's not the centre of attention for five minutes and he storms off? This is because I'm here.'

Chloe sighed and hung her head. 'It's not that,' she said, touching my sleeve. 'He's worried about me.'

'About you? Why? What's there to worry about?'

'He thinks I'm going to leave him.'

❖

Noises from the laneway outside drifted through the window. Neighbours talking to their children. Merchants with wheelbarrows selling fresh vegetables. The sounds of the little kitchen selling baozi and noodles.

I didn't dare speak, fearing any word from me might disrupt the moment, and prove the very possibility that she was going to leave him merely an illusion.

'My father has asked me to join his company in Africa,' she said. 'Sebastian doesn't want me to go.'

I nodded, remaining outwardly calm while my mind churned with calculation. Which of the two options was worse? That she ended the relationship and left for Africa? Or she stayed living with Sebastian? Neither scenario aided my hopes of rekindling what we'd had in Hong Kong. But while I knew sending her back to her father was the worst option for Chloe, I ached for her to be free of Sebastian. They were living together. That was serious. Who knew what was next? If there was an option to break her away …

'What's in Africa?'

'There is so much work I could do there,' she said. 'My father would give me a role with his company.'

'Doing what?'

Her eyes flashed. 'Working on projects like these.' She gestured at the photos still on the table. 'Only on a much larger scale. Africa needs infrastructure. They are as China was thirty years ago. We know how to help them.'

'Is it because your father knows about Sebastian? Is that why he summoned you?'

In my mind, Zheng was a tyrant. He had struck his only daughter for keeping a photo of her dead mother.

'My father wants to give me an opportunity.' Chloe tidied her portfolio, placing the images back into their folder. 'He wants to give me purpose.' She held up an image of the project in Xinjiang. She was sitting outside the school she'd built, two little girls, pupils, on either side of her. 'This work cured me, Charlie. I can't explain. When you knew me in Hong Kong, I was desolate. When you left, it got worse. I got worse. This work saved me.'

I licked my lips. 'Sebastian told me your father sent you to work with the Foundation as a punishment for being with him. He said he stopped you going back to MIT, and he forced Sebastian out of China.'

She shook her head. 'My father was trying to save me.'

'But he wanted you to end it with Sebastian.'

She sighed.

'He did. He forced Sebastian to leave. My father is stubborn.' She smiled. 'But so is Sebastian. My father ensured that he'd never get a student or a tourist visa back to China, so what did he do? He became a diplomat. He returned as an official. We can be together for at least four years. And maybe there will be other postings too. He did that for me.'

Looking at her face, filled with love for my rival, I understood Sebastian's drive in these last years. His myopic focus on DFAT success. It wasn't just ego. He'd had a purpose. To return to Chloe. To find a way around her father. All that, he'd done for her. Christ.

'I didn't know that. He didn't tell me.'

'I think he was embarrassed.'

'About what?'

'He knows what he did to you.' She glanced at me. I stared back, unable to find the words. Did she mean what I thought? That Sebastian was embarrassed because he'd stolen Chloe from me? She continued before I could ask.

'And with Liu Hui, it was worse than what he told you.'

'Worse, how?'

She went to a drawer and withdrew a Moleskine notebook. From between the pages, she handed me a photograph. I don't know why, but I expected it to be of her mother. It wasn't. It was

Sebastian. In a hospital bed. His face was bruised and bandaged. His arm in a sling.

'They did this to him. In Beijing. Afterwards I told him to leave China. He wasn't safe here. But he came back for me, Charlie. And now they can't touch him.'

I winced, looking at my childhood friend, alone in the hospital bed.

'Who did this to him?' I demanded. 'Was it Liu Hui?'

She nodded sadly.

Why would he keep this from me? Why wouldn't he have called me and asked me to come to Beijing, to care for him? There was a time, no matter how long ago, we always cared for each other. After his father died. Even before, at school, when we were bullied. A memory bloomed in my mind. Walking to his father's car after our beating by Mallet. What was his mantra? *Don't show it. Don't show it. Don't show it.*

'Sebastian asked me not to go to Africa. He proposed to me.'

'Jesus.'

'He said he'd give up his job for me. If we were married, we could move to Sydney.'

I felt my mouth fall open.

'I'm torn. I want to do good work in Africa, but I look at that picture of him ...' She touched the bruised image of Sebastian. 'I know he loves me. He is committed to me.' She breathed out. 'Advise me. Tell me what to do, Charlie.'

I stared at the photo of Sebastian's bruised face. He had been nothing but loyal to her. He'd struggled for her. Taken beatings for her. Laboured to get back to her.

But he would not have her.

Not if I could stop him.

CHAPTER TWENTY-TWO

Sebastian left town, but my delegation was in Shanghai for a week. The itinerary was full for Watkins, but I was largely left to my own devices. I had to tag along with the MPs, but the Trade Commission staff were in the lead and I wasn't missed when I separated myself from the group and went off with my laptop to write. I felt exhilarated.

I have never murdered a man, but perhaps this was a close approximation to how it would feel. To murder your brother. I set out to murder Sebastian's character. I applied all the dark arts I would come to be known for in the Party, and use later to tear down a sitting prime minister. All the viciousness that, back then, only people like Ronnie who had crossed me in university knew I possessed. I was the nice guy. The guy to be trusted. But now I revealed my true self. My secret Iago. And I murdered my friend.

The thought of it made me sweat and tremble as I opened my laptop and entered the email address Chloe had given me. I bombarded her with emails, writing of my happiness at seeing her again. Reminiscing about our time in Hong Kong. Telling her about my life since: at Sydney Uni and my move to Canberra. And then telling her about my time with Sebastian in Canberra. The half-truths and lies pouring naturally across the screen. How committed he was to graduating as a diplomat. How hard he worked, and yet how he was still able to be the life and soul of the party. How popular he was. How admired. How adored.

When I'd said in their apartment, 'We can't all get around as much as you, Sebastian,' Chloe had been quick to defend him. Too quick. I was sure some doubt still lingered.

And so I fed the slowly blossoming uncertainty I detected in her replies.

Oh, but I was subtle. I was clever. My assassination was artistry. When I had deliberately taken a half-step too far, I pulled back. Making excuses for him. Covering his tracks. Email by email I brought back to life that earlier Sebastian we'd seen and gently mocked as students in Hong Kong. The flirt, the chaser of skirts. There was an elegant beauty to my approach. I was planting seeds that even his straight denial could never fully smother. Finally, the night before we were due to leave, she asked me directly. She demanded I tell her if Sebastian had been faithful to her. I prevaricated. I contorted. I clumsily deflected. And then I sent her a scan of that photograph I'd taken with the disposable camera. Sebastian, predatory and callous, locked in a sexual embrace with a stranger. While partygoers cheered him on.

❖

I left Shanghai the next afternoon. Or at least, I attempted to. Our plane to Shenzhen was delayed and we waited another four hours at Hongqiao airport before boarding. The dread that would build over the next twenty-four hours was still laced by adrenaline and that sense of having achieved something monumental. Of having realised my superhuman power. In Shenzhen, they whisked us across the city in minivans, touring factories in industrial zones. Cavernous rooms filled with workers bent over conveyor belts. Textiles, electronics, consumer goods for export. The low-cost, mass-produced model that had inspired further special economic zones across other Chinese regions like Jiangsu, Zhejiang and Tianjin.

I stumbled through these tours like a zombie, seeing nothing, composing in my head another email to Chloe. I was plotting my next move. When would it be appropriate to call her? She'd given me her mobile number, along with her email. She'd called me her 'precious friend' and thanked me for saving her from a 'mistake'.

I checked my email that night at the hotel. I was hoping for a response from Chloe. I must have sent her fifty emails already. Less than twenty-four hours had passed. But when I opened my personal inbox, I saw only one new mail. It was from Sebastian. My heart pounded as I clicked on my best friend's name.

What did you do?

It was all he had written, and I knew beyond any doubt these were the words of a defeated man. I had won.

She had left him.

It wasn't until the delegation reached Hong Kong, two weeks after I'd seen Chloe and Sebastian in Shanghai, that I became aware that something dreadful had happened.

Stepping from the plane onto the airbridge at the new Lantau airport, the scent of the Fragrant Harbour was already distinguishable. It grew stronger as we waited at the taxi rank, our clothing sticking to our bodies amid the soupy humidity, then again through the filtered arctic blast of the taxi's air conditioning.

I closed my eyes and experienced that same anticipation I'd felt staring out into the street on my first night in Lan Kwai Fong. The night we'd met Chloe.

If only things had turned out differently. If only he hadn't forced me to do what I had done.

My BlackBerry rang as the taxi pulled onto the Lantau Link. Sebastian's name lit up the screen. My heartbeat increased. I let the call ring out. He redialled immediately. I rejected the call. Then came the pinging alerts for voicemail.

I folded my arms in the front seat of the taxi. Watkins was on his phone in the back, berating someone with the reptilian lisp that all us staffers mocked behind his back. I should have been concentrating on his tirade, and on whom he would later deploy me to inflict his factional revenge, but my phone was still vibrating and I couldn't focus.

What was Sebastian doing? Was this his response? Calling incessantly? Voicemail blitzkrieg?

I wouldn't listen.

Why should I feel ashamed or concerned about what happened in Shanghai? Hadn't I done to Sebastian exactly what he had done to me? I'd snatched her away. That's what he did that night in Hong Kong. The handover. Chloe was handed over. Well, now I'd taken her back.

Not for the first time I was glad no one could hear the dialogue in my head. I knew how I sounded. But I didn't care. For once, I was the popular one. For once, I was the bully, not the bullied. Tell that to Henry fucking Mallet.

The taxi crossed the Tsing Ma Bridge, which Chloe had once told us was her inspiration for becoming an engineer. I saw skyscrapers lining the foreshore as we approached the city, their lights shimmering in reflection across the waters of Victoria Harbour.

The island came into view, and I raised my gaze above the familiar city skyline, my heart missing a beat as I discerned the vague location of Chloe's father's home, nestled in the darkness amid the jungles of the Peak.

My phone continued to vibrate silently as we entered Kowloon, and the red taxi cab moved slowly through the bustling streets of Tsim Sha Tsui, the evening darkness now exorcised by the glare of neon signs and digital billboards up and down Nathan Road towards the hotel.

We were staying at the Marco Polo and it was at reception, after I'd checked in, that the concierge pulled me aside.

'Excuse me, sir, are you Charlie Westcott? I have a message for you.'

I glanced at Watkins, worried he may hear.

'Is the message from Sebastian Adler? If so, I don't want it.'

'No, sir. It is the Central Police Station.'

I stared at him, a local Hong Konger in a white uniform. He had a British accent and trembled with the effort of holding himself at attention as he delivered this news.

'Who?' I demanded, thinking I had misheard.

'The Central Police Station. You have been asked to call.'

I took my bags to the room, telling Watkins I felt unwell and would forgo the delegation dinner. Then I dialled the number the concierge had given me.

'Mr Westcott. Thank you for calling, sir. We need you to come and pick up Sebastian Adler.'

It made no sense to me.

'Sebastian is not in Hong Kong,' I stuttered.

'He is in Hong Kong, sir. He is in the Central Police Station. He was arrested yesterday evening. We are only able to release him into your care. We have been trying to reach you on his phone. The doctor has indicated he needs someone with him, that he may be at risk of ...' He cleared his throat. 'Self harm.'

Noises screaming in my head. It was like I was listening to a radio play, or I'd picked up the phone and received news intended for someone else.

'Mr Adler arrived in Hong Kong two days ago, sir. He was involved in a car accident late last night, early this morning. I think it's best if he tells you the rest. He is being brought up now. I will put him on.'

'No,' I said, but it was too late.

'Charlie?' It was him. It was Sebastian.

'Sebastian? What's happened? Why are you in Hong Kong? Why are you at the police station?'

'I need you to pick me up. They won't release me unless someone takes me. I need you to come. I know you're here. I remembered the delegation schedule ...'

My hotel room was still dark. Through the windows, the lights of Tsim Sha Tsui twinkled. The cool air conditioning carried the scent of chemicals, rotting food and the open sea.

'Sebastian, what's happened?'

I heard him sob. The sound of the phone receiver as he swapped hands or held his fist to his head and wiped sweat from his brow. Then his breathing, ragged and hysterical, returned, and he said the words that have haunted me to this day.

'Chloe is dead.'

CHAPTER TWENTY-THREE

'They let him go? Why wasn't Adler charged?' Ronnie demanded.

'He was, initially, then the charges were dropped. That's when he gave them my number and they called me.'

'Why were the charges dropped?' Katrina snapped.

'Sebastian said Zheng had intervened.'

'Zheng told him that?'

'No, that's what the police said. Sebastian never spoke to Zheng. He said he saw him at the police station, but he was ushered away. The police told him Zheng had "made arrangements" and Sebastian was free to go.'

Ronnie lurched to his feet, heaving his angular body around the room. 'A young woman had died, and the police were willing to pretend it didn't happen? That's nonsense.'

'I guess Zheng had sway.'

'But why wouldn't he want Adler punished if he was responsible for his daughter's death?'

'Like I said, I don't know.'

'What do you assume?'

'I assume that having left Beijing to avoid the shame surrounding his wife's death, he saw the death of his daughter as another scandal. If it got out that she'd been killed, high on drugs, while with a western diplomat whom she was secretly living with, that would have been just as destructive for Zheng as for Sebastian. Probably worse.'

I knew I needed to keep descriptions narrow, brief, reduce details that would prompt further questions. I was no longer a storyteller but a tightrope walker, balancing my way over a fatal drop as Ronnie and Katrina held their breath, wanting me to fall.

I told them about waiting outside the police station. The bent figure of Sebastian appearing through the grate, clutching his belt and shoes in bandaged hand. His face battered from the crash, covered in bruises and dried blood. The police officer spoke to him as a child. 'Go with your friend. He'll look after you.' And I was struck by how similar this was to what my mother had said the first day we'd met.

I could see he was unwell. He trembled as he embraced me. Muttering into my ear with foul prison breath. 'She's dead, Charlie. She's dead.'

I put my arm around him and took him to a waiting taxi, but when I said the address of the Marco Polo, Sebastian lurched from his torpor.

'No, we can't.' I tried to reassure him, but he insisted. He couldn't be seen. The MP Delegation. The staff. They'd all seen him in Shanghai, briefing alongside the CG. He'd be recognised. No one could know he'd been in Hong Kong. No one could know what had happened. I tried to reason with him, but he clutched at the lapels of my jacket and pleaded until I relented. 'You owe me, Charlie. You owe me.' What I owed him for was left unsaid.

He told me about a room he and Chloe had rented in the small village of Yung Shue Wan on Lamma Island. He wanted to go there. It was secluded and he could pull himself together without being seen. We directed the taxi to Central Pier 4, running down the gangplank to catch the last ferry to Lamma.

We sat outside, huddled together as the ferry passed through Victoria Harbour. After twenty minutes, the lights from the city faded and we were amid the darkness of the South China Sea. The ferry passed smoothly through the tranquil waters, disturbed only by the occasional bow wave from a freighter or junk passing by our side.

The cool air and gentle rise and fall of the vessel was calming. Neither of us spoke. We stared into the darkness, the warmth of our bodies together, comforting, like brothers.

Then, out of the darkness ahead, small lights appeared on the horizon and we saw the low rise houses of Yung Shue Wan, nestled against the shadowed jungle hills of Lamma.

We disembarked under lamplight, with a handful of other passengers, and made our way along the shoreline promenade towards the village. A cool breeze blew off the sea, relieving the humidity and carrying the sound of fishing boat rigging and seabirds still flying beyond the setting of the sun. Somewhere a temple bell rang. We could hear the voices of villagers, cutlery and saucepans scrubbed in the back of a local restaurant kitchen.

Sebastian wove through the streets past two-storey houses with colourful facades and traditional Chinese tiling. He located the guesthouse he was looking for, off the main street with a line of sight to the ferry. After ringing the bell and knocking for a few minutes, an old woman appeared. She recognised Sebastian, who spoke to her in Cantonese, and then we were upstairs in a sparse room, looking out towards the sea.

Over the next two days, it was like watching someone withdraw from addiction. He would shiver and moan, never quite finding sleep. He would sob, and I would hold him. When staying in the room became unbearable, I took him to walk by the water's edge, a blanket around his shoulders, as the villagers slept. The moon was high in the sky, reflecting off the waves. He collapsed in the shallows, crying and shivering, and pounding on his head.

Caring for Sebastian helped me to not think about Chloe. The concept of her being dead was too much to comprehend. I would mourn for her later. But over those two nights and three days, I was there for Sebastian.

'And did he know what you'd done?' Ronnie was looking at me, aghast.

'He knew Chloe had left because of something I'd said. He didn't know about the photograph. Or my lies.'

'You never told him?'

I shook my head, and a shiver passed down my spine. I was sure now he knew. Now he was dead. He'd know it all. That was my belief. That in death you see everything that has been hidden from you, not only by your enemies, but by those you love, those you have called your friends, your family. This is why ghosts howl and spirits roam.

❖

'Go back to how Chloe died. What happened?' Katrina's staccato questioning was relentless. Every time I blocked, she came back like a boxer off the ropes.

'After I left Shanghai she'd argued with Sebastian, telling him she couldn't live with a man she couldn't trust. Sebastian denied everything of course, but the suspicions I'd created went deep. She ran, and he followed to Hong Kong to search for her. He went to her house on the Peak, but she wasn't there, they wouldn't let him in. He found her instead at a party. Mutual friends. She was high, or drunk, or out of her mind on something. He dragged her from the party, desperate to talk, to understand why she had run from him. Somehow, he got her into the car. But they argued and didn't make it off the Peak. She'd struck him, screaming at him, punching him, he lost control and they went off the road.'

'So, he wasn't drunk, as you said.'

'No.'

'You really are a fucking grub, aren't you, Charlie?' Ronnie said quietly.

Katrina ignored him. 'How long were you on Lamma?'

'Two nights, three days.'

'And on the third day?'

'He returned to Shanghai.'

'Just like that? He was well enough to leave? You weren't worried about his safety?'

'Of course, I was. But on the second night, he was more in control. There was no more sobbing. He went for a walk. When he came back, he was calm. We sat on the balcony staring at the sea. Then he said he had to go back. That they would miss him at the Consulate if he was away any longer. He said he had no choice, and when I woke up the next morning, he was gone.'

'Three days later?' Ronnie shook his head.

'Where did he walk?' Katrina persisted.

'What?'

'You said he came back from a walk. Where had he walked?'

'I don't know.' I shrugged. 'Along the promenade, up the hill to the temple. I don't know …'

'You don't know.' Katrina fixed me with a stare, and I felt the tightrope begin to sway dangerously. I nodded, feeling dizzy.

'Did he meet anyone one? When he was out walking in the night?' she asked again.

I stopped myself from reacting and stared back at her as impassively as I could. The murmur I'd been trying to block out since I'd sat down in front of Katrina had now become a full-blown chorus.

I shook my head and denied it. But I could no longer hear my own voice. Instead, I was standing by the window in that little apartment in Yung Shue Wan, watching Sebastian wander the promenade. I could see him walking to the main street. His head bent, his hands in his pocket. He hesitated and looked towards a storefront. A conversation with a figure who remained hidden. The pointing finger of a man in the shadows, now drilling into Sebastian's chest. He nodded as he made commitments. He took instruction, until the anonymous figure was satisfied, and sent Sebastian on his way. Wandering in a daze down the street towards the ferry pier.

The light from the store, spilling out onto the quiet road, now illuminated a figure, stepping out beneath the eve, watching Sebastian stumble away.

'No one. He met no one. I was the only person he spoke to while we were on Lamma.'

Katrina breathed out through her nose and turned.

I had made it across the tightrope.

I'd kept my defences around this last truth. *I need you to keep a secret …*

An unspeakable, lurking truth, with a burnt face, staring after my friend in the main street of Yung Shue Wan. The secret that made me feel sick. The unformed terror in the darkness, stepping into the light.

The secret friendships I couldn't explain.

Why had Liu Hui been there?

CHAPTER TWENTY-FOUR

The lights in Parliament House dipped, flickered, then burnt at a lower wattage. There was a sharp knock on the door and Jacob stood back to let a wispy-haired man enter.

'Power is off.'

'Where?' Katrina said, rising to her feet.

'Everywhere. The whole NEM is down, except here. Except in Canberra.'

'Jesus,' breathed Ronnie, turning to his phone. 'Someone is sending a message.'

'Wait here,' Katrina said as she marched towards the door.

But Ronnie also leapt to his feet. 'No. I have to go too. The PM has texted me. The National Security Committee is meeting. It can't wait.'

Katrina nodded. 'They've also summoned me.' She collected her notebooks. 'Charlie, we need to break, I'm not sure how long for tonight. We will recommence at 8.30 am tomorrow at ASIO headquarters. Ask for me at reception and I'll send someone down. I understand the police are encouraging people to return to their homes tonight and stay off the streets. There is a risk of power failures here in Canberra too. I advise that you go straight home and we will speak in the morning.'

My heart lurched. For a moment I had thought I was free and that it was over. But this was worse. Not just an informal discussion, but reporting to ASIO's headquarters. That could only mean worse to come.

'I've told you everything I know,' I stammered. 'You already know it all anyway.'

Katrina looked at me and in her face I saw the product of my story, the aim I'd sought from the moment I sat down. Disgust. She found me disgusting.

'Our discussion is far from over, Charlie. We have many more questions about Mr Adler's life after the death of Chloe Zheng. Do you know the ASIO building, or would you like me to send Jacob to collect you?'

The veiled threat told me now was not the time to argue. I agreed to meet her, then pulled on my coat and hurried to the door. Eager to get away.

'Charlie. One more thing ...'

I braced and turned back.

'Adler never saw Zheng again?' Her gaze was sharpened to a point. 'After that night, in the police station. He never met him again. Is that what you're saying?'

I looked her in the eye, forcing from my head any recollection of what Tang had told me that very morning. Lying to her face. 'He had no contact with Zheng. He wrote to him. He tried to apologise. He tried to see him; Zheng never responded. Sebastian never heard from him again.'

Katrina raised her eyebrow.

'Until this morning,' she said.

❖

The cool evening air hit me as I made my way out of Parliament House, through the security gate and across to the staff carpark, some hundred metres away beyond the gum trees.

The sky was still filled with aeroplanes, and I briefly wondered how they would be managing air traffic control in the states where the energy network was out. I presumed there were generators, some sort of contingency plan. We always assume a contingency plan exists, trusting that somewhere, grown ups are in charge.

I now needed a contingency plan for tomorrow morning. All afternoon I'd tried to be a loyal friend to Sebastian. But I was sure Katrina and ASIO had already known all of what I'd confessed. The only revelation I had offered was the role my treachery had played in ending Chloe's life, and while the guilt had haunted me for twenty years, it wasn't enough to satisfy ASIO. They were searching for something else, something more sinister or scandalous. It was there in the final questions from Katrina. Had Sebastian been in contact with Zheng? As if she could read my mind. See into my thoughts. Or as if she too had spoken with Tang. Whatever it was, there would be more questions to come in the morning. I needed to be prepared.

Unlocking the passenger side of my Mazda Astina, I reached into the glove box and took out my personal mobile phone. I'd had the foresight to leave it in the car. It had been sloppy of Ronnie not to ask where it was when ASIO had seized my work phone. He should have known I'd have a backup. What political operative would conspire in the dark arts using their FOI'able government-issued mobile?

Missed calls and text messages pinged onto the cracked screen as I turned it on. Thank God the Telstra network was still working.

A series of those ghostly 'error' news alerts that I'd seen on Ronnie's phone now pinged across my screen. I deleted them immediately, finding their presence on my mobile disturbing.

I checked my missed calls. There were half a dozen from Swanny earlier in the day when he had tried to contact me for comment. There were missed calls from Cassie, and I sighed, realising I'd probably have to call her too.

I found two messages in my inbox from unfamiliar numbers. The first was from local police about the power outage.

<EMERGENCY ALERT: *Due to the risk of power outages, Police request all residents to return home immediately. Please limit travel to essential needs only. Stay safe and follow updates on the ACT Government Website. Stay Home. Stay Safe.*>

The second unfamiliar number was from a +1 country code, meaning a United States caller.

I opened the message.

<Charlie. This is Henry Mallet. Call me.>

Then another message.

<Charlie, This is Henry Mallet. I heard about Sebastian. Please call me.>

Then another.

<It's important, Charlie. Call me back. HM>

In addition to the messages, he'd tried to call me, at least five or six times.

Mallet never called or texted me. Usually when he or Kai Birch wanted to arrange a meeting with Sebastian it was done through executive assistants. I was left out, with the understanding that I'd be neither interested nor welcome to join them for whatever pursuit they had in store for Sebastian's next visit to Silicon Valley. Maybe eighteen holes at Kai's Los Altos Golf and Country Club? Drinks at the Sequoia Yacht Club then a cruise around the San Francisco Bay on Mallet's motor yacht? A weekend in the Napa Valley?

After thirty-five years of excluding me, Mallet was reaching out. Fuck him, I decided, and deleted his messages. I didn't have time to console him and answer any more questions about Sebastian's suicide. I needed a contingency plan.

Andrew Swann answered my call after a single ring.

'Swanny. It's me.'

'They let you go, Charlie?' He sounded surprised.

'Of course they let me go. Did you think I'd been arrested?' I said, not enjoying the surprise in his voice.

Swanny made a rumbling sound in the back of his throat, an attempt to laugh perhaps, but it came off more like a gargle. 'Who can say tonight, with everything going on. You heard about the energy networks going down?'

'Everywhere but Canberra.'

'I hear the west is still on.'

I glanced at my watch, anxious about time even though it was still only early evening. Tomorrow morning seemed to be coming on fast.

'Swanny, I need to talk to you about that other yarn you mentioned this arvo. The cautionary tale.'

'You want to comment, Charlie. On the record?'

'Background only.' I said. 'Deep background. And I need information from you in exchange. I need to know what McCubbin has given you.'

'Who said McCubbin has given me anything, Charlie?' he asked slyly.

'I know he's your source, Swanny.'

He didn't reply, but I could feel him listening intently. There were voices in the background, and the chinking of glasses. 'Where are you?'

'Press Club bar.' Swanny swallowed a burp. 'Nothing else is open. The police have told everyone to close down. But this joint's open because there's going to be press briefings through the night.'

'Are you with other journos?' I asked. 'Can you lose them and meet me outside in fifteen minutes?'

Swanny cleared his throat. The background noise lowered as he walked to a secluded corner.

'Alright come on over. I'll hear you out.'

'See you in fifteen.'

I hung up, unsure what my plan was or what information I had to trade. But I knew I needed a sense of the yarn ASIO had pitched him. What was the angle? How were they framing Sebastian's suicide and revelations about a secret relationship with Chloe or alleged blackmail? If I knew, I could be more prepared for Katrina tomorrow morning. And I needed to be prepared. I had already told her everything I was able to disclose. Anything further and I'd be into that darkness where truths that I hadn't divulged, even to myself, lurked ...

I tossed my phone onto the passenger seat and walked around to the driver's side. As I got into the car, I thrust my hand into my pocket searching for cigarettes, but my thumb struck a sharp edge. I withdrew a plastic case from my jacket, wondering what it was.

A cassette case.

Chloe's mix tape.

I'd kept it in my pocket since Sebastian's house.

I turned it over in my hands, opening it and again examining the handwritten track listing. The faded cover picture of two hands, snipped out of the *South China Morning Post*.

Just waiting to be free.

I pressed the cassette into the stereo and drove out of the carpark along Parliamentary Drive, heading for the Press Club, bracing myself for the first track. I still knew them all by heart. All the songs Chloe and I had shared: 'Disarm', 'Indifference', 'Dancing in the Moonlight', 'Restless', 'Hunger Strike'.

As I turned onto Kings Avenue I scowled at the stereo, turning up the volume. Still no song. No chord. A vague static. Maybe the tape was too old.

The roads were eerily empty. The street lamps were off, but I could still see lights in distant buildings. I wondered briefly if what was happening interstate was now happening here, and I felt a growing dread.

Moths bounced against my headlights. I leant forwards over the wheel, trying to see, feeling alone in the darkness, missing my friend, realising that in a few hours it would be the end of Sebastian's last day on earth.

Hello, Charlie.

I slammed my foot on the brake and the car came to a screeching halt. My heart pounded in my ears. I turned, staring around the dark cabin, the backseat.

Charlie Westcott. My best friend. My lifelong friend …

Now I was out of the car. Stumbling out of the door, uncaring of any other traffic (there was none), on hands and knees, tripping and falling, scrabbling away, fleeing that voice. The ghostly voice. A spectral voice coming from the car.

Charlie. Charlie. Charlie.

Sebastian was chanting.

It's almost over. It's almost done. Time for the truth. Time to tell you the truth.

My mouth was wide open. I dragged myself to my feet, fighting to contain myself, my body braced for danger. I crept back towards the Astina. The voice kept talking. Kept saying my name. But as I approached, I realised it wasn't his spectre. It was on the stereo. The mix tape. He'd recorded over it. A message? For me?

Time to tell you the truth, Charlie. What you haven't known all these years.

He swallowed, and I saw again the study, the chair facing the painting of Hong Kong Island, the tumbler of Scotch by the decanter.

I'm telling the truth now. You don't know the truth. You've never known the truth.

The chink of glass. More whisky poured.

She's not dead, Charlie. She's not dead.

PART THREE
Sebastian

CHAPTER TWENTY-FIVE

I pulled the Astina onto the shoulder of the road and turned off the engine. My hazard lights flickered on and off, like lamps at a seance.

I was breathless with excitement. It was him. It was Sebastian. Why had he recorded over Chloe's tape? I knew it was a deliberate act. He had mocked me so many times for persisting with my tapes and CDs when the world had moved on to music streaming. He knew only I would be so nostalgic as to listen. It was a message for me. He'd been thinking of me.

I rewound the cassette and pressed play, turning up the stereo volume. This time round, after the silence, then the hiss, I heard the thump of the Play and Record button. Mechanical sounds of a 1990s tape player. Nothing digital. An analogue machine. I recalled it among the books and photographs in his study. The same I'd used in Hong Kong.

Hello Charlie. Charlie Westcott. My best friend. My lifelong friend. Charlie. Charlie. Charlie. It's almost over. It's almost done. Time for the truth. Time to tell you the truth. Time to tell you the truth, Charlie. What you haven't known all these years. I'm telling the truth now. You don't know the truth. You've never known the truth. She's not dead, Charlie. She's not dead. That's the truth. Chloe's not dead. She's still alive, but she needs to die.

The smile drained from my face. Chloe was alive? Chloe needed to die? What the fuck was he saying?

I know that's a lot to take in, Charlie. It's a lot to dump on you. But I'm trying to help you, because if you have this tape, then it's already happening. Chloe needs to die. I've been trying to help her for years, for twenty-five fucking years. But there's been nothing like this. I've done nothing like this before.

I could feel my pulse quickening. All thought of Swanny and the Press Club deserted me. There was something terrible in Sebastian's voice, low and slurred from alcohol. But it was the words that filled me with dread.

It's bad, Charlie. It's the worst. The worst betrayal. I had to do it. Do you understand? For her.

The sound of the tumbler: pouring another drink. He swallowed down the liquid. I imagined the burning, peaty fragrance filling my nose.

Charlie, I'm recording this at the end of June. We've just got back. I've been unwell for three days …

End of June. That was the last trip. The Sea-Air-Space Expo in Maryland, USA. Meetings and an overnighter with Kai Birch and Mallet in California. Home via Hong Kong. Meeting Tang.

Blood pounding in the vein at my temple.

The night Tang saw him at the China Club with Zheng.

The next morning in the hotel foyer, he'd shown up sick.

It wasn't food poisoning, Charlie …

He sniffed hard. I could practically hear the snot and tears on his face.

I said it was gastro, but I was sick to the stomach. Sickened by what I'd done. There's something else going on, Charlie. As Kai says, 'secrets beneath the surface' … Jesus, tell Kai I'm sorry. Tell Henry …

His voice trailed off. Getting himself under control as if conscious his wife and children were asleep in adjoining rooms.

You know, I've imagined confessing to you a thousand times, Charlie. I've imagined coming right up to the edge of the confession. Like our toes curled over the edge of the school swimming pool when they'd make us dive in during winter. I know as soon as I speak, everything will change. I've imagined your face. How you'd go from being my friend, to seeing me as a traitor and an enemy. It's why I'm obfuscating now, savouring this moment before the revelation. But it's not real, is it? Because if you're listening, it means things must already be in motion. Time is not neutral. It's borrowed. We are on borrowed time, Charlie.

The sound of the microphone plugged into the tape deck thudding as he moved it between his hands, his voice growing in urgency.

This is only a ninety-minute tape. You need to listen now, Charlie. I am going to tell you what happened to Chloe and why she needs to die. And then I will explain the terrible thing I have done, what I have bargained to bring her relief. I'm telling you this, not to ask your forgiveness, but so you can tell others why I did what I did. You'll know who I mean. Explain that, even though it seemed I didn't care, I cared very much, Charlie. He'll understand it coming from you ...

Already I was confused. Explain to whom? Who was he talking about? What did he want me to explain?

I'm doing you a favour too, Charlie. This isn't just a confession. It's a get out of jail free card for you. When they come for you, give them this. Let them listen and they'll know you've had nothing to do with it. I acted alone. I am the trusted insider that McCubbin fears. You had nothing to do with it. Which is, of course, ironic, isn't it, Charlie? As you are the most guilty person I know.

But you didn't do this ...

❖

Sebastian launched into his story. While he was not physically present, I could almost feel him sitting next to me in the car. He spoke as if this was less a confession in monologue than a conversation. He anticipated and responded to the questions he knew I'd want to ask. He assumed a tone of sympathy when his words made me grind my jaw in fury or the shock made tears well in my eyes.

He was unrelenting, speaking at a pace to ensure there was time to tell it all. He was brutal with the truth and often I felt he relished the bluntness of his revelations.

But I took him at his word. He was trying to help me. He was arming me with the truth, which had been in the shadows all day. The truth, previously indiscernible, spoken of in code by Katrina M of ASIO, as if she were already aware of Sebastian's secrets, or at least understood the shape of the terrible thing, still looming in darkness. Now my friend was determined to protect me by tearing open the curtains and revealing all his actions in the harsh light of day.

By the time he had finished his confession, I would loathe him …

But I couldn't say what I would have done in his place.

CHAPTER TWENTY-SIX

Sebastian began on the night of the crash at the Peak. Blurting it out as if 'abruptly' was the only way he could begin tearing down years of silence and subterfuge. He'd arrived in Hong Kong in a panic, worried about what Chloe might do.

I knew she was in a rage. I knew it was because of something you'd said.

He paused, letting his meaning hang in the silence, as if he wanted me to savour and suffer each word.

She was pregnant, Charlie. Five months. Beginning to show. You didn't notice, did you? I've never told you. That's why I didn't want her to leave for Africa. You understand? That's what we were fighting about when you came to see us. It wasn't just because of my selfishness.

His words were like a fist to my belly. I couldn't breathe. I couldn't believe he'd kept this from me for all these years.

She was coming to Hong Kong to terminate the pregnancy. She'd threatened it before.

He told me how he'd chased her. Found her at a party on the Peak. She'd told him her appointment was for the morning and he rushed after her as she stormed towards her friend's Porsche. She was high on grief and drugs and all the bile that I had poured into her system over that week in Shanghai. Sebastian fought his way into the passenger side of the vehicle, her fists pounding against his face as she screamed at him to get out. He wouldn't go. She drove fast, as if to punish him, burning around those hairpin turns, the dark jungle whizzing by the window. They almost collided with a taxi, coming up the other way. Sebastian screamed at her to slow down, but Chloe kept gunning the engine. That's when she lost control.

It's the silence that stays with me, Charlie. It can't have been absolute, but after the skidding of the wheels, our screams, the grinding of the car against the metal guardrail, the crashing through the vines, the impact against the earth, our brains shaken out of our heads, in those moments that occurred afterwards as the jungle settled around us, it felt like the silence at the bottom of the ocean.

It took him a moment to focus his eyes. Then he saw her slumped over the steering wheel. He drew her upright and saw the blood. He thought she was unconscious, but her lips were moving. Then came the sound of fire igniting, and heat was all around them. Sebastian had to get her out of the car, but the door was wedged closed. He kicked out the windshield and crawled across the bonnet. He was pulling at the driver's door when the explosion occurred. It threw him backwards, and he lay, staring in horror as the fire consumed the cabin. He could hear her screaming. He tore at the door handle, the skin of his palm melting away as he hauled it open and pulled her from the car.

Her body was on fire, Charlie. I could smell her burning flesh as I threw myself onto her, beating out the flames. She writhed in agony on the jungle floor. Her cries have haunted me ever since.

He didn't know how to get back onto the road and call for help. Instead, he sank to his knees and prayed. We hadn't prayed since the school chapel. In the cabin of my Mazda Astina I held my breath, wanting to join him in prayer. I knew that as the moment she'd died. Sebastian had told me so in the days that followed. That was always the moment she'd passed away. On the jungle floor. The flames from the burning car illuminating the canopy of banyan trees.

But then her phone rang. It must have flown from the vehicle as we made our descent. Its illuminated face shone in the darkness a few metres away, amid the tangled roots and vines.

A phone call he'd never divulged.

He rushed over and recognised the name flashing on the screen. It said 'bàba'. He recognised Zheng's voice.

'*Where's my daughter?*'

But Zheng? Zheng had never been in the story before.

Sebastian explained the situation. Zheng told him people would come. He told Sebastian to check the car for drugs. To remove anything and get rid of it. He seemed so focused on removing evidence that his daughter's condition was secondary.

I couldn't make him understand the car was an inferno, and that Chloe's clothes were burnt from her body and what was left was now fused against her skin.

Sebastian hung up and waited, keeping watch over Chloe. It felt like hours. He fixed his entire concentration on her shallow breathing. Willing each intake of breath, terrified it would be her last. He was leaning over her like that when they arrived. Medics on ropes, descending into the jungle. At least ten of them. Police. Special forces. He didn't know which. They appeared out of nowhere, as if summoned by Zheng, and, ignoring him, they began treating Chloe. Sebastian stood helpless, saying, 'Her breathing's stopped.'

It was then that one of them turned around. It was Liu Hui.

He hit me hard with a night stick and I fell into darkness.

❖

I could hear Sebastian moving in the leather armchair. I could hear his hands rubbing at his face, and for a moment I was worried he might be tiring and would end the recording. But the relentless confession continued.

I don't know how much later it was, Charlie. I remember the police station in Central, stinking of disinfectant. They had fans bolted into the blue concrete walls, but the heat was still overpowering. The fluorescent lights. The roar of the fax machine, the white static between calls on the police radio. They bandaged my burnt hands and gave me a compress to hold against my head. Whenever anyone came near me, I begged them for news of Chloe.

It was the early hours of the morning and there was only a skeleton staff on duty in the police station. Sebastian asked the young constable in short sleeves why he had been breathalysed when he hadn't been driving the car. The constable looked confused, and muttered he'd been told Sebastian was the driver, reassuring him that the tests showed no alcohol in his bloodstream.

This was the first sign there were competing factions in the police station that night. Those professionals trying to do their job. And those others, working for Zheng.

A group appeared, dressed in fatigues, Liu Hui among them.

I shouted his name as soon as I saw him. I was desperate to know what had happened with Chloe. He glanced up, then looked away.

And then the office was full of raised voices arguing over what should be done with Sebastian. Liu's group demanded his arrest, shouting over the young constable, who held his ground, waving the zero alcohol reading and repeating Sebastian's claim he wasn't driving.

A fat sergeant pushed aside the constable, still chewing on his dinner and making fawning apologies to Liu and his group for the constable's 'mistake'. He dragged Sebastian's burnt hand forward to take his fingerprints, ignoring his cries of pain.

But the young constable didn't give up. Now exiled to the corner of the room, he waved Sebastian's red Australian diplomatic passport and gestured to the phone, insisting they call their superiors. This caused another stir, multiple hands passing around the document and turning its pages. But Liu Hui was adamant.

'Fuck the passport. He killed the girl. Arrest him …'

On the tape, Sebastian took a deep, quivering breath. I could hear in his voice the trauma of that recollection.

My Cantonese wasn't fluent then, Charlie, so I hadn't followed all the arguing. But when Liu spoke in Mandarin, the words had brutal clarity. Killed. He'd said I'd killed the girl. That meant Chloe.

I can't describe it. I was fucking hysterical …

He had to be restrained, dragged to a cell, begging Liu to confirm it wasn't true. The only confirmation Liu offered was of his own viciousness. As the cell door closed, he repeated the accusation.

She's dead. You killed her.

And the words rang in Sebastian's head.

It was the cruellest torture, Charlie. To have just said that. Then to leave me alone with the knowledge. It must have been hours.

When they returned to him, he was half mad with grief and could hardly focus his eyes. Liu Hui's faction had won the argument to arrest Sebastian. The young constable with the kind face was nowhere to be seen. Now it was just the corpulent sergeant and Liu Hui. They dragged Sebastian into a cold basement room with a single chair. Concrete floors and walls with a naked fluorescent light in the ceiling. No security cameras.

The fat sergeant paced. Liu egged him on.

I realised it wasn't an interview, Charlie. It was more a briefing. They were getting the story straight as if preparing for questions from someone else, and needing to ensure Zheng's daughter was in the clear.

They asked Sebastian who was driving the car and, when he insisted Chloe was driving, they asked the question again. When he failed a second time, they coached him.

'*You were driving the car. You were drunk. You were on drugs.*'

It went on like this as they pressured him to accept their script. Presumably, it was Zheng's doing. It was the cover-up Sebastian had told me about and that I had described to Katrina and Ronnie. The sergeant, along with Liu, was on Zheng's payroll. They were preparing Sebastian for other investigators less loyal, who may have wanted the truth about Zheng's wayward daughter. Who would have used that truth against him.

It was bullshit, Charlie. A disgusting fucking lie. They wanted me to say I was drunk. That I'd just met Chloe at a party, never seen her before. I lost it and shouted back that I loved her, that I'd asked her to marry me, that she was carrying my fucking child.

That drew Liu forwards. He was on top of Sebastian, punching his face, when the door opened and the young constable entered, together with a shorter man wearing grey suit pants and a salmon-pink polo shirt.

This newcomer held a folder and Sebastian's diplomatic passport in his hand. His presence had an immediate effect on Liu, who stepped back from Sebastian as if awaiting orders. With a gesture of his head, Salmon Shirt dismissed the sergeant and the constable.

I remember he had oval-shaped glasses that kept slipping from the bridge of his nose, which was covered in droplets of sweat in the humidity. He had a thick mainland accent. He introduced himself as Qiu and asked me if I was an Australian diplomat.

The streetlights along State Circuit, previously dark, now flickered to life. Their glow was weak but provided a slight illumination in the darkness of the Astina. I held my hand in front of my face and saw it trembling. Why had Sebastian never told me about this?

Qiu asked for Sebastian's rank at the consulate. Sebastian explained he was just a Consul, that it was his first posting. Qiu seemed disappointed and checked Sebastian's credentials in his passport to make sure. His eyebrows raised. He remarked to Liu that Sebastian was accredited to the Australian Consulate General in Shanghai, rather than Hong Kong.

The thought of any Australian consulate made me nauseous, Charlie. If Chloe was dead, I'd rather stay in the cell and mourn. I didn't want to hear Australian accents, or be rescued by consular staff.

But then the questioning shifted. Qiu asked Sebastian for his security clearance. What level of clearance did a Consul have? How long had he held his clearance?

Something was turning. Edging in a different direction. It was not just a police matter anymore. The questions grew more pointed and rapid fire. Qiu wanted to know about Sebastian's access to the Consulate's IT systems, the level of his secure emails. He asked details about his job description, his responsibilities. He wanted to know about Sebastian's political reporting. Who did Sebastian speak with to research his analysis? Were these reports turned into diplomatic cables? They made him list every cable he had written or contributed to since going to the post. He was asked to list each minister that had visited. Each dignitary. Each business leader.

The volume and specificity of so many questions about his work jerked Sebastian from his daze. He pushed back, refusing to answer anything more until they told him what had happened to Chloe. And what about Zheng? Had Zheng been told? This question got a reaction from both of them. Liu turned his face away, but Qiu leant forwards and drilled his finger into the table.

'Zheng knows where you are, and where his daughter is.'

Sebastian sighed, and I knew something awful was coming.

They tried to continue the questioning, but I'd clammed up, Charlie. Not another word until I saw Chloe. I wasn't ready to accept she was gone. I needed to see her.

That's when Qiu shrugged and gestured to Liu, who grabbed me by the hair.

Liu, who was clearly loyal to Qiu despite being Zheng's 'security', led him down a long corridor in the basement of the police station to a door marked 'morgue'. Inside there was a slab and a body, burnt and charred.

I tried to enter the room. But Liu slammed the door and threw me against the wall. His elbow was against my throat and he kept spitting accusations.

'You did this, Guǐzǐ. You did this. I told you to leave her alone.'

Then he hit me in the belly and I slid down the wall, sobbing and gasping for air.

Qiu was beside him. He reached down and clasped Sebastian's shoulder, acknowledging how painful the loss of 'the girl' must be. Her death was a terrible thing. He was sympathetic and told Sebastian he should take some time to recover after such a traumatic experience.

Qiu asked if there was anyone Sebastian knew in Hong Kong who could come and pick him up. He was explicit. No one from the consulate. If they called the consulate, it would be official. For now, things could stay unofficial. They would keep his secret. They were doing him a favour.

Of course I thought of you, Charlie. I knew you were flying in from Shenzhen. I gave them your details. It wasn't long after this they took me upstairs and put me on the phone with you. I remember as I heard your voice, I could still smell her burnt flesh.

Sebastian was silent for a long while as I heard him replenish his glass and gulp the whisky like water. He had never told me any of this before. About the interrogation. About seeing her body. About agreeing to keep Chloe's death a secret with this mysterious Qiu.

Understand, Charlie, it was all a blur. I thought I was going to prison. I thought I was going to rot in that place and, frankly, I thought I deserved it. I wanted punishment. I felt responsible for her death. I'd seen her burnt body on the slab. Then they told me I could leave. That you were coming. That they hadn't called the consulate. I was a zombie. I just did what they told me.

Here, Sebastian hesitated. I imagined him looking back at me in the darkness.

They took him down to the courtyard, where the police vehicles arrived and departed before the main entrance to the station. I was waiting for him on the other side of that gate. That's when he saw Zheng. They were bringing him in. He was getting out of a car. It wasn't his car. There was a tall man with him. He had him under the arm, as if assisting him, like they'd 'assisted' Sebastian into the station.

I've told you before about the look of hatred on Zheng's face when he saw me there. I told you how I tried to step towards him, but they held me back.

Sebastian called to him, saying he was sorry. He shouted it in English, Cantonese and Mandarin. He had told me this before.

But I never told you that Qiu was there, too. He greeted the man accompanying Zheng in Mandarin, touching him lightly on the arm as if he were a subordinate. He was less friendly to Zheng, grabbing his wrist and whispering to him, punctuating his words with a finger raised in the air, as if giving instructions.

Zheng nodded and seemed to shrivel. He looked beaten and frail and Sebastian realised it was no longer Zheng orchestrating the cover-up. If he had ever tried, he had failed.

I know I told you he was in control, Charlie. But by the end, it wasn't true. Zheng wasn't in control. And as they led him upstairs, I caught his eye one more time. He didn't look furious anymore, Charlie. He looked scared.

Qiu walked across the courtyard and put his hand on Sebastian's back like the host at a party, greeting a new guest while showing another to the door. He led him toward the gate, telling him he understood Sebastian wanted to speak to Zheng, but that Zheng was indisposed. Zheng had his own questions to answer.

He promised me, though, Charlie, that a meeting would be arranged in the coming days. We would all meet again. I would be able to apologise to Zheng. There would be more questions and we would all discuss next steps. Meanwhile, I couldn't leave Hong Kong. He was keeping my passport. I was instructed not to contact the consulate. Not to spend time with Australians in Hong Kong who might know me. He cautioned me that if, for whatever reason, I was confronted by other officials, if other police arrested me, if there were people I had not seen that night, who I could not trust, I knew what to say.

That was when they thrust me out into the night towards you, Charlie. And do you remember what I said?

That he was driving. That he'd been drunk. That he'd killed Chloe.

He'd recited their lines perfectly.

CHAPTER TWENTY-SEVEN

I stared into my last packet of cigarettes. I was almost out, but given the circumstances, I couldn't stop myself. Why hadn't Sebastian trusted me? Yes, I'd betrayed him, but I wasn't DFAT, I wasn't the Hong Kong police. How could he have bottled it all up? Why had he lied about Zheng running a cover-up? And if Qiu sent him away on the condition that they would meet again soon, had that occurred? Had he met with Zheng again after that night?

And what of Chloe? He'd said she was alive. But he'd described seeing her body. What had happened to her? Why the fuck was he torturing me like this?

I flicked the cigarette lighter, and as the flame ignited, the streetlights also returned to their usual strength. It was a reassuring moment, like Canberra was bravely fighting off the virus that had plunged the rest of the country into darkness. In the renewed illumination, I noticed a tall man in a dark suit with a backpack hanging off one shoulder. He emerged from a clump of banksias and bottlebrush shrubs as if, having abandoned the footpath from Parliament House, he'd charged through the wild gardens from Capital Circle, down to State Circle. Now revealed in the light, he slowed his pace to a walk, and made a deliberate show of not looking in my direction. I found this strange given the eyesore of my clapped-out Astina with its hazard lights on, pulled up on the side of a usually busy motorway. I was at least worthy of a glance.

Instead, he looked straight ahead, crossed the deserted road, then kept walking through the uncut kangaroo grass towards

Barton, disappearing into the darkness in the direction of the RG Casey building. Was he a DFAT boffin working late? A staffer or a lobbyist heeding the police alerts on his phone and racing home to be with his family? Or was he something else? Someone who wasn't looking at me precisely because he had been sent to watch me and had now been exposed?

It was disconcerting, but everything was disconcerting. What was happening around Australia was throwing any concept of normal out the window.

I turned away, trying to convince myself it was nothing. I focused on the tape and Sebastian's confession, forgetting other people in the world existed.

Before I could hit play and return my full attention back to Sebastian, my phone lit up with an incoming call. I glanced at the clock on the dashboard, thinking it might be Swanny checking where I was. I'd said I would be with him in fifteen minutes, and I'd been at least twenty. But it was the +1 number again. Henry Mallet in California. I rejected him and returned to Sebastian's confession.

I remember being on Lamma Island with you, Charlie, after they released me from the police station. I remember not being able to walk without your arm around me. I remember you spooning rice into my mouth like a child. And bathing me after I vomited over myself. You were so caring. That night you were my saviour.

Warmth flushed across my chest.

It was beginning down a road to forgiveness that we are still on to this day, Charlie.

The smile drained from my face. My body tensed.

Because we both know you carry the blame. If you hadn't done what you did, she would never have fled to Hong Kong. That is your cross to bear.

I bowed my head in pain, clutching the steering wheel with both hands.

That night on Lamma, I took refuge in memories of Chloe. Lamma was our special place. Chloe took me there the day after the handover. The day after you'd departed Hong Kong without saying goodbye.

They had taken a ferry to Sok Kwu Wan, the little village on the eastern side of the island, just a line of restaurants on the seafront. She chose one called Peach Garden Seafood. They shared a bottle of cold Tsingtao beer and Sebastian realised it was the first time he'd seen her drink alcohol.

I think it was because we were both miserable. Your absence changed the whole dynamic. We sat in silence, staring at the fresh fish rafts floating in the bay. She asked why you had left without saying goodbye, and I told her in my experience you judged your friends harshly, and often disapproved …

Was he seeking solace in the memory, or just drunk now and forgetting about the confession? Punishing me instead with decades-old crimes.

They walked across Lamma Island through the jungle trails, emerging into the sunlight as they crested the hill and gazed out across the island. In the stillness, Chloe spoke about her mother's suicide, the pain of her mother's abandonment of her.

It was playing on her mind. You'd abandoned us. The British had abandoned Hong Kong. But I knew exactly what she meant about her mother.

You can get used to a person no longer being alive. Even with the idea they have chosen to take their own life. But you never recover from the shock that someone you love has decided to abandon you, with such finality, such violence.

That's what suicide is. A violent act of abandonment.

It was as if they were sharing the lessons they'd learnt but kept secret as wounded children. Now, they'd each found a soulmate with whom they could share the trauma they'd kept locked inside for years.

Chloe said she'd never do what her mother did, just as I said I'd never be like my father. She believed the only time to voluntarily 'give up' your life would be if you had some fatal disease and there was no more life to live. Only then, only when there was no hope left and it was a decision made for love, and mercy, not abandonment or surrender, would she be willing to end her own life.

It was a morbid discussion about death, amid the sunshine and sea air, but it was the source of their connection. Something deeper than I could understand. Through abandonment, they'd come to value loyalty. Through their parents' deaths, they'd agreed on the sanctity of life. Two resilient children who had lost a parent in the worst way, but gained one another …

… and it had been me who had brought them together.

After hours of walking and talking, they arrived at Yung Shue Wan, the main village of Lamma. They were holding hands by then and it was all so perfectly romantic, walking into the narrow laneways, between two-storey flat-roofed buildings with fishing nets and awnings strung across the road. That's when they found the room in a cherry red building, near the playground. It was the same room he took me to that night as we fled the police station.

Mrs Lam, I don't know if you remember her, Charlie. She showed us in and touched a finger to her lips. She said, 'It's private. And if anyone comes, I say I didn't see you.'

Sitting in the Astina, I could still see the room without even closing my eyes. It was on the second floor. Lemon-coloured walls. Sparsely furnished with a high bed and embroided pillow cases. The light fixture was blown glass, shaped like an orchid. A simple wooden chair was positioned beside a Ming-style dressing table and mirror. I'd sat there watching him sleep, staring at the same painting of the Peak that now hangs in his study. For me, the recollection of that room is traumatic. But Sebastian clung to happier memories.

I can't tell you the joy we experienced that night. Chloe's body, in the moonlight, pressed against mine. Her skin was soft and salty and hungry for my touch. We made love with the windows wide and a view of the sky.

For fuck's sake! I hammered the steering wheel. The intensity of my rage came as a shock, both to me, and for a moment I thought also to Sebastian. He had gone silent on the tape. Then I heard a door opening. His wife's voice.

What are you doing in here so late?

The sound of movement. Fumbled pages. Was it the photo album being set aside? Then his body shifting against the leather seat.

Go back to bed.

It was a bitter, unfamiliar tone, imbuing his words with a grinding contempt, shocking in its contrast to his public fawning over his wife on the campaign trail.

I heard the 'thunk' of the tape being stopped. My heart sank. I feared that was it. The end of his confession.

❖

And maybe it would have been better if the confession had ended there, because when the tape recorder clunked again, Sebastian's voice returned, hard and bitter. He went straight to the second night after I'd taken him from the police station. By then, he was strong enough to stand without my support. The panic he'd felt the day before had receded to numbness. He'd told me he wanted to get air. He was going to find the Tin Hau temple. Tin Hau was the goddess of the sea.

But I didn't make it to her, Charlie. In the dark of the street, Liu Hui was there. Qiu had sent him.

It was time to see Zheng.

I sucked a breath through my nose and glanced around, terrified someone may hear. Sebastian had just confirmed what I'd denied to Katrina M. The narrow street was illuminated by light from a single store. A figure with a burnt face, his finger drilling into Sebastian's chest.

Liu Hui.

Liu Hui had been on Lamma Island.

And now Sebastian's confession picked up pace.

I left you sleeping the next morning. I took the first ferry back to Hong Kong Island then a taxi from Central. The address Liu had given me was on the Peak, and to my horror, the driver chose a route past the site of the crash. Police tape fluttered like decorations on the twisted metal barricade.

They continued around Peak Road, towards Mount Kellet, where the lane veers off through an iron gate into the courtyard of Matilda International Hospital. It looked more like a luxury hotel than a medical facility. A neoclassical lodge, with a portico surrounded by rows of arched windows, a second storey crowned with a pediment, and grounds cleared of jungle on a cliff face, towering over the sea.

I was shocked, Charlie. Zheng was in the hospital. I presumed the trauma of Chloe's death had given him a stroke or something. I had come to plead his forgiveness, only to find that I'd ruined him, too.

Liu Hui met him in the foyer. His arms folded in a tight black T-shirt. Sebastian followed him along the mosaic-tiled hallways, and across a concourse, into an elevator in the modern wing of the facility. In the elevator, he rehearsed his apology.

I wanted to commit to Zheng. I wanted to tell him how much I loved Chloe, that I'd never cease to mourn her. That I would be as loyal to her in death as I had been in life. No one would replace her. I would be faithful to her memory.

The elevator doors opened onto a maternity ward. It seemed like a cruel joke. The sound of wailing babies, new life, laughing parents and beaming grandparents holding balloons and fluffy toys. Nurses glanced with disapproval at Liu but didn't question their presence.

Liu opened a set of heavy double doors with a keycard. As they closed behind them, the sounds of new life and family were silenced. The rooms on either side of the carpeted hallway were all empty maternity suites, as luxurious as the most prestigious hotel.

Liu gestured with a jerk of his head towards a suite on the left. This room was unique. Even before Sebastian entered, he could hear the pinging and humming of machines. Life support systems, like some overbearing praetorian guard, crowded around the bed in which lay a small, human shape, covered in bandages and unrecognisable. By the window, Zheng sat in a chair with his head in his hands. His face was ravaged. A grey fuzz of hair covered his usually close-shaven scalp and face.

We stared at each other a moment. Then he sighed and turned towards the figure in the bed. I understood. It was her. It was Chloe.

I felt the breath catch in the back of my throat. He'd said at the beginning of the tape that Chloe was alive, but as he'd told his story I'd begun to doubt if he'd been telling me the truth. I'd imagined nothing like this. That she was actually alive. That she'd survived the accident? The body in the morgue wasn't her? Light and sound burst in my head like the fireworks over Hong Kong during handover. I was lost in conflicting emotions. Outraged that Sebastian had kept this from me for so many years. Joy at realising Chloe was still alive.

I raced to get close to her, Charlie. Clutching at her bandaged hand with my own. Not a patch of skin was visible, but hope brimmed over. Bandages meant wounds could heal. All these machines meant treatment and recovery.

Sebastian turned to Zheng, peppering him with questions in English and Mandarin. He was certain this must be Zheng's doing. Zheng had been in control after all, and now his daughter was receiving care at this exclusive private facility. But why had Qiu lied? What about the body in the morgue? What had happened?

'They kept her alive.' That's all Zheng said. He had his hands locked behind his neck, not looking at me. I couldn't understand why he wasn't more ecstatic. Then it occurred to me … What about the baby? The look on Zheng's face was one of shock, and I guessed he had no idea what I was talking about.

Zheng, staring aghast at Sebastian, began clambering to his feet, but before he could speak, the door opened. Qiu entered wearing the same salmon-coloured polo. He looked pleased at finding Zheng and Sebastian together, and with a wide smile remarked how important it was for families and friends to be together at such times. He apologised for the 'mistake' with the 'other' (meaning 'other body') at the police station. There had been a mix up by some local officers, but at least that had given his people time to make Miss Zheng comfortable in this excellent facility, where arrangements had been made for her to remain.

It was a strange choice of words, Charlie. 'Arrangements had been made for her to remain.' Zheng heard it too. I could tell by the twitch of his head. He sat back down, as if deflated.

Qiu walked to the bed and began unwinding the dressing by Chloe's ear. He spoke as he worked, explaining she had sustained extensive burns to her body which would be treated and monitored for infection. His calmness made his words more brutal.

She hadn't regained consciousness since the accident, and now she was in an induced coma. With the very best care (and this, he stressed) there was the potential for some recovery, but given the extent of her injuries, we were not to expect miracles. Maybe she would regain some limited movement. Maybe she would be able to communicate. Maybe just to open her eyes. She would never be who she was. But with the 'best care', she would live.

Qiu had stepped back then, revealing her face, or what was left of it. She was melted wax. Her skin was brown and blistered. Her features were almost indistinguishable. Sebastian couldn't see where the ridge of her nose began, or discern her mouth as anything but a rounded hole amid bubbling skin. Almost as an afterthought, Qiu added that the trauma she had sustained had caused her pregnancy to be lost.

Sebastian relayed all this over the tape, unable to stifle his sobs.

Her beautiful face, Charlie. She'd become a pile of tortured clay. Beaten and unformed. And then he just throws that in at the end. The pregnancy was lost ...

Qiu nodded, as sympathetic as he had been in the police station, lying to Sebastian about the anonymous corpse. He assumed a reassuring manner, reiterating that Chloe would be well taken care of in this facility. They had the best care, the best doctors. It had been built in the early 1900s for colonial expats and now catered to the elite of Asia. Millionaires across mainland China came here for care. Qiu would see to it that Chloe received the best support. His agency would make the arrangements. They would manage any complexities and costs. It was a beautiful room. A premium room, and he pointed to the balcony outside overlooking the ocean.

Only the best for an old friend like Mr Zheng.

And he turned to Sebastian and added with that same wide smile: *And our new friend from the Australian Consulate in Shanghai.*

I listened to this, my arms locked across my body. I knew what this was. It was familiar to me. I know all about pursuing political influence through seduction and compromise. First, we seduce our target by offering something their heart secretly desires. Then we compromise them by threatening to use their desires against them. I listened to Sebastian's description of Qiu, recognising a fellow traveller.

Qiu said what had happened could remain our secret.

He said he would deal with the Hong Kong police. And knowledge of 'the incident' was limited to a small trusted group within his own agency (he didn't say what this agency was). It was also not in the interests of Zheng to have his daughter's 'behaviours' exposed, given his important work in Beijing, not to mention his family's history (and here Sebastian presumed Qiu was referencing Chloe's mother). As for Sebastian, it would be sensible for him to tell no one at the Consulate, his superiors in Canberra or the security agencies in Australia. After all, Qiu understood that his relationship with Chloe had not been disclosed, and he didn't want to see Sebastian get into trouble.

He'd done his homework. He knew Chloe lived with me in Shanghai and that it wasn't allowed. He knew I'd lied in my security clearance interview.

Maybe Sebastian didn't understand Qiu's manipulations. Maybe he did and was already trying to negotiate. But he turned the conversation back to Chloe. Now, for the first time since the accident, he had hope. Chloe was alive. Chloe would live. He didn't allow his mind to consider what shape or form that life might take. Yesterday she was dead and today she was alive, and that was enough. He asked how long her recovery might take. How long, therefore, would Qiu's arrangement last?

Once again, Qiu's avuncular matter-of-factness belied the awfulness of his words.

He said full recovery was impossible, Charlie. She would remain in need of high-level care for the rest of her life. Then he said, luckily, such care was possible here.

Qiu gestured around the light, sunny room, at the modern machines, the sense of order and competence, before sadly shaking his head and admitting that not all hospitals in China could offer such care.

Perhaps if she had been unlucky enough to have ended up in a public hospital, she would not be alive now. Perhaps if she went to one now, the story could end differently. Overcrowding, lack of staff, fewer doctors, infection. A patient in her condition could easily succumb. His voice was regretful. But the threat was clear.

She would live only as long as they cared for her.

❖

The balcony from Chloe's room had a view off the coast, south-west towards Tin Wan and Aberdeen Harbour. I imagine that day the channels and waterways had been filled with freighters, fishing boats and the occasional naval vessel. The island chain would have been visible in a blue silhouette: Ap Lei Chau, Po Toi, Lamma, and beyond, the South China Sea stretching to the horizon, its deep waters mirroring the endless blue sky, punctuated with cumulus clouds.

Zheng had been silent throughout Qiu's remarks, staring through the balcony doors yet not seeming to see the immense view. He had appeared resigned, as if he'd known all along that this would be the outcome. Perhaps in acknowledgement of the gravity of what he'd said, Qiu left the room without a word. After a long moment, Zheng took a breath and looked at Sebastian. His voice was firm. He told Sebastian they had to do what Qiu said. That Qiu had saved Chloe's life. They had to trust him. They needed to accept the situation.

I was still in shock, Charlie. Chloe was alive, and yet her care and survival were now in the hands of a total stranger. A man who was capable of using a charred corpse as a prop if it would serve his interests. I told him I didn't trust Qiu. I told him we had to get Chloe away from there.

Zheng's face hardened, and he growled. Sebastian didn't understand the situation. Zheng explained that for a man of his position to not know his daughter was living with a foreign diplomat, or that she was carrying a foreigner's child, was a grave transgression, and a violation of Party discipline and standards. He was compromised and in danger himself, which explained why he had attempted to cover up the car crash.

I told him I didn't care about his fucking Party discipline. I asked what was more important: his daughter or his ideology.

This caused an eruption. Zheng's sharp cheek bones inflated, his lip curled into a snarl and that look of hatred Sebastian had seen at the police station returned.

He jabbed his finger into my chest like my father used to.

'This is your fault. Your influence. You corrupted her. I told you to leave her alone. You are responsible.'

When this tirade had blown itself out, his expression grew ravaged. He glanced again at the view from the balcony. Then turned back to Sebastian and muttered three words that made everything clear.

Qiu is MSS.

I could almost hear Sebastian's body shuddering against the leather couch as he recited these words. He placed such weight on the acronym that I could feel the heaviness of each letter as they unfurled in my head.

Qiu is MSS.

The Ministry of State Security. The intelligence, security and secret police apparatus of the Chinese Communist Party. We had all received the briefings. ASIO's cautionary tales. Jesus, it was McCubbin himself who had bludgeoned us with the threat assessments (and accusations) as he'd rammed his foreign interference laws through parliament under the last government. We had been lectured endlessly on the dangers of MSS 'influence operations' in Australia: the United Front Work Department; manipulation of the Chinese diaspora, of prominent individuals in the community; political donations and compromise to gain influence, sway policy direction to Beijing's favour and undermine public institutions. I'd always thought it was a beat up. A political curmudgeon deployed by the opposition to tarnish our reputation and make us seem unfit for office. That's why Sebastian joining the party had been such a coup. It had neutered this line of attack, because how could anyone accuse Alec McCubbin's son–in–law?

But now he accused himself.

Sebastian had already confessed to lying about Chloe, Liu Hui, Qiu and Zheng: lies I'd denied multiple times throughout the day, including during the interview with ASIO. But this new revelation was something worse altogether.

Sebastian had been compromised.

Beyond lying on his security clearance, beyond the undeclared relationship and living arrangements with Chloe, now he found himself in a conspiracy with the Chinese Ministry of State Security. He'd collaborated with the foreign intelligence services of China. He had followed their instructions not to notify his consulate, or any other appropriate authorities in Australia. He had been utterly compromised and his voice on the tape, weary and defeated, couldn't disguise that he'd known it was true, and that I would be thinking as much as I listened to his confession.

I tried not to show my panic. It was hard. But I kept my face set, trying to show no expression. I said I didn't care if Qiu worked for the MSS. I told Zheng we needed to get Chloe away from him.

But Zheng dismissed me with a shake of his head. He told me that moving Chloe was not an option. The question was simply whether the MSS would care for her, or let her die.

I saw the fear in his wide eyes, Charlie. His lips trembled as he spoke. He said we needed to help Chloe. He said he was scared for his daughter. He said he knew Chloe loved me and that he was talking to me now like a son-in-law. We needed to work together to save her.

Qiu's people would continue looking after Chloe. They would make sure she had the best care and did not suffer. Everything that had happened would be kept a secret. Zheng and Sebastian would go on with their lives, knowing Chloe was safe and not in pain.

We needed to go on living, he said.

And here, again, I heard Sebastian bring the glass of whisky to his lips. He gulped a mouthful, then spoke quickly as the Scotch burnt his throat.

In return, we would both be expected to assist Qiu and the MSS with various favours. Zheng said he had 'ongoing obligations'. But for me, it would be nothing unreasonable. They knew I was only junior in the Consulate, but they also played the long game. They recognised my career was on an upward trajectory. Zheng said we would support each other. He had already agreed to be the intermediary. He would help me, help Qiu, help the MSS ... to help Chloe.

Or in other words, in return for Chloe's care, Sebastian would become their asset.

He asked me to think about the alternatives, and I quickly realised there were none. If I rejected them and reported everything to DFAT, then there was no guarantee the MSS wouldn't just turn Chloe's life support off. Zheng would not be able to stop them.

Zheng did not look smug or triumphant, or in any way pleased with the situation as he explained the bargain to Sebastian. He kept repeating that Qiu was MSS, and there was nothing they could do. The most important thing was Chloe's welfare. He was begging Sebastian, a father to a son-in-law.

I knew I was trapped, Charlie. I told him I would leave my job and move to Hong Kong to be with her. He shook his head, that same tortured expression on his face. He said once I embarked on this path, it would be too dangerous to return. Perhaps dangerous for Chloe. People would be watching. We had to keep the relationship a secret. This was of the utmost importance. I must not be distracted. I would receive weekly updates on Chloe's health to show that Qiu was keeping his side of the bargain. There would be photographs. One a week, when I met with the MSS. But I must continue in my role working for the Australian government.

And I would not see Chloe in person again.

Like an iron weight in his belly, this revelation almost dragged Sebastian to his knees. He protested, but Zheng clutched at him, his face mirroring Sebastian's panic.

A photograph, once a week, he said, shaking Sebastian. A photograph showing she was cared for and healing. Wasn't that better than knowing she suffered, or worse?

He told me I shouldn't argue. Now was the time to show loyalty and take responsibility. If I really loved her, if I was really loyal to her, I had to accept ...

It was an impossible commitment, but Sebastian had no choice. He nodded and submitted. Zheng called Qiu back into Chloe's room. He explained the situation to Qiu, who, acting surprised and slightly hurt, agreed on the spot to provide all necessary care for Chloe's condition and to organise for Sebastian to receive regular evidence of her recovery.

He said they would do whatever needed to be done to ensure the best outcomes for Chloe. We were friends now, he told me, and friends helped each other.

Liu Hui entered, carrying a red box and three shot glasses. It was baijiu, the highly alcoholic white spirit. Sebastian hesitated, but Qiu nodded to the security camera in the corner of the room and told him the occasion needed to be marked.

Qiu said gānbēi, and we drank a toast over Chloe's hospital bed.

CHAPTER TWENTY-EIGHT

I jumped at the ringing of my mobile phone. Nerves on edge. Emotionally wrought. Flicking off the stereo, I snatched up my phone, ready to reject another call from Mallet. But it was Swanny.

'Swanny, I know I'm late —'

He cut me off. Still good natured, but frustrated, as if he had his adrenaline up.

'Where are you, Charlie? You said fifteen minutes.'

'I'm sorry, mate. I don't think I'm going to make it.'

There were too many things going through my head after Sebastian's revelation. I didn't trust myself talking to anyone, let alone a fucking journalist.

'Well, I would make it if I were you, son …'

My hands gripped the steering wheel. I ground my head into the leather stitching. The MSS. Sebastian had just confessed to being recruited by the MSS. How could I talk to Swanny now?

'I'm not coming, Swanny. Something's come up.'

'Well, more has come up here too, Charlie.' I heard him walking as he spoke, the vibration of his footfalls coming through his chest, as if he was pacing with nervous energy. 'I've been on the phone with your mates at ASIO. The yarn has just got a few more arms and legs now, Charlie. I'm gonna need a comment from you …'

I sighed, realising I couldn't reject him. If ASIO was talking to Swanny about Sebastian, I needed to know what they were saying and why. Meeting Katrina at headquarters tomorrow morning had grown more complicated. What loyalties did I have to Sebastian after this last confession? What did this mean for my status with ASIO? I was not only responsible for covering up an undeclared romance, but however unwittingly, I had withheld proof that a minister of the Crown, a trusted insider, had been an asset to the Chinese Ministry of State Security. I didn't know what I was going to say tomorrow, but I'd need to be prepared.

'Are you still at the Press Club?'

'Yep. Still here.'

'I'll meet you out the front in three minutes.'

I turned over the engine and pulled back onto the road. The stereo came on and Sebastian continued to speak on the cassette. His voice was louder now, as if he were giving a deposition or addressing a courtroom.

Since that day, Charlie, I have worked for the MSS. I have stolen vast quantities of classified information and provided it to the MSS via Zheng. I have contributed intelligence and logistical support to MSS influence operations designed to woo significant political and business support for Beijing's preferred policy settings in Australia. I have worked to compromise significant individuals of importance in the Australian business and political community to undermine community faith in democracy. I have done all this for Chloe ...

For fuck's sake!

I punched the off button. I couldn't take any more. There was something self righteous in Sebastian's tone as he dumped one revelation after the other. A steaming pile in front of me.

I couldn't restrain the anger boiling over. I roared in fury. My friend had led a double life. He had lied to me. He had kept her from me all this time ...

I need you to keep a secret for me, Charlie ...

❖

Swanny was standing outside the entrance to the National Press Club of Australia. I saw his tall, stooped form flagging me down, and I sucked in a breath, forcing myself under control.

He was in the same wrinkled brown suit from earlier in the day. Behind him, the Press Club was lit up. The journos must be hitting it hard, and I longed for life to be as it had been twenty-four hours earlier. Only yesterday it would not have been out of place for us to go for a steak and a dozen Sydney rock oysters at the Press Club's Chatham House Restaurant, or order a bowl of fries (or as Swanny called it, 'a man salad') and a couple of negronis in the bar, then have a cheeky cigarette in the stairwell leading up to the carpark. We'd trade intel, leads, gossip, scandals. I'd swap him dirt on our opponents for tip offs about hit jobs on my mob. It was all part of the political game, and seeing him by the side of the road, I felt nostalgic for something that now seemed lost and irretrievable amid all the nightmares of the day.

I slowed and opened the window.

'You want to talk in the car?'

'How about we leave our phones in there and take a walk?'

I looked at him. Did he think ASIO were bugging our devices? I didn't ask, just locked both devices in the glove box. Swanny's paranoia was contagious. On impulse, I reached back into the cabin and ejected the mix tape from the cassette deck, putting it in my jacket pocket.

We walked up National Circuit, heading north on the loop back towards Old Parliament House and the Museum of Democracy. It was dark with few streetlights; there was no one on the street and few cars to be seen. It seemed everyone had followed police orders and was at home, glued to their television sets or phones or, if they were in the cities where the lights had gone out, sitting in the dark, clutching their families, waiting to see what would happen next on this mad night.

Voices and tinkling glass carried on the night air from the Press Club bar. Other than the eucalypts leaning over us as if eavesdropping on our conversation, we had the footpath to ourselves.

'Police are enforcing curfews in cities with power outages,' Swanny said, his own bleak version of small talk. 'It's another lockdown, only worse than COVID. The cops are going to have to keep people in their houses, because when they wake up and realise the shops are empty – no fresh bread, vegetables, milk – things are going to get ugly. Social media is already going feral. Conspiracy theories. Bullshit about police going door to door in Western Sydney.' He halted abruptly in the dark and turned to me. 'I mean, Charlie, how the fuck does anyone know what's actually going on? We're filing reports ... but nothing's going up online. All the newspaper websites are down. The television networks are out. There's no radio. Everyone's relying on social media for news. So who the fuck knows what's real ...'

I realised Swanny, like everyone else, was shaken by the unfurling chaos of the night. He jabbered nervously, giving me updates on the impacted cities, as if by cataloguing everything that was going to hell, he could somehow bring things under control. Maybe it just helped him feel he was doing his job as a journo; now at least he had an audience (of one) for his reporting.

I touched his arm, a gesture to stop. I needed him to focus.

'Tell me about ASIO,' I muttered.

He sighed and we commenced walking again.

'Okay. So I got a follow up from your mates at ASIO.'

'McCubbin?' I asked, trying to keep my voice under control.

'It was McCubbin who gave me the first drop. You were right. Called earlier, said he had a story. It was on background. Like I told you, he was running a line that Sebastian Adler killed himself because he was being blackmailed about an undeclared relationship he'd had with a Chinese lover back in the noughties, who had died in a car crash. He was responsible for the crash, drink-driving. All this happened while he was on a diplomatic posting to Shanghai. Sounds like a real shitshow.'

'And you believe that?' I asked, dragging on my cigarette and trying to find the strength for my usual prickliness. I needed to pour cold water on this story, but if Swanny had the bit between his teeth, there would be no turning him.

'You can deny it all you want in a sec, Charlie,' he said. 'Tell you the truth, I didn't think it made much sense at first. Why would McCubbin want to be dancing on his own son-in-law's grave so soon?'

I glanced behind us, ensuring there was no one in earshot. 'Because he hates this government ...'

'Yeah, I know that. But even McCubbin wouldn't leverage his own son-in-law's suicide just to sink the boot into the government. There must be something more important at play.'

My hand went to the cassette in my breast pocket. I felt a sense of dread about what was waiting for me tomorrow morning. That same sense I'd had with Katrina all afternoon, the feeling that ASIO knew more than they were letting on. Could McCubbin have known about Sebastian and the MSS? Could he be leaking the story as part of some counter-intelligence move or ...

Or, were more base motives at play?

Veteran that he was, Swanny's mind had already gone there. 'So then I got thinking: what if McCubbin wanted to leak the yarn, not because he wanted to beat up the government, but because he was covering his own arse ...'

A couple were walking towards us along the footpath, and Swanny touched me lightly on the elbow, indicating we should cross the road.

'I mean, if all this about blackmail is true, then McCubbin is going to be humiliated, right? He's the national security tsar. The guy who convinced the last government to triple ASIO's budget. Who forced far-reaching foreign interference laws through Parliament, and when your mob complained, called you "soft on national security". If it comes out that McCubbin's own son-in-law had these skeletons in his cupboard and the security tsar didn't have a clue ...' He blew a raspberry and bounced his eyebrows. 'Well, it's not just humiliation. His job would be on the line, wouldn't it?'

I hadn't thought about that earlier, in the aftermath of Sebastian's suicide. Neither had Ronnie. We'd been too concerned about what McCubbin could do to us. But Swanny was right. It would be the end of McCubbin's career, and we wouldn't be sad to see him go.

'So then, why would McCubbin be shopping a yarn that is likely to damage him?'

Swanny shrugged. 'Maybe he's trying to get out in front of the story. Shape it early, so the heat doesn't fall on him.'

'How would he do that?' I asked, nervousness returning to my gut.

'By serving up a bigger villain, framing the narrative in a way that gets both him and the government off the hook.'

We were across the road from the Kurrajong Hotel. When I'd first come to Canberra, I'd stayed there, still young and moved by the romance of our bush capital. I'd loved the idea of staying in the iconic establishment where former Prime Minister Ben Chifley had died. These days I knew there was nothing romantic about political ghosts.

'Who's the bigger villain then?' I asked, as we came to a halt on the footpath. In the evening breeze, Swanny's red hair was a tangled mess. He turned and smiled at me through his greying goatie.

'Well, that brings me to the second call I had from ASIO today.'

'McCubbin again?'

He shook his head. 'Katrina somebody.'

I threw my cigarette butt onto the concrete and ground it out beneath my heel.

'Katrina M?' I asked, not looking up

'That's it. She was calling to tell me they had identified the responsible party.'

'Responsible for the blackmail?'

'She said they were following up some last leads, but they'd be making arrests tomorrow morning.'

I squinted my eyes in the moonlight. Tomorrow morning, Katrina was meeting with me.

'She said the yarn was mine if I wanted to run it. It was on embargo until tomorrow. But after the arrest, I could have it. Exclusive. They'd want it on the front page. They'd give me a twenty-four-hour exclusive to get it out far and wide, then ASIO will put out a statement.'

'A cautionary tale ...' I muttered.

'They would have moved on it today, only this shit with the cyberattack got in the way. It sounds like a big deal, Charlie. They're willing to declassify evidence ...'

'What evidence do they have?'

'She said they could link the identity of this person to a car crash in Hong Kong and the secret relationship between Adler and this girl. The information used for the blackmail.'

I shook my head and swore under my breath. Were they going to expose Zheng? Did they know about Sebastian's connections with the MSS, or was this just some random shot in the dark from McCubbin, desperate to protect his job and avoid a scandal?

'Katrina M also said the person has extensive links to the government. It sounded to me like they were a trusted insider. Someone from within the Party.'

Black dots swam in front of my eyes. I had to take a step back to steady myself. Why hadn't I seen this coming? It now seemed the obvious play. Something I might have thought up if the roles had been reversed.

Swanny pulled out his packet of cigarettes and handed me one.

'So, any comment?'

'About what?' Deny. Feign ignorance. Distract. Point the finger at someone else. Deny again. These were the rules of the game I'd played for decades. Rules that had become muscle memory to me, even when the world was crumbling around me.

'About the fact that I reckon it's you that ASIO is going to arrest tomorrow morning for the blackmail of Sebastian Adler?'

❖

I laughed in Swanny's face, summoning all the bravado I had left. It sounded hollow in my ears.

'So that's a "no comment", mate? Or are you denying the charges?'

'I'm denying you have a fucking story, Swanny.'

But he wasn't to be deterred.

'Why's it such a long shot, Charlie? Everyone knows you and Adler have a long history. Katrina M told me she had evidence dating back to the time of the car crash. Photos. Emails. Whoever was blackmailing Adler likely knew him back then. That narrows the field. Then if it's someone with links into the Party ...' He stuck out his bottom lip. 'Doesn't seem beyond the realm of possibility.'

My face felt frozen, but I forced it into a look that I hoped suggested outrage. 'You think I was blackmailing my best friend?'

'Well, you've always jealously guarded access to your boy. I've seen you get pissed off when he's dared to have relationships that don't include you —'

'Come off it, Swanny. You could say that about any chief of staff.'

'How many times have I heard you bitch and moan about his footy mates? Or old boys from your school? So maybe you had similar jealousy issues with whoever the girl from Hong Kong was.'

Before I could tell him to go fuck himself, he held up a defensive hand. He'd stopped smiling.

'Mate, of course, I don't think you've done this. I'm just coming to you as a friend, and saying this is what I've heard. I'm giving you a heads up, like you asked for, about what you might be walking into tomorrow at ASIO.'

My Machiavellian brain, slow and distracted by all the trauma of the day, was now kicking back into action. If McCubbin was looking to save his job, he needed someone to blame. And what was a better story than the failure of a father-in-law to detect blackmail? That the blackmailer was the victim's childhood friend.

I thought of the mountains of evidence ASIO now had linking me to Chloe. The photograph album. The emails hacked from my account. My statement. If they wanted to paint a picture of me as a jealous scorned lover, it would be easy ... because I was.

Swanny was smoking and watching me pace. He'd seen me like this many times before, trying to untangle a smear campaign. He knew if he waited, I would start to negotiate and he was liable to walk away with a counter story, twice as good.

But he'd set my thoughts on a path now. Whether or not I told ASIO about Sebastian's confession, I would likely be guilty in their eyes. I had already lied for him. Could those lies be twisted into support for not only Sebastian but for Zheng or the MSS? Just as allegations of blackmail could be tangled, so too could evidence of espionage and foreign interference. I was too close to Sebastian, and Sebastian was toxic. And if McCubbin was motivated to find a scapegoat …

It was with this thought that I panicked. If they made any of this stick against me, then it wasn't just about newspaper articles and my reputation. I would be charged under the Espionage and Foreign Interference Act and go to jail for a very long time. I needed to be more than prepared for the morning. I needed insurance.

My hand shot out and grabbed Swanny's wrist, making his cigarette spill ash like a bomber's payload into the darkness at our feet.

'What if I could give you a better yarn?'

'Well, I presumed you would,' Swanny said, wiping ash off his trousers.

He looked up at me for a moment and I saw his face soften. 'What have you got?' he asked.

I took the cassette tape from my pocket and held it up in the low light. 'How about a confession from Sebastian Adler that he was an asset for China's Ministry of State Security?'

Back in the car, I handed Swanny his mobile through the window and bid him farewell. I felt confident I had done the right thing. I had told him everything about Sebastian's confession, of the secret relationship with Chloe, the car crash, Qiu and Zheng at the police station, Liu Hui on Lamma Island, and poor Chloe alive in the hospital. His face had twisted from disbelief to astonishment, but when I'd finished, he locked me with that veteran journo gaze. Better than any lie detector and finely honed after a career sniffing out political bullshit and scandal. He could also sniff out a story.

We'd agreed I would make him a copy of the cassette (I still had a tape player at home to listen to my beloved bootlegs and mix tapes). Swanny and I would meet again in two hours. I'd give him a copy of the confession and he'd have it in safe keeping should I, for whatever reason, not make it out from ASIO after the discussion tomorrow morning.

Swanny, of course, had wanted to take the cassette on the spot, but I told him no. I needed a copy for ASIO, and I needed to listen to it all by myself first. 'It's worth waiting for, Swanny. I promise. When you hear it, you'll understand. It's in his voice. Every word is true.'

I felt a pang of guilt then, for laying bare all the secrets about Sebastian that I'd kept safe for twenty-five years. Secrets I'd spent the day protecting. But I knew I had done what Sebastian wanted me to do.

This isn't just a confession. It is a get out of jail free card. When they come for you, give them this.

I remembered Sebastian's words from the cassette. In my anger at his revelations, I had forgotten why he had confessed in the first place.

I'm telling you this, not to ask your forgiveness, but so you can tell others why I did what I did. You'll know who I mean. Explain that, even though it seemed I didn't care, I cared very much, Charlie. He'll understand it coming from you …

Maybe he meant ASIO. McCubbin. I was still unclear.

But he'd called the cassette a get out of jail free card. He'd meant it would be my redemption.

I'd use the confession as he intended. A wave of gratitude flooded over of me, almost bringing tears to my eyes. Yet at the edges of my tired mind there were still more unknowns. Things that I sensed, but couldn't yet properly see.

I was sure the rest of the tape was going to detail exactly what Sebastian had done for the MSS, and what that had meant for

Chloe (was she alive or dead?). But there was something else. The way Sebastian had started his confession. All that stuff about him trying to help me, about being on borrowed time.

... because if you have this tape, then it's already happening. Chloe needs to die. I've been trying to help her for years, for twenty-five fucking years. But there's been nothing like this. I've done nothing like this before.

And I still didn't understand the meaning of Zheng's message. *It's done.* It made me nervous. What did that mean? What more had he done? What else was coming? Why had he killed himself?

I couldn't hand the cassette over to Swanny without discovering these answers first. I needed to listen alone. This was between Sebastian and me. It was personal and I needed to understand.

I slid the cassette back into the car stereo and prepared to find out, turning the key in the ignition and flicking on the lights.

That was when I saw him again. The tall, thin man, wearing a suit, a backpack on one shoulder. The same man I had seen running across State Circuit. He was standing on the other side of the road, just beyond the reach of my headlights, watching me from the shadows. I wondered how long he'd been there, and how much he'd heard.

CHAPTER TWENTY-NINE

My apartment in Kingston was only a ten-minute drive from the Press Club. Rather than going directly there, I kept driving, listening to Sebastian's tape. I needed to know its full contents before I gave it to Swanny. Afterwards, it would only be a matter of dropping in at home, making a copy (thirty minutes on my tape recorder's 'high speed dubbing' setting) and then back to the Press Club to hand it over and lock in my insurance before the interview with ASIO tomorrow.

I drove north on National Circuit, past the Attorney General's Department and Prime Minister and Cabinet. Then onto the King's Avenue, accelerating over the bridge on the four-lane road towards Russell. Something strange was happening with the streetlights that arced like thin, splayed fingers along the side of the avenue. They'd lost the brave resolve that had comforted me earlier. Now they flickered. Each at random, every second or third light coming on, or going off, as if the power was ebbing and surging through the utility.

I wondered how long it would take for the outage to hit Canberra. What had Katrina's advice to Ronnie's father been? Get in groceries, collect water in buckets in the bath. My fridge was all but empty, just a few slices of cold pizza and some beer. Thinking about food now, my stomach growled, and I was reminded I hadn't eaten anything all day. I was unprepared for any disruption should the hackers target Canberra next. Why hadn't they yet, I wondered? Why turn the lights out everywhere across Australia and leave the capital? Maybe Ronnie was right. Someone was sending a message.

I didn't have bandwidth in my mind to ponder these questions. My attention was back on Sebastian, and I turned up the volume on the stereo.

❖

Sebastian's treachery began in bite-sized chunks, likely calibrated that way by the MSS so as not to overwhelm him. The first task was as simple as inserting a USB (designed with the Australian coat of arms to appear like a sanctioned device) into the port on his terminal at the Consulate.

I still remember holding it between my fingers, Charlie. I could hear my colleagues bustling around me, conversations down the hall, people typing emails. No one looked my way, no one suspected me. But I felt myself withdrawing. With this one act, I was abandoning those that trusted me. There was no turning back.

While I am sure a part of Sebastian was pained by this treachery, he smothered it, focusing on a greater sense of moral purpose.

I did it because I couldn't sleep at night. Every time I closed my eyes, I saw her bandaged body on that bed.

Once the extraction was complete, he set out on foot from the Consulate on Nanjing West Road, the USB in his pocket, blending with pedestrians as he wove away from the luxury malls into the quieter residential areas of Jing'an District. A few hundred metres away, fashion boutiques were replaced by lane houses and a primary school. The streets were quiet but for the sound of bicycle pedals and children in red scarves walking into class.

Just as his MSS handlers had instructed, Sebastian made an abrupt stop halfway down the lane. He leant against a plane tree and waited, watching back the way he'd come. When he'd satisfied himself he hadn't been followed, he hailed a taxi and directed the driver to the Garden Bridge entrance of the Bund. From there, he walked along the promenade until he saw Zheng seated on a bench. They sat, not looking at each other, as if perfect strangers.

Zheng had chosen the Puxi side of the Huangpu River, with his back to the old colonial buildings, gazing across to Pudong's financial district. It had an almost space-age skyline, shaped by the iconic Oriental Pearl TV Tower, the Shanghai World Financial Center, the Shanghai Tower.

Keeping his hands on the bench at his side, Sebastian palmed the USB into Zheng's waiting fingers. Zheng snatched it and stuffed it into the inner pocket of his suit jacket as if he, too, were afraid of being seen.

His eyes still fixed on Pudong, Zheng then recited instructions from Qiu about how their operation was going to work, how they would cooperate as asset and intermediary. Zheng listed the type of information the MSS wanted Sebastian to collect and detailed how he was to pass intel to his handlers. Sebastian would report to an MSS agent for briefings and intelligence exchange on a weekly basis. Zheng and Sebastian would meet together only once a month.

I asked him about Chloe and he said she was still receiving intensive care. Her burns and head trauma required further surgery. He mentioned skin grafts and neurological interventions, but reassured me Qiu was keeping up his part of the deal. Chloe was getting the best care. There was continued hope for modest recovery.

Zheng handed him a memory card from a digital camera, explaining it contained photos of his daughter. Sebastian would receive a memory card every time he met his handler. It would have a time stamped photo of Chloe in it. This first card had more than one photo. Zheng had taken the images himself a week ago when he'd been granted time with Chloe.

Turning the card over in his fingers, Sebastian wondered out loud why Zheng needed to be 'granted' time to visit his own daughter?

I watched him flinch a little, as if my question stung. He muttered that he too had obligations because of what had happened. He'd been forced to undergo 'self-criticism' – a result of having allowed his daughter to live with a foreign diplomat. This had impacted how often he could see Chloe. It had also implications for his career. He was no longer involved in daily operations at China Overland. He had been directed to various projects with the PLA Navy's Engineering Corps as part of a process of 'self-improvement'.

Sebastian recalled the obvious duress Zheng had been under in Chloe's hospital room. He had tried to cover up the car crash and his daughter's behaviour. That had failed, and he had to atone.

I knew we needed to work together for Chloe's sake. I tried to build a relationship. I told him Chloe had admired his work. That the job he'd found for her at the Foundation had inspired her and she had wanted to go to Africa and work for China Overland and 'build bridges over the sea' like her father.

Zheng was silent for a moment, then nodded and thanked Sebastian for sharing his daughter's words. Thawing a little, he recalled how he had brought her to Shanghai more than once over the years, and they'd sat in this very spot looking at the emerging Pudong skyline.

Possibly repeating a lecture he'd given to Chloe on the same bench, Zheng explained to Sebastian that only twenty years ago, everything in front of them had been marsh and rice fields. One of the biggest engineering complications had been land reclamation. They'd had to dredge and fill in areas of the Huangpu River to create the solid base for development, the new apartments and homes, the skyscrapers, the financial and trade zones. They had experience from work on the Shekou Peninsula in Shenzhen.

It was good, Charlie. We'd never had a proper conversation. But now I needed us to have a relationship. The minute I'd walked out of that consulate, the minute I'd handed him the USB, I'd left all my old relationships behind. This was my life now. What he'd said about being like father and son-in-law, it had already begun to mean something to me. He was the only one in the world who shared my concern for Chloe.

Sebastian asked whether land reclamation would feature in the work he was doing for the PLA. Scratching his chin, Zheng answered technically yes. But those projects involved more complex land reclamation, to help improve the living conditions and infrastructure on the islands and reefs in the South China Sea.

Then I fucked it. I said they were lucky to have the man who had managed the Pudong reclamation project. His face darkened, and he shook his head. For Pudong, they'd used his planning and ideas only. He could not work on it. When construction started in 1990, he had already moved his family to Hong Kong.

I knew, as Sebastian did, that this was a coded reference to the suicide of Chloe's mother, and the deep freeze that followed for Zheng's career.

The memory affected him and his face grew tense. And then he got nasty, Charlie. He wanted to know why I was asking about any of this. Why would a foreigner who lived in the French Concession care? An arrogant 'lǎowài' who lived beside a park where there used to be a sign that said 'No dogs, or Chinese'.

Zheng gestured over his shoulder at the imposing colonial architecture along the Bund: the HSBC building, the Peace Hotel, Customs House, the precincts beyond, that for much of the 20th century had been under the control of foreign powers. That was all architecture of shame, he said. Monuments to a century of humiliation that should fill any patriotic Chinese person with rage.

Now he was leaning over me, not caring who saw us. He pointed his finger into my chest. He said he agreed with Qiu, and that it was shameful that his daughter had been living in Luwan District, the heart of the French Concession.

Sebastian, shocked by the sudden mood change, stammered that Chloe was happy in Luwan. But this only brought Zheng to his feet, and he spat his words over his shoulder as he stormed off along the promenade.

And what good did happiness bring her?

The first meeting of asset and intermediary was over.

These sorts of ideological lectures became a feature of Sebastian's meetings with Zheng. I suspect it was a way for Zheng to evade speaking of anything personal. Sebastian, who understood clearly that even after one act of espionage there was no going back to an 'uncompromised' life, was not deterred. In fact, Zheng triggered something primal in him. Memories arose of his father drilling him about sports or reminiscing about his success at school. Zheng's bitterness over historical inequities reminded him of Paul Adler's rage over the conspiracies that had disappointed all his potential: the injury that ended his rowing aspirations, the recession that tanked his career at the investment bank. And as a result, Sebastian was drawn to Zheng. He applied himself to being an MSS asset with the same fervour he had brought to his school career, seeking the approval of his new father. There was no turning back. He committed to 'do more, work harder' and the frequency and volume of the classified reports and cables he stole from the Consulate increased.

Besides what he could steal with the USB, he used his initiative to make detailed summaries of meetings with his Consul-General in Shanghai, other heads of Australian Consular Posts across China, and the Ambassador in Beijing. He also reported on discussions with ministerial offices and other agencies, including DFAT in Canberra, and collated records of conversations on meetings between the consulate and political and business contacts in Shanghai.

After that first time on the Bund, all his meetings with Zheng and the MSS handlers took place in a sprawling subterranean children's market in Xuhui District, specialising in kids' clothes and accessories. He'd ride an escalator beneath street level, as if descending into the subway, to find stores selling fairy costumes, pirate outfits and remote control cars. The sounds of children's laughter and tantrums grated in the echoing chamber. He pushed by doting grandparents waving at their babies riding on miniature trains, or clutching a unicorn on a slowly turning merry-go-round. At a shop selling counterfeit Disney apparel, he would slip through a storeroom door. There, behind the artificial walls, the sounds of children grew muffled and the real purpose of the underground chamber became apparent. It was a bomb shelter, one of many, left untouched since Mao had ordered their construction at the height of the Cultural Revolution.

A shadowed corridor strewn with rubble was lit for a few metres by a series of construction lamps, then continued into infinite darkness, giving the impression that the bunkers sprawled all the way beneath the brand malls and shopping districts of the international city above.

Sebastian would follow the lights only a few metres, to a door that opened into a small room, once a canteen, its walls still decorated with faded propaganda posters and instructions about what to do when the bombings began. There were two handlers waiting inside. A man and a woman, Mr Fu and Ms Chen. Both were in their mid-fifties, dressed like factory workers in denim jeans and jackets. Sebastian wondered if they'd been in the tunnels since the seventies, and had not been told the Cultural Revolution was over.

Fu smoked from a packet of Double Happiness cigarettes. Chen fussed with a thermos of tea, never offering any to Sebastian, but spitting bits of leaf and twig from her mouth as she took notes with a pencil and notebook.

The three of them would sit together at a wooden table, debriefing Sebastian. Little of the information he handed over represented high value intelligence. The cables and reports that were accessible to him as a Consul were no more enlightening than what he could have read in the pages of *The Economist*, or the *Australian Financial Review*. He remarked at other times to Zheng that it felt like the MSS was an industrial strength vacuum, hoovering up everything and anything that could be classified as intelligence. Zheng, again, corrected his thinking, explaining that Sebastian's value to the MSS was not his access to information, but to people.

As an official at the Consulate, Sebastian's job brought him into contact with Australian delegations visiting Shanghai. Sebastian supported at least one delegation a month, if not more. There were CEOs of ASX listed companies, SMEs, educational institutions and travelling scholars, industry bodies, commonwealth or state government ministers, officials and boards of not-for-profit bodies, not to mention the 'mega missions' where hundreds of companies would travel in sector-specific streams, led by the Prime Minister and Minister for Trade, to promote Australian goods and services to the Chinese market.

They all came to marvel at the Chinese economic miracle, believing in the same platitudes Sebastian had uttered to Chloe and me in Hong Kong. That China's economic reforms would lead to political reforms, that just as Beijing would embrace the global economic order, it would one day also embrace democracy. Only now these weren't Sebastian's personal views, but a script of influence provided by the MSS.

Zheng explained that the MSS, along with the leadership of the CCP, believed that the west wanted to undermine the Chinese political system and replace it with American-style democracy. That Beijing was expected to join the US-led international order without challenging it, and meanwhile American culture, technology, education, religion and civil society were being deployed as blackhand operations to inspire unrest among the middle class, encouraging demands for greater political freedom and a colour revolution against the CCP.

According to Zheng, to defend China, a grand influence operation was conceived by the MSS to convince the world that China was on a liberalising path, willing to submit to the existing global order and remain subordinate to the US. By appearing to submit, Beijing continued to access the capital, technology and resources within the world markets it required to grow its strength. It could also ask for accommodations or cultural support from the west, which meant all the benefits of WTO accession, brushing aside western concerns about currency manipulation, IP theft, human rights issues, the problem of Taiwan, the authoritarian government in Beijing, the shadow of Tiananmen. All these 'issues' could be overlooked, as China needed time and was already on a path. It was called a 'peaceful rise', but what it was doing, according to Zheng, was buying time for Beijing to strengthen its arm.

I asked him what would happen when China was strong again. His reply was simple.

'China will stand up.'

In all this, as a junior Australian official in the Shanghai Consulate in the early 2000s, Sebastian played a minor role. He would share lists of delegates and their bios with Fu and Chen, along with calendars of their planned arrivals in China. He would make recommendations as to which delegate held a particular level of influence within their given sectors in Australia. Or, more often than not, which were the 'up and comers' destined for a position of leadership and power in Australian society. The next week, their roles would swap and Fu and Chen would take him through the list again, only this time the names of those delegates the MSS were interested in would be circled in red.

This is what it was all about, you see, Charlie. The delegates of interest were embraced and feted. They were given access to top Beijing officials, meetings that were arranged through benign organisations to hide the presence of MSS agents. The Australians would come away from meetings excited by the progressive view of China's future, but they had been meeting with MSS agents and went home amplifying the key messages MSS wanted to get out to the world.

The MSS would 'help' these delegates once they returned home. If they were a politician, they would be helped through donations (usually funnelled via property developers); if they were an academic, they'd get research funding and fieldwork opportunities; if they were in the private sector, of course there were endless business opportunities.

I'm not just talking naive small fry exporters, Charlie, but 'big whales'. Mining magnates, former ministers, former prime ministers. And I heard them back in Australia, reciting the lines Zheng had told me were crafted by the MSS. A peaceful rise …

It wasn't all as salubrious. Sometimes the lists of travelling delegates would be returned to Sebastian with marks next to names of Australians who were to receive 'the treatment'. For whatever reason, the MSS wanted to take these individuals deeper under their control. And for that, a more belligerent approach was required.

You would have been at home with this work, Charlie. It was worthy of your factional dark arts. I would take them to Judy's Too on Mao Ming

Road. Moutai. Baijiu. Tsingtao beer. The free house cocktail when you walked in the door. Something sweet with vodka. I would text Mr Fu when we were coming, and they'd mix up a strong batch. If the alcohol didn't do the trick, then something stronger would be slipped into their drink, so by the time the girls were leading them home to their hotel rooms, with cameras in the television and behind the bathroom mirror, they didn't protest in the slightest.

The stings in regional hotels, in Jiangsu and Zhejiang, were more elaborate and alarming for the victims. MSS operatives posing as police would pound on the door at 3 am, when the girls were still with the Australians.

I'd find CEOs whimpering on their knees in their boxer shorts, and deliver consular advice so dire they'd agree to any proposition Fu or Chen would put to them after I left the room.

It was like a production line of compromise. They were hooked. Through ambition, lust or greed, or via more direct threats from the MSS that photos would be released, careers and marriages destroyed. One after the other, the compromised were sent back to Australia, to influence public opinion positively for the CCP and erode trust in democratic institutions. Whether knowingly or just through manipulation, they all became tools of foreign interference.

To be honest, I found them all disgusting, Charlie. They were all the same. The respectable ones with their hands out for business opportunities or research funding, or those grubby ones on the floor of a massage parlour. Their corruption was fuelled by personal indulgence and desire to save their own skin. I was nothing like them. I was a traitor. But at least I believed in loyalty. I was doing it for Chloe. I would have torn the flesh from my own shoulders if it meant giving her a chance to live.

The only person who had ever called Sebastian out for keeping company with MSS agents was Kai Birch.

Five or six years Sebastian's senior, Kai was in Shanghai working as Head of Innovation for a US tech giant. He dressed straight out of a Brooks Brothers catalogue and possessed a confidence born of privilege and success. A Yale graduate and Oxford Rhodes scholar, he had served in the US Navy, then went into banking, making millions in deals across Asia before he was thirty. His confidence, in a way, reflected Sebastian's own. Sebastian looked up to him, almost idolised him.

Mallet had introduced them after he'd moved to Shanghai, about a year into Sebastian's posting, also working for one of the investment banks. Of course, Sebastian kept me in the dark about this and I didn't know until his wedding that the old boys' club had reconvened in Shanghai. They'd all had a ball living it up amid the Australian community, playing rugby in the Expat Cup and competitions against the British and New Zealanders in the Shanghai Cricket Club League.

I recall innumerable references at Sebastian's wedding to nights on bar streets in Shanghai between the three of them. I was disgusted at the time, not understanding how Sebastian could turn the page on Chloe and go back to revelling with Mallet. But in his confession, Sebastian was quite frank about the utility of his relationship.

Henry showing up in Shanghai was a godsend, Charlie. As a banker, he knew so many people not just from the Australian community, but across his client network, which was filled with Americans, Europeans and Japanese – all based in Shanghai. Zheng and the MSS loved how this extended the reach of my activities.

He began making connections between Henry's contacts and the same groups with embedded MSS agents. I admit I flushed with pleasure, imagining Sebastian exploiting Henry in this way. I know it was terrible, but I'd spent a quarter of a century thinking that Sebastian was a sociopath going back to his bachelor life in Shanghai after Chloe's death. Now everything fell into perspective, and despite the horrific nature of all these revelations, I felt a tremor of relief.

But then, Kai Birch threatened to upend all his hard work.

Kai and I were having coffee in Xintiandi one morning and he dropped it on me. He'd hosted an event for his company, and among the guest list he'd invited various contacts he'd made via Henry, and by extension, through me. Apparently, he'd been tipped off by his head of security, who he described as 'former CIA', that there were MSS operatives in the invite group. I remember he looked at me with those piercing blue eyes. I don't think he was making an accusation, but my heart stopped.

Sebastian waited for a week before telling his MSS handler about the discussion. He was nervous not only about exposure by Kai's former CIA colleague, but also about what the MSS would instruct him to do to mitigate the risk.

I was terrified they were going to put a mark next to his name, and I'd have to take Kai to Judy Toos. We'd become friends by then, Charlie. Kai, Henry, me. They were a relief in some of my darkest times in Shanghai. I didn't want to corrupt Kai. Not that he'd have been interested in the girls at Judy's …

To Sebastian's relief, the instructions from Fu and Chen were strictly 'hands off Kai Birch'. Background checks had been run on him, various discussions had been had. Sebastian was to remain close, cultivate the friendship, but wait. Birch would be of use to them in the future.

With Kai, it was a long game. I didn't realise then how long. So long, I almost forgot we were playing. I considered him a friend, even when the time came …

CHAPTER THIRTY

As promised, at each weekly meeting with his handlers, Sebastian was rewarded for his efforts with a memory card containing a single image of Chloe. He would walk from the bomb shelter behind the children's market, clutching it in his pocket, feeling the sense of anticipation that a drug addict must feel walking away from a score. Once home, he would access the images using a card reader and a laptop that he kept in his apartment.

I would obsess over every detail, examining each photograph as if it were a relic. And in fact, for most of those first years, she appeared as an Egyptian mummy, wrapped from head to toe in bandages, with a respirator for breathing support and monitors for vital signs.

Sebastian always knew when it was Zheng who had taken the photograph. Rather than a thoughtless image, snapped from the doorway on a nurse's mobile phone, underexposed or blurred, Zheng's images were detailed and there was often more than one on the memory card.

Despite all his ideological rants and occasional furies, I took his photos as a kindness to me, Charlie. Part of the bond between father and son-in-law.

Zheng had an engineer's eye for details and Sebastian imagined him spending hours in Chloe's room seeking the perfectly framed photograph to sustain hope and locate the woman they loved beneath the bandages of the patient in that hospital bed.

He took close up photos of her closed eyes. Her eyelashes, burnt away in the fire, slowly returning, follicles of hair like the spines of insects reemerging through her skin. Or her hands, by her sides, where the bandage was worn away, exposing the pink of her fingertip.

Losing himself in these images, zooming in on details, seeking signs of improvement, sustained Sebastian through lonely and sleepless nights in the lane house he'd once shared with Chloe.

The images brought her back to me, Charlie. I know that sounds mad. But often I'd feel she was behind me. Her arms around my neck, looking at the photos together. I would talk to her.

Chloe's recovery was slow, and the changes Sebastian perceived in these images in the months after the accident were minimal. But Zheng had a way of making him feel there was momentum. He always had progress to report at their monthly meetings. Sebastian would lean over the table, hanging off his every word as the sound of children's laughter echoed around the bomb shelter.

He'd update me about her treatments and surgeries. They were working to manage complications with wound breakdown and nerve damage. He'd tell me, with a tremble in his voice, how she'd opened her eyes, or squeezed his hand and we'd laugh and almost weep together in the darkness at these minor signs of improvement. I'd be high as a kite for the rest of the day.

The greatest milestone in Chloe's progress came after eighteen months. Finally, the bandages around her head were removed, and Sebastian could see her face again.

I remember that first time – I bit into my knuckle as I traced the scarring and the red swelling of the skin grafts across her cheeks. There were still tubes for feeding and medications and, as Zheng explained, intermittent periods of induced coma to manage the pain. But her hair was growing back and, despite the scarring, her face was still Chloe's.

Sebastian spent nights flipping through these images in chronological order, watching her recovery and sustaining himself with the faith that this was why he was doing what he was doing. Each week of treachery, each month of living a double life as an MSS asset, was rewarded with a photograph and a conversation with Zheng, justifying all of Sebastian's actions.

❖

This life lived through Zheng's photos of Chloe continued through the rest of Sebastian's posting in Shanghai. Signs of Chloe's improvement increased in frequency. In one photograph her eyes opened, in another she sat hunched on the edge of the bed. There was a particular image that he loved, where she seemed to be in conversation. Her arms outstretched, her mouth open, showing teeth in almost a smile, head thrown back as if responding to a joke.

I told Zheng I couldn't believe it and quizzed him on what they'd been talking about, and who had been in the room.

Zheng was vague but encouraging. He grasped Sebastian's arm over the table in the bomb shelter cafeteria and said, 'She is doing very well.'

I saw her improving, Charlie, and I couldn't help but fantasize she was going to recover. I knew they'd said she would never be herself again, but a flame of hope ignited.

Hope turned to urgency as the end of his posting approached. DFAT told him he was destined for the Foreign Minister's office in Canberra, a brilliant career move based on his 'China expertise' and a coup for the MSS, who wished him godspeed. Zheng told him it was a great opportunity to further deliver on the bargain with Qiu.

But I panicked. I was leaving the apartment we'd shared. I had to get rid of Chloe's clothes and belongings. I felt like I was deserting her. I told Zheng we should make plans for when she recovered. How we would get her out of that hospital room, away from Qiu and the MSS. Maybe we could go to Australia, or she and I could hide out on Lamma Island …

These fantasies didn't survive contact with reality. When Sebastian talked about these plans with Zheng, the gates came crashing down.

He reminded me of our commitments. We had to deliver on what we had committed to Qiu. Me in Canberra. Him with his projects for the PLA. There was no going back on that.

Sebastian tried to argue, and on more than one occasion their meetings ended with him storming out of the canteen in frustration. But Zheng wouldn't budge. The only way to aid Chloe, in his mind, was to serve Qiu as they had promised.

I wondered for the first time about Zheng's priorities. What was more important to him? His daughter or his duty to the Party?

In frustration, Sebastian recalled a visit with Chloe to a propaganda museum in Shanghai. Chloe had taken him to a nondescript building in an apartment complex on Hua Shan Road. A security guard handed them a small card, which gave directions to a basement apartment filled with thousands of wood block posters. It was communist propaganda art, vibrant coloured illustrations of heroic peasants, the Mao Personality Cult, the Chairman as the red sun shining over sunflowers, then posters celebrating the victory of the proletarian Cultural Revolution, denouncing reactionary capitalists and US imperialism.

Chloe knew the owner of the museum, who let them into a locked room not open to the public. It was filled with 'big character' posters. Large sheets of yellowing paper, covered in black and red characters, denouncing fellow citizens as 'anti-socialist' or 'anti-party' or 'counter-revolutionary'. The museum owner explained these posters had been weapons of political rage, plastered across buildings in cities around China during the Cultural Revolution.

Chloe said they'd also been pasted over her grandfather and grandmother's home in Beijing.

Zheng's parents had been denounced.

I recalled the images Katrina had shown me earlier that day with shock. Zheng as the CEO of China Overland. Zheng meeting the Chinese President at the CPPCC meeting in the Hall of the People. How had Zheng made it so far, with so much baggage? Not only after his wife's suicide, but his daughter's relationship with a foreign diplomat, and now this other secret from his childhood. His parents, denounced as reactionaries.

They were academics. Scientists and engineers at the university, members of professional associations targeted by the Red Guards intent on dismantling the old system to create a new revolutionary order.

The denouncement was damning. Zheng's parents were accused of being intellectual elites and bourgeoisie. They were guilty of expressing counter-revolutionary views critical of the communist movement. Worse, they had political connections to undesirable counter-revolutionary groups and links to spies and traitors spreading foreign ideology.

While the worst of these accusations couldn't be proved, it had been enough to devastate Zheng's family. They were ostracised, submitted to struggle sessions and public humiliation. They lost their jobs and their home. The family was relocated to a reeducation camp where they could reshape their thinking to align with revolutionary ideology.

And here Sebastian took a breath, as if shaking his head in astonishment.

But, Charlie … Chloe told me. It was Zheng who denounced them.

She'd heard it from her grandfather. Zheng denounced his own family to the Red Guards, and they called him a hero.

He'd been in love with a girl: Huang Mei. She came from a poor, uneducated family. They attended rallies and organised study groups. Zheng's father criticised her family's revolutionary fervour. They'd denounced his colleagues at the university, and his friend's family had suffered. He banned Zheng from seeing Mei.

Sebastian gave a mirthless laugh on the cassette.

Does that sound familiar, Charlie?

Of course, there was a falling out within the family. Tension boiled over into anger and they shouted hostilities.

And at some point, Zheng went to the Red Guards and told them his father was a counter-revolutionary. He did all that to be with the girl he loved.

There was a long pause on the cassette, and I took my eyes off the road a minute to ensure it was still playing. Sebastian was waiting, as if leaving room for me to wonder what more of Chloe's sad family background explained Zheng's obsequiousness to authority.

Can you think who that girl was?

My mind had already drawn the conclusion. The girl, Huang Mei, later became Zheng's wife. Chloe's mother. Who was working in a hospital when they brought in the students from Tiananmen Square.

She must have recognised something in those young protestors, Charlie. Something that reminded her of her own youth, and the resolve she felt back then. Only to see the protests smashed and the students broken. She lost faith. I'm sure that's what happened.

But Zheng couldn't lose faith. If the Party was not correct, then Zheng's betrayal of his family was not the noble act that the Red Guards had told him it was, but was a brutal, selfish thing for his own indulgence.

He lost faith in his wife instead. He tried purging her from his daughter's memory. Her photograph wasn't even allowed in the house.

There was wonder in Sebastian's voice.

Zheng couldn't forgive his wife for killing herself in a way that could be perceived as a protest against the CCP's actions. He could countenance no criticism of the Party, because to do so would be like falling dominoes back to his original betrayal.

That's how I understand his mind and his actions, Charlie. To Zheng, the Party must be infallible, its leadership always correct, and its ideology followed without question. Why? Because if the Party can be wrong, then so too Zheng may have been wrong to do what he did, and everything that flows from that first act is compromised and becomes part of a lie that he's been living. It would be like unpicking an entire history in which, rather than being the hero, he'd realise he was a villain.

It was clear Sebastian was using this story to illustrate his growing concerns that Zheng was prioritising the Party over his own daughter. But I couldn't help wondering if, even for a moment, he perceived a likeness between Zheng and himself.

❖

In the last fortnight of Sebastian's posting to Shanghai, he decided to confront Zheng about his concerns. Waiting in the darkness of the bomb shelter canteen, he paced by the noticeboard of faded posters and timetables rehearsing how he would renegotiate their bargain. It had been five years since he had agreed to Qiu's terms under the duress of finding Chloe alive and in critical condition.

Now he would insist that, given her progress, she be released from the hospital and he be allowed to see her.

But this determination vanished when Zheng entered the room, his face grave with concern.

'There has been a problem,' he said, taking me by the wrist. Chloe had experienced a massive seizure. It had come out of nowhere. The doctors had put her back into an induced coma while they ran tests, fearing brain damage.

Sebastian collapsed into a chair, all the strength draining from his legs.

Zheng lowered himself down across from me. He'd gone quiet. I had to prompt him. I remember asking at least three times. 'What did the tests find? Was her brain damaged? How bad was it?'

When still Zheng didn't answer, Sebastian leant over the table and repeated himself, loud and urgent. Needing to know. Zheng just stared at him, licking his lips. His eyes were moving, like a man trapped, trying to decide which way to flee.

He didn't want to tell me. I knew it was the worst thing possible. I knew she must be damaged beyond recovery. But then he squared his shoulders and shook his head.

The tests showed no negative impact on her cognitive function. She didn't have brain damage.

He said this looking me dead in the eye, Charlie.

Then Zheng took Sebastian's wrist again. He explained that while she was not brain damaged, the trauma from the seizure had been considerable, resulting in a significant side effect.

He said she had locked-in syndrome.

On the tape, Sebastian's voice was again close to the microphone, as if he were speaking bent over, his head in his hands.

It's like being a quadriplegic, Charlie. There was damage to the brain stem and she couldn't move her body. She couldn't speak either – but she was conscious. She could think and she could see. She could move her eyes. But she was locked inside her head.

Sebastian rushed his words, as if determined to tear the Band-Aid off and deliver the horrendous events before his emotions could get the better of him. My emotions weren't in control. I felt pain in my heart for Chloe. It was unbearable to think of her suffering like that. After such a long recovery from the horrific injuries caused by the car accident, now this.

I remember gripping the table as I listened to Zheng describe the situation. My first instinct was to go to her, to comfort her.

He told Zheng he wanted to see her, that he would detour through Hong Kong on the way back to Canberra. That he would delay his return to Australia.

'You can't see her.' Zheng dismissed me, not considering it for a second. I shouted at him. I insisted. But then he lost his shit. He pounded on the table and told me that locked-in syndrome was not curable. That we needed to focus on Chloe's care for the long-term now.

Zheng said he had already struggled to get commitment from Qiu to ensure Chloe received the treatments she required. She needed physical therapy to maintain her muscle strength and function. She'd been recieving speech therapy and now there would be a whole new raft of technologies and support to help her communicate. She had to learn to work with assistive technology to help with daily tasks. She would require a whole multidisciplinary team to help her adapt to the condition and achieve the highest level of function.

He said to me, 'All of this requires money and resources. None of this will happen if you betray our commitments now. You will put her care in jeopardy.' He was back on his feet, back to pointing his finger into my chest. Once more, he wore that furious expression on his face, as if I were to blame. 'You need to go back to Australia and do more, work harder. This is the only priority if you are truly loyal to my daughter.'

I flung the steering wheel to the left and dragged the car from the road in a shower of gravel. I had driven out of the CBD and was beyond the airport. Residential Canberra had been replaced with business parks. The road was deserted, uncurbed and semi-rural. Beyond a sagging barbed wire fence, I could make out the faint silhouettes of rusted sheds and water tanks. No other streetlights.

I didn't remember having driven here, so fixed had I been on Sebastian's narrative.

The revelation was shocking.

Oh my God. Chloe. But my mind was again racing and my political instinct was calling bullshit. While I didn't doubt Zheng would have despaired at his daughter's condition, Chloe's seizure seemed to have occurred at precisely the moment Sebastian was pulling against the yoke of his commitment to the MSS. This new condition forced him to recommit to Qiu indefinitely. This felt convenient for Zheng, who increasingly reminded me of Sebastian's father, forcing his son to grind through exhaustion to do as he was commanded, fists raised in a sparring stance, shouting at his son: 'Jab, cross, slip, roll.' And Sebastian, as if triggered by a stage hypnotist, moving faster, slapped when he slowed, increasing his pace, continuing to drill through the burn as sweat poured into his eyes and his lungs felt as if they were going to explode.

Sebastian had committed to 'do more, work harder' and Zheng approved and sent him on to Australia, promising that in return for his efforts, Chloe would be given all the care she needed.

They were allies again.

I trusted him, Charlie. Nothing mattered more to either of us than Chloe's care.

I think I groaned out loud as he said this … but then the squealing of tires on bitumen tore me from my thoughts, and the concern I felt towards Sebastian drained away, replaced with concern for myself.

A black SUV, headlights blinding on high beam, skidded to a halt in a shower of gravel in front of my Astina.

The doors opened and two men climbed out. As they began walking towards me, I recognised both of them. One tall, but this time without his backpack. The other, stockier, his beard like a sea captain's. Jacob.

Even as they shouted at me, I dragged the Astina into reverse, backing away from them as quickly as the old car would go. They chased at first, my door handle just out of reach, which is what saved me in the end. By the time they realised they wouldn't catch me on foot, they were over 100 metres from their SUV. Slamming on the brakes, I crunched the transmission into drive and accelerated straight back up the road again. They flung themselves out of the way, and my last sight as I accelerated around the abandoned SUV was of them picking themselves up from the dusty verge.

CHAPTER THIRTY-ONE

Dust and moths in headlights. The Astina's back wheels sliding on the road, the engine grinding as I pushed the accelerator to the floor, hoping to Christ the head gasket didn't blow. I kept glancing into the rear-view mirror. Looking to see if the SUV was following me. There was no sign of them yet, but it wouldn't take long.

The road wound through paddocks. The darkness was broken at intervals by lonely farm houses. I cursed myself for speeding away from the CBD, the opposite direction to my home, my tape recorder, and the plan to make Swanny a copy of Sebastian's confession.

At least I knew now who had been following me since I left Parliament House. But why had they pursued me out here?

Swanny's voice. *I reckon it's you ASIO is going to arrest tomorrow morning for the blackmail of Sebastian Adler.*

A chill seized my body then, as in the rear-view mirror distant headlights pierced the dark. ASIO again. It had to be. Coming on fast along the empty night road.

Jesus Christ! I pounded the steering wheel. Why were they doing this? Had Jacob and his mate driven all this way out here to arrest me? Why couldn't it wait a few more hours until the meeting tomorrow? What had made things so urgent they needed to swoop in tonight?

My mind strained to understand, to think through the politics and conspiracy of what was happening. But I couldn't think over

Sebastian's voice. His narrative had increased in urgency, as if he was channeling the determination he'd felt leaving Shanghai. He insisted I focus on his confession, as if he somehow knew my attention was diverted by those headlights now following in my rear-view mirror.

Locked-in syndrome, Charlie. Can you imagine it? I couldn't think of anything else as I arrived home in Australia. You met me at the airport with that sympathetic look in your eyes. But I had no time for your kindness. I was watching videos about patients with locked-in syndrome. Those that had recovered partial movements, or the ability to communicate using technology. They gave me hope, but they also filled me with horror. They told stories of being in pain in their hospital bed, unable to move, or speak, or ask for help. Just screaming in their head, like a prisoner in the darkest dungeon, while lying silently, surrounded by family. I imagined it as hell.

And as he went about reintegrating with Canberra colleagues and starting his new job in the Foreign Minister's office, outwardly he was charming and capable, a dependable ministerial advisor. Inside, he too was screaming.

The photos changed. Or maybe I changed, looking at them. No longer was I searching for signs of her recovery. Rather, I saw myself reflected in her gaze. Her eyes staring into the camera lens, as if knowing I was staring back and desperate to send me a message. Her face, while still bearing scars from the burns, had mostly recovered, and yet now the left side had collapsed, paralysed like her body. It drooped, lower than the right. Zheng said it was positive that she could control the right side of her face. She could blink, and there were technologies that could help her, computer systems that she could learn to use to communicate. But, he said, all of that costed hundreds of thousands of US dollars. He needed to convince Qiu and his people that they should pay. This was just one of many costs for her medical team, for her hospital room, her rehabilitation.

Sebastian needed to do more, work harder, to make sure Chloe had the best care.

Fortunately, he was well positioned. The intelligence he could access assigned to the Foreign Minister's office as a departmental advisor eclipsed anything he could get his hands on in Shanghai.

He threw himself into the task.

I gave them Cabinet papers, briefings from the National Security Committee, classified Five Eyes intelligence. Anything that I could get my hands on.

His MSS handlers were delighted, yet cautious. No longer on their home turf, the weekly exchange became a dead drop. The memory card and a USB stick in an empty packet of Winfield Blues, wedged between the wood of a park bench on Federation Mall, a short walk from Parliament House, where Sebastian would eat his lunch.

It was information about the Chinese diaspora that interested them most. The MSS were obsessed with suppressing 'five poisons'. Democracy activists, Taiwanese activists, Uyghur activists, Tibetan activists, and Falun Gong. They wanted to know who was making representations to the Minister on behalf of these groups.

And Sebastian gave them all up.

Records of conversations, names and addresses of individuals and their families, Australian citizens, intimidated in their homes in Sydney and Melbourne, their families in China threatened unless they returned to face charges. Australian citizens disappearing the moment they got off the plane.

Jesus Christ.

I betrayed them all, Charlie. And I didn't care.

His fear for Chloe, and his determination to help her, made him harder. If he had retained any capacity to feel for others, or reflect on his actions while in Shanghai, by the time he was back in Canberra, he had none.

I didn't think of what I was doing as a crime. When I started working for the MSS in Shanghai, I didn't have time to think about it. By the time I was back in Canberra, I didn't think about it because it had become a way of life. There was no debate in my mind. I just had to do what needed to be done.

A farm driveway was coming up on my left, a hundred metres away, with a line of ghost gums shading the front fence, breaking the line of sight from the road into the property. I couldn't outrun the SUV, so I needed to hide. I snapped off my headlights and brought the car to a halt in a cloud of dust and squealing brakes.

Then I was out, cursing my unfit body as I wheezed towards the gate. My hands shaking, I unhooked the chain, working fast before the SUV lights emerged over the ridge. With a heave that twisted something painful in my shoulder, I shoved it open, then limped back to the car and drove through, stumbling to close the gate behind me before parking in the shadow of the gums.

I sat in the dark cabin, waiting for the SUV to arrive, hoping to God it would drive on past and I'd be able to head back the way we'd come to the relative safety of Canberra.

Fucking ASIO, Charlie …

I did a double take at the stereo. It was as though Sebastian were sitting beside me, his eyes like mine locked on the headlights approaching.

Everything got harder when McCubbin became Director-General.

'Did they chase people through the night in black SUVs?' I whispered in the darkness.

He ignored me.

McCubbin released a risk assessment saying foreign intelligence services were trying to compromise Australian politicians. He said this was the tip of the iceberg in a concerted influence operation to make Australia the weak link in Five Eyes. I don't know where he got his intelligence from. The MSS went apeshit.

They activated their influencers. The property developer peak bodies, the wine makers, the universities, the farming bodies, the international students, all condemning the new ASIO head's 'fear mongering' and 'Cold War mindset', accusing McCubbin of risking the lucrative trade relationship with China.

But McCubbin didn't stop. He pushed the PM and the Foreign Minister to drive far-reaching counter-espionage laws through Parliament.

The MSS were aghast when I told them it was coming.

I heard him swallow, then take in a deep breath, preparing for something he'd been working up to.

That's when they told me to seduce McCubbin's daughter …

The SUV hurtled by as Sebastian's words reverberated in the Astina's silent darkness.

What had he said? McCubbin's daughter? He meant Cassie. The marriage, his family ... Jesus, his kids too? All a sham? All at the instruction of the MSS, because he was so intent on saving Chloe? Because betrayal was a way of life now and he was beyond caring about anyone or anything.

I shuddered as the other vehicle disappeared over the ridge and darkness consumed my reflection.

Unable to process this new revelation, I opened the farm gate and floored the accelerator. The wheels spun, the back of the car fishtailed. I skidded out of the gate and onto the road, driving back towards Canberra.

I had given ASIO the slip for the moment.

If only I could have outrun Sebastian's confession.

By the time I reached home, I no longer admired Sebastian's determination to help Chloe. I thought he was a monster. If he'd been standing in front of me, I would have spat in his face.

Tell them I cared, even though they'll think I didn't care.

I snarled in the darkness, recollecting his words from the beginning of the confession. Jesus Christ, did he really expect me to tell people he cared? He didn't care! He didn't fucking care. He cared about nothing but his obsession ...

I dragged the cassette from the tape deck of the Astina and stuffed it in my pocket. I just wanted to get inside. To lock myself in a darkened room with a drink and a smoke and not hear another word.

My mid-century townhouse had a garden that opened into Telopea Park. Rather than putting the Astina into the garage, I parked down the road and then, with an excess of caution, detoured through the historic Atlas pines and old, established hedges towards my back door. From here, I could just glimpse the street and keep my eye out for the black SUV.

As I walked, I thought through Sebastian's shocking confession about his wife.

Zheng had given him the instruction to seduce Cassandra McCubbin during one of their monthly meetings, which occurred when Sebastian travelled to Sydney to visit his mother.

The uni near Mum's house had a Confucius Institute. One of the language tutors was an MSS operative, and when I came, they'd put me in a study room with a laptop. Zheng would be waiting online.

As he had in Shanghai, Zheng fed Sebastian's determination during these exchanges by telling him about the improvements in Chloe's condition. They'd detected movements in her fingers. They were working with her to make sounds with her mouth.

At first, Sebastian resisted the instruction to seduce McCubbin's daughter. He accused Zheng of driving a wedge between him and Chloe, but Zheng had played his cards to perfection.

He upped the ante, Charlie. He told me he had a message from Chloe, and I stopped fighting.

Sebastian explained Zheng had had the idea of asking Chloe to spell a message in English. It was like a game Chloe had played with her mother when she was a child. He would read the alphabet out loud carefully, giving her an opportunity to blink when she wanted to form a word. Each time she blinked, he noted the letter, then started the alphabet again. It was exhausting for Chloe, who still struggled to manipulate the right side of her face, but Zheng said she was getting stronger each day. On the video chat, he held up a sheet of paper to show her transcribed message.

It said, 'From my bed, I see Lamma Island and think of you.'

A sob broke from Sebastian's mouth. Then the sound of him sucking in air. I could imagine him squeezing his fists together. Steadying himself.

Zheng had other messages for him, words of gratitude and love and encouragement – which must have sounded so foreign in his mouth, rather than hearing directly from Chloe.

It was like we were reconnected, Charlie. The possibility that we could communicate, beyond just imagining her voice in my head, or trying to see messages in her eyes. Now she could speak and listen.

Zheng said it was proof that what Sebastian was doing was

paying off. He told Sebastian he could send messages to Chloe at any time.

Zheng said this was all progress, and that we needed to make sure that her treatment continued to ensure more progress. Qiu was paying for specialists. Breakthroughs were happening every week. We couldn't stop it now!

And so Sebastian recommitted himself. Just as he always did, accepting the circumstances thrust upon him, putting his head down and doing his best, just as he had done in the face of his father's bullying, or his mother's neglect. He did more, he worked harder. He agreed to Zheng's demands, insisting only that Zheng would promise never to tell Chloe about his infidelity.

All this made me recalibrate my memory of that night before the wedding, how he'd drunk himself delirious in a speakeasy bar in Canberra. He'd clutched me across the table and said, 'I love her,' and at first I'd thought he meant Cassie. I'd thought his marriage was an act of selfishness. But he did it because he had hope. Zheng kept giving him hope. And this, in Sebastian's own twisted logic, justified his next actions. The relationship with Cassie, the marriage, conceiving the twins.

All acts of obsessive loyalty to Chloe.

Further into the double life he went, locking himself deeper into his own mind. It must have taken so much energy to hide this secret life from the world. The roaring tragedy playing out in his head. But in a way, it was like any other long-term addiction. Ever the high-functioning addict, just like his father, he was maintaining a successful outer life while hiding the deep flaws in his character and lifestyle. An entire secret existence. A hidden family. In his own way, he was just as locked-in as Chloe.

A year after the MSS had instructed Sebastian to seduce McCubbin's daughter, both Sebastian and Cassie were posted to the Australian Embassy in Beijing. It was unclear if some other asset had pulled the strings to get this done. They were promoted into new roles: Sebastian as Commercial Counsellor, Cassie as the Assistant Defence Attaché, supporting the Australia China Defence Strategic Dialogue.

Being thrown together gave Sebastian the opportunity to build the relationship as instructed. They stayed late at the Embassy, writing briefs, organising the minister's folders, checking venues and other logistics to prepare for the strategic dialogue. Car pick ups, translation, media releases, hotel bookings.

I can still hear Sebastian retelling the story of their romance to his kids, yet he never mentioned how during those long nights he coaxed her to let slip classified intel that perhaps, of itself, was immaterial, but as with pieces in a jigsaw, he could assemble a picture over time and report back to his MSS handlers.

They talked about the western response to Beijing's unilateral declaration of an Air Defence Identification Zone that included disputed territories with Japan and South Korea; about regional reactions to the Scarborough Shoal standoff, Japan's nationalisation of the Senkaku/Diaoyu Islands; of the West's appetite to accept Beijing's crackdowns in Xinjiang as legitimate actions in the War Against Terror.

This way of extracting intel through conversation was Sebastian's attempt to avoid an intimate relationship with Cassie. But after she was promoted to her boss's job, her value to the MSS increased. Zheng visited Sebastian one morning and, almost apologetically, explained that reporting on conversations with Cassie was no longer enough. The MSS required real-time intelligence. Sebastian was issued an encrypted USB device, smaller than the one he'd used in Shanghai, and was told to make regular extractions from Cassie's laptop.

I had no choice, Charlie. We became intimate. It wasn't easy for me.

On the tape, his voice was hostile, as if covering his shame with anger.

I started staying the night in her apartment in the diplomatic compound. We would turn out the light around 11 pm. I'd doze until 2 am, then leave her sleeping and creep downstairs to conduct the extraction. It became a ritual that has continued to this day.

The extraction took around seven to ten minutes, which is why he did it in the small hours of the morning. It was also why such a small device was ideal. It was subtle enough to be overlooked, if not scrutinised. In emergencies, it bought him some time.

Only once did Cassie wake up and come looking for me. I feigned sleeplessness because of stress at the office, and we made love on the lounge as the USB did its work. That was a long time ago, Charlie.

Waves of revulsion shook me as I imagined Sebastian prowling round his house late at night, betraying his wife. While I had never liked Cassie, what Sebastian had done to her was a desecration of trust and intimacy, and I hated him as he played for sympathy on the cassette.

Was it to Cassie he wanted me to give his message? *Tell them I cared, even though they'll think I didn't care.* Because if it was, I didn't believe him. I wouldn't do it.

I knew this was likely the hardest part of his confession. He couldn't stand the idea of anyone not loving him, even when confessing to something as shameful as this.

Not everything in that relationship was a lie, Charlie. Not the twins. I love my kids. You tell them what I said.

I didn't want to listen anymore. I didn't want to know the hideous secret he was still to reveal: what he'd done to Kai Birch or what had happened in Hong Kong. I just wanted it to stop. To copy the cassette, to hand it over to ASIO and Swanny, and never think of Sebastian again.

But there was still Chloe.

I needed to know what had happened to her.

Of course I had to listen. Of course I'd finish it.

But I'd need a stiff drink first.

There was a bottle of Lagavulin and a fresh pack of cigarettes on my study table, beside a pile of books and newspapers. With these creature comforts, I could make it through the final side of the cassette. Then I'd make the copy for Swanny. Then I'd be done.

❖

I reached out to unlock the back door, but found it swinging in the evening breeze. The wood around the lock was splintered, as if it had been opened with a crowbar. I stepped into the kitchen. The lights were off, but the big mid-century windows allowed moonlight to illuminate the room. The place had been turned over. Kitchen drawers hung open and cabinets spilled their contents onto the floor. I stood motionless in the dark, listening for signs of movement, terrified that whoever had done this might still be there. I wanted to turn on my heels and run, but I knew I needed that tape recorder. I had to make a copy of the confession and get it to Swanny.

I crept forwards into the lounge room, navigating by my phone's torchlight. Here too, the room had been trashed. Books pulled from the shelf, drawers left open. What the fuck had they been looking for? And who was 'they'? It had to be ASIO. But would ASIO come in the dead of night and do this without a warrant?

I paused, listening for footsteps on the floor above, then moved, as quietly as I could, to the bottom of the stairs, using the torchlight to step over fallen debris.

I was halfway up the stairs when the torch on my phone went out. The screen burst with colour and the old-fashioned telephone ring shattered the silence. My heart pounded, trying to cancel the incoming call.

Henry fucking Mallet again!

I punched the reject button and stood listening in the darkness, feeling my pulse pounding in my neck. If anyone was upstairs, they sure as hell knew I was here now.

With a sigh, I climbed to the second floor, expecting at any moment to be attacked or arrested. But upstairs, it was just the same carnage. In my bedroom and the spare room. Wardrobes open. Clothing on the bed, mattresses thrown against the wall.

Outrage overcame fear. This was a fucking violation. How dare they come into my home and do this? How had I become so tainted that ASIO felt they could treat me like this? It was fucking Sebastian's fault. It was my proximity to him that had made me a person of interest, that had compromised me. Guilt by association. With Sebastian, with his secrets, and now with his dirty villainous fucking confession.

My hand went to the tape in my jacket pocket, realisation chiming like a bell.

Sebastian's confession. They must know about it. That must be what they were looking for.

I remembered the thin man in the suit, standing in the shadows outside the Press Club. Had he been listening to Swanny and me? Did he know about the taped confession? Did he know I was trying to get a copy to Swanny as insurance before the meeting tomorrow morning?

My heart skipped a beat, and I ran, stumbling into the study. Newspapers on the floor, my desk drawers turned over, bookshelves a shambles and then, dread seizing my throat, I saw the tape recorder on the floor. It was smashed. Like someone had put the heel of their boot into it. A pile of busted plastic and springs. Beyond repair. The little case next to it where I kept my bootlegs and mix tapes. Cassettes I'd had since high school, all empty. All gone. They'd known. They must have known about the confession and they'd taken everything, hoping to find it.

Headlights in the street drew me to the window. The black SUV had pulled up outside the townhouse. I ran down the stairs, into the kitchen, and out the back door as an aggressive banging came from the front of the house. I was scared and overwhelmed, but most of all, I was confused. If it was ASIO who had trashed my house, why would they come back? Why would they knock, if earlier they'd broken in with crowbars?

❖

I ran into Telopea Park, wheezing and feeling an icy chill down my spine, cringing away from the shadows of trees that now looked like the silhouettes of hidden watchers, a camouflaged pursuit. If ASIO hadn't broken in, then who? Who else would be threatened by Sebastian's confession?

The answer was suddenly obvious. A horrid, simple logic.

It must be the MSS. Sebastian's handlers. He said they had people in Canberra. Of course, they'd want to cover their tracks. Any confession he'd made would be dangerous to their enterprise in Australia. They wouldn't want the tape getting out. I was being hunted by ASIO *and* the MSS.

I ran, shaking my head and cursing into the wind. Gum trees, like a line of jeering schoolboys on either side of the path, thrust their limbs into the sky, as if delighting in my misfortune.

I was fucked. They'd smashed my tape recorder. How could I make a copy of Sebastian's confession now?

Telopea Park is narrow. A storm water drain runs down its centre, criss-crossed by a handful of bridges along the length of the park. I crossed at the nearest point, then knelt, sweating and heaving for breath in the shadows of a waratah shrub, looking back the way I came, waiting for pursuers. When I satisfied myself I wasn't being followed, I pulled out my phone with trembling hands and called Swanny. He answered almost immediately, and I felt a flood of relief to hear his familiar voice. At that precise moment, he felt like the only person in the world I could trust.

'Charlie. What's happening?'

I swallowed, unsure about what I should say on the phone. But what else could I do? I needed to tell him about the situation.

'Mate, someone's been inside my house. They've turned it over.'

I heard the concern in his voice. 'Do you still have the tape?'

'I've got it. But it looks like the only thing that's gone from the house is old cassette tapes. Same vintage.'

'Jesus. You think they were looking for ...?' He let his words trail off as if he, too, was conscious of others listening.

'Yeah. I do. They also smashed my tape recorder. It's fucked.'

I could hear him calculating. I knew he'd be worried about me. But the lure of the story was also taking hold of him. If intruders looking for the tape had turned my house over, then likely my story was the massive scoop I had said it was.

'Well mate, maybe you should just give me the tape. I can keep it safe.'

But I was already shaking my head. I couldn't give it to him. I needed to give it to ASIO. If Swanny was right and Katrina was intent on arresting me tomorrow for blackmail or whatever trumped up charge, the cassette was, as Sebastian had described, my 'get out of jail free card'. I needed it with me when I went to rebut their charges. But I also needed Swanny to have a copy, in case ASIO wanted to make both me and the cassette disappear.

'I need to make a copy, Swanny. I need a tape recorder.'

'Yeah, okay,' he said, and I imagined his tangle of red and grey eyebrows creasing as he racked his brain. 'Look, there's an old tape recorder in the press rooms in Parliament House.'

'I can't go back up the Hill, Swanny. They'll have people up there. If I'm seen ...'

'Yeah, right. I can get the press club to check?'

'No, mate. The same thing. I can't go anywhere anyone might see me. Journos, ASIO, other staffers. I need to keep out of sight until I have a copy and it's with you.'

I could hear voices now behind him. Some sort of commotion. It didn't sound like the Press Club bar.

'Where are you, Swanny?'

'I'm at Parliament House. The PM's holding a press conference.'

I checked my watch. It was almost 10 pm, an extraordinary time for a presser.

'There's shit going down in Sydney and Melbourne. Many people defying curfew and out on the streets protesting. Apparently, there's a massive push on social media, all the conspiracy channels that came up during COVID. They're saying the government is going to institute martial law because the financial system is collapsing. Apparently there are lines for blocks of people trying to get cash out from automatic tellers. Police are responding to incidents where ATMs are being rammed by cars, or detonated with explosives because they can't get their money. The PM's coming out to call for calm. It's pretty hairy out there. Lots of clashes between police and protestors. So much for social cohesion during a crisis.'

Between the horrors of Sebastian's confession and the stress of being chased by ASIO and the MSS, I had forgotten about what was going on in the rest of the country. A thought flickered in my mind, wondering whether the social media disinformation came from the same players who'd hacked the energy network, or whether these days it was just the automatic reaction of a polarised society to any form of chaos. But what was going on in the wider world would have to wait, pushed aside by the immediacy of my own dire circumstances.

'Charlie, I've got to go. The PM's coming out. I'll see you in an hour. You're going to need to work out a way to copy that tape, or I'm going to need to take yours. I'm sorry, mate. If I think of anything, I'll text you. Got to go. The presser's starting.'

He hung up, and I was alone in the darkness.

I walked hopelessly back to the Astina, constantly checking behind me, and once more got in the driver's seat. I cupped my forehead in my palm. In the dashboard light, I could see my reflection. I looked haggard. I felt old and alone and wished Swanny had blown off the presser and driven over to meet me so we could work this out together. I needed a friend.

I knocked on the glass. Two knocks with my knuckle, like a confident adolescent. Then whispered, hearing my mother's voice, 'Go with this boy. He'll look after you.'

But Sebastian wasn't looking after me anymore. He'd abandoned me. Not just today, but years ago. That night, when Hong Kong was being handed back to China. Ever since that night, he hadn't looked after me. He'd used me. Just like he'd used the trust his government put in him. Just like he'd used his own wife.

Poor Cassie. It was so awful. I winced, trying to understand how this man who I'd admired all my life could be the same grub who sat in his study confessing such awful things, when only a wall divided him from his wife and his kids.

And then it hit me …

He'd sat in his study confessing. Confessing into a tape recorder. I'd seen it in his study when I'd visited earlier in the day, the same one on which years ago I'd made the original mix tape for Chloe. ASIO hadn't taken it. I was a fool for not having thought of this before. Cassie had even called me earlier in the night. She'd wanted to talk. So why not? I'd go to her and check in and somehow make a copy of his confession.

I sent Cassie a message, and she replied almost immediately. It was late, but she wasn't sleeping. Yes, she wanted to talk. Come for a drink.

I had hope again. A way of getting my insurance. Of protecting myself. From ASIO, from the MSS.

From everyone.

I turned on the Astina, and pressed the cassette back into the stereo.

CHAPTER THIRTY-TWO

In the years that followed his marriage to Cassie, Sebastian had two more postings in China (as Consul-General to Chengdu, then back to the Embassy as Deputy Head of Mission), and a six-month period in Canberra when he and Cassie returned to Australia for the birth of the twins. He never stopped working for the MSS, or doing Zheng's bidding, and by the time his last posting in Beijing was concluding he felt closer than ever to the man he really considered his father-in-law.

Sebastian would meet Zheng in a pavilion in the Temple of the Sun Park near the Australian Embassy in Chaoyang District. It was a strategic location, chosen so they could observe their surroundings and benefit from the natural cover of the elderly locals dancing and watching Tai Chi practitioners beneath the cherry blossoms and gingko trees. The ambient noise generated by the folk songs or the tour groups along the shaded paths around the lake masked their conversations, and if they saw any foreigners walking towards them, they would melt away into the crowds before being seen.

Amid this privacy, they confided in each other with the familiarity and mutual reliance of a father and son–in–law, even as they tiptoed around the fact that Sebastian now had a family with another woman.

Zheng avoided discussing Cassie. He left the MSS handlers to receive the weekly USB rip from her laptop and spoke of the relationship only through euphemism, referring to Sebastian's wedding in Canberra as his 'personal engagements in Australia'.

The birth of Sebastian's twins was 'recent progress' 'worthy of congratulations'.

Sebastian took Zheng's discretion as kindness, as he did Zheng's generosity in helping him deepen his relationship with Chloe.

For many years, Sebastian had continued to receive the weekly photographs of Chloe, but over time, the images grew much the same. Chloe propped up in bed, one side of her face paralysed and drooping lower than the other.

I confess I stopped looking at her, Charlie. Her gaze made me sad. She seemed blank and void. And it was hard to discern the progress Zheng described.

It was Zheng who suggested they replace the photographs with correspondence. He explained how Qiu's people had installed an eye tracking system connected to a computer interface in her hospital room. It still relied on Chloe winking, but now the computer could track her gaze, detecting letters and predicting the words she was after. It was exhausting, and her progress was slow, but over time she could write longer messages, expressing herself and reconnecting with Sebastian in a deeper way. Zheng would be their intermediary. A discreet chaperone, ferrying correspondence between them.

I was self-conscious at first, and I'd just say something stilted and conservative. 'Tell her I love her, and I am working hard for her ...'

But Zheng urged Sebastian to write down his messages to Chloe, allowing him to express himself more openly.

It was strange, in a way, Charlie. Where once we had hidden our relationship from Zheng, now he encouraged us to be more intimate.

In the cabin of the Astina, I sucked in a breath through my nose, realising I was grinding my jaw again. There was much I didn't like about what I was hearing.

Writing to her became a sort of outlet for me. It's hard to explain. I would tell her how much I longed for her, how I thought about her always as I led this double life, stuck in my head.

Many of Chloe's early replies seemed self-conscious too. Sebastian described some of them as reading like a motivational manual.

||*Thank you for working hard for me. You must keep going. You are making a difference.*||

But then, around the time the photographs stopped, her messages changed, and it was like Chloe had returned. Sebastian could only ever read each message once, before Zheng would snatch away the correspondence written on the letterhead of Matilda Hospital. But some lines or phrases stayed with him and he could recite them as if they were the quotations he'd learnt by heart for an English exam or debating tournament

||*I exist beneath this suffocating veil. I won't be snuffed out. I dream of making a difference. I dream of freedom.*||

||*In all this fucking isolation, I cling to the memories of freedom that flicker within me, refusing to be extinguished ...*||

I felt a shiver down my spine as Sebastian recited her words and I recognised Chloe's voice. That turn of phrase seemed unchanged from when we'd met. Poetic lines, influenced by the angst-ridden lyrics of the bands we both loved. It was her voice. Sad yet ferocious, determined to rebel against her situation.

||*I am a prisoner in my own head. I won't stop until I'm free.*||

Over time, Sebastian observed a desperate tone to her messages, which made him worry.

||*I feel laden with unspoken truths. Love weighs me down like the sea.*||

||*I ache to break free from my mind, to reclaim the thoughts and emotions muted by this repression.*||

Zheng dismissed Sebastian's questions about Chloe's mental state with the same old refrain. 'She is improving. Of course she is angry and troubled by her condition. That is why we must keep helping her.'

I asked him to let me talk to her. A web chat online. I knew there was technology that could give voice to her words or at least let her type and respond in real time.

Zheng refused. He said it was too much for Chloe. It took her more than a minute to spell out a word. She didn't want to talk to Sebastian this way. Of course, this only made Sebastian more desperate to see her. Zheng told him it could never happen. He reminded Sebastian how, more than ever, with all the support Chloe required, they couldn't risk angering Qiu.

Not long after this, Zheng informed him that at the end of his posting in Beijing, it had been decided that Sebastian needed to leverage his father-in-law for a position with ASIO.

It was a gut blow, Charlie.

Out of nowhere, he said the MSS needed me in Canberra. McCubbin's Foreign Interference legislation had passed Parliament after years of delay. The MSS wanted intel about ASIO's efforts to disrupt its influence operations. And just like that, I was meant to go home and desert her …

But, for the first time since becoming an asset of the MSS, Sebastian disobeyed. Rather than use his influence to get a job with McCubbin, he leveraged his father-in-law to secure the role of Australian Consul-General in Hong Kong.

It was perfect. A four-year posting in the same city as Chloe. I was sure Zheng would come around, given all our discussions and all the messages between Chloe and I that I knew he had read. I presumed he'd understand. I presumed he too was worried about her mental health and that, for once, he'd forget his obligations to the Party and put his daughter first. I even hoped he'd help me find a way of getting the MSS over the line.

But to Sebastian's surprise, Qiu and the MSS were not the problem. His MSS handlers were supportive of the senior diplomatic posting. It was Zheng who was furious. He exploded at Sebastian for disobeying instructions. He called him unreliable and self-interested, and he refused to meet with him for the remainder of his posting in Beijing. It would be six months before they spoke again.

And meanwhile, the correspondence with Chloe went silent.

❖

Despite the fallout with Zheng, the posting to Hong Kong went ahead, only for Sebastian to arrive and find the city in flames. Tear gas and rubber bullets had been fired at a group protesting outside the LegCo complex against the Chief Executive's extradition bill. Footage of street battles between riot police and black-clad protestors with yellow hard hats, goggles and gas masks was all over the internet. Global news and social media were filled with conspiracies, triads in white T-shirts beating protestors, tanks and armoured vehicles on the border of Shenzhen threatening to cross into Hong Kong and restore order.

Sebastian was thrown into this chaos, and Zheng could ignore him no longer. Only weeks after arriving, he was summoned to a private dining room upstairs at the China Club – the very same place where Tang would see them together, years later. Zheng explained the MSS needed intel fast. The political situation in the city was deteriorating. Sebastian was to acquire intelligence on any plans from Five Eyes partners to criticise the heavy-handed Hong Kong police response to the protestors, or to make allegations that Beijing was tearing up the principle of One Country, Two Systems.

They were so sensitive about public statements and embarrassing Beijing. They wanted any whisper of criticism and support so they could use influence or other means to shut it down. Frankly, I just saw it as an opportunity to return myself to Zheng's good graces.

Just like high school, when he'd detect my anger and come rushing back to our friendship, so he now recommitted himself to Zheng, unable to disappoint his master after so many years. Unable to tolerate the thought he was not loved, overachieving in his career as an MSS asset, to which he suborned all the access and privilege of his role as Australia's Consul-General to Hong Kong.

He delivered. As he always delivered.

He provided advanced copies of statements from the British and Australian governments, as well as intelligence from the US Consulate detailing Congress considerations on revoking Hong Kong's special trading status, the State Department deliberations on sanctions. He used his position as Consul-General to identify and collect names of influential members of Hong Kong society who were supportive of the protestors, and he handed their details over to Zheng and the MSS.

I didn't care about any of the politics, Charlie. I gave them all the intel that came across my desk as Consul-General. I was desperate to reconnect with Zheng, but most of all to talk to him again about Chloe, to hear from her again. Six months had passed without news of her progress, and when last I'd received her messages, she seemed so despondent. I needed to know she was okay.

But as the city began to resemble a war zone, Zheng grew incoherent with rage. Every time they met, he only fumed about western double standards, US influence operations, the 'brainwashed' young protestors.

When he raged like this, he had no time for talking about Chloe. My role returned to that of a pupil he needed to convince, reciting a roll call of US betrayals: The Opium Wars, US troops deployed against the Boxer Uprising, President Wilson ceding Shandong territories to the Japanese, US denying military support against the Japanese invasion of Manchuria, rapacious US capital seeking to undermine CCP rule, increased weapon sales to Taiwan, US incursions in China's territorial waters, US interference in CCP authority via religious groups and civil organisations, NGOs and black hands. A century of humiliation, the Thucydides trap, a new Cold War …

Zheng would shut down any conversation about Chloe before it could start. At their first meeting, he warned Sebastian not to try to visit her. Police guarded her ward. The MSS would know if he tried, and any unsanctioned visit would jeopardise Qiu's support for her treatment.

'She is fine. She is improving. There is no time for sending love letters. We need to focus our minds on our work.' That's what he insisted every time I brought her up, Charlie. And if I pushed?

'You know the answer to that question.'

'I knew this is what would happen if you came here.'

'Do not ask me again.'

After two months of these rejections, Sebastian realised Zheng was as fixated on keeping him away from Chloe as he had been when they first met in Hong Kong. So he did what he should have done the minute he got off the plane. He took a taxi to Matilda Hospital.

❖

Sebastian's heart pounded as he walked along the hospital's mosaic-tiled passage where Liu Hui had led him a lifetime earlier. He had no plan as to what he would do if he were stopped by security. The memories of his Hong Kong incarceration were still vivid in his mind and made his palms sweat as he walked.

But the fear of arrest was secondary.

I was more concerned about what I'd say to Chloe. I didn't want it to be awkward.

It would have been a nerve-wracking experience under normal circumstances, having not seen each other for so long. But the unknown of how he would communicate with Chloe through the various machines that Zheng had described heightened his anxiety.

Zheng had said it took her over a minute to blink each letter. That she grew exhausted. I didn't want to embarrass her. I just wanted to lie beside her on the bed, staring out towards Lamma.

There were no police officers guarding her door. That was the first thing. Rather than MSS agents, there were friendly, albeit surprised, nurses, who welcomed Sebastian to the maternity ward.

A female nurse with short hair led him through the locked doors to Chloe's wing. She exclaimed over her shoulder that Chloe was the longest patient in residence at the hospital. It was nice to see someone new visiting. Maybe something could be done.

Before Sebastian had time to dwell on what she meant, the nurse thrust her ample hip against a heavy door, and they were standing in Chloe's room.

I knew as soon as I entered, everything was wrong, Charlie. It smelt wrong. It felt wrong. There was no hope in that room ...

It was dark. The curtains were drawn, hiding the ocean view. The nurse turned on the lamp, and Sebastian's eyes, expecting to see a room filled with rehabilitation equipment, instead found a sterile space, sparse and all but empty except for a few life support machines gathered like mourners in the corner.

Then he saw the figure in the bed, and couldn't stifle his cry.

I realised why the photos had stopped, Charlie. She had deteriorated. I saw how her face drooped on one side. But it was worse than that. She looked older, frail and grey. Fresh bandages wrapped around her chest and back as she heaved with coughing fits. Her face had lesions.

The nurse who had followed him into the room explained that she'd had pneumonia. Her lungs were damaged. She had ulcers because she hardly moved. She was growing resistant to the drugs and experiencing increased pain. The marks on her face were self inflicted ...

Before he could ask more, Chloe's eyes snapped open.

I stepped forwards, putting on a brave face.

He took her hand, bent before her intense gaze and whispered to rouse her, smiling hard.

I was struggling to comprehend. Where was her computer? The brain interface? The speech synthesis software? I asked the nurse. She didn't reply.

He asked Chloe to wink, as Zheng had recounted. Just give me a yes or no. Do you recognise me?

I recited the alphabet. Watching her eyes. Waiting for her to select a letter. Spell a word. Show me she was still there.

Chloe stared blindly.

Then her head twitched, her limbs strained, and I noticed the restraints.

Sebastian's voice on the cassette trembled.

She writhed, her back arching as her head snapped from side to side. Her arms pulled against the restraints, making the bed shake. And those eyes I'd stared at in the photographs, that I'd imagined speaking messages ...

They rolled back into her fucking head.

Christ, how could this happen the day I came, Charlie? Had Zheng been right to tell me to stay away? Was it my fault?

The nurse tried to calm him. This was nothing new, she said. The patient had been this way for years – before any of the current nursing staff had come to the hospital.

That made no sense, Charlie. I demanded to know about her rehabilitation. But the nurse said she knew nothing about any of that and ran off to fetch the doctor.

Sebastian backed away from the bed, unable to take his eyes off the writhing figure.

Her fingers were splayed as if she were casting a spell or the victim of some satanic curse. Her tongue lolled from her mouth.

A doctor hurried into the room and introduced himself in a quiet voice as Dr Lee. Sebastian said he was Chloe's fiancé and the young doctor looked surprised. He'd been caring for Chloe for at least six years, and had never heard there was a fiancé.

I tried to control my voice as I told him I had not been aware of her condition. That now I was here, I needed to know what was wrong with her …

Lee explained Chloe had experienced a massive seizure during a period of her induced coma. The impact on her cognitive function had been catastrophic. She had been in a vegetative state ever since.

Ever since … Ever since when? Had it happened in recent weeks? Or months?

Lee shook his head, consulted Chloe's chart and stated a date that placed the seizure at the time Sebastian was preparing to depart from his first posting in Shanghai.

Truth like a vicious blade pierced his lungs, and Sebastian couldn't breathe. His body trembled, and he felt his knees weakening beneath him.

They had lied. Zheng had lied to him.

I knew the exact conversation, Charlie. The Shanghai bomb shelter. Zheng looking me in the eye and telling me she was okay. That her body, not her mind, had suffered …

I was transfixed, listening to Sebastian's pain and fury. I was furious too. How could Sebastian have ever believed Zheng? Listening to his sorry tale, I'd had suspicions of Zheng from the outset – suspicions that were now vindicated. But I took no pleasure in it.

Poor, stupid, lovesick Sebastian. Desperate to believe in a future for him and Chloe. So desperate it blinded him to everything else. He was a clever guy, an intelligent guy. But never a political mind. Never an ounce of dog cunning that would have allowed him to conceive Zheng's deceit. They'd tricked him. Tricked him into returning to Canberra from Shanghai and continuing his service to the MSS. They'd tricked him into marriage. Into children. Betraying his country. He'd thought he was saving Chloe. But

Chloe was already gone, and they needed to keep him on the hook all these years.

The doctor confided that he had explained many times to the patient's father that recovery from her vegetative state was impossible. Most families in such a situation would not wish for the condition to be prolonged. Zheng, however, was insistent. The hospital must continue providing life-sustaining interventions. There were notes from Chloe's original medical team: artificial nutrition and hydration were to be provided to sustain Miss Zheng indefinitely.

The doctor touched Sebastian's wrist. The proposed alternative options to relieve Chloe's suffering were still available. Palliative medications could be administered to provide comfort and speed up the end-of-life process.

He could assist Chloe to die with dignity if I could convince the family that this was the kindest option.

Lee said he believed Zheng loved his daughter. He came often and sat beside Chloe. He spoke to her and read to her, holding her hand. But he knew the father was not acting in the interests of his daughter. That the decision should have been made years ago. Something had obstructed the father from acting, either his own grief or – and here he brought his lips closer to Sebastian's ear – some other external factor. Now Sebastian was here, perhaps he had the opportunity to make a difference.

Zheng's treachery made me want to scream, Charlie. But despite the doctor's explanation, there was one thing that still made no sense.

Who had written the messages Zheng had passed off as correspondence from Chloe?

I had been so convinced she was writing to me, Charlie. It was Chloe's voice. Chloe's frustration at being locked in. Zheng couldn't have written these all himself.

When Dr Lee left him alone, Sebastian rifled through the cupboards and drawers of Chloe's room. All the storage was empty, until he came to the drawers by her bedside table. Here he found a pile of softcover Moleskine notebooks in a rubber band.

I knew what they were, Charlie.

So did I. I remembered her writing in them as we spent those days together in Hong Kong. I remember one of these notebooks pressed inside the pages of her concrete textbook, and later her pulling a photograph of Sebastian, battered and bruised in a hospital ward.

They were her diaries, which, as I opened the cover of each, I realised covered the years before and after 1997.

Snatching them up, he noticed pages marked, passages of her diary entries circled. Alongside the diaries, a notepad, with the letter head of Matilda Hospital.

The nurse, still in the doorway, smiled sadly. 'Her father and the other young man. They copy them. I guess it's all they'll have left to remember what she was like.'

And it all fell into place.

He'd taken words from her diaries. She hadn't intended those lines for me. Zheng and Liu Hui had violated her secrets. They'd used them against me.

The messages he'd received from Chloe weren't descriptions of her life under paralysis. They were diary entries from a young woman, experiencing life under the paralysis of being Zheng's daughter. Of being dragged from Beijing to Hong Kong and told to forget what had happened to her mother. They were diary entries craving freedom, yet feeling shackled by her father's love and ideology.

I couldn't stand it any longer, Charlie. I called him on the phone right then. We never used the phone. I didn't care. I screamed down the line into his voicemail, calling him a liar and a cunt. That I knew he'd left her here like this. And that he'd lied about everything. I told him I was out. I was done with him and Qiu and all of it …

❖

He stayed another hour with her after that, gazing down at this woman he'd loved. To whom he'd been devoted for years. She looked old. But when he glanced at his own reflection in the mirror above the bed, he realised he was old, too. There were lines on his face. His hairline slightly receding. His lips thinning. Both their lives had been wasted. Used. Exploited.

As if made nervous by his brooding presence in the room, the nurses now began to linger in the doorway, keeping a watchful eye on him, and finally saying visiting time was over. Preparing to leave, he put the pile of her diaries into his satchel, then turned back to look at her one last time. He touched her hand as tears fell down his cheeks.

I was looking for any glimmer, Charlie. If she'd shown any glimmer of recognition, or that she was still there, it would have changed everything.

Instead, her body reacted violently to his tenderness. Once more, the lurching commenced, and in her spasms and grinding on the bed, he confirmed this was no longer Chloe. She was no longer the woman he had committed himself to. He turned and walked from the room.

For the first time in almost twenty years, he felt his priorities changing. He couldn't leave her like this. The doctor was right. She needed dignity and to rest in peace. He left the room with one simple notion chiming in his head.

Chloe's alive, but she needs to die.

CHAPTER THIRTY-THREE

When Sebastian emerged from the hospital, Liu Hui was leaning against a black Mercedes in the carpark. He nodded to the backseat and instructed Sebastian to get in, pulling up his white T-shirt to show the handgun in the top of his jeans.

As soon as I bent my head to get in the car, I saw Zheng. I needed no further prompting.

He lunged at his father-in-law, shouting, consumed by the rage of discovering the truth about Chloe.

I was ready to kill him, Charlie. I had him by the throat.

But the driver turned and cracked a heavy aluminium thermos across Sebastian's head. Pain shot through his temple, making him clutch his face and close his eyes. He heard Liu Hui getting into the car. Then that same voice that had told him in the Hong Kong police station that Chloe was dead.

'Hey Guĭzĭ, don't think I won't …'

He opened his eyes and saw the gun pointing at his chest.

The Mercedes pulled out of the hospital compound onto Mount Kellet Road, driving toward Central. Sebastian hunched against the door. The blow from the thermos had broken the skin at his temple. There was blood on his fingertips as he touched the wound.

Liu Hui kept his weapon trained on him as they drove.

Zheng spoke in a low tone, almost a murmur.

I remembered the night I'd hidden in Chloe's wardrobe watching him 'educating' his daughter, his hand on her shoulder, murmuring like a priest reciting a catechism.

He told me I shouldn't have gone to the hospital. That I'd betrayed him and betrayed Chloe. That this would be bad for her. That Qiu would be unhappy and we may have jeopardised Chloe's treatment.

When Sebastian spat that he knew Chloe wasn't receiving treatment, Zheng folded his arms and muttered that the treatment was keeping her alive.

'She's not fucking alive,' Sebastian roared.

Zheng cringed. Liu flexed his grip on the handle of the gun.

I told him I'd spoken to the doctor. I knew everything. I knew he'd been lying to my face all these years. I reminded him he'd looked me in the eye in that bunker in Shanghai and told me she wasn't brain-damaged after the seizure.

I could hear Sebastian standing up and walking. I imagined him in his study, pacing and gesturing as he spoke.

Zheng responded by blaming Qiu. Qiu had instructed Zheng not to tell me about Chloe.

They hadn't wanted to jeopardise Sebastian's return to Australia. The opportunity of having him in the Foreign Minister's office was too important, and Qiu feared knowing the truth about Chloe might impact his commitment.

'*What about your commitment to your fucking daughter?*' *I snarled at him. How could he have left her in that state for so long when the doctor was clear there was no chance of recovery?*

Zheng refolded his arms, clasping his thin biceps. Up close, Sebastian could see the age on him. His neck had grown gaunt and seemed too weak to hold his head, which bowed forwards. The skin on his face, once a rich, oiled olive, was now pale and paper thin. There were lines across his forehead and down the side of his mouth. Trenches excavated with an unceasing scowl.

Ignoring Sebastian's comments about Chloe's condition, Zheng justified his commitment to her. He visited her as often as he could. He sat with her, just as the doctor had described, speaking to her like they had sitting on that bench looking out to Pudong when she was a little girl.

It made me sick to the stomach, Charlie. I accused him of taking satisfaction in her vegetative state. She was finally compliant and that's what he had always wanted. Even if her life amounted to nothing more than a long and useless death, she was finally under his control and that was the most important thing to him …

They were crossing Chater Road. It was deserted but filled with debris from protests. Water bottles, a few battered umbrellas, broken barricades, torn posters reading *#freedomHK*. A protestor, wearing all black with a yellow helmet, came running at speed out of the MTR.

Zheng could not restrain himself at this point and lurched forwards in his seat, spitting his words at Sebastian through gritted teeth.

'She … was … not useless.'

It was like a veil had dropped from Sebastian's eyes. There was silence in the car. From the other side of the square, two more figures dressed in black came racing towards the road.

She was not useless? I realised from his tone that he was proud of her. Proud that he'd been able to use her to manipulate me and give Qiu what he wanted. After all the shame she had brought him, following in the footsteps of her mother, Chloe had been rehabilitated because they had used her to force me to serve the Party.

In a rage-choked voice, Sebastian repeated his accusation that Zheng was selfish and cruel for keeping Chloe alive.

I said the doctor was right. We needed to end Chloe's suffering. She needed relief. She needed to die.

Zheng exploded, stabbing his finger into Sebastian's chest. He swore he'd never agree to murder his daughter. He accused Sebastian of abandoning Chloe. Sebastian spat back that his obsessive control of Chloe was a torture both before and after the car crash.

That's when I pulled her diaries from my bag and waved them in his face. I told him to read the fucking words she'd written. All those descriptions about suffocating and being locked in. They weren't written about locked-in syndrome, they were written about him!

Zheng seized the diaries, and they struggled over them as outside the car more protestors materialised from the laneways between buildings and pedestrian bridges. The driver pounded his horn, trying to clear the road. The car jerked. Zheng lost his grip and lurched forwards. Sebastian pulled on the door handle, and despite Liu Hui's grasping hands made it out of the vehicle and into the street.

Outside the vacuum of the car, Sebastian was overwhelmed by the noise and press of bodies. Another group was marching down Queensway with a red banner unfurled: *If we burn, you burn with us.*

Young men. Young women. No one older than early twenties, many still teenagers with soft skin and baby faces. But when they roared, their voices echoed through the streets.

Ng daai soukau, kyut jat bat ho! (Five demands, not one less!)

Hoenggong jan, gaa jau! (Hong Kongers, add oil!)

Gwongfuk Hoenggong! Sidoi gaakming! (Reclaim Hong Kong! Revolution of our times!)

The front passenger door opened, and Liu Hui pushed his way around the front of the car. Sebastian clutched the diaries to his chest, turning and fleeing into the crowd.

It was in that dense press of bodies that he saw a girl holding the arm of a taller boy. She had short hair. A fringe over her eyes. Black-rimmed glasses.

She could have been Chloe's double, Charlie. She threw her fist in the air and joined in the chanting. Gwongfuk Hoenggong! Sidoi gaakming!

Haak kei! Haak kei! Protestors looked around. Those with gas masks pulled them on. People screamed. Others shouted insults at what they called 'dirty cops'. *Sei hak ging! Sei hak ging!*

In the mayhem, someone fell or pushed Sebastian, striking him square in his back. He stumbled forwards, using his hands to break his fall as he hit the road.

Her diaries, Charlie. I dropped them, and they were immediately kicked away by the feet of fleeing protestors.

A sound like popping champagne corks.

'Gas masks! Protect yourselves!'

'Open umbrellas!'

Tear gas rounds arced into the air. Shells hit the road, making a pinging sound, spitting and sparking as they skidded across the asphalt. Sebastian clambered through people's legs, desperately trying to regain what was left of the diaries. But noxious smoke poured from the aluminium canisters and the street was draped in cloud.

My eyes were stinging, my nose and throat burning. I felt like I was being choked. The nausea made me double over. Chloe's lookalike was on her knees beside me, spitting and gagging. The diaries were disintegrating before my eyes. Their covers ripped, their pages trampled on, torn and shredded across the streets of Hong Kong.

Protestors were scattering as the police marched through the crowds, truncheons beating on their shields. The black flag was raised again. More gas came. Protestors kept low and ran.

I was still on the ground when the police charged. I saw them coming in hard, arms flailing with truncheons, striking out, beating anything that moved. Protestors fought to protect themselves, but they were overwhelmed. Police struck at their heads, behind their knees, binding their wrists. They screamed as they were dragged towards prison buses.

A group of riot police pointed at Sebastian. They came running towards him and he rolled on his side, bracing for the impact of their truncheons. Then he felt hands on his clothes, beneath his arms, dragging him to his feet. He opened his eyes and saw a burnt face close to his own. Liu Hui, shouting at the police, holding up an identification card, giving orders.

Like a group of robots, Charlie. When they saw Liu Hui's credentials, the entire line halted, turned, and charged off, realising we weren't their target.

❖

When Liu Hui pushed Sebastian inside the private dining room at the China Club, Zheng was at the window watching a helicopter fly low over the central business district. Seeing Sebastian, he nodded to the corner of the room, where Qiu sat at a chair pulled from the banquet table.

I was still in a daze from the madness in the street, but when I saw Qiu, my nails bit into my palms. He was older and frailer, but that made me hate him no less for all his lies and manipulations.

Qiu acted as if he were reuniting with a dear friend. He gestured to Liu Hui, who rushed over and helped him to his feet, then walked him over to Sebastian.

'Mr Consul-General. It has been so long. We have all grown older. Even you are no longer the fresh-faced young man I met in Hong Kong – in better days than these.'

His hair had turned grey, and while he still had a paunch, his face looked wasted. The excess skin hung from his jowls. He still wore rimless glasses, but had given up his polo for a short-sleeved white shirt and grey pants. He carried a leather document case in one hand, gesturing Sebastian to the table with the other, then slapping him on the back like an old colleague.

'The Chinese people owe you an enormous debt for what you have done.'

He cupped his cheeks, his elbows on the table, and sighed.

'You deserve to burn in hell for what you've done,' I spat.

Liu marched around the table and seized Sebastian by the hair. But Qiu raised his hand, signalling for him to be released. He carried on in a calm tone, as if they were all still friends.

'I am so sorry to hear you are upset, Mr Consul-General. I understand what happened to Miss Zheng is a tragedy. After all your efforts, for it to come to this … I cannot imagine how you are feeling. It must be terrible to realise you have been lied to for so long.'

He gestured with his head for Zheng to sit with them. He obeyed, taking a seat between Qiu and Sebastian.

'You are the ones that did the fucking lying,' I said, despite Liu Hui glaring at me.

But Qiu only shrugged. 'We also kept Miss Zheng alive. We ensured she was without pain. That her living conditions were superior. We have kept up our side of the bargain.' He took off his glasses and polished them. 'As for any lies you've been told, I am not responsible for them. Mr Zheng is accountable for his own decisions, as he has always been.'

I saw the way Zheng looked at him then, Charlie. A look of unvarnished hatred.

But Qiu ignored him and got straight to the point. He said he was saddened to hear Sebastian had threatened to be 'done with' their friendship.

I realised that was the point of the meeting. They were reacting to my phone call to Zheng from the hospital.

The smile left Qiu's face and he told Sebastian that, despite what he had discovered about the true nature of Chloe's condition, it would be an error to think there was no longer anything binding him to the MSS.

Qiu unzipped his document pouch and produced a sky-blue manila folder, which he opened like a lawyer's brief, licking his fingertips before withdrawing each exhibit.

Photographs. Evidence of my crimes …

Image after image was laid on the table between them. Photographs of Sebastian meeting Zheng on the Bund, in the Shanghai bunker, in the Temple of the Sun Park. There were images of the classified documents Sebastian had downloaded from secure systems, Sebastian's name clearly displayed in watermark across each page.

'And we musn't forget this one.' Qiu laid a final image on top of the others.

Sebastian saw himself, a younger man, standing with Zheng and Qiu, and Liu Hui in the background, drinking a toast over Chloe's hospital bed, marking the occasion, so many years ago, when he'd first entered into the bargain from which now Qiu was telling him there was no escape.

It was blackmail after all.

Qiu leant forwards to drive home the point. 'What would happen if we exposed you now, Mr Consul-General? You must realise that after all these years, there is no going back. You are a traitor to your country. Imagine what would happen. The impact on your reputation, your friends, your family …'

And for a moment I thought I understood how Qiu had trapped him. How they'd kept him locked into his allegiance to the MSS for another five years with this threat to expose him.

But I again had misunderstood my friend.

I said he was wasting his fucking time threatening me, Charlie. I didn't need to be reminded of what I was or what I'd done. I'd known from the first fucking moment I pushed that USB into my machine at the Shanghai consulate, there was no going back.

'How about going to prison?' Qiu growled. 'In China, you'd be executed as a traitor.'

I told him I didn't care. How could I care what would happen to me? After what I'd seen in that hospital room? All the hope that Qiu and Zheng had manufactured to keep driving me, to manipulate me for so many years … it was all gone. They had nothing to compel me.

Sebastian had already decided what he was going to do. As soon as he was free of the China Club, he'd return to the hospital and tell the young doctor everything. He'd convince him to deliver on the advice Zheng had ignored. The palliative medications to provide comfort, allowing Chloe to die with dignity.

Her relief was all he cared about.

And if the doctor wouldn't care for her, Charlie, then, Jesus Christ, I was prepared to do it myself. I'd give her relief, even if it meant … doing the worst thing. I'd do it to set her free.

Qiu seemed to understand the level of resistance he was confronting. He nodded to himself. Then, with a glance at Zheng, who stiffened but continued to stare straight ahead, he reached into his document pouch and withdrew an envelope.

More photographs, smaller, like holiday snaps. He laid them on the table, dealing each one like a gambler with his cards.

Zheng pushed back his chair and strode to the window, muttering to himself. Qiu ignored him and kept dealing.

Sebastian's voice grew haunted.

It was a boy, Charlie. A little Eurasian boy.

With blue eyes …

I ceased breathing. This could not be what I thought it was.

A little boy. First as a baby, just his face visible, with a little hat to keep his head warm. Another of him crawling, smiling. Then maybe age four, dressed in so many layers of jackets he could hardly lower his arms, walking in a garden, holding Zheng's hand. Then another photo, in blue shorts and a red scarf around his neck ...

Sebastian sucked in a breath, and his words gushed forth in a torrent.

... then, standing by Chloe's bed ... looking down on his mother ... as Zheng watched from a fucking chair.

Jesus Christ. Jesus Christ!

A child? Chloe had a child?

It was the pregnancy they'd told me she'd lost. Twenty-four hours after the car crash. They told me the child was lost. But they'd been lying all this time. Chloe had given birth to my son. MY SON! They'd hidden him from me.

The Astina lurched over a speed bump. I'd been too transfixed by the revelation to notice, and my body jolted forwards, crushing my finger between my leg and the steering wheel. I cried out, unsure if from the pain or the anguish I felt for Sebastian.

So this was Qiu's ace in the hole. A new compromise, a new way to keep Sebastian in harness.

He reached back into the envelope for more photos ...

The little boy had gone, Charlie ...

The next images were of a young man in his twenties. A young man in the dark blue dress uniform and white gloves of a military academy. The same young man in camouflage fatigues, holding up a small medallion.

Now in a suit and tie ... standing by Chloe's bed ... a visit to the hospital for Chinese New Year.

And in each photo, Zheng stood beside him, his chin raised with pride.

It was everything he'd ever wanted. A daughter, subdued, who could never leave him. A grandson, raised to be complicit, to ask no questions.

Qiu waited for a reaction. But Sebastian was immobilised by the compounding trauma of the day. Incapable of words. Unable to concentrate on anything but the roar of grief inside his head.

It wasn't just that I was learning I had a child, Charlie ... I was losing a child. These pictures of a grown man meant the little boy in the other photographs was already gone.

I heard the torment in my friend's voice and recalled again his oath in the darkness of his childhood bedroom that night after his father's treacheries were revealed. He'd sworn that he'd be loyal to the woman he loved. That he'd devote himself to their children.

But the opportunity to be a father to this son had been lost.

The agony of those photographs was that ... just like my own father, I hadn't been there for him. I'd missed everything. Every day of his life. Our child! Every moment laid out in those photos was a moment lost to me and Chloe.

And now it was too late.

I pressed my knuckle into my mouth, unable to stifle a sob. I had seen Sebastian's face searching for his father from the choir stage or from the football field too many times not to be moved by the agony in his words.

But Qiu was growing impatient. He removed his glasses and polished them with a handkerchief.

'You can see Mr Zheng is very proud of his grandson.'

He gestured towards the pile of photographs with his glasses.

'It's a pity you, too, don't have a relationship with your son. It's not too late, of course ... for a family to be reunited.'

Maybe perceiving Sebastian's growing defiance in his silence, Qiu switched from temptation to malice. He stood up and edged his way around the table, easing himself into the chair that Zheng had vacated. Sebastian could smell the nicotine on him.

'Your son is a bright young man, with a bright future ... But he may miss out on promotions. He may lose his job ...'

Zheng stirred by the window.

'... he may be found guilty of some crime and be sent to prison. He may not make it out of prison ...'

Zheng crossed back to the table, shaking his head, his voice filled with alarm.

'No ... No ... That is not right ...'

Liu Hui stood up, his eyebrows raised. Zheng pulled up short, then collapsed into a chair, mopping sweat from his forehead with a napkin.

'Surely you don't wish another loss on this family that has suffered so much.' Qiu sighed.

It was at this point that Sebastian made a decision. He understood where Qiu was going, and he acted quickly to head him off.

I couldn't let it go on, Charlie. I knew what he was doing. If I let him turn this into a negotiation over the welfare of my son, then it would be like with Chloe all over again. While I'd never had the opportunity to be a father to that little boy ... I could at least spare him from becoming another bargaining chip in Qiu's game.

Sebastian reached out to the photographs in front of him, shuffled them into a pile, and dropped them face down in front of Qiu. He then turned to confront him, their faces so close he could feel the other man's breath on his lips.

I looked him in the eye, Charlie, and said: 'I don't care.'

I could imagine Sebastian's features drawn, drained of life, the way he'd looked when I collected him from the police station the night of Chloe's death.

I don't care.

If I hadn't been driving the Astina, I would have closed my eyes.

I don't care.

Qiu's brow furrowed.

'You don't care about your child?' He leant away, as if seeing Sebastian at a distance would make more sense of this rejection. 'You don't want to meet your son? You don't care if he suffers?'

Zheng silently implored Sebastian across the table. The fear on his face was sincere. It was the same expression he'd worn that very first morning beside Chloe's hospital bed.

But this time, Sebastian ignored him.

I told Qiu again, I didn't care about my son. I wasn't interested in a relationship with him. I wanted nothing to do with him. Zheng could have him ... He meant nothing to me ...

I bit into my knuckle. I knew what Sebastian was trying to do, but hearing him deny this young man sent a shiver up my spine.

As if expecting my reaction, Sebastian reprimanded me from the tape.

What else could I have done, Charlie? Every fibre of my body was screaming at me to demand they take me at once to my son, that I be allowed to meet him! But it was the same old trap. They wanted to use him as a pawn, just as they'd used Chloe. The best thing I could do for him was to deny him.

I couldn't be distracted again from doing what was right for Chloe.

The agony in his voice was back.

I told Qiu that if they wanted me to keep working for the MSS, they needed to offer me something I wanted, not something I didn't care about.

I wondered whether Qiu was sceptical about Sebastian's disinterest. Whether he smiled with recognition. Or whether he nodded with understanding, one cold-blooded animal to another.

Whatever the case, I'm sure he sensed a breakthrough.

Touching his fingers to his chest, he asked innocently what payment Sebastian would prefer.

That was my chance, Charlie … I told him my price had never changed. I cared only about Chloe. She needed to be released. She should be allowed to die with dignity, just as the doctor in the hospital had recommended.

Qiu was silent for a long time, staring at Sebastian.

I could see him calculating. For him it was just a transaction. A price for my service. Be it access to my son, or Chloe's life. It didn't matter. As long as I was under his control.

Finally, Qiu nodded. He said he understood. That he sympathised. That Sebastian's strength and loyalty to Miss Zheng impressed him above all else.

And yet …

And here he pivoted like a fucking dancer, Charlie. A seasoned negotiator, always looking for the better deal.

And yet, of course, it would take time …

The death of any citizen, particularly one of such a notable family, was a grave matter. Even more so as the state had invested such resources in her treatment. Qiu could see many difficulties in persuading the necessary authorities to let such a death happen. And of course we were speaking of Mr Zheng's daughter, and clearly he was not in favour of her being allowed to die.

Sebastian saw realisation breaking over Zheng's face. He knew the negotiation had shifted and his eyes turned back to Sebastian, full of loathing.

Qiu continued in that sing-song voice of his, sipping from a cup of jasmine tea.

And yet ... perhaps, just perhaps, he said. If I were to prove myself once and for all ... Then perhaps there might be a way they could all agree to let Miss Zheng die with dignity, and there would be no need for any disturbances to the wellbeing of her son.

Zheng's hand grasped the table. A gesture so emphatic the tea spilt from the cups and the plates and crockery rattled. Liu once more stood up, and this time walked around the table and stood behind him.

Liu wasn't there to protect him anymore, Charlie.

Zheng released the table and bowed his head. Qiu nodded and became matter-of-fact.

'Good, then we are agreed.'

❖

And just like that, we were on to the final stretch ...

Perhaps betraying a certain sense of urgency, the negotiations and disagreements of a moment ago were now forgotten. Qiu was quick to focus Sebastian on his new orders.

He explained that Sebastian's service to the MSS would continue, but that his diplomatic career needed to end. He was required to return to Australia and run for political office.

This must always have been their plan, Charlie.

Qiu explained Beijing had been wounded by the current Australian Government. Foreign interference laws had thrown China's generosity back in its face and hurt the feelings of the Chinese people.

I was to return to Australia and help defeat the government at the next election. They wanted someone on the inside.

I slowed the Astina outside Cassie and Sebastian's house. I was shaking my head. At least now it all made sense. Sebastian's urgent desire to quit his diplomatic post and run for office. His appeal for my help. Exploiting my guilt about what happened to Chloe, and my ambition for my own career. Of course. Why not? He had manipulated every other relationship in his life. Sacrificed everyone else to help Chloe, and now, I realised, to save his own son. Why wouldn't he exploit me, too?

I was beyond surprise.

There were other conditions too, Charlie. They wanted to know if I was still in contact with Kai Birch …

I confess, rather than thinking what this could mean, and what purpose the MSS could have with Kai, I felt a brief moment of smug relief. So Kai and Henry, too, had been exploited. Maybe all those trips to California hadn't just been a preference to spend time with his other friends. It gave me a brief flush of delight, for which I feel ashamed now.

But Qiu hadn't finished.

He repeated that for Sebastian to have what he desired, there would need to be something special, something of the utmost importance to the Party, to China. At some stage in the future, a sacrifice may have to be made by Sebastian. When and if it came, Sebastian should see it as a last sacrifice for Chloe.

Sebastian reassured him he would do what was necessary. But Qiu continued as if swept up in his own thoughts.

He said, in time, we might all be called to make sacrifices to help China. That's what would be needed to correct history.

He explained, with a gesture to the helicopter still hovering over the city outside, that the west was determined to contain China's rise. They were using these ignorant students in Hong Kong in an attempt to destabilise China.

But these efforts would fail, he said.

The protestors would be brought to heel. Beijing would purge its territory of colonialists and troublemakers. Historic wrongs must be righted. The Chinese people were preparing for a historic struggle to safeguard their national sovereignty and territorial integrity. China would assert its interests on the world stage. It would take back what had been stolen.

Everyone would need to sacrifice.

He gripped Sebastian's arm and leant close. His dark eyes were magnified through his rimless glasses, taking Sebastian back to the first time they'd met in the Central Police Station prison cell.

How important is Miss Zheng to you? How loyal are you? Will you do what needs to be done to let her die?

His grip on Sebastian's arm became stronger. His nails pierced Sebastian's skin.

Because if you fail us, if you are disloyal, if you attempt to see her again before your work is done … her suffering will continue, indefinitely … and do not think for a minute that your son will avoid suffering too.

And finally I understood how the MSS had kept him in harness over these final years.

He said Chloe would be kept alive until what they required was done. Meanwhile, my son would stay with Zheng. He wouldn't suffer … but Qiu wouldn't rule it out …

Until it was done.

I could hardly hear him now. Sebastian's voice was so soft, I had to lean forwards, concentrating hard to not miss a word.

That's why I said yes, Charlie. I committed everything to Qiu. Even before understanding what they wanted. I had no choice. I had to end Chloe's pain.

I had to protect my son.

His voice was barely audible, a last breath through parted lips.

Qiu told me the plan. The awful thing I've been struggling for ninety minutes to tell you … I still don't know how to tell you … I'm so close now, after what I've done. What I did in California. And in Hong Kong. It's just time. Borrowed time. Any day now, Zheng will make contact. He'll tell me, it's done …

I jumped in my seat as my mobile phone began ringing.

Mallet again.

296

I rejected the call, not wanting to be distracted as Sebastian reached his final revelation, but then a pounding on the window made me spin around, quickly turning off the ignition to silence the stereo. I squinted into the darkness, fearing the thin man with the backpack or some faceless MSS operative.

Cassie, in a dressing gown, hair and eyes wild, pointing at my hand which still held my phone. I opened the door and the smell of alcohol stung my nose. Had she been drinking gin since I left her?

'Answer it. You have to answer it. He's desperate,' she said, pointing again at my mobile.

'Henry Mallet?' I asked, looking at my device.

'Yes. He's been trying to call you all night. He's been calling me too. Something's happened to Kai.'

They wanted to know if I was still in contact with Kai Birch.

CHAPTER THIRTY-FOUR

I followed Cassie inside the house, fighting to order my thoughts. I felt burdened by the weight of Sebastian's secrets. The MSS, the lies about his marriage and, Jesus Christ, the existence of a child ...

The lounge room now looked like the aftermath of a slumber party rather than a set for *Interior Design Monthly*. Illuminated in blue light from the television screen, the leather sofa was covered in blankets and doonas. There were pizza boxes on the coffee table and empty sleeping bags on the floor. I guessed Cassie had watched a movie earlier with the twins. As we walked through to the kitchen, I wondered whether she had told them yet about their father's death.

I wondered too if Sebastian's son knew. What he had been told. Would he be grieving now?

'We're out of gin. But I've just opened a bottle of shiraz.'

Cassie was holding out a glass of red wine. She wore no makeup and looked old and exhausted in the stark kitchen light. Deep lines ran from the corner of her lips in parallel tracks down her chin. Her forehead was lined, with crow's feet at her eyes. After a day stuck in memories of our youth, it was a rude reminder that we had all passed beyond middle age. It was so many years since Sebastian, Chloe and I were kids in Hong Kong. I'd always taken heart in the idea that, unlike us, Chloe had escaped the ravages of age by dying young. Now I knew from Sebastian's confession that wasn't true. She had aged, like the rest of us. In fact, as I sipped Cassie's wine and took a seat at the kitchen table, it occurred to me that Chloe had likely only died a few days ago. What else could Zheng's message to Tang have meant? *It's done.* But if that were true, as little as seventy-two hours ago, Chloe had still been alive.

I let out a long sigh and shook my head. I'd been grieving for her all this time, and she'd been alive.

So much wasted time.

And what the hell had Sebastian been doing? Chloe had been kept in her tortured limbo for over five years by Qiu. What was a big enough 'sacrifice' to have persuaded the MSS to finally let her die? What final act had Sebastian committed for them? And what had that meant for his son?

'Here.' Cassie plonked a packet of cigarettes down on the table in front of me. 'Uber Eats. Cigarettes came with the pizza and wine.'

My hands shook with anticipation, peeling back the plastic, pulling away the silver paper and taking in the comforting smell of tobacco.

'You have to call Mallet.' She was leaning across the table, holding out her lighter.

'I do not,' I snorted, taking my first reassuring drag of the cigarette.

'You need to call him, Charlie. He's beside himself.'

'We're all fucking beside ourselves. Why does he need special attention?'

'He said Kai is in trouble.'

I caught her eye a moment, but looked away, thinking about Sebastian's confession. Whatever the ultimate mission Qiu had given him, it somehow involved Kai Birch.

'What sort of trouble?'

'He wouldn't say what it was on the phone. Or at least not to me. He wanted to talk to you.'

I folded my arms across my chest. I was torn, but not enough to jump to a summons from Henry Mallet.

'I'm sorry, Cassie. Why the fuck do I care?'

'They're your friends.'

'They're Sebastian's friends.'

'You went to school with Henry.'

'And he beat the shit out of me every day.'

'You were always staying with them in California.'

'Sebastian stayed at Kai's Los Altos Hills villa. I'd stay in a hotel to avoid them.'

This seemed to surprise her, and she cocked her head to one side. 'What did they do together?'

'I have no clue. Played poker, watched football, got drunk. They could have been ordering showgirls and strippers to the house for all I know.'

Cassie snorted in response. 'If they were strippers, they wouldn't have been show*girls*.'

Seeing my confusion, she laughed and shook her head. 'You didn't know? Jesus, Sebastian knew how to keep a secret, didn't he? Kai and Henry. They're a couple. That was Henry and Sebastian's big point of connection. Henry came out to him at school when they were boarders. Sebastian protected him. I can't believe you didn't know that.'

On top of all the other revelations, Mallet was gay? And he'd come out to Sebastian at that school? Such a thing was unimaginable back then. For those vicious schoolboys, homosexuality was considered worse than being fat or weak. It would have been worse for Mallet, as a first eight rower, a footballer and school captain. The other boys would have seen it as a betrayal. Extraordinary to think that Mallet must have lived a life of repression at that school. His true self locked deep inside. Yet another of us with locked-in syndrome.

Still, I felt no sympathy. In a way, it made my persecution at his hands seem even more cruel and hypocritical.

'Kai and Henry have been partners since they met in Shanghai. Wasn't that obvious at the wedding when they were dancing with each other?'

I shrugged. How could I tell her I'd left early?

As surprising as all this was, I knew I needed to get on with what I came for. My eyes flicked towards the study door. I needed to make a copy of the tape. The only question was how could I get into the study and use Sebastian's tape recorder without revealing all to Cassie?

The answer came with the old-fashioned ringing of my phone. Mallet again. I pulled it out and showed Cassie Mallet's name.

'I'll take it in the study,' I said.

❖

'Jesus Christ, Charlie, I've wanted to speak to you for hours. Why didn't you pick up?'

A bolt of teenage rage burst in my temple.

'Because I'm not fucking beholden to you, Mallet.'

There was a pause on the other end of the phone. I expected him to roar at me. That old snorting through his nose he used to do as he held me down. But when he spoke, his voice was gentle and placating. 'Look, Charlie, I'm sorry. I know you must be upset about Sebastian. So am I.'

'I was there, Henry. I was with him.' Stupidly competitive. I knew how immature I sounded, but I couldn't help it.

'I can't imagine. It must have been awful. You two were so close. You were his best friend, Charlie.'

Now I knew he wanted something. Such a concession didn't come cheap. But hearing Mallet acknowledge I was Sebastian's best friend still made me shiver with pleasure.

'But Charlie, I need your help. Kai's in trouble.'

'What's happened to him?'

'He's been arrested ...' There was a pause at the other end of the phone. Mallet's voice caught in his throat. 'On espionage charges.'

Alarm bells rang in my head. Whatever this was about, it had to be related to Sebastian. I was standing just inside the door of his study, staring at the leather armchair where he had recorded the confession.

'Kai's got mates inside the DCSA. They wouldn't tell me much, but it relates to an EDR incident —'

'For fuck's sake, Henry, can you stop talking in acronyms? What is the DCSA?'

'Sorry, I've been moving in Defence circles too long. DCSA is the Defence Counterintelligence and Security Agency. EDR stands for Endpoint Detection and Response. It's an advanced cybersecurity solution that detects threats in real time as they occur at endpoints, like laptops, desktops, servers and even networked mobile phones. You can understand that given Kai's job and his clearance level at the Innovation Expansion Unit, all his devices were protected by Department of Defence grade EDR solutions.'

'So what happened?'

'The Feds say they have evidence that an unauthorised device was used to extract classified information from Kai's secure laptop.'

Sebastian's method of operation. The USB that he used in the Consulate, on Cassie, and again when he was in Beijing and Hong Kong.

'What's any of this got to do with Sebastian?' I asked, marvelling that my first instinct was still to protect him.

'Nothing at all, other than I've found out when the alleged unauthorised extraction took place and it was the same night Sebastian stayed with Kai. I wanted to know if he'd told you anything. Did anyone come over that night?'

'Well, weren't you there too? I presumed you lived with Kai … given your relationship.'

There was a pause on the line. His voice returned, hardened and defensive. 'No, Charlie, I wasn't home.'

I opened and closed my mouth a few times, blushing and unable to find words. 'I just meant, I understood it was always the three of you for poker nights …'

'Less and less. Sebastian's dates kept clashing with mine. I've been travelling the last few times he's been here.'

This was suspicious. Given what I knew now, it sounded like Sebastian had been cultivating Kai and trying to get him alone, leading up to where he extracted information from the laptop.

'Did Sebastian say anything to you about that night? You were travelling with him, weren't you?' Mullet pressed.

'He didn't tell me anything, and I wasn't with him.'

But he'd feigned food poisoning two days later, after he'd handed whatever he stole from Kai to Zheng at the China Club. It all fit together now.

'What was extracted from Kai's computer?' I asked.

'They're not telling me. But you know the type of stuff Kai has access to. Any extraction from his laptop would have been extremely serious. I've looked at Kai's diary for the day,' Mallet continued. 'He met with a delegation of Australian businesses, led by Sebastian. They went for a briefing to a secure offsite location. I don't know where. Afterwards, rather than returning to the office, where he should have securely stored his laptop, he went home. Sebastian must have been with him.'

'This sounds like an accusation, Henry. You think Sebastian somehow lured Kai back to his house, subdued him, then hacked his laptop?'

'Jesus, Charlie! I didn't say any of that. I just wanted to know if Sebastian had said anything, or seen anything that could help Kai ...'

This was the terrible thing Sebastian had done. The reason he looked so ill and claimed he had food poisoning. He'd persuaded Kai, against all protocol, to go straight home after the briefing. He'd then found a way, late at night, creeping around the villa, to access the laptop and make an extraction.

'Do you at least know what Kai was briefing Sebastian and the delegation on? Maybe that can give us some answers?'

'I told you, Henry, I wasn't there.'

'But you're his fucking Chief of Staff, Charlie, surely you know ...' Mallet gulped, swallowing his impatience. He tried again in a voice so exhausted it made me realise it was still before dawn in California. He must have been up all night. 'There must have been a briefing for the meeting, Charlie. Could you at least check that? Maybe that could help explain what's going on.'

There was no way I could get that briefing, as it was saved on the computer in Sebastian's office at Parliament House. But there was an easier way. I glanced at the bookshelf and saw the tape recorder. The last five minutes of the tape would tell me, once and for all, what Sebastian had done. What he had stolen that was so important it had resulted in Kai being arrested. The 'most awful thing' he'd struggled so much to reveal.

I reached into my pocket for the cassette.

And realised it wasn't there.

My head pounded. Jesus. I had left it in the car. I'd forgotten to eject the cassette. I'd got out of the Astina and left it in the stereo.

'I'll call you back, Henry. I'll look into it.'

Mallet was protesting as I hung up.

Tearing open the study door, I ran down the hall, out the front door, to my car. Even before I reached the vehicle, I saw the light in the cabin was on. The driver's side door was open. There were footsteps ringing out along the pavement. Someone running. I raced to the Astina. In the distance, I heard the screeching of tires. I pushed eject again, again, again. No reassuring sound. No movement from within. The stereo was empty.

The cassette was gone.

And so too evidence of my innocence, and Sebastian's confession of what he had done to Kai Birch.

❖

I staggered back to the study and poured myself a long glass of Sebastian's whisky, then collapsed into his leather armchair, fighting to stop myself hyperventilating.

'Did I hear you go outside?' Cassie walked in and pulled herself onto Sebastian's desk, where she sat cross-legged. 'How was Henry? Can you help him?'

'I need a cigarette,' I stammered, and she threw me the pack. I couldn't hide the fact that my hands were shaking and I could hardly pluck the cigarette from its box. I got up, intending to walk outside and smoke. I needed to calm my nerves, but I also needed to think.

'Charlie, what happened to Kai?' Cassie persisted.

'He's arrested on espionage charges,' I said, too consumed with my situation to notice the heavy silence in the room.

I stopped in front of the painting of Hong Kong Island on the wall. The dark ink shading over the Peak looked more ominous than ever. A storm, or a tsunami, a calamity of some sort waiting to fall on the city, like fate pitching me headlong into the disaster of Sebastian's making. Or was it the other way around? I had pitched Sebastian and Chloe into calamity. I had brought the storm.

'I hate that fucking painting,' Cassie sniffed, drawing me out of my reverie. I glanced around and saw her lighting a cigarette, not caring about the smoke in the house.

'He was cruel hanging it up.' She pointed at the painting, exhaling smoke from her nose. 'It's from Lamma Island. A house in Yung Shue Wan. It was cherry red.' She saw my eyes open wide, and smiled ferociously. 'You know which one I'm talking about, don't you?' She gestured again. 'That was on the wall.' She nodded, seeing my recognition, and began to speak of a weekend trip to Hong Kong that they'd taken together, when Cassie and Sebastian had lived in Beijing.

'There was an old woman downstairs, muttering to Sebastian in Cantonese, calling me a whore. When we got upstairs, he walked into that room with such fucking reverence it could have been a shrine.'

'You … were suspicious?' I asked.

'Of course. Even in the restaurant, it was obvious we were reliving a ritual. We could only sit at a certain table or eat certain things.'

I could imagine Chloe's favourites: salt and pepper squid, razor clams, steamed fish, fried rice.

Cassie was allergic to seafood.

She folded her arms and took a deep drag on the cigarette, blowing smoke into the room as she spoke.

'Then he called out her name when we were having sex. He didn't know he'd done it until I told him the next morning. Then I made him tell me.'

Shocked, I turned to her. She nodded in reply. 'He told me she'd been the love of his life. How she died in a car crash and he still thought of her. I asked if he still loved her. He said he did, and

I left. He let me go. It took him two hours to follow me. Getting down on his knees in the Qantas lounge at Hong Kong airport and asking me to marry him.' She sighed and flicked ash from the cigarette onto the leather pad across Sebastian's desk. 'I told him to never speak of her again. Then years later, after we were married, after the kids showed up, after he'd stopped touching me or showing any affection ... that turned up' – she pointed with hatred at the painting – 'and I knew he was trying to say something. He somehow needed to testify his loyalty to her, even if he didn't have the courage to say it out loud.'

She got off the table and walked to the painting, rubbing her hand along the deep timber frame.

'I wanted him to leave it in Hong Kong. But he had it reframed and mounted when we came here.'

She turned back to me then. 'Is Sebastian responsible for Kai being arrested?'

I was too stunned for words, and just stared at her.

'Tell me the truth, Charlie,' she said again. 'What did he do that he was so ashamed of, that he had to kill himself? Was it ... was it also something to do with espionage?'

I considered for a moment, then nodded. She deserved to know.

Now she squared her shoulders as if facing a verdict.

'Did he spy on me, too? Is that why he was with me? Was I just a source for him all along?'

'No, of course ... I can't say ...' I cleared my throat, appalled for her. 'I can't say if that is all you were.'

'Jesus,' she said, leaning against the wall. 'He did. He did it to me too. He spied on me.'

I nodded. Hiding anything now seemed pointless. I told her about the cassette tape and the confession, holding back only about the existence of Sebastian and Chloe's son. Somehow I felt protective of this final piece of information and needed to keep it to myself. I told Cassie everything else and watched her turn pale as I explained it all, but she deserved to know. After all that he had done to her, she didn't deserve to mourn a person who had never existed. She should be given relief from that obligation. I wanted to help her. And yet, no. I'll confess my political operative's mind had not deserted me. I wanted her to help me. To help with her father. If she believed what I said, maybe that would help me with McCubbin.

'But without the cassette, you have no proof?' She had slid down the wall and I had brought her a tumbler of Sebastian's whisky. 'And you reckon ASIO is gunning for you? They think you were blackmailing him, and that's why he killed himself.'

'That's what your father thinks, and now I don't have evidence to convince him otherwise.'

She contemplated that for a moment, then stood and lifted the picture from its place on the wall. There was a letter opener in the small barrel of pens on the desk. She seized it and stabbed it into the back of the frame. Slicing downwards through cardboard backing and brown paper. Despite the alcohol, her movements were purposeful. Her eyes narrowed in concentration. She was breathing through her nose.

She stripped back the paper and gestured for me to look. There was a narrow roll of plastic sandwich wrap sitting neatly against the inside of the timber frame. I prised it off and realised I was looking at a card reader and two rows of memory cards wrapped together. I knew what was on them: the pictures of Chloe that he'd received each week when he was in Shanghai. The images of her in the hospital bed.

Waves of curiosity crashed over me. I wanted to see Chloe. I wanted to see what Sebastian had seen. But then I noticed something else still taped down against the frame. The USB device. The size of a fingernail. The tool of his trade.

'You knew all this was here?'

She stared at me, her eyes filling with tears, her face trembling as if she were fighting against the will to nod her head, to confirm what she had done. But she didn't break down. She was stronger than that. She jutted her chin forwards, sniffed hard, and wiped at her eyes with the back of her hand.

'I knew something was there.' She looked down at the USB. 'I was loyal to my husband and my kids,' she said, sounding angry.

'Have you looked at it?'

She shook her head, pursing her lips.

'I didn't want to know. I saw him removing the back of the painting and then replacing it. He did it himself, after trips with you. I knew it was something secret. Something awful. I didn't want to look. To look would have made it real.'

I nodded, trying to keep my voice under control. This might give me the insurance I needed. Not only pictures of Chloe in his possession, but if that was the USB he had used to extract whatever he'd taken from Kai's laptop, then I'd have everything I needed … as long as I could make a copy and buy myself insurance, just as I had intended with the confession.

'Do you have a laptop? I need to see what is on all of this.'

Cassie shook her head.

'ASIO took everything, remember? We don't have a computer in the house.'

I sighed and ran my fingers through my hair. There were no laptops here, and I couldn't go home.

I could think of no other option. I'd have to return to Parliament House.

CHAPTER THIRTY-FIVE

I got in the Astina and drove to Parliament House. The way I saw it, I had nothing left to lose. Without the cassette I had no evidence, no 'get out of jail' card to distance myself from Sebastian's crimes, or defend myself against any accusation I was blackmailing him. It was almost midnight. A matter of hours before I was due to meet Katrina again. I needed to see what was on the USB stick. If it still contained whatever Sebastian had stolen from Kai's computer, I'd have the evidence I needed. If it didn't, then at least I could access the briefing materials from the last trip to California and, hopefully, join the dots to understand what Sebastian had done. What was the awful thing that he had been working towards telling me? If I could map it out myself, I'd have some insurance for the interview with ASIO. Either way, I would still get the findings to Swanny.

I cursed myself for not having paid more attention on those trips to the US. Not just the trips, but all of it. Sebastian's responsibility as an assistant minister. The Foreign Affairs and Trade stuff I'd never been interested in. I was his Chief of Staff for Christ's sake, but I'd left all the policy substance to the advisors and the department. My only interest was the politics. Even when I travelled with Sebastian, I spent most of my time on calls back to Canberra, so focused on guarding his back against the ruthless cut and thrust of factional positioning that the actual details of his trips were mostly a hectic white-out of planes, hotels and endless meetings. Shocking to think now that I too had unwittingly been working in the interests of the MSS. I had dreamt of manoeuvring him into the leadership. Sebastian as prime minister. I had mapped it out. A five- or six-year plan. It was why Ronnie hated me: he knew we were coming for him. I had form tearing down prime ministers. And all this intrigue and politicking meant I had never focused on the substance of what Sebastian did. I only read the political briefs, rarely anything that came up from the department. I sat through meetings with senior officials and international partners, emailing and texting colleagues in Australia. I was uninterested in anything about Sebastian's work, unless it helped me further his political career.

And now I was paying the price.

I pulled up in the underground carpark and entered Parliament House via the basement security checkpoint. There was a moment of tension as I pressed my parliamentary pass against the scanner and the guard inspected his monitor. I half expected him to tell me my credentials had been cancelled, or worse, for sirens to start wailing. Instead he just nodded to me and made some remark about the cyberattacks. As I stepped through the large steel doors I could see scenes of rioting in Sydney on the television beside his desk. Fires were burning. Police on horseback were overwhelmed as crowds charged, smashing shop windows and overturning cars.

Jesus Christ. Everything, everywhere seemed to be getting worse.

'Albert's out of hospital, if you want to know.'

Another young security guard handed me a tray for my phone as I walked through the metal detector. I blinked at him, not realising whom he was referring to in the moment's stress.

'The guard. Your assistant minister beat him over the head and stole his weapon. He's going to be okay. But he'll lose his job for allowing himself to be disarmed. He's pretty messed up about the death. Feels responsible ...'

I muttered my sympathies and hurried through the security doors into the concrete underbelly of Parliament House. I had no bandwidth to dwell on yet another of Sebastian's victims.

The lights were bright in the labyrinth of tunnels, and still alive with cleaning and maintenance staff preparing the House for the morning. I was less concerned about them than I was with meeting a staffer or a politician who would recognise me. Thankfully, the lift at the end of the passageway brought me out close to our office. I hurried down the corridor, head lowered, heart racing. It was the Senate wing, and each office I passed had a window plastered with various campaign slogans, or cartoons cut from the newspaper, sledging opponents, or advocating pet political projects.

The clocks ticked heavily in the silence. I passed the small meeting room where I'd spent the better part of the day being interrogated by Katrina and Ronnie. Then on to our office, where police tape covered the locked door. I had my key and, slipping beneath the tape, entered through the foyer and into Sebastian's office, stopping dead at the doorway when I saw the blood soaked into the carpet by the coffee table. The memory of his body, sitting propped up against the stained lounge, was fresh in my mind. A shiver ran over me, as if he were still there, staring at me, trying to communicate.

I need you to keep a secret for me ...

As I'd hoped, ASIO had only been interested in taking the laptops from Sebastian's home. His office desktop, monitored by departmental security software and linked and accessible by secretaries and assistants, was far too open a machine for secret communications. None of that concerned me now. I sat down at his desk and booted up the computer. As it loaded (it always took forever), I laid out the USB, memory cards and card reader on the desk in front of me. All my desire fell on the memory cards. If these were the photos Sebastian had been granted as payment all those years, I longed to see them, to see Chloe again. The idea filled me with anticipation, and also fear. Seeing her with my own eyes would make all of Sebastian's confession true. There would be nowhere left to hide. I had to admit to myself that, even now, after all that had happened, a small refuge in my mind still doubted all I had heard. It couldn't be true. The world could not be like that. My best friend would not have done that. I knew seeing images of Chloe in her hospital would strip me of this last scrap of denial. And yet I had to see. I needed to see again the woman I had not seen since that week in Shanghai, years ago. The woman I had loved. The woman to whom, through my jealous actions, I had brought torture and ruin.

This final thought made my jaw spasm. Not yet. I wasn't ready to see her yet. First the USB. I turned it in my hand as the computer completed its boot up protocol. Start here. Start with the comfort of knowing that I had proof of Sebastian's crimes … before turning to my own crimes and seeing Chloe in that hospital bed.

When the computer was ready, I reached with the USB towards the port, remembering how Sebastian had described doing the same in the Shanghai consulate, surrounded by friends and colleagues, the trusted insider, about to start down a path of treachery that would consume the rest of his life.

But before I could press the USB home, a voice from the doorway made me lurch forwards, almost overbalancing in my chair.

'Get the fuck away from that machine.'

Three figures burst through the door. Two AFP guards and Jacob, the bearded ASIO operative. Then someone else, thrusting himself between the others. Charging into the room with his bald, gnarled head and his meaty clenched fists, stamping forwards onto the patch of bloodstained carpet, desecrating the scene of Sebastian's death.

The Prime Minister's hammer.

Alec McCubbin. Furious. And ready to kill.

PART FOUR

McCubbin

CHAPTER THIRTY-SIX

'Get up and step away from the desk,' McCubbin barked. 'If you touch the computer, if you insert anything in it, we will use lethal force.'

Two AFP guards flanked him with drawn weapons. The day was ending as it started, with guns pointed at me for crimes I had not committed.

I knew how this looked. USB poised over a parliamentary computer. I looked like Sebastian. Now I was the spy. I was the traitor.

'Get away from that fucking machine!' McCubbin shouted again.

There was a madness to his tone, and in the way he held up his hand, palm out, as if ejecting a drunk from a country pub.

I'd only ever seen him from a distance. An ominous figure standing behind the Prime Minister, or beside Sebastian at the wedding. An amateur boxer during his jackarooing years, his squashed snout gave him a perpetual snarl. He had a stocky build with wide shoulders. But he was always immaculately dressed. Pocket squares and matching Windsor knotted tie. Not tonight. His collar was open, tie dragged from his neck. He wore no jacket, just a creased shirt rolled at the sleeves, exposing massive forearms.

I failed to respond to his instruction quickly enough, so he threw his bald head in the air and charged, snorting through his nose. He grasped the back of my chair and dragged it away from the desk, causing me to crash into the windowsill, making photographs of the last US trip fall to the floor.

Then he was over me, seizing my wrist and prising open my fingers to release the USB.

McCubbin's aggression was legendary. He was called the PM's hammer because he smashed things. People's careers. Mass public servant layoffs. Foreign interference. Now he wanted to bring the hammer down on me.

Jacob moved forwards quickly.

'Sir?' he asked, like a nurse trying to calm an asylum patient.

McCubbin stuck his finger in my face.

'Disobey me again and I will have you shot. You understand? I can do it. I have provisions under Australian Counter Terrorism laws. You are an imminent threat. Caught red-fucking-handed.'

He gave my wrist a twist, even though he already had the USB. Pain shot through my arm.

'I'm not fucking resisting,' I cried.

He raised his chin, breathing through his mouth so I could see his strong, yellow teeth, then leant forwards, bringing his face towards mine. 'I've always suspected you, Westcott. I know your type. Anyone that tears down a sitting prime minister is no patriot.'

I stuttered a protest, but he shouted over me, waving the USB.

'What's on this?'

'I don't know.'

'Bullshit, you don't know,' he roared, seizing my shirt and dragging me closer to him. 'What were you going to do with it?'

'It's nothing like that. It's not mine.'

'Bullshit. What is it? Malware? Sabotage? We know it's linked to the cyberattack.'

I was trembling, my eyes clouding with panic. I thought I might faint. It was worse than I'd feared if they thought I was involved in the cyberattacks.

'I got the USB from your daughter,' I cried, the words only just making it out of my lips before the back of his hand connected with my cheek. I saw stars, and my head snapped back with the impact. Pain followed, shooting through my cheek. Tears in my eyes. Fury, welling up. It was Mallet all over again.

'Call your fucking daughter. Call Cassie,' I spat, tasting blood in my mouth. 'I was just there. We found the USB together. It belonged to Sebastian.'

McCubbin froze, glaring at me, as if struggling to decide. Finally, he muttered at Jacob, who signalled for the two AFP guards to lower their weapons and leave the room. He closed the door as they left, turning back to watch us with impassive eyes.

McCubbin waved his finger in my face. The skin around his knuckles seemed tight and stretched, like a leathered hide.

'What the fuck are you saying about my daughter,' he spat.

I explained as best I could. How we had found the USB in Sebastian's study, behind the painting of the Peak.

'You knew where to look.' He cut me off. 'Why that painting? Why did you find it when my fucking people couldn't?'

'Because I know Sebastian. I know what the painting meant to him. So did Cassie.'

Again his face twitched, and he raised his chin.

'Stop talking about my daughter. Right now, I need you to tell me what is on this USB. It is a matter of national security.'

'I don't know what's on it,' I wailed as he twisted my wrist again. 'I think it's whatever he took off Kai Birch's laptop.'

'Who the fuck is Kai Birch?'

'He's a friend of Sebastian's from Shanghai. He was at the wedding. He runs the Innovation Expansion Unit at the US Department of Defence.'

'What is the Innovation Expansion Unit?' McCubbin grunted, glancing at Jacob. 'Defence procurement?'

I tried to string words together to explain Kai's job, but the pain in my arm was throbbing and I made no sense. Jacob spoke over the top of me, reading aloud from his mobile phone.

'"The Innovation Expansion Unit fast tracks defence technology and national security innovation into the US military. It consults across the defence forces from the Joint Chiefs to front line operators to identify 'problems', then works with private sector companies to prototype and scale technology solutions into the hands of war fighters. We apply a Silicon Valley model to defence procurement …'" He lowered his phone. 'Want me to find a liaison point in Defence and contact them?'

'Wait.' McCubbin waved him into silence, his eyes never leaving my face. 'You're saying Adler used this USB to extract something off a US DOD laptop?'

I nodded. Taking a breath, I tried to overcome the pain enough to communicate.

'Kai Birch's laptop. Yes. His partner, Henry Mallet, called me and Cassie —'

'He called Cassandra?'

'Kai was arrested after Defence detected information had been extracted from his laptop while in an insecure environment.'

'And you think Sebastian extracted something linked to defence innovation?'

'I think he handed over the contents to a contact in Hong Kong.'

This made an impact. McCubbin looked at Jacob.

'Was the contact Zheng?' he asked, turning back to me.

'I believe so.'

'And why would he have done that?' McCubbin growled, leaning forwards. Beneath the office lights, I saw a sheen of sweat across his scalp. All day I had dreaded this moment. All day I'd attempted to protect Sebastian from being exposed before the probing of his father-in-law.

'Why give it to Zheng?' McCubbin roared and twisted my wrist. I cried out again in pain, trying to free myself from his grip.

I need you to keep a secret for me.

I'm sorry, Sebastian, but I can't. I can't anymore.

The truth came in a rush. The levy broke. The dam burst.

'Zheng and Sebastian both work for the Ministry of State Security. They've been blackmailing him. The MSS. They turned him after the car crash.'

'But that was years ago.'

'Chloe didn't die in the crash. Sebastian worked in return for her care and treatment. The MSS gave him the USB. It was the way he extracted information. They taught him in Shanghai. He did it throughout the Consulates. And when he worked in the minister's office. He used it to extract information from Cassie's computer. It makes sense he would have done the same to Kai. I think he passed the contents of the USB to Zheng during our last trip to Hong Kong. SK Tang said they met. Late one night at the China Club.'

'Jesus,' breathed Jacob, looking at McCubbin. 'That's it. That's the connection with Zheng.'

McCubbin ran his gnarled hand over his pockmarked skull. His face clenched like a fist, and I thought he was going to smash his forehead into my nose. When he spoke, his words trembled with anger. 'Why the fuck should I trust you, Westcott?' His fist crushed my wrist. 'You're the one we've found holding the fucking USB. You could be making this all up to cover your own arse. You could be just throwing your dead mate under the bus. You have no proof that whatever is on that USB wasn't put there by you. No evidence to incriminate Adler, or prove he was working for the MSS.'

He wrenched my wrist sideways, and I felt something tear or break. I howled. Tears burnt my eyes. I could hardly speak. Christ, how I needed the cassette. Sebastian's confession. The proof of my innocence.

Then I remembered the memory cards.

Still in clingwrap on the desk.

I bounced my head. Desperate to show him.

'There. We found them with the USB. The MSS gave them to him. Pictures of Chloe. Proof she was alive. One a week at first, to compel him to work.'

McCubbin's eyes darted to the desk. I saw him calculating, gritting his teeth. Without releasing me, he took up the clingwrapped package and studied it. After an excruciating moment, he dropped the cards back on the desk beside the USB.

The violence of his movement slowed, as if the adrenaline that had driven him from the moment he burst into the room was now draining. At last, he released my wrist and pointed at the items on the desk as he spoke to Jacob.

'Get it all onto an air-gapped machine. Tell me what you find. Come back to me. Only to me.'

'Yes sir,' Jacob said.

'Tell no one about what's been said here. About the USB. About Adler. Or …' He glanced at me. 'Or about my daughter.'

Jacob nodded and left the room, clutching what I hoped was proof of my innocence.

❖

McCubbin seized me by the collar and thrust me into the chair I'd sat in that morning, across from Sebastian. I could still see a few crumbs and droplets of egg yolk left over from my bacon and egg roll. McCubbin stood, leaning against the desk, glaring down at me.

'I've read your interview with my operative today. You're a fucking liar.'

'I wasn't lying,' I whimpered, massaging my wounded wrist. 'I didn't know any of what I've told you when I spoke to your agent.'

'Well, what happened? How did you become enlightened this evening?'

'He left a confession.'

McCubbin stood up from the desk.

'What the fuck are you talking about?'

'I found it in his study.'

'Where? Jesus, you're telling me my people missed something else?'

'It was recorded over a mix tape cassette I made when we were kids in Hong Kong.'

I still had the empty cassette cover in my pocket, and as I pulled it out, I saw again the cutting from the *South China Morning Post*. An image of hands clutching each other. I passed it to him.

'"Just waiting to be free?"' He sneered. 'What the fuck is this?'

I told him as quickly as I could all I'd learnt from the cassette. He pulled up Sebastian's chair in front of me, and as he listened, hearing more of the devastating confession from his son-in-law, the father of his grandchildren, McCubbin's body hunched forwards. His elbows were on his knees, his head in his hands. If anyone had entered at that moment, it may have looked like he was praying for me.

I spoke without pause, bombarding him with the truth of what Sebastian had done, everything but the existence of Sebastian's child. I told McCubbin everything else, all the time watching the scars and lumps across his naked scalp. He let me tell it in full, up to the abrupt conclusion when I turned off the tape, disturbed by Mallet's phone call and Cassie knocking at the car window.

McCubbin looked up, as if surprised by the unsatisfactory conclusion.

'But what did Qiu and Zheng want him to do? What was the last sacrifice before they let her die?'

'I don't know.' I shrugged.

McCubbin's eyes widened with urgency.

'It's vital. If Zheng said it's done, then it's what's happening now. We need to hear the rest of the confession to explain *what* he's done.'

'I know, but I told you I don't have the tape. It was stolen.'

'Fuck!' McCubbin bellowed, leaping to his feet and striding away, then turning back and gesturing towards me with furious outstretched arms. 'Why the fuck didn't you come to me as soon as you had this? You've wasted hours.'

'I thought ... I needed to hear it first.' I cringed, fearing more violence. 'I needed to make a copy ... for insurance.'

'Insurance?'

'In case you took the cassette and covered it up ...'

The look of outrage on his face made me stutter. I stumbled on as he clenched his fists.

'I know how this works. You need a fall guy. Why else are you leaking about me in the newspaper?'

'I leaked to get you to tell the truth. You looked as guilty as hell. You were the only one who knew about the girl. I wanted to put some pressure on and shake the truth out of you. I thought you might have been blackmailing him on behalf of Tang, or even Zheng. Frankly, I'm still not convinced you aren't.'

'And that's why I needed a copy of the confession,' I retorted, clambering to my feet. 'I was going to leave it with Andrew Swann.'

'Andrew Swann? The journalist?'

McCubbin's eyes were wide and keen.

'Did you speak to Swann about the confession?' he persisted. 'When? When did you last speak to him?'

That familiar sense of foreboding. The certainty McCubbin knew more than I did.

Nausea swelled in my stomach.

'Around 10 pm. It was just before the PM's presser ...'

I stopped speaking. McCubbin was shaking his head.

'Swann's dead,' he said, flicking through his phone. 'Murdered ...'

He held his mobile screen so I could see. An image of Swanny crumpled beside a car door, as untidy in death as he was in life, his brown jacket rucked up around him, his untucked shirt drenched by the gaping wound in his chest.

'Oh, Jesus.'

Swanny was the closest thing I had to a friend after Sebastian.

'Shot through the heart. Close range. Professional job.'

'Why? Why would he have been ...? Who would have done that?'

McCubbin stuffed his phone into his back pocket and folded his arms.

'Well, if what you're saying is true, I presume it was someone with connections to the MSS. They would have seen you with Swann and presumed you'd given him a copy of the tape. Your house was turned over earlier today. Did you know that? Lucky you weren't there. You'd have ended up in the same way. That confession was a loose end. The MSS wouldn't have wanted that kind of exposure, even if their asset was dead.'

I stuffed my knuckle into my eye, the weight of guilt crushing me into the chair.

Swanny had been killed because of me. Because I'd involved him in this. But he wasn't the only one. I was thinking of all the others who had died or been damaged because of what I'd done, decades ago in Shanghai. Sebastian, dead, Chloe dead; Henry, Kai and Cassie all shattered, their lives in ruins. The trail of destruction that my actions had wreaked on so many lives.

McCubbin sighed and walked to the window. When he spoke again, his tone was more gentle. 'I'm sorry if he was your mate. But this happens ...' He gazed out. I could still see the blinking orange and red lights of aeroplanes in the sky. 'This happens when people don't take this shit seriously. You should have come to me. I had people looking for you all evening. Katrina shouldn't have let you leave. We know who Zheng is. We knew you were connected to him.'

'I'm not connected to him.'

He turned, pressing the tips of his stumpy fingers together. 'Did you know Zheng hasn't had an operational role with China Overland for over a decade?' He stepped closer, his voice raising again. 'That he holds the rank of general in the PLA Navy's Engineering Corps? That he is on the US sanctions list with respect to being responsible for China's activities in the South China Sea and the East China Sea?'

'Island building?' I said, remembering Sebastian's description of his conversation with Zheng about land reclamation and the stories he had told Chloe as they sat on the bench by the Huangpu River and stared at the emerging Pudong skyline.

'Exactly. And after that, he played a pivotal role in the modernisation of China's defence forces, drawing on his logistics experience with Overland. He was brought in to shake things up. Zheng spearheaded projects, from the construction of new military bases to developing transportation networks, enhanced force mobility and' – he nodded at me – 'operational readiness. He received honours from the President for this work that "defends our national sovereignty and paves the way for the reunification and future security of China".'

'Katrina showed me the photo of him shaking hands with the President. I had no idea …' I still had no idea of the enormity of this thing that Sebastian had got himself into.

'When we started looking into his background in connection to Adler and the girl in the car accident, our US counterparts alerted us. That's when we knew this was more than a couple of fuckwits covering up a love affair.'

It made more sense now. This was why the tone of the discussion with Katrina and Ronnie had changed after they'd received details of who Zheng was from the Americans.

Before I could reply, the door was thrown open and Jacob returned. I watched his expression, eager to know if he brought details of what had been stolen from Kai's laptop, and therefore proof of my innocence.

But he shook his head.

'Nothing,' he said. 'The USB was blank. Wiped.'

McCubbin glanced with accusing eyes at me.

Jacob continued. 'The USB is defence grade tech for data exfiltration. It could rip an entire hard drive in five to ten minutes. It's got a bunch of built-in stealth and anti-forensic capabilities to bypass EDR systems, using encryption, timestamp manipulation, altered metadata, obfuscating copied data to evade detection …'

'But it's fucking empty, right?' shouted McCubbin, grinding his fist into his palm and turning on me. 'You said it would have whatever data he took from Birch —'

'I said I didn't know!' I cried, my voice high. 'I presumed that was the last time he'd used it. Maybe the contents were deleted after he uploaded them with Zheng? I don't know.'

'Well, that's pretty fucking awkward for you then, isn't it?' he snarled. 'Because now we have no way of verifying your fanciful fucking story about my son-in-law. All we have is you, caught red-handed with a defence grade exfiltration device, about to commit espionage on a Parliament House computer.'

'Sir …' Jacob touched McCubbin's arm.

'What?'

The bearded officer handed McCubbin an iPad, similar to the one Katrina had used earlier in the day to show images of Sebastian's security clearance.

'We found these images on the memory cards.' He tapped the glass and an image I couldn't make out lit the screen. McCubbin's eyes widened. He glanced up at me. Then back down. He swiped the screen. Once. Twice. Flicking through image after image.

'What is it?' I asked, moving in my seat.

'How many are there?' McCubbin kept swiping, ignoring me.

'Hundreds. The first ones contained only one image per card. Later ones, attempts have been made to consolidate —'

'Show me. Show me the pictures.' I was on my feet, grasping for the iPad. I knew what it was now. I had to see those photos.

I lunged at McCubbin. He saw me coming and thrust out the iPad so I caught it in my guts, winding me. I clutched the device as I sank to my knees.

But I felt no pain.

Only relief.

I could see the pictures now. It was her. It was Chloe. In the hospital bed. Her face scarred, older, ravaged by the years like the rest of us. But still Chloe and still alive. Proving everything Sebastian had said was true.

She stared into the camera. As if she knew that she'd saved me.

I was so overwhelemed to see her again, it took me a moment to realise ...

Her son was standing beside her.

CHAPTER THIRTY-SEVEN

His blue eyes were unmistakenly Sebastian's, but there was a softness on his face as he gazed down at his mother in her bed, in which I immediately saw Chloe. I'd seen that same expression on her face when she'd told me about those projects with the Foundation, helping lift communities in regional China out of poverty.

It was a sensitive face, not yet marred by skepticism or ideology.

His hair was slightly long and cut in a fringe over his forehead. If he'd worn thick black glasses, he would have been her double, only he was taller and more powerfully built.

There was no way of knowing when the photo was taken. He was younger than Sebastian had described him on the tape. Maybe nineteen.

But these features were just a prelude to the detail that shot a thrill of joy through my body.

He was wearing a Blinding Love T-shirt.

I recognised it immediately as it was identical to the one I'd worn in Hong Kong and that Chloe had coveted. The *Restless* album cover on the front. On the back, the lyrics:

And I'm just waiting to be free.
With someone else like me.

Something caught in my throat, and then I was back with Chloe on our first night in Hong Kong, at the Wanch in Lan Kwai Fong, singing along with the band.

I could have laughed out loud, or sobbed.

How had he discovered Blinding Love? Was he wearing it to visit Chloe because he knew it was important to her? But how ... How did he know?

I realised the answer. I'd been thinking about Sebastian finding the diaries in Chloe's hospital room. What if her son had found them too? What if he had read, in Chloe's own words, her account of those years from the nineties? Her desperate attempts to break free. The release she found in her relationship with Sebastian. Their struggle to be together. What if he knew it all? Was it so improbable? How else could he have known about Blinding Love? Surely wearing that T-shirt to visit his mother was more than a coincidence.

I felt a rush of affection for him. He was the product of Chloe and Sebastian's love. He was the continuation of something I thought lost with the ringing of a gunshot in Parliament House that morning. I wished to Christ I still had the cassette tape. I wanted desperately to know if Sebastian had ever met him. What had happened to him? Jesus, why hadn't Sebastian started his confession with this revelation?

And then I realised that he had.

I'm telling you this, not to ask your forgiveness, but so you can tell others why I did what I did. You'll know who I mean. Explain that, even though it seemed I didn't care, I cared very much, Charlie. He'll understand it coming from you ...

At last, I realised what Sebastian wanted me to do ...

'Who is that?' McCubbin interrupted my trail of thought, snatching back the iPad.

'I have no idea.' I shrugged, turning away so he couldn't see the expression on my face.

I sure as hell wasn't going to share my revelation with him.

He looked at me skeptically. His face was grey and his voice had softened. The images of Chloe were irrefutable evidence that my explanation was true, and his son-in-law was an asset of the Ministry of State Security.

I could see his mind spinning, considering his options, maybe his career, his reputation. There was something almost human in the way he seemed to breathe more heavily, and the creases across his brow grew deeper. The truth took its toll, even for this spy chief who had seen so much. A betrayal of this magnitude struck deep and personally. I was sure that it would have felled a lesser man. Not McCubbin. Not tonight.

He turned on me again, stabbing his finger towards my face.

'You must have known something about this,' he said, using blame to stifle his loss. 'You've been covering for him for years.'

'I told you I didn't know.'

'But you've had suspicions for years. Suspicions are reportable. Suspicions are not an excuse not to act. You should have spoken up.'

'Did your daughter?' I growled in return. 'Did you?'

He sprang at me, seizing my jacket with both hands. 'You bastard. If I'd had the slightest sense there'd been something wrong with him, I would have thrown him in a cell. If I thought for a second my daughter knew and was covering for him, I'd have thrown her in the one beside him. Do you understand?'

He flung me away from him, and I fell into a chair, wiping the spittle from my cheek.

'Do you have any concept of what is happening tonight?'

Before I could speak, he answered his own question, bending over me in the chair.

'We are under attack. Do you understand? Our country is being attacked. All major utilities are down across the entire country. Transport. Energy. Water. Communications. Our financial system. We are cut off from the world. A neutered island.'

He jabbed a meaty finger at the lights still burning in the ceiling.

'So why are they still on? All the lights across the country are off, except here in Canberra. Why do you think that is, when whoever is doing this has unfettered access to our energy grid?'

'Because they're sending a message.'

He shook his head.

'The lights are on in Canberra to show the rest of the country that the solution to the disaster that's overtaken the whole of fucking Australia is right here.' He twirled his finger around as if taking in all of Parliament House. 'That if the government rolls over, life goes back to normal.'

He flicked through his phone, then held it out again so I could see the screen. There were still images, similar to what I'd seen on the guards' television downstairs. Masked protestors clashing with police in Sydney and Melbourne. Fires burning.

'People are already demanding the government do what it takes to end the crisis, including capitulate to those responsible. That's how coercion works. They know' – he pointed again at the light – 'that as soon as our fat, privileged democracy is put under strain, civil unrest will put the government under further pressure to surrender. Look how quickly business turned against us when Beijing threatened sanctions as we dared institute foreign interference laws. The miners, the winemakers, the education institutions – all turned on the government. Just like these pricks ...' He pointed at the phone. 'Driven by self interest. Rather than standing by their government, they leverage people's fear to their advantage. And they're just the extreme. Despite most of the country not having access to television, the opposition has been on cable news for the last four hours, blaming the government's energy policy and loose cybersecurity settings for the crisis. Have you wondered why, if the power is off, the majority of the phone networks are still online? It's so all this self-defeating shit can be pumped through social media and further undermine any sense of social cohesion.'

'I presumed you agreed with the opposition.'

He shook his head. 'Even if I do, now is not the time. Now is the time for unity of purpose. We cannot be divided. Or self-interested. Or pursuing competing loyalties. Pain is being inflicted on us to coerce an outcome.'

'Yes, but what outcome?'

'That's what I needed you to tell me!' he roared. 'That's why you should have brought me his fucking confession.'

'You think Sebastian is behind this —'

'I don't have a fucking clue!' He threw up his hands, pacing the room. 'I don't know what "this" is. All I know is that everything so far is overture and we are on borrowed time. When the power goes off, when those lights go out, then we are in trouble. Because that's when it starts. That's when "it's done".' He stood, staring out the window.

I closed my eyes. I could hear Sebastian's voice.

It's bad, Charlie. It's the worst. The worst betrayal. I had to do it. Do you understand? For her.

McCubbin seemed to shake himself from his nightmare. As if he considered his own rant an indulgence. Now he whirled back to me, returning with focus and energy.

'We need to know what intel Adler extracted from Kai Birch's laptop. Tell me about the trip to the US. What were you doing there? Why did he meet Birch?'

'It was Sebastian's pet project as Assistant Minister for Foreign Affairs and Trade. He wanted to get Australian companies selling into the American defence supply chain.'

'What sort of companies?'

'All sorts. But particularly tech companies. AI, data analytics, quantum. Sebastian's relationship with Kai Birch was a positive for getting outcomes for Australian businesses, which have a tough time of it navigating US export controls and licensing arrangements. In fact, his relationship with Kai Birch was one reason I could get him into the outer ministry. The PM and Ronnie Durban didn't want him. But given the existing relationship with Kai, along with ...'

'Along with what?'

'The fact he was your son-in-law.'

I could see McCubbin's jaw clench. 'And on this trip you did what?'

I explained about the delegation to the Sea-Air-Space Expo in Maryland. Our lobbying in Washington, then the trip to California.

'So Adler took a smaller group to meet Birch, to get a briefing on a project DOD required technology for. That is important. What was the project?'

I opened and closed my mouth. 'I don't know,' I admitted. 'I wasn't involved in the detail.'

'You were his fucking Chief of Staff. You were with him.'

'I was in the hotel. Making calls back to Canberra.'

'About what?'

'There was a preselection battle. I was exploring support for Sebastian to move from the Senate to the lower house.'

McCubbin's face creased in disgust. 'You were lining him up for a run at prime minister?' He didn't pause for me to respond. 'And so you were negligent in your responsibilities. You don't know what he did in California. Which companies were with him? What project they discussed?'

My face was flaming red. Feeling ashamed and exposed, I leapt to my feet. 'The briefings. They'll all be in our system.'

Before I could take a step forwards, Jacob was between me and Sebastian's desk, his hand on my shoulder like a vice. I struggled against his grip as McCubbin stared at me.

'Listen, I can get the briefing. It will tell us everything we need.'

'You don't seem to understand you will never touch a government computer again,' McCubbin said coldly. The words had their intended effect as the weight of realisation hit me and I understood fully that my career was over. Once he had seen it sink in, he nodded at Jacob.

'Show Jacob where. He'll operate the computer. You touch nothing. Show him where to find the files.'

❖

Jacob sat down at Sebastian's desk. I stood beside him, McCubbin next to me as if ready to wrestle me to the ground should I try to touch the keyboard. I gave them my login and directed them to a shared drive where the staffers kept an archive of all the briefs. It was arranged by week, and when there were a group of briefings related to an overseas trip, a sub-folder stored the travel brief from DFAT and anything the advisors had prepared.

'There. It's the briefing book for the last US trip.'

'Two hundred pages ...' Jacob whistled, scrolling to the index.

We had always complained to the Department Liaison Officer about how dense these briefing books were, but now I was grateful for the detail. All the travel and meeting logistics were recorded. We could see every meeting Sebastian had, from our time at the Sea–Air–Space Exposition in Maryland, through to lobbying calls in Washington and on to California.

'The schedule shows times and dates, along with meeting participants,' I said, as Jacob pulled up the itinerary on the screen. I pointed to the meeting participant column, where a series of initials were listed. 'See, I was with him throughout engagements at the Expo and in Washington. Then when we hit California, my initials disappear.'

'That's convenient,' McCubbin growled in my ear.

'I didn't want to spend the evening with Kai and Mallet and Sebastian. We didn't … get on.'

My schoolboy reasons sounded petty and childish now. McCubbin didn't need to point out that it meant I had missed something vital. Something awful. Maybe if I'd been a better person, I could have stopped Sebastian.

'Looks like they didn't stay in Mountain View,' Jacob said, highlighting a box on the schedule. 'Adler and the delegation went with Birch and his team to Moffett Federal Airfield. From there, they hitched a ride on a C-130 to Naval Base Coronado, in San Diego. Do you know what that is?'

'Henry Mallet said they'd gone offsite for a secure briefing on the sort of technology capability Defence were looking for. The companies were going to test prototypes.'

'According to the brief,' Jacob said, scanning the words on the computer screen, 'the base specialises in undersea operations. It hosts several submarines and naval vessels and, given its proximity to the Pacific Ocean, is used for submarine warfare training.'

He stopped reading and turned to look at McCubbin. There was a silence between them and I felt pressure building in the room.

'Which companies were with him?' McCubbin asked, his voice constricted.

'Go to the appendix,' I said. 'Company backgrounds and profiles will be detailed.'

Jacob scrolled through to Appendix A, locating a topline summary of each of the Australian companies travelling with Sebastian.

1. Pythia AI specialises in algorithms and models to optimise decision-making and enhance autonomous systems for underwater operations.
2. Dataverse processes and analyses data collected from undersea sensors, sonar systems and other sources that support decision-making in undersea warfare scenarios.
3. AquaSentinel develops robotic systems and autonomous underwater vehicles for undersea warfare applications.
4. HydraSonar specialises in advanced sonar systems and underwater acoustic sensors to detect and track threats across the underwater domain.
5. CommsShield specialises in secure communication and networking solutions for undersea warfare operations, ensuring reliable and encrypted communication between underwater assets, submarines, and other naval platforms.

'It's all undersea warfare capability,' Jacob breathed.

I didn't understand his surprise. This was normal. Most of our discussions with Defence related to undersea warfare.

'Everyone knows the DOD spends a fortune on that stuff. Keeping the technological advantage over the PLA is their key priority. Those companies were the best of the lot that went to expo. It makes sense they'd go for a more detailed briefing at Coronado,' I said, feeling like I was explaining the obvious.

Again, there was silence. I felt the crushing weight of something unsaid between the two men on either side of me.

McCubbin's voice. 'Go to the detailed event and brief for the session at Coronado.'

Jacob scrolled back up to the detailed brief. I felt embarrassed that I was reading all this for the first time. As chief of staff, I should have cleared his briefing. But I'd left it to the advisors.

'That's unusual,' I said, pointing at the screen as Jacob scrolled through the brief. While the details of the companies pitching were there, the usual background on the purpose of the meeting, and what work the Australian companies were pitching for, was curtailed. There were no key messages or further details about the substance of the meeting. Only a single bold line of text, which Jacob highlighted and then turned to McCubbin with eyebrows raised, his face paling.

THE MINISTER'S BUSINESS DELEGATION WILL RECEIVE A BRIEFING ON THE DEPARTMENT OF DEFENCE KRAKEN PROJECT. FOR DETAILS OF KRAKEN REFER TO CLASSIFIED BRIEFING.

'There was another briefing?' I frowned, then touched Jacob on the shoulder. 'Click back to the folder on the server. See if there's another brief on Kraken.'

'There will be nothing about Kraken on this system.' McCubbin's voice was heavy.

'Well, do you know what it is?' I asked, looking between them. 'Can we check the other system? It's in the minister's brief, so there must be more detail. We can check the classified system.'

My words seemed to drop into a void. McCubbin had grown still, yet his tension felt almost palpable, a current crackling with concern.

'I need to speak to our US counterparts. We know enough now,' he said to Jacob, walking towards the door. 'You stay with him.' He pointed at me. Once more, there was something dreadful moving in the shadows that everyone else could see but me.

'What do you mean, we know enough? Who are you going to talk to? What is Kraken?' I demanded as Jacob stood and pushed me back to the chair on the other side of the desk. McCubbin ignored me and left, and I appealed to Jacob. 'What is it? What is Kraken?'

'I have no idea,' he whispered. 'But it looks like the end of the fucking world.'

It's bad Charlie. It's the worst. The worst betrayal.

Whatever the 'worst' thing was that Sebastian had done, that last sacrifice demanded by Qiu and Zheng involved the Kraken.

❖

Jacob and I didn't speak as we waited for McCubbin's return. It reminded me of that forever time, earlier in the day, when I'd sat in the meeting room after Sebastian's suicide, planning how I would protect his secrets. Now I was desperate for them to be revealed, for McCubbin to return and tear away the final curtain.

I regretted this wish as soon as I saw his face.

McCubbin entered the room, looking like a condemned man. He held himself erect, trying to maintain his dignity, but in his eyes it was like he was seeing a firing squad. He closed the door of the office and leant against it, his hands behind his back.

'We have confirmation from partner agencies in the United States,' he announced, staring at the window and the planes passing in the night sky. 'Kai Birch has been arrested on suspicion of espionage. He has confessed under interrogation to —'

His head fell forwards, his finger adjusting his watchband.

'To what?' I urged.

He thrust up his chin.

'To an affair and intimate relations with Sebastian Adler.'

My mouth fell open. Jacob turned and stared at me. I was astonished. Lost for words.

McCubbin ploughed on.

'On the night in question, Adler convinced Birch to return to his home after a briefing session at Naval Base Coronado, in San Diego. Birch was carrying an air-gapped laptop that should have been returned and stored in a secure location. Instead, they went to Birch's Los Altos villa. They took drugs. They had sex. At some point, Adler gained access to the laptop, which required biometrics to open it. He must have somehow compelled Birch to use both his eyes and fingers to gain access. Birch doesn't remember. The stealth and anti-forensic capability on the USB bypassed DOD

EDR systems, and the extraction was missed. Our counterparts have confirmed now that the files stolen from Birch's air-gapped laptop were indeed related to Project Kraken.'

My mind swam. I longed for Sebastian's voice, wishing I'd heard this final confession on the cassette spoken by him. The voice I had known since high school. That had called to me through the window of my mother's car, or laughed as we played *Castle Wolfenstein* in his bedroom, or whispered into the night about loyalty and betrayal in the aftermath of his father's death. Without his voice, I was left with only his actions. Treachery in the stark and sterile light of his office. Betrayal of everything, laid bare by the brutal voice of his father-in-law. Everything and everyone betrayed but Chloe. The Sebastian I knew, fading like a figure in receding light.

'What is Kraken?' I asked in a whisper.

McCubbin turned to look at me, as if only just remembering I was present. He let out a long breath. Then rallied, balling his fingers into fists, as if reinflating his resolve.

'Kraken is a deterrent that protects us from the end of the world,' he proclaimed, stepping into the room. 'Kraken protects the global order which has benefitted Australia and its allies since the end of the Second World War.'

No doubt reading the incomprehension on my face, McCubbin paused, as if considering how much more he could say. A weighing up of the current circumstances. A decision made. Secrets that no longer had value. 'Kraken is the crown jewel of the US military. Imagine if you could look through the ocean as if it were glass. Imagine if we could see their submarines as clearly as fish in a tank. Imagine if our submarines could see their surface ships from beyond the horizon, then deploy swarms of autonomous remote-controlled unmanned underwater vehicles, equipped with advanced torpedoes and other weaponry, at massive scale and speed. We could target anything that moved in the Taiwan Strait long before they could target us. That's what Kraken is. The most advanced and sophisticated integrated defence system the world has ever seen. From satellites to undersea drones using quantum-entangled photons that make sonar look as outdated as a bow and arrow. The Chinese knew we had it, and it scared the shit out of them. All their vast investments in anti-ship missile systems, naval assets, air defence, all that area-denial capability that they needed to push the US out of the region. It was all meaningless. Because of Kraken. Because they, as yet, have no answer to it.' McCubbin stopped. When he spoke again his voice sounded hollow, his expression appalled. 'But the secret of secrets. The one thing the Chinese could never know. Kraken didn't work. It never did what we claimed it did. The intent was there. Hundreds of billions of dollars was spent to try to make it work. It's what your mate Birch did. Maybe a bit of Silicon Valley know-how could solve what traditional defence companies couldn't. It's why our tech companies were there. But in the meantime, we pretended it worked. And the Chinese believed it. That's what Adler's done. That's what he's given away. He showed them Kraken is as useless as tits on a bull. And from Birch's own fucking laptop.'

The room fell still. Jacob was staring at his boss. My gaze was fixed on the patch of dried blood on the carpet. I dragged my eyes away. 'What does it mean?'

'It means everything is in motion. It's happening.'

'What is happening?' I asked, feeling that dread-filled anxiety that made me want to vomit when Mallet and his pack followed me for a beating.

'The Americans have shared satellite imagery over the last three days, showing massive deployment of PLA units to the Eastern Theatre Command. The Liaoning Carrier Strike Group has moved up the Taiwan Strait, accompanied by amphibious assault ships. The ninth fighter division and tenth bomber brigade have been deployed to airbases nearby. This explains the cyberattack. It is intended to neuter us. The cyberattack is the start. Now they know about Kraken, they have everything. Taiwan's laid bare. We thought it was the usual PLA posturing. Until now. With Kraken off the table it suggests we've got less than twenty-four hours until missile strikes.'

'Jesus Christ. Strikes on what?'

'Beijing's first step in an invasion of Taiwan will be to attack US bases in the region. US Marines stationed in Okinawa and the Air Force in Guam will evacuate to avoid being destroyed. In twenty-four hours, we will have a quarter of a million US troops retreating to Northern Australia. From that point on, Australia will become the southern base for Americans, operating its combat forces out of Darwin. That's when there will be preemptive strikes on US forwards deployments here ...' He listed on his fingers. 'RAAF Tindal and the US Bomber rotation in the North, the Larrakeyah defence precinct in Darwin. Pine Gap. They'll have a go at HMAS Stirling in WA, targeting the US Submarine Rotational Force-West. Anything to do with US force structure or strategic capability based in Australia will be a priority target.'

I made an inarticulate noise of horror.

'Terrifying, isn't it?' McCubbin sneered. 'These are the things grown-ups think about while you play university politics up and down the halls of Parliament House.'

He bent and brushed his hand across the red stain darkening the carpet, as if he felt the need to point out what spilt blood actually looked like.

'For the last two decades, the Americans have had their eye off the ball and failed to meet the challenge of a rising China. They've lost control of critical supply chains, they've let alliances drift, they've cut military funding as men like Zheng have worked tirelessly to modernise the capabilities of the PLA. They've talked for ten years about pivoting to Asia, but where is the evidence? They've held meetings and press conferences and launched defence papers, and labelled China a major strategic rival. But what have they committed to uphold their pre-eminence in East Asia?'

McCubbin shook his head, staring at his hand. He rubbed his fingers together until clots of dried blood crumpled to the carpet.

'The biggest threat to Australian security is not the rise of China but a crumbling of US resolve. They've already withdrawn from the Middle East. Ukraine slowed them in Europe, but there are calls for a further retreat. There is a real risk they will abandon us too, and do it when Australia needs them to commit to fight, no matter the cost, to keep their pre-eminence in East Asia. Kraken gave us a breathing space. Working together to keep technological primacy in the Pacific, to develop a technology advantage and deterrence, that rallied the alliance. We saw the resurgence of the allied collective will. That's why Adler was sent in to target it. Now Beijing thinks that, without technological preeminence, the US will not commit to the fight.'

'What does commit to fight mean?'

'It means committing to the biggest war the US has fought since 1945, and with an adversary not dwarfed by US military and economic resources. A war where the US will be disadvantaged by distance, with their supply chains stretching across the Pacific. And Beijing has the advantage of fighting in its backyard.'

I felt my knees weakening beneath me. I couldn't hold his unblinking gaze.

'The Chinese are counting on the US not having the stomach for it. They can see their divided domestic politics. They know Taiwan means more to China than it does to people in the US, who are suspicious of overseas adventures after the failures of Iraq and Afghanistan. They think the American people want a return to isolationism. That they want to lock down, safe in their western hemisphere.'

He was pacing now, those gnarled boxer's fists punctuating his dissertation.

'And now they have the truth about Kraken, they believe they can defeat the US militarily in the Taiwan Strait and pinch out their regional bases. But if Beijing hits those US bases in Okinawa and Guam, if there are massive US casualties – American blood in the Pacific, a bloody spectacle, a terrible sacrifice – think what that would do to the will of the American people. A Dunkirk moment of national resilience, combined with the rallying fury of 9/11. A million would soon replace those 250,000 troops, along with aircraft, ships and submarines, the goddamn inter-continental ballistic missiles I've been arguing we need in Australia for years. It would no longer be a war of technological preeminence, it would be two superpowers bludgeoning each other, slugging it out in the waters to our north ... Both sides will have the capacity to fight each other to a grinding standstill, at which point the conventional war goes nuclear, and we're ploughing headlong towards the end of the world.'

McCubbin's energy had returned. He strode the confines of the room like a general on his battlefield, radiating intensity. I couldn't work out if he was terrified by the catastrophe he was describing or delighted by the actualisation of a long held hypothesis.

I was about to challenge him with this very question.

But then the lights went out.

CHAPTER THIRTY-EIGHT

Soon after the power went out across Canberra, McCubbin left. Not because of the outage, or what was about to happen in the Taiwan Strait or Okinawa, but because of Cassie. He'd sent officers to her house after I'd told him about the USB. Whether to check on her welfare or to arrest her was unclear. But they'd arrived and it had not gone well. She'd been distraught, inconsolable. They'd sedated her. And McCubbin had gone off to control the situation. A man who was used to being in control …

Now losing control.

Before he left, by the light of the torches the AFP guards had brought us, he threw me a yellow writing pad. I recognised my handwriting across seven pages and realised he'd found the narrative I'd written earlier. The tragedy of Paul Adler. Trying to explain Sebastian's actions through the sins of his father.

'Write it,' McCubbin had insisted, pointing at the pad, just as Ronnie had done that morning. 'Tell them everything that has happened. Everything your friend Adler has done.'

'Tell who? The PM? Cabinet?'

McCubbin shrugged, then changed his mind and took a step forwards, thrusting up his head as if challenging me to a fight in a pub.

'No. I want you to write it for everyone. We'll put it on the front page of all the papers. All over the internet, radio, TV news. Whatever still works, wherever there are still people to see. I want them all to know what's happened and why. Make them understand the world has changed and that we need to be prepared.'

'A cautionary tale,' I muttered.

McCubbin nodded. 'People need to know.'

And so, I've done what he said. I've been writing for hours, with no news about what is happening out there in the world. Are there missiles landing in Okinawa? In Guam? On Darwin? What is occurring in the Taiwan Strait?

I have no idea.

McCubbin wants me to write a cautionary tale of foreign interference, of what happens when people like me stop listening to the 'grown-ups', of what we might all be facing tomorrow and the day after.

I just wanted to know what happened to my best friend. But with every word I have written he's seemed to drift further from me, like a body sinking into the sea.

People will say Sebastian shot himself because he couldn't stand the repercussions of his betrayal, that his children would know of his treachery, that they might see him as no better than his own father who had betrayed him. I think that's only half true. He was a traitor, but he was also the most loyal person I have ever known. The world might believe that once he committed that first act of treason all those decades ago he was acting out of self-interest, to preserve himself and receive the benefits that I suspect the MSS pushed his way – the postings, the promotions that made his career look so stellar. But I don't believe that. I believe he did it for Chloe, as he said he did. I contrast all that he sacrificed for her with my own cowardice that night at the Peak, quivering in front of Liu Hui as he dragged her away. And I know Sebastian was the better man. A stronger man. The more loyal man.

That's why I betrayed him.

And why everything that followed is a product of my frailty. My ego.

I am to blame.

I wonder if that is what McCubbin really wanted me to tell you. That this is how the world ends. Not by ideology or some grand historical force or unstoppable geopolitical current, but by humans being human. The cumulative experience of human frailty. The sum of those failures to be courageous, to be loyal, to be more than individuals servicing individual desires.

What Sebastian did was not ideological – he considered his despicable actions an expression of love. Chloe deserted her father's beliefs for that same love and the pursuit of the freedom that she felt listening to the music of the nineties. Paul Adler felt a right to betray his family because life had not delivered as promised. Zheng denounced his wife and tortured his daughter because to do otherwise would be to admit to his betrayal of his own father. Kai Birch sacrificed his freedom for passion and infatuation. Chloe's mother abandoned her daughter to indulge her grief. Cassie let a traitor walk free because she couldn't blow up her family.

They were human. And frail. Like me. And we let the world burn.

McCubbin has long gone, but the last thing he told me before leaving was to keep writing. 'We have to prepare them,' he said, jabbing a finger at me. 'You have to tell them what Sebastian has done. Tell them that tomorrow when they wake up, it will be the end of the world.'

And yet ... I realise I gave up writing for McCubbin hours ago. I can't shake the thought that Sebastian, from the very start, had another audience in mind. He wanted me to tell you what he's done. To explain that, even though it seemed he didn't care, he cared very much ...

And now he's gone to join Chloe. He's done what he's always done. He's taken her beyond my reach. They've gone together, withdrawing into the grey morning light. And I'm on the side of the football field, watching them go. They catch my eye a moment, then look away.

They're looking at someone else. A small Eurasian boy, with sky-blue eyes.

How can you leave him? I want to ask as they turn away.

But I can hear Chloe's voice now, calling back to her son ...

Go with this boy. He'll look after you.

AUTHOR'S NOTE

Although this novel is a work of fiction and all characters are fictional, many aspects are rooted in fact.

My career has provided me the opportunity to live and work in the locations portrayed in the novel and to interact with many of its issues and character 'types', but I owe a debt of gratitude to the scholars, writers and experts whose work I have drawn on to shape the historical and geostrategic context in which the story is set.

I provide the following references both to acknowledge my sources, but also as a recommendation for readers looking to learn more about the subject matter.

The Hong Kong setting is predominantly drawn from my own experience, but I found inspiration in Louisa Lim's *Indelible City*, a beautiful meditation on the history and culture of Hong Kong written not long after the 2019 protests. I also drew on Antony Dapiran's *City on Fire*, for his visceral descriptions of the sounds, slogans and frontline clashes between police and protestors. Chris Patten's *The Hong Kong Diaries* was also very useful capturing the atmosphere in the months leading up to the handover.

Alex Joske is one of Australia's most insightful writers on the CCP and I owe a debt to his *Spies and Lies*.

On foreign interference, I consulted former Australian prime minister Malcolm Turnbull's *A Bigger Picture*, which offers unique insight into the creation of Australia's foreign interference laws and the opposition Turnbull faced from business and other groups concerned that national security measures would damage Australia's relationship with China.

I also drew on the work of another former Australian prime minister, Kevin Rudd, currently Ambassador to Washington.

Rudd's *The Avoidable War* is a balanced examination of the history of suspicion between China and the west.

On the geostrategic forces shaping Australia's relationship with the United States and China, there is ongoing public debate within Australian foreign affairs and defence circles.

I would recommend Sam Roggeveen's essay, 'Target Australia' in the periodical *Australian Foreign Affairs,* Issue 18, titled 'We Need to Talk About America' and his book *The Echidna Strategy,* which considers Australia's capacity to defend itself in the context of its alliance with the United States. Roggeveen picks up on themes contemplated by Hugh White, including his essay from *Quarterly Essay,* 'Sleepwalk to War'.

Issue 19 of *Australian Foreign Affairs* entitled 'The New Domino Theory' provided a useful examination of the conventional wisdom shaping Australia's foreign policy towards China. The article by James Curran 'Excess Baggage: Is China a genuine threat to Australia?' was particularly insightful.

Finally, for the imagined experience of Australia during an invasion of Taiwan, I drew on 'Red Alert', the provocative series of reports by the Nine newspapers, written by Peter Hartcher and Matthew Knott with scenarios developed by an expert panel including Lesley Seebeck, Mick Ryan, Alan Finkel, Lavina Lee and Peter Jennings.

ACKNOWLEDGEMENTS

I owe debts of gratitude to many who supported bringing this novel into existence. Tom Gilliat, my agent, whose passion for the book and unwavering support for me as a writer has sustained and inspired me. Catherine Milne, my publisher (and a diplomat's daughter), with whom I felt an immediate creative connection, and whose vision and insight immeasurably enhanced the book's clarity and power. Morgan Springett, my UK editor, whose insight and passionate stewardship prepared the novel for an international audience. Shannon Kelly, who guided me through the editorial process with such care, insight and attention to detail. Felicity Blunt, my UK agent, who generously took on an unknown first time author from Australia and landed him a deal. And all the amazing teams at HarperCollins in Australia and the UK for their enthusiasm, trust and commitment.

Love and gratitude to my family for their support: Amanda and Oliver (who pushed me to use a cassette for Sebastian's confession), Susan and Graeme, Yvonne and James.

To the amazing Philippa King for her unwavering encouragement insight and advice. Thanks also to Justin Bassi for generously reading the manuscript and offering sage counsel and support. To other dear friends who read the book(s) and provided feedback, particularly Creina Chapman, Peter Rainey and Tasman Armytage. And my original mentor Kathryn Heyman.

And finally, special thanks to Rebecca Mann for our writing salon, and all the empathy, reassurance, constructive feedback and friendship that sustained me throughout this journey.